The Dragon's Emissary

The Dragon's Emissary

Legend of the Fragmentum
Book One

Robin Arnette

Rosewood
Avenue

PUBLISHING

Cover Art and Maps by Alina Lalik, alalikart.com
Robin Arnette Logo, Rosewood Avenue Publishing Logo, Cover and additional miscellaneous graphic design by Sean Hilferty, hilfertyhouse.com
Cover Copyright © 2025 by Robin Arnette
Print book interior design by Cristi Green
Author Photograph by Sean and Victoria Hilferty
Rosewood Avenue Publishing
Northridge, California
United States of America
First Edition: August 2025.
Identifiers: PCN 2025907186 | ISBN 979-8-218-64449-9 (paperback) | ISBN 979-8-218-64450-5 (ebook)

For Mum,
This book isn't just my triumph.
It's our triumph.

Content Warning:
This book includes themes directly or indirectly related
to grief, depression, alcohol consumption, child abuse,
Post Traumatic Stress Disorder, panic attacks, and
magic-related self-harm.

For more details about placement and the extent of
these themes, please visit: robinarnette.com

The Court of Kings and Queens
Goldhaven
Weareely Marshes
Lake Lockloreain
Alaspinor
The Old Barrows
Torrin's Lair
Bimblebarrow
Castle Veloria
Ethnadian

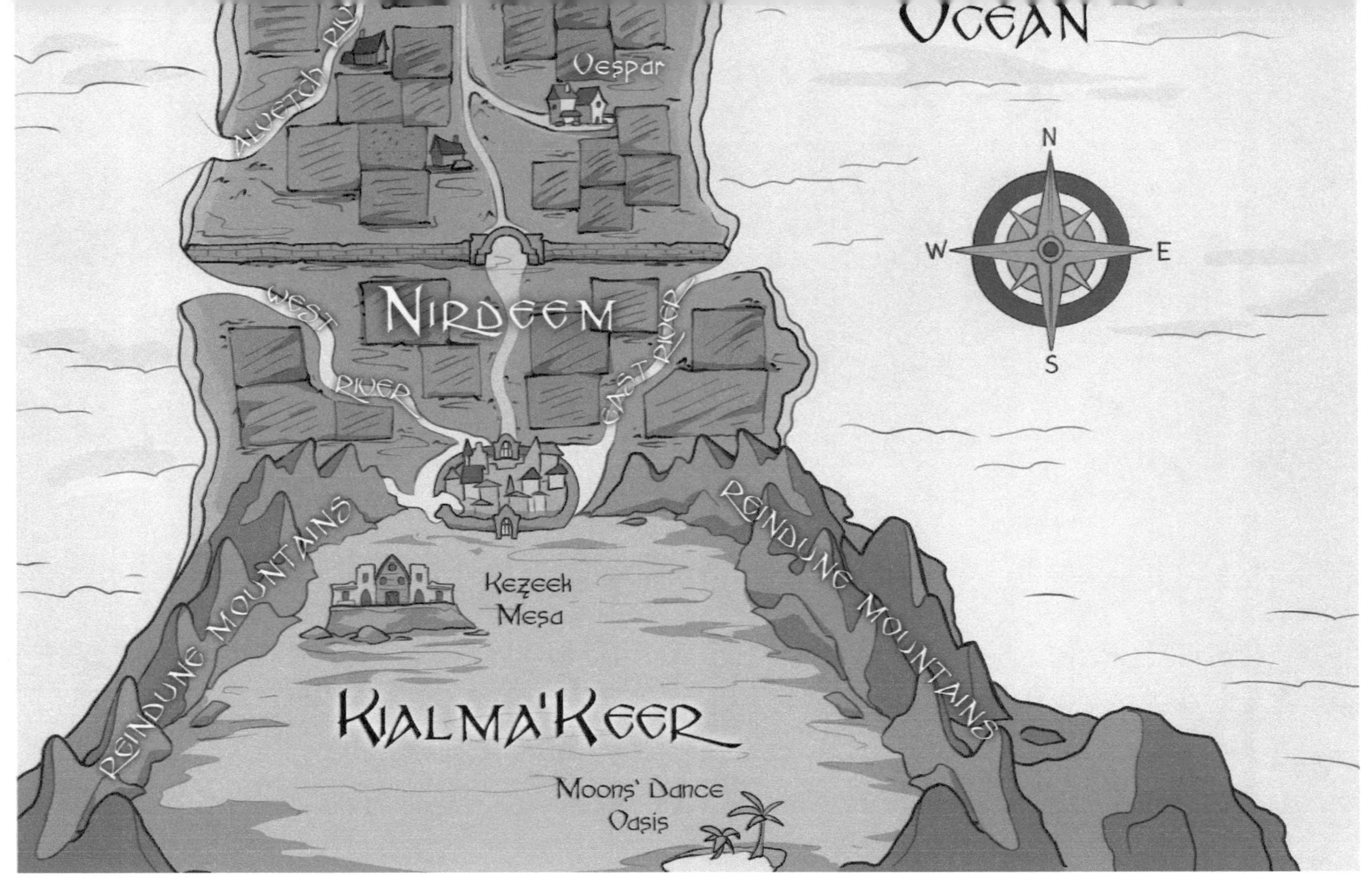

OCEAN
N
E
S
W
Vespar
Alveral River
NIRDEEM
WEST RIVER
EAST RIVER
REINDUNE MOUNTAINS
REINDUNE MOUNTAINS
Kezeek Mesa
KIALMA'KEER
Moons' Dance Oasis

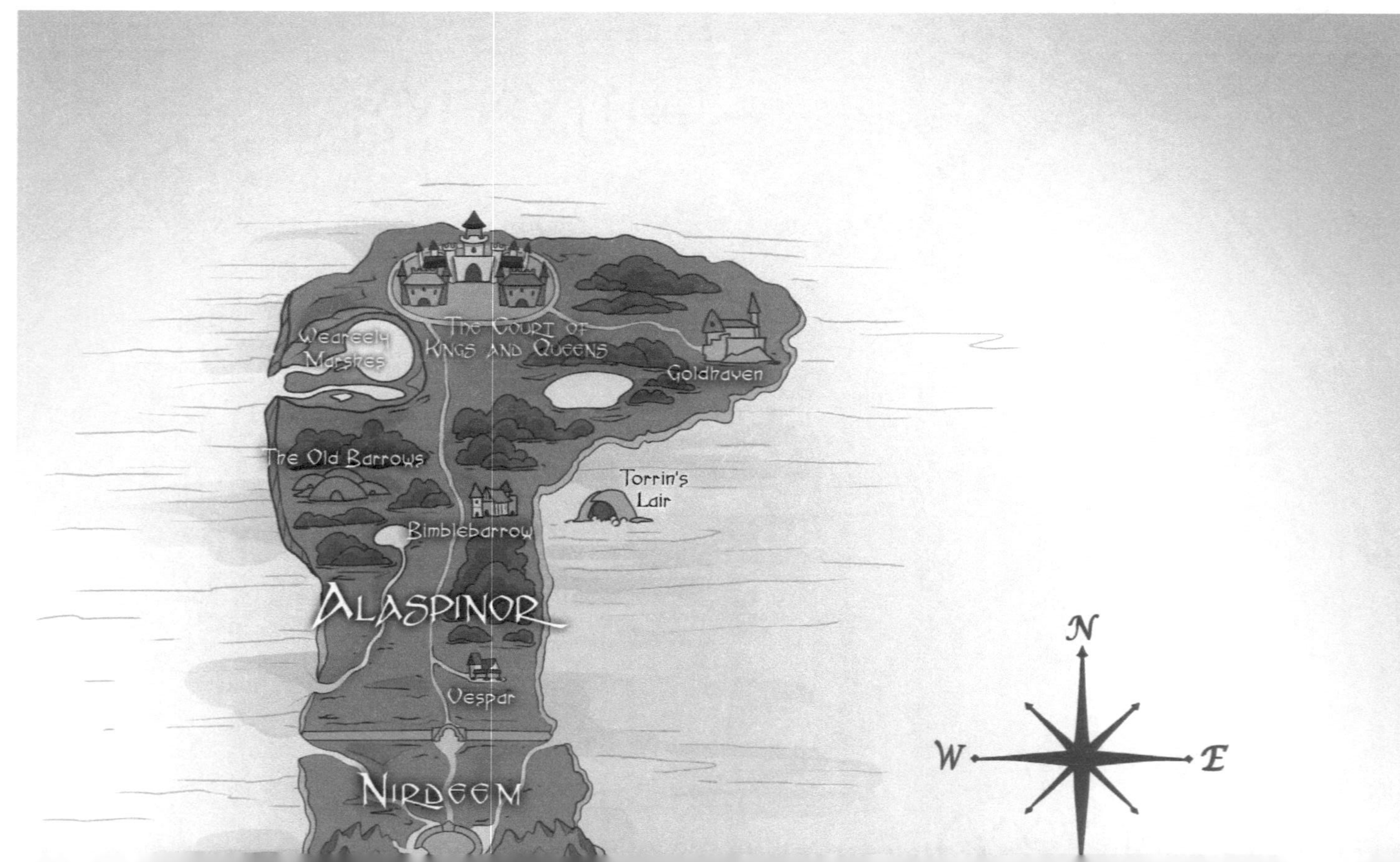

Weareely Marshes
The Court of Kings and Queens
Goldhaven
The Old Barrows
Torrin's Lair
Bimblebarrow
ALASPINOR
Vespar
NIRDEEM
N
W
E

Kezeek Mesa
REINDUNG MOUNTAINS
REINDUNG MOUNTAINS
Moons' Dance Oasis
KIALMA'KEER
Mysterious Cave
Bokest al'Bar
FELSHA'ROR CANYON
Zoh'kret University
S

Chapter One
The Petty Thief

Zelnor shifted one of the wooden beams up and stepped inside the crumbling cottage. The scent of ash still lingered in the air, bitter on her tongue. She pressed her fingers into her eyelids; the pressure spawned dark silhouettes in blossoming browns and reds. One of the silhouettes looked far too much like a human, no older than she was now, doubled over in front of a pile of charred rubble. The afterimages faded, but the memory wouldn't—not until she found the ring and got away from this place.

Stooping to sort through the black debris, Zelnor's thin braid slipped over her slightly pointed ears. She straightened, tucking it back into her short ponytail with the rest of her white hair. A dark blue sparkle caught her eye. She dove for it and emerged with a silver ring. The glistening stone set in its center shifted between emerald and sapphire in the fading sunlight.

Zelnor tugged at her beard. The jewelry looked expensive… She might make more gold from selling the ring than the noble was

paying her, but it wasn't worth it. Stealing something this valuable would put an unnecessary target on her back, and this commission was already the most high-profile job she'd ever taken.

There was so much about the commission that she still didn't understand. Why would a prevator ask a vagabond like Zelnor to retrieve her ring? Why would someone of her standing want to meet up in a farming village? Not even a real village at that, more like a collection of a dozen or so houses and farms. It was almost unheard of to even see a prevator outside the Court of Kings and Queens, but somehow Zelnor, a scruffy, bearded half-elf, had been hired by one?

The entire deal was suspect, but Zelnor didn't have much of a choice. She made some coppers mending roofs and fences, but more often farmers paid in homecooked meals and a bed for the night. It just wasn't worth the risk. She needed a solution to her money problems that kept her far away from other people.

Prevator Apalandis had offered a substantial payment of gold; this one job would be enough to sustain Zelnor for a long time, without endangering others. Better to just finish the task quickly and never think about it again.

Zelnor pocketed the trinket and carefully climbed back out of the rubble. She couldn't help but wonder how the fire had started and whether Prevator Apalandis had anything to do with it. *No. Do not get involved, Zelnor.* She pulled her cowl over her head, and turned away from the wreckage.

Fortunately, the walk back to the "village" wasn't that far. As she drew closer, she passed through the farms. Dark clouds overhead threatened a downpour, but it was nearing the end of the Bitter Season, and the constant storms had started letting up a little. Wind brushed over the countryside, leaving a brisk chill in its wake and rippling through the long grasses of the open plains. Figures moved through the fields, tending to their daily chores and praying to

Primitha for a bountiful harvest.

Zelnor gave them a wide berth. *Soon,* she reminded herself. It would all be over soon. She would meet briefly with Prevator Apalandis and refill her dwindling supplies, and then she could focus solely on removing her curse. Their meeting place was just off the main road in a small clearing of trees. A few more turns, and she'd be there.

A hand shoved her to the ground. Zelnor was still reeling from the first blow when two more men gripped her shoulders and hauled her back up again. A group of thugs had ambushed her. Their weapons, still slick with the sheen of fresh blood, stayed tucked into belts of fraying rope.

They probably assumed Zelnor was a frail old man. Her white beard, slight frame, and androgenous features led most people to that conclusion. Unfortunately, that also made her look like an easy target for lazy bandits—ones who found merchant caravans too troublesome to rob.

Felsha'kor's feathers! Zelnor could've easily avoided these men if she had just paid more attention.

"Where's a scruffy bum like you going so quick, huh?" the leader asked.

Zelnor kept her mouth shut. If they had *any* reason to think she had something valuable, it was over. She would have to use elemental magic on them, and gods only knew what would happen then. *But,* if they thought she was a poor, old man with nothing worth stealing, maybe they would leave her alone.

"He ain't talking," the man to her left said.

The leader stepped up into her face.

"Guess he has something to hide then," he said. "Out with it, or we get *real* friendly."

Damn them. So much for leaving her alone.

They had Zelnor's arms pinned to her sides. Struggling was pointless, they were too strong. She had no choice. She needed to use her cursed magic on them.

She opened her hand toward the leader without breaking eye contact, hoping he wouldn't notice the movement. The two thugs holding her tightened their grip.

Zelnor felt the core of her magic swirling inside like a never-ending storm. The power leaped into her palm. She'd put off casting again, and after days of trying to suppress it, the magic practically sparked at her fingertips, *desperate* to be unleashed.

A single white dot flickered into existence in front of her. Another appeared. Then another. A silver thread connected each one as they materialized, until the six dots surrounded her. A pinprick of heat sparked to life in her otherwise cold hands. She channeled her energy into it, and it grew to the size of a small walnut. Zelnor hid the little ball of fire in her fist, waiting for an opening.

She glanced up at the thugs: like everyone else, they wouldn't see the white dots. Sometimes, she wondered if the dots were even really there, or if seeing them was just another side effect of her magic. Either way, they were incredibly dangerous. She needed to be far away when the dots hit her. They might've been bandits, but Zelnor *really* didn't want to be responsible for their deaths.

Zelnor tried to keep the points at bay, to prevent them from closing in. Dividing her attention between the fiery orb in her fist and the points surrounding her, she took her focus off her attackers.

Big mistake. One of them punched her stomach, and she almost dropped the fire in her hand. She needed to act now, or she would lose control!

Lowering her fist to her side, the spurt of flame rocketed toward the pants of the man who'd punched her. The material caught fire and spread unnaturally fast. He screeched and shook his leg, trying

to put out the flames. Losing his balance, he knocked into his companions and toppled them sideways.

As soon as they released Zelnor, she sprinted away. The dots closed in around her, surging into her. She braced herself. After a moment of anticipation, a little shock ran up her spine.

That was the only side effect this time? *Oh, thank the gods!* She'd had much worse second spells than that. She felt a prickling sensation on the skin behind her right knee.

Footsteps and shouting followed her. The bandits did not look happy. Their weapons were out now, and they were catching up.

The road was busier up ahead. If Zelnor could get into one of those carts, she could lose them. A wagon filled with goods pulled over to the side, while the owner checked his horse's feet. This was her chance! She leaped into the cart before the merchant noticed her.

After a tense moment, Zelnor heard the men run a few feet beyond the wagon and come to a halt, arguing loudly over whose fault her escape was. Thank Felsha'kor the thieves were as intelligent as cathmals. *No, that would be an insult to cathmals.* Zelnor smiled thinking of the little calves she'd raised as a child. Actually, cathmals were much smarter than these dolts. No comparison, really.

Zelnor crawled deeper into the mound of boxes. She rolled up her pant leg to check behind her right knee. As expected, she found a new lock of white fur, tip tinged in gold. How many was that now? *Too many…* She ran her hands through the matching fur on her chin. Vel'erma, what was happening to her?

Zelnor had hoped that understanding the fur's growth might give her insight into her elemental magic. She had watched closely for any kind of pattern that dictated where it grew, but aside from it *always* happening after she used her magic, she'd found nothing.

What would happen after the fur covered her completely? Would other parts of her body change? What if it started to affect her mind?

How long did she have to figure it out? A year? Two?

Zelnor wished she could just stop casting spells altogether. It was the only way she could think of to prevent the transformation, but casting elemental magic was an instinct that kicked in whenever she was stressed or in danger. And even in the best, most ideal conditions, the magic still slowly swelled inside her, until the energy grew so strong that she couldn't physically hold it back anymore. Releasing the magic into a spell quelled the urge temporarily, but never for long enough. She needed a way out of this cycle.

No matter how many books she scoured, everything from technical tomes to pamphlets, she had yet to find anything that even mentioned elemental magic. At this point, she would take the most *useless* piece of information. She just needed somewhere to start, a rumor that could give her something to build on.

One of the cart's wheels passed over a bump, nearly knocking Zelnor out onto the ground. While she'd been lost in thought, the wagon must have started moving. She poked her head out of the boxes. They were much farther than she'd expected.

The silver-haired merchant started to turn toward her, and Zelnor quickly ducked back down. She stayed perfectly still.

Her tension only eased when she felt the continued gentle sway of the cart and rumble of the rough road beneath her. Had the man seen her, he would've stopped immediately and brought an end to her free ride. It seemed she'd gotten away with it.

Zelnor crawled back into the boxes to wait for the merchant to make another stop. Then, she would be able to sneak out, and the man wouldn't get angry that she'd hitched a ride. She would get far away from the thieves and find the closest library or bookshop.

She straightened her jacket and found the ring still in her pocket. Oh gods, this was the *exact* situation she'd been trying to avoid. She didn't know much about prevators, but she at least knew that you should never cross them.

It was fine. Zelnor just needed to sell it. Fast. That way if Prevator Apalandis ever found her, she could pretend the bandits had stolen it, and everything would be fine. Zelnor would get her gold and the noble would be none the wiser. That is, provided nothing else went wrong.

She shut her eyes and prayed to Ireeshnem that, for *once*, things might go her way.

Zelnor found herself waking to the bright sun hanging low in the sky. Afternoon? When she'd fallen asleep it had been *dusk*. How far was this stranger going? She peeked her head out over the side of the cart and saw they'd stopped in a town. *Godsdammit*. She *really* shouldn't be in a place with this many people. Well, there was no helping it now. At least she'd cast a spell recently. It should be all right for a while.

Zelnor jumped from the wagon. A couple of kids stared at her and scattered. That was the advantage of looking like a vagrant in the nicer places; most people already avoided her, saving her the trouble of trying to keep them at arm's length.

The town was the most developed piece of land Zelnor had seen in a while. Most of the settlements in Alaspinor were just simple villages. But here, the buildings were packed together on either side of the street, as though they hoped to squeeze in as many places as possible. Almost every business in sight was either a tavern or a bakery.

The cart had taken Zelnor to Bimblebarrow. She'd been here once or twice, but as one of the largest towns in Alaspinor, she generally tried to avoid it. Bimblebarrow was famed for its cuisine, the

best in the country, apart from Goldhaven. Aspiring chefs, hoping to escape poverty for a successful career in food, flocked here from all over to showcase their talent and throw in their lot with a brick-and-mortar shop.

Signs swung gently in a light breeze that had picked up, carrying the scents of sweet treats and fresh bread. She passed at least half a dozen bakeries and three separate taverns, each bigger than the last. They all looked a little too grand for the three coppers in her pocket.

Finally, Zelnor found a tavern with weathered shutters. The windows' flaking plum paint made the building look shabbier than the ones surrounding it, but the hourglass shape of its sign caught her eye, as did the curvy human woman in a tight purple dress drawn under the words *The Violet Temptress.* Someone had painted an extra "n" on the sign so that it read *The Violent Temptress* instead. Zelnor wasn't sure whether to feel flustered over the painting of the provocative woman or nervous over the name change, but her stomach overruled her misgivings.

Taverns formed the hub of towns in Alaspinor, teeming with gossip and nosy patrons looking to add to the rumors. None of that was of any interest to Zelnor—far from it. She only went to taverns when absolutely necessary, usually to ask around for jobs or grab some food when she was desperate.

Now *libraries*, those were worth the risk of nearby casualties. If she wanted to get rid of her elemental magic, she needed more information, and it was better than having to spend precious coppers buying books. Unfortunately, she hadn't found a good library in a while, so she had visited far more taverns than she would prefer.

She found a seat at a table in the corner, with her back to the wall and a good view of everyone else around her. A server wandered over, took her order, and ambled back to the kitchen again. As Zelnor waited for her food, she took stock of the unique tavern.

The Violent Temptress clearly had a theme, from the amethyst-colored barstool cushions to the various purple liquors on the shelves and the lilacs on the lavender wallpaper. Despite its unsavory name, the tavern was clean and well-maintained.

The only downside was the massive crowd that had formed unexpectedly over the past few minutes. People packed into the moderately sized room. Several patrons whistled and whooped; others catcalled. The noise spread until everyone was shouting so loudly that Zelnor had to shove her fingers in her ears.

The only thing worse than a crowd was a *rowdy* crowd. Unfortunately, Zelnor had already ordered and paid. It was too late to leave. *Might as well see what they're so worked up about.* She arched her back, almost standing from her chair.

A crystal clear, high voice cut through the cacophony, silencing everyone instantly. An ishlanian woman climbed onto a table near the bartender. Zelnor gasped. She'd read about ishlanians once—although they were barely mentioned in the text, just a footnote of a footnote. They were a reclusive race that who lived deep under the waves of the Ethnarian Ocean.

Zelnor only recognized the stunning woman as an ishlanian by the flutter of gills at her neck; she was nothing like the half-fish, half-woman that the text had described. In fact, the woman almost looked like an elf, but the slight downturn of her long, pointed ears, wavy lavender hair, and pale teal skin made it obvious she wasn't one. She wore black leather pants cropped impractically short, barely covering her thighs, and a tight, black leather jerkin tailored to her curves. Her breasts were pushed up so high they almost seemed to fall out of her plunging neckline.

Zelnor hid her face in her hands; some people were absolutely shameless. Thanks to her embarrassment, she only caught glimpses of the performer's languid dance. But the haunting aria the woman sang was more than enough to captivate Zelnor.

The ishlanian sang a series of slow melodies, accompanied by a steadily increasing, soft luminescence that the half-elf could see through the gaps between her fingers. By the time Zelnor worked up the courage to look at her fully, the singer glowed pale blue, her light filling the tavern and transfixing everyone around her. She finished her set and hopped off the table, her body bouncing with the movement.

As the bewitching performer made her rounds, Zelnor's head dipped and she noticed the cold plate of herb-roasted lamb and butter leek puree had arrived while her eyes were closed. The food had kept well considering how long Zelnor had been…*gawking*. She flushed, wanting suddenly to get out of *The Violent Temptress* as soon as possible.

As Zelnor wolfed down her food, her eyes were drawn back to the ishlanian singer. The performer swished gracefully around the other customers. Some of the patrons reached out to try and touch her as she expertly weaved outside their range.

Zelnor felt a twinge of sympathy as she considered the unwanted attention this woman must often draw. It was unfortunate, and she wished the woman well, but Zelnor still wasn't inclined to linger. Frankly, she had already spent more than enough time amid such a large crowd. But before Zelnor could leave, the bard pivoted, heading directly toward her.

Zelnor felt as though she were chained to her seat underneath the singer's intense gaze. The woman slipped into the chair next to her. The ishlanian was no longer glowing, but she looked no less enchanting for it. Up close, her irises sparkled a pale silvery blue that reminded Zelnor of bright moonslight, the kind you only saw when Parenus and Cytho were both full.

Zelnor cringed, realizing suddenly that she'd been eyeing the woman. Gods, the singer was harassed enough without someone who looked like a scruffy old man hitting on her! But the ishlanian's lips quirked upward. She didn't look uncomfortable, she looked… interested. Zelnor leaned forward, her heart racing.

The bard's hand hovered over Zelnor's leg, and Zelnor nodded, urging the woman on. She gently laid her hand on Zelnor's knee, slowly working it higher and higher. Zelnor swallowed. A distant part of her screamed that this was a bad idea. It was risky for her to even stand close to someone; how could she even consider doing something like—like *that?*

Her thoughts stalled as the ishlanian leaned in to whisper, moving her other hand to Zelnor's shoulder. Zelnor felt herself drifting farther forward. She could hardly breathe as the performer drew even closer.

"Erianna Orvash'na. Pleasure to meet you."

The bard's low, smooth voice erased every doubt in Zelnor's mind. For once, she could hardly think at all, and it felt *really* good not to think.

With another nod from Zelnor, Erianna slid her hand higher on Zelnor's thigh, and let her other hand slip down to Zelnor's chest. Feeling the bard's hand *there,* Zelnor suddenly regained her senses and jumped backward, clamping a hand over her mouth. How had she let herself get so *intimate* with someone she'd *just* met? She wrapped her cloak tightly around herself.

"Why do you…?" Erianna trailed off.

At a normal volume, Erianna's voice had a lilting, bubbly quality that made it sound even prettier. Zelnor flushed. What had she been thinking, leading this poor singer on? Gods, she needed to apologize to this woman. Zelnor was acting like a Thorns-dammed lunatic.

Erianna scooted forward in her chair, and something small and silver slipped out of her hand, clattering against the table.

The prevator's ring! The bard must have taken it while Zelnor had been distracted. Zelnor snatched it up and glared at the singer, but Erianna ignored her hostility. She reached toward Zelnor's beard, stopping just shy of it.

"I have never met a half-elven woman with a beard. Oh, sorry, I should ask, do you consider yourself a woman? In case you're worried, I don't have a preference either way." Erianna winked.

"You—You took my ring!" Zelnor spluttered.

"Ring?" Erianna asked. "You mean the one that fell on the table?"

"Fell? You *stole* it!" Zelnor accused.

"Quiet with the s-word." Erianna glanced around the bar. "Besides, you can't steal something that's already been stolen."

"This is my ring. I didn't steal it from anyone," Zelnor lied.

"Really?" the bard asked.

"Yes, *really*. Maybe you shouldn't judge someone based on their appearance."

"All right. Then get me kicked out," Erianna said. "I'm sure it won't bother you if rumors start going around about your expensive ring. It's not like you're trying to hide it from anyone."

The woman propped her long legs up on the table and leaned back in her chair. She had backed Zelnor into a corner, and she knew it. Zelnor willed the annoying songstress to leave, but the other woman's smile only *widened*.

Zelnor refused to let this petty thief have the last laugh. She pinched the ring between two fingers, and slowly, passive aggressively, moved to return it to her pocket. The two-toned gem's surface gleamed in the candlelight.

With deceptive speed, Erianna caught her wrist.

Too startled to react, Zelnor just watched as Erianna dragged her hand closer. Erianna examined the ring with a deep frown. Shaking off her stupor, Zelnor yanked her hand away. The bard's eyes stayed fixed on the jewelry.

"Where did you find that cursed gem?" Erianna asked.

"Cursed?" Zelnor asked.

"Well." She scowled. "Not *everyone* thinks of a pact as a curse."

Just her rotten luck. She had no idea what a pact was, but the last thing she needed was another curse. The sooner she got rid of this thing, the better.

"Well, thankfully, I'll be selling it soon," Zelnor said.

The ishlanian nearly fell out of her chair. "You can't sell this!"

"It's mine," Zelnor said. "I can do whatever I want with it."

"You don't know what you're getting yourself into," Erianna hissed.

"Well, that's not your problem, is it?" Zelnor bolted upward, knocking her chair onto the ground. Erianna's perfectly shaped eyebrows drew together in a scowl, and Zelnor glared right back at her.

Petty thief thinks she *can tell me what to do? Ha!* The two stared at each other, but neither backed down. Then, in an instant, Zelnor spun around and strode out of the room. And of course, Erianna was right behind her. Gods, Zelnor wished the stupid thief would just leave her alone.

Chapter Two
The Idiot Mage

Erianna followed the half-elf to the middle of a narrow footbridge. A small brook trickled beneath their feet. Under any other circumstances, it might have been pleasant. It *should* have been pleasant, taking a leisurely stroll with a handsome half-elf—who was much younger than their white hair implied—and adorably inexperienced.

But right now, Erianna had just about had it with this simpleton. She would much rather go back to *The Violent Temptress,* find some other beautiful individual, take them up to her room, and actually enjoy herself.

Instead, she was responsible for this unwitting idiot.

The half-elf had seemed so promising at first, far more intriguing than Erianna's usual fare. While she had certainly met people whose gender didn't match their birth, none of them had ever been able to grow a beard. In fact, she had slept with a few people who would pay serious gold for that ability. Erianna had been looking forward to an interesting conversation with the half-elf after they had their fun, but before she could smooth over the misunderstanding about the "stolen" ring, that familiar blue and green stone had ruined everything.

How had a pact gem gotten into a *ring?* With the way pacts worked, it shouldn't have even been possible. Probably some new trick to lure this poor soul into making a choice they would deeply regret. And without Erianna, it would've worked. This dumb half-elf should be thanking her. Instead, she had been forced to follow the stranger around like a damned puppy, because they couldn't see how stupid they were being. Really? Selling it? Liscuntia only knew who'd end up with it then!

Erianna blocked the half-elf's path. She towered over the bearded stranger, standing almost a foot taller than them.

"That gem is dangerous," Erianna said.

"Can you just leave already?" the bearded half-elf asked.

"You have to bring it back where it came from."

At this point, Erianna was absolutely willing to just take it from the half-elf. It was for their own good. She darted forward, but the half-elf was ready. Before Erianna could even try to grab it, they whipped the ring out of their pocket and held it over the river.

"Do you even *know* what you stole?" Erianna asked.

"I told you. I didn't. Steal. Anything."

"It's a dragon's scale," Erianna said. "Do you really want to be in a pact with a dragon?"

The half-elf's eyes widened, and the ring slipped through their fingers. Erianna managed to catch it before it fell in the river, careful not to touch the gem. She held it above her head, just in case the half-elf made a grab for it again.

"A dragon's scale…" the half-elf muttered.

"Now do you understand why you can't sell it?" Erianna asked.

The stranger *still* had the gall to look unconvinced.

"What is it now?" Erianna sighed.

"I need the money," they said.

For Liscuntia's sake! Erianna wanted to throttle this dimwit, but this bickering wasn't getting them anywhere. It wasn't the half-elf's fault they didn't recognize a dragon scale. Most people wouldn't. But *still,* now that the half-elf knew it was from a dragon, they shouldn't even be contemplating selling it. Clearly, they didn't understand what they were suggesting.

"You want to be responsible for some other idiot unknowingly forging a pact with a dragon?" Erianna asked.

"I've been holding it for more than half a day, and I'm fine."

The half-elf tried to snatch it out of her hand, but Erianna easily kept it away.

"Maybe that's exactly what the dragon *wants* you to think. Maybe he's waiting for you to pass it along to the right person," Erianna said.

"Or *maybe* it's just a normal ring with a normal stone," the idiot argued.

Oh, it was most certainly a pact gem. The way the "stone" shimmered between two colors was undeniable proof, and unfortunately, Erianna knew exactly which green and blue bastard the scale had come from. But that wasn't any of this stranger's business.

"Are you willing to take that risk?" Erianna challenged.

The half-elf winced. At least they had *some* conscience.

"If I could get the scale out of the ring, *then* I could sell it?" they asked.

"No!" Erianna chastised, balking at the very idea. "Absolutely not. It might have some sort of residual magic in it or something. Dragons are powerful creatures!"

"But I...I have to," the half-elf said. "I really need to get rid of it."

"Because you stole it?" Erianna asked.

The stranger glowered at her, and Erianna raised an eyebrow. There was no denying it anymore.

"Fine, I stole it. On accident," the half-elf finally admitted.

"On accident?" Erianna asked.

"As if a thief like *you* has the moral high ground," they grumbled.

"I'm not judging. I'm just wondering how you steal something accidentally."

"It doesn't matter!" the half-elf said. "The point is I—"

"Can't be found with it. I understand," she said.

Whoever the half-elf had stolen the ring from, they seemed to think the person would seek it out. If the original owner found it, that would just put that person at risk instead. There was only one solution: destroy the ring and chuck the scale right back at the dragon it came from.

"Fine," Erianna said. "Come on. Let's go."

"Go where?" the half-elf asked, jogging to catch up with her.

"You'll see."

Erianna smiled at the prospect of seeing Hrik'nar again. She didn't know many people in this town, but she was lucky to count the blacksmith among her acquaintances. Hrik'nar was great at his craft, wasn't greedy, and, most importantly, wouldn't ask any questions. He was the only one she trusted to handle the ring.

As the two walked together, Erianna glanced sideways at the stranger. Now that her annoyance had faded, she started to feel curious again.

"So, you already know I'm Erianna. And you…?"

"Zelnor," the half-elf said.

"Last name?" she asked.

"Don't have one," Zelnor said.

"Hmm. Interesting." Erianna hummed. "So. Pronouns? Which ones do you use?"

Zelnor was quiet for a *long* time before answering.

"I guess…you can use 'she' if you want, since you already know,

but please use 'he' in front of other people."

"That's different," Erianna said.

"Well," Zelnor sighed. "I'm used to 'she,' I was called that for a long time, but now when people find out that I'm a woman with a beard, they…"

"Gasp and drop your stolen ring on the table?" Erianna joked.

"Something like that," Zelnor muttered. "It's just easier if I go by 'he.' I don't want to draw any attention."

Zelnor's answers only made Erianna even more curious. It sounded like she hadn't had this beard her whole life. How had she gotten it? And why was she trying so hard to avoid notice? Sure, she had stolen a ring, but Erianna doubted that was the full reason. The bearded woman was a first-time criminal at best. She was far too easy to read to be any sort of professional. Either way, she certainly wasn't lying low because of petty thievery—there was no authority to hide from in Alaspinor. So who was she running from? Was the ring's owner that powerful?

Erianna stumbled, just barely catching herself. Surely, Zelnor wasn't running from the Broken Claim…

There was no point in wondering. As soon as they got this dragon scale situation sorted out, they'd go their separate ways. Erianna just wanted to prevent another hapless idiot from getting entrapped by that dragon. That was all.

"Although, as long as you're traveling with me, people are looking anyway," Zelnor grumbled.

"Because I'm so beautiful?" Erianna teased.

"Because you're an ishlanian," Zelnor said quickly.

"A *beautiful* ishlanian."

Zelnor rolled her eyes, but Erianna could see her blushing. The bearded woman was fun to tease, when she wasn't being stupid.

At this late hour, Hrik'nar's Smithy was empty. The particularly short, gray-feathered kunari was shaping a piece of wood into a long bow. He narrowed his beady black eyes, focusing intently on the weapon. It took all his weight thrown backward to curve it the way he wanted. His talons pierced deeply into the supple wood, leaving holes in the midsection of the bow. The puncture marks were a signature of sorts, one of the reasons the kunari had come to be so well known in Bimblebarrow.

Hrik'nar put down the bow and tilted his head up to look at Erianna, nearly folding himself in half to properly to see her.

"Good evening, Erianna," Hrik'nar said. The kunari spoke in a deep voice. She still remembered her shock when she'd first heard it.

"Hello Hrik'nar! How are you?" Erianna asked.

"Well, thank you. Little Sreet'nar has been asking after you."

Erianna had met the blacksmith for the first time when her knife had broken. She'd been directed to him as "the best blacksmith in town."

Meeting with Hrik'nar was the first lengthy conversation she'd struck up in quite a while. Usually, she only sought out others to collect payment for her singing or to satiate her desires. Neither activity involved much talking. Not that she wasn't a *sparkling* conversationalist, but her particular lifestyle—selling her voice, never staying in one town too long—didn't leave much room for friendships.

Hrik'nar wasn't necessarily a friend either, but he was kind and a genuine pleasure to talk with. The middle-aged kunari had several hatchlings that he doted on, and Erianna enjoyed listening to him recount their misadventures with fondness. There was a certain comfort in hearing about a happy family like his, but as much as she would like to catch up, they needed to get this matter resolved as soon as possible.

"Unfortunately, I have urgent business to discuss with you," Erianna said. "Please tell your daughter hello from me, though."

"Of course," Hrik'nar said. "Now, what sort of business have you brought this time?"

Erianna pulled the ring out and handed it over.

"It's something dangerous. Something only you should handle," she said.

Hrik'nar delicately balanced the metal loop in his talons and held the ring close to one black eye, scrutinizing it, before shaking his head.

"I have never seen such a gem before. Although it does interest me greatly, perhaps a jeweler would be more suited to—"

"No!" Erianna shouted. "I don't need it appraised. I need the gem removed. It's…" She lowered her voice. "It's a pact gem."

Hrik'nar's eye widened, and he craned his neck, staring at the ring with a new intensity.

"A pact gem…" the blacksmith repeated in wonder. "I have never heard of one set into a ring before…"

"I don't know how it happened," Erianna said. "But I would like the ring melted down and the scale removed. Please."

Zelnor stiffened upon learning that they would be destroying the ring, but thankfully, she didn't argue.

"I can melt it down, and I've got something that'll pry the gem out, but…" Hrik'nar inhaled sharply. "Jewelry is not my line of expertise. I may damage the gem."

"Dragons scales are unbreakable," Erianna said, almost instantly.

Zelnor frowned, and Erianna could almost feel the question coming. Thankfully the half-elf didn't ask how Erianna knew so much about dragon scales, and Hrik'nar simply hummed at new the information. He had always respected Erianna's privacy, for which she was incredibly grateful.

"Very well. That being the case, it shouldn't be any trouble," the blacksmith confirmed.

"Thank you," Erianna said. "How much do I owe you?"

"No charge," the blacksmith replied.

"But Hrik'nar—"

"Just come visit the hatchlings the next time you find yourself in Bimblebarrow."

"All right," Erianna agreed hesitantly. "I promise."

Hrik'nar turned around, gripping a slim metal lever in his talons. He hunched over his anvil. As he pried the little tool into the setting, the ring slipped out of his other talon. Hrik'nar muttered grumpily under his breath.

To Erianna's shock, Zelnor stepped forward and held the ring in place for the blacksmith. The half-elf hadn't said a word since they'd arrived. Erianna had assumed the bearded woman had been sulking, but now, she wondered if Zelnor was simply shy. *Well, around everyone except me.* Erianna snickered.

With Zelnor's help, Hrik'nar was able to lodge the thin piece of metal under the scale with a *pop,* the gem separating from the ring. Erianna let out a long breath. She hadn't realized how tense she'd been until he had finished. She had been so worried that the gem would resist being removed, or react badly to being touched, or *something.*

We're lucky that nothing—

Before Erianna could even finish the thought, the gem started glowing. It crackled with tiny bolts of blue and green energy. The lightning reached out toward the half-elf.

"Get away from it!" Erianna shouted.

The tendrils of light shot out toward Zelnor, wrapping around her wrist. She shook her arm, desperately trying to dislodge the sapphire and emerald energy, but it just kept climbing higher. When the energy dissipated, the pact gem had imbedded itself into Zelnor's right wrist.

Liscuntia, this was the worst outcome imaginable! Somehow, the half-elf had inadvertently accepted the dragon's "gift," and now she was stuck at the mercy of a monster. Not just any monster either. *Torrin.* Torrin had claimed another, and it was all Erianna's fault.

Chapter Three
Cursed

Zelnor ran her hands over the gem embedded in her wrist. Smooth but warm, the same temperature as her skin. The once two-toned gem swirled with movement, emerald and sapphire bleeding together.

She had been nursing the same tankard of ale for the last hour, wondering what in the Seven Afterworlds she was supposed to do now. She had just stood there, dumbfounded, as the blacksmith apologized profusely. She knew that it wasn't his fault, but his apology might as well have been a eulogy for all the good it did. She was done for! A pact with a dragon? On top of everything else?

When Erianna suggested returning to *The Violent Temptress*, Zelnor had numbly let the bard lead her away. The drink was calming her nerves somewhat, but it was just a distraction. A distraction from the fact that she had somehow entered into a *pact* with a *dragon!* She could already feel the magic in the scale. Buzzing and tingling, just itching to emerge and do gods-only-knew-what. As if she

23

wasn't already unstable enough.

"Did you know this place used to be called *The Violet Temptress?*" Erianna asked suddenly.

Zelnor squinted at her, confused by the unprompted fact.

"The owner's sign was vandalized. Someone added the 'n' and he decided to keep it," Erianna continued. "He's pretty easygoing."

Zelnor stared incredulously at the bard. Did she care *at all* about what she'd done? Zelnor could have—no, *should* have—just thrown the ring in the river. Now, she had an entirely new problem to deal with.

"This is all your fault," Zelnor said.

Erianna's eyes darted toward the stone.

"It is not my fault. I didn't know that this would happen," she said. "How could I have?"

Erianna's skin emitted a bright blue light. A couple of farmers at a nearby table gaped openly at them. A few older merchants muttered to each other and pointed in their direction. Zelnor sank farther into her seat.

"People are *looking*." Zelnor hissed.

"You should've thought of that before you decided to blame me for everything!" Erianna yelled.

Zelnor's elemental magic swelled. Everyone's eyes were on her. Her heart started beating faster. Energy strained toward her palms. *Not now! Please, please not now!* She couldn't cast a spell in a room this crowded.

"*Please* calm down," Zelnor said.

"Calm down?" Erianna glowed brighter. "You expect me to just—"

"I'm sorry. I'm sorry." Zelnor's breathing went shallow. "I—I'm just—Just forget it."

Zelnor needed to get away. She could still feel everyone's eyes on her. What if she hurt someone again? *This is bad.* What if someone *died* again?

"Zelnor," Erianna said softly, snapping Zelnor's attention back to her. "Let's talk in my room."

Zelnor nodded, grateful for the chance to escape this nightmare situation, and followed the bard upstairs. Erianna unlocked a door and pushed it open, guiding Zelnor into a small bedroom. There was a single bed, simple straw with clean sheets and blankets, beside an end table with a small oil lamp. An elegant blue dress had been hung up on the opposite wall. The only other thing of interest was the *giant* backpack propped against the back corner.

Erianna sat down on the bed, crossing her legs and patting the spot in front of her. And that was the moment Zelnor realized she had gone alone into a room with a stranger. She sat in front of the bard. If it came down to it, Zelnor could protect herself, but she didn't want to accidentally destroy the inn trying to escape. (It had happened before.)

"It's still not my fault, but…" The bard sighed. "I'll help you get rid of it, all right?"

"Why?" Zelnor asked.

Zelnor barely knew this woman, and yet she was going out of her way to help. Erianna was a thief (not to mention pushy and annoying); she didn't exactly seem the charitable type. What did Erianna have to gain from this? Zelnor was going to turn her down either way, but she wanted that answer first.

"Because I'm the only one who can," Erianna said.

"Ha," Zelnor scoffed. "No, thank you. You've done *more* than enough. I'll deal with it on my own."

"Oh really," Erianna said. "And how are you going to deal with it?"

Zelnor would deal with the problem the same way she was dealing with her other curse. First, she would need to research dragon pacts. Then, maybe she could find some way to reject it. Or some sort of loophole? Whatever she did, it would require caution and planning. Dragons had been around for a long time, at least as long as mortals had—maybe more.

"I'll find a way to get rid of it," Zelnor said.

"And how long will that take you?" Erianna asked. "You clearly know nothing about pacts."

"And you do?" Zelnor retorted.

"I happen to know a lot about pacts, actually," Erianna said.

Erianna did seem to know a lot about dragons. She had immediately recognized the dragon scale and known that it was unbreakable. Now that said gem was imbedded into her wrist, Zelnor really needed to know where Erianna had gotten her information from. Zelnor doubted Erianna had read about pacts. There was no way this woman had the patience for intensive study. But if that were the case, then...

"You have a pact with a dragon?" Zelnor concluded—half asking, half accusing.

Erianna's expression twisted into a scowl, somber for the first time since Zelnor had met her.

"I don't," she said, not meeting Zelnor's eyes, "but I know about them. Don't be tempted by his powerful magic. It isn't worth the price."

More magic? That was the last thing she would ever want. Gods only knew she had enough magic-related problems.

"I don't want a dragon's magic. I don't want *anything* to do with a dragon."

"That's...surprising," the bard said. "Most people I've met want power."

Erianna eyed Zelnor, and Zelnor scooted back a bit under her intense gaze.

"Well, I don't. So...how do I get rid of it?" Zelnor asked.

"You haven't agreed to the pact yet, so I'm guessing the scale just latched on to whoever was closest. All you need to do is go to him and refuse the pact."

"You mean go to…the *dragon?*" Zelnor gaped. "As in, giant monster with teeth? What if it eats me?"

"He isn't going eat you," Erianna said. "Well, probably."

"*Probably?*" Zelnor screeched.

"Oh, calm down," the ishlanian said. "I'm pretty sure dragons don't eat mortals."

"Then what do they eat?"

"I don't know, actually," Erianna said.

"You're crazy. I'm not doing that," Zelnor said.

"So, you'd rather be at the beast's beck and call?" Erianna asked. "Whatever plans you had, whatever you wanted from life, you can say goodbye to all of it, because Torrin only cares about himself."

"How do you know the dragon's name?" Zelnor asked.

"I've…" Erianna's eyes widened for a split second before she regained her composure. "I've heard it mentioned. His lair is nearby. People talk. You know, rumors."

There was obviously something Erianna wasn't telling her. Still… the bard seemed to know a lot more about pacts that Zelnor did. In fact, she knew a suspicious amount about them for someone who didn't have one. While Zelnor couldn't trust the woman, there was no harm in asking for directions.

"I'm assuming you know where this Torrin's lair is?" Zelnor asked.

"It's close. Only a few days east of here," Erianna said.

"I'll leave tomorrow, then," Zelnor said.

"*We'll* leave tomorrow," Erianna corrected.

"I don't need an escort."

"You can stay here for the night," Erianna continued, ignoring Zelnor's protests.

"I told you I don't—Wait. Are you asking me to stay with you? No thanks, I'll sleep outside," Zelnor said.

"Outside? On a night like this? Do you really hate me that much?" Erianna asked. "How many times do I have to apologize?"

"At least once," Zelnor said.

"Oh, for—Fine," Erianna grumbled. "I'm *sorry* for trying to steal the ring you'd already stolen. Happy?"

"Ecstatic," Zelnor said. "Have a nice life."

"Please," Erianna said before Zelnor could get up, "just sleep here tonight."

"What? Afraid I'll run away?" Zelnor asked.

"Well, you are a flight risk," Erianna said, "but no. No one should have to sleep in the rain."

Normally, Zelnor didn't mind sleeping outside on the streets, finding a secluded place and avoiding people as much as possible, but Erianna was right. It would be miserable sleeping outside tonight. It was a tempting offer, provided this wasn't some sort of trick… But Zelnor had nothing left to steal. Besides, it had been a very long time since she had slept in a bed. *Wait a moment.*

"There's only one bed," Zelnor said.

"It's large, we can share," Erianna said.

Zelnor flushed and shook her head vigorously. The ishlanian frowned, looking hurt.

"I'm not going to do anything. I would *never*," Erianna said.

"No! I didn't mean. I just…I'm sleeping on the floor," Zelnor finished awkwardly. She placed her coat on the ground and slid off the bed to lie on top of it.

"All right. Goodnight then," Erianna said.

"Goodnight," Zelnor said.

Too late, Zelnor realized that she'd never gotten the chance to actually turn down Erianna's aggressive offer to guide her. The situation was far from ideal. Zelnor was relying solely on an unapologetic thief, and tomorrow, they would start heading toward a *dragon*. Somehow, after two careful years, Zelnor had broken her vow to travel alone for a selfish, overconfident, attention whore.

Unfortunately, Zelnor couldn't see a way out of it. Even if she snuck out in the middle of the night, Erianna would certainly follow her. She knew where Zelnor was going, after all. It was better to appease the bard for now. They would travel together for two days, three at most, and then Zelnor would get rid of this gem and would never have to see the annoying bard again.

A pillow hit Zelnor's head. Erianna was looking down at her expectantly. Zelnor contemplated throwing it right back, just to see what the smug bard thought of a face full of feathers, but she was too tired to be petty, and the pillow was softer than anything she'd ever slept on. Zelnor let out a little sigh, sinking deeply into it.

The bard smiled at her. Zelnor really hated that stupid, satisfied expression. The teal woman's smirk was absolutely insufferable.

Two days, Zelnor decided. They had to reach that dragon in two days. If the trip took three, she was pretty sure she would kill this woman. On purpose.

Zelnor dreamed she was back in her mother's shelter in the desert. The spacious barn—home to countless refugees—was uncharacteristically empty. It was a large, open building with a huge ground floor. The second and third floors were more like wide balconies that wrapped around the interior. The third floor was the smallest, and her mom called it the loft. The mage's chest clenched with a warm burst of nostalgia. The loft had been one of Zelnor and

Heeden's favorite places to play when they were little.

Zelnor wasn't herself. She was a passenger in another body with no control over its movements. The knowledge didn't surprise or scare her. It had happened before. She just wondered whose eyes was she looking out of this time.

Zelnor didn't recognize the person's sleeping area, but then again, they all looked mostly the same. There was a small cot, low to the ground, and a bag filled with clothes. The woman she was inhabiting bent down and placed a neatly folded black tunic on top of the pile. *She must be leaving.* As the woman leaned over, a lock of short red hair fell in front of her face. Her scarred, pale hand moved to tuck it behind her ear.

The woman closed the bag and crossed her arms over her chest, looking around the shelter for the last time. The shelter felt lonely without its usual bustle. It was the people, the community that Zelnor's mom had created, that made the vast shelter feel so warm and inviting. She breathed in deeply. The arid scent of sand lingered on the air, so dry it stung her nose. The smell of home.

"I'll miss this," Zelnor heard herself mutter in the woman's unfamiliar accent.

The woman turned back to pick up her bag but froze when she heard a loud *bang* downstairs. She slipped a dagger from her side and slid it across her calf, adding another cut to her heavily scarred leg. Little tendrils of darkness curled from her fingertips and spread across her body. The woman faded into the dim light of the loft.

Shadow magic! It was the first time Zelnor had ever seen the practice in person. Although, she wasn't sure seeing it in a dream counted.

The woman jumped nimbly to avoid the creaky boards. Zelnor could tell that this woman had years of experience moving quietly; it was in every graceful, surefooted step. Soon, she reached the railing and peered at the scene down below.

A young girl had rushed into the shelter, dragging along a satchel too big for her. The bag had belonged to her father. She was nine years old, with long, light brown hair and tan skin. The little girl gestured frantically to a dark-skinned boy a few years older than her. Even from this distance, Zelnor could see the girl tugging anxiously on a streak of white hair.

"You did *what?*" the boy shouted.

The little girl walked toward the boy, speaking urgently, and he clasped a hand over his mouth. It took a little while for his shock to wear off. But when it did, he put his hand on her shoulder and asked something.

"She lied to me!" the girl shouted. "I can't—I can't stay here!"

The girl flung her arms about wildly, describing the situation, before finally ending with a question. The words the young girl said were inaudible. The person that Zelnor was—this pale, scarred redhead—was too far away to hear them. But Zelnor knew what the girl had asked. She even knew the exact words the girl had used.

This was the night Zelnor had asked Heeden to run away from home with her.

Heeden had agreed. Of course he had. He was Zelnor's best friend. He would've done anything for her.

The little girl sprang forward and wrapped her arms around the boy, squeezing him for a moment before they broke apart. He disappeared from view, returning with a small bag, and the two left the shelter together.

The scarred woman slowly lowered herself onto her cot. It whined and bowed beneath her. She stared at her fully packed bag and pulled down the hem of her high-collared tunic. She ran her fingertips lightly over the right side of her neck, just above her clavicle. The skin there was raised, but it didn't feel like a normal scar. The shape and texture weren't quite right. A tattoo maybe?

"Anya. I am so sorry. Soon…I promise," the woman whispered. "Soon…"

The woman leaped up from the cot and sped down the stairs, taking them two at a time, before rushing outside. She ran past the eclectic mix of wood and adobe buildings until she came to Zelnor's home. The woman paused with her fist raised to knock at the door. Zelnor watched the woman's hand shake. They both took a deep breath, and Zelnor felt the woman steady herself. Finally, they knocked on the door.

"Lia!" the woman shouted. "LIA! Please—"

"Get up!" Erianna shouted.

Zelnor squinted against blinding sunlight filtering in from the window and realized, after a few groggy blinks, that Erianna had shaken her awake. In fact, the ishlanian was *still* shaking her. Why was she waking Zelnor at this gods-awful hour? Clearly, the bard ran on a completely different schedule than Zelnor. She shoved her head back into the pillow, trying to ignore the overly cheerful ishlanian.

"Good, you're finally up," Erianna said.

"No, I'm not," Zelnor mumbled.

Just when Zelnor started feeling herself drift off again, Erianna snatched the pillow out from under her, and Zelnor's head hit the floor with a quiet *thump*.

"We need to set out as soon as possible," Erianna said. "Besides, you don't want to miss breakfast."

Erianna snickered, and Zelnor realized the ishlanian was looking at her hair. Pursing her lips, Zelnor smoothed her white hair down. She knew it looked wild in the morning, sticking up at strange angles, and Erianna obviously found the unfortunate look amusing.

"I'm already finished getting ready," Erianna said, hiking her enormous bag higher on her shoulders. "I'll wait for you outside the door."

And with that, the ishlanian left to give Zelnor some privacy.

Zelnor pulled her spare tunic out and sniffed it. It smelled *ripe,* caked in mud and covered in sweat stains. Keeping it in her bag had not done it any favors, but there was no point in washing it any time soon. She would just get it dirty all over again with a whole new round of chores, after this Torrin business was over, since she *still* didn't have any gold…or silver, or copper…or anything resembling currency.

Zelnor stuffed the shirt back into her bag and thought of her dream. She often dreamed of her past. She would close her eyes and see a different moment on Kezeek Mesa or relive a day in Alaspinor. She assumed it was some form of torture, courtesy of her curse—seeing people she'd lost or left behind. As if a second random spell and fur growth weren't bad enough.

Thankfully, she sometimes had dreams about other people entirely. Those were the strangest ones, though; inhabiting another person's body and seeing through their eyes, occasionally even hearing their thoughts. It was always someone she knew. Sometimes it was someone she'd only briefly met, sometimes a loved one, but there was always some connection between Zelnor and the person she dreamed about. So why didn't she recognize the scarred woman who'd spied on her and Heeden?

Who was this pale stranger? How did the woman know Zelnor's mother? And who was Anya? The woman's lover? A sister? Zelnor wanted answers, and she was tempted to go back to sleep to get them.

While unlikely, it was possible she would have another dream that continued where the last left off. The stranger's conversation with Zelnor's mother might reveal some of the secrets Zelnor was still desperate to uncover. Either way, she wouldn't mind the extra sleep. A few more minutes wouldn't hurt, right?

But as she lay back down, the smell of sausage and eggs wafted down the hall and into the room. She also smelled sweet pastries and bitter coffee. She hadn't been awake early enough for breakfast in a long time. She supposed being up early had *some* benefits…and as long as the bard was paying, she might as well get a meal out of this ordeal.

As promised, Erianna was waiting for Zelnor outside.

"You're wearing the same tunic you did yesterday," Erianna said.

For the first time, Zelnor noticed Erianna's outfit: a soft pink dress that fluttered around her mid-calf. A tightly fitted, leather cuirass decorated with pale pink flowers over the bodice offered protection. The combination of brown and pink went well with the teal of her skin and her lavender hair.

Zelnor awkwardly adjusted her threadbare tunic.

"The other one's dirty," she mumbled.

"You only have two outfits?" Erianna asked.

Feeling self-conscious about wearing her rumpled clothes from the previous day, Zelnor rushed past Erianna downstairs to the main room of the tavern. Despite leaving first, the ishlanian easily pulled ahead of Zelnor, leading the way to an open table. She hoisted her bulky bag more securely onto her back as she weaved through the crowd, setting it down on the ground with a muffled *thump* and looping one strap around her ankle so no one would steal it. *Ironic considering, the ishlanian herself is a thief.*

What did Erianna keep in that gigantic monstrosity, anyway? Based on her reaction to Zelnor's old tunic, probably three dozen outfits. Either way, it seemed cumbersome, impractical, and wholly unsuited for a life on the road traveling between towns. The bard seemed fine with it, though, so who was Zelnor to comment?

The same server from the previous night set two plates of the breakfast Zelnor had smelled down on their table. Erianna winked at him as she took slow, deliberate bites of her food. The young man smiled bashfully. *Ugh.* Zelnor wished she were at another table. It was too early for this nonsense, but Zelnor refused to let the bard's over-the-top flirting ruin her appetite.

"You're going to choke eating that fast," Erianna said. "You act like this is your last meal."

Zelnor swallowed the fried egg she'd just stuffed into her mouth.

"Well, since I can't sell the ring anymore, it might be," she replied.

"Right… In that case, I'll pay for breakfast," Erianna said.

"I hope so, or else I would have to run *really* fast." Zelnor smirked.

Erianna leaned forward.

"Did you just make a joke? I didn't know you were capable of that," she teased.

"You're hearing things," Zelnor said.

Erianna started to speak again, but Zelnor held up a hand. She had to finish her coffee first. It was her only defense against the bard's sunny disposition. She drank it in a few gulps and rejoiced when the server brought more. It her took two full cups to feel like a person again.

"So," Zelnor said. "Torrin?"

"Well, when you're a traveling performer you run into all sorts of people. I once met someone who made bad choices. One of those choices involved a dragon named Torrin," Erianna said, and then added, "People talk when they're drunk."

Did Erianna really expect Zelnor to believe that her extensive knowledge of dragons had come from a few conversations?

"If it was just some drunk patron, then how is it you recognized exactly which dragon this scale came from with just a *glance?*" she asked.

Erianna shifted in her seat, fixing her eyes on her half-empty plate. There it was. Yet another reminder not to trust her. This woman had already stolen from Zelnor once, and now she was clearly hiding things.

Zelnor scoffed, and Erianna's head snapped back up again. Her teal skin glowed faintly.

"What about you, then? Where did you get that gem? Why were you so eager to sell it?" Erianna asked.

"None of your business," Zelnor said.

Zelnor could have just told Erianna the truth. Apart from the prevator, the explanation behind the ring was mundane enough. With the number of roving bandits littering the country, any reasonable person would believe that she'd accidentally stolen the ring. Erianna, however, did not strike Zelnor as someone reasonable. And besides, she didn't owe this petty thief *any* explanations.

The two glared at each other, both ignoring their food. Their intense staring match lasted a few minutes, until Erianna finally broke eye contact.

HAH! I WON! Zelnor winced when she realized how childish she was being. Thankfully, she had cheered in her head and not out loud...

"Listen, Zelnor," Erianna said. "We'll be together for a couple days, so could we put aside the hostility? At least temporarily."

Zelnor had forgotten their plans for a moment. She couldn't spend two full days with this woman. She might not be particularly fond of Erianna, but the bard didn't deserve a grievous injury or worse. Zelnor didn't want any more blood on her hands. She should at least *try* to dissuade the woman.

"We really don't have to go together," Zelnor said.

"You think you can find the lair, the *secret* lair, without a guide?" Erianna asked.

"Dragons are giant lizards. How hard could it be to find?"

"You'd be surprised," Erianna said.

Zelnor was already directionally challenged. Who knew how much time she would waste looking for Torrin's hidden lair on her own? Damn it all. She did need a guide. There was no helping it. As long as Zelnor didn't cast any spells and slept a healthy distance from the bard, she *should* be able to avoid any nasty accidents.

"… Fine," the mage said. "I'll agree to a temporary truce."

Zelnor held out her right hand. Erianna beamed. Her face lit up, both literally and metaphorically.

"Fantastic!" she said.

Erianna took Zelnor's hand and firmly shook it. Her eyes darted toward the gem on Zelnor's wrist, and Erianna's grip lingered as she stared at it. Her brow furrowed briefly, before the ishlanian let go and settled back into her chair.

"Did you know," Erianna started with a gleam in her eye, "that this place has a rivalry with the inn across the road?"

Zelnor slowly shook her head, surprised by the abrupt topic change.

"They're called *Nestle Down* and claim to have real teriact feathers in their pillows and beds." Erianna leaned forward, resting her head in her cradled hands. "Of course, my loyalty is to *The Violent Temptress,* so I've never slept there myself, but I heard…"

The ishlanian bard continued recounting the ridiculous competition between the two establishments, and Zelnor let the words wash over her, only giving occasional one-word responses when the other woman asked a question. So much had happened in less than a day. And the next couple of days would probably feel even longer, if this animated yet one-sided conversation was anything to go by.

This was going to be a long journey.

Erianna and Zelnor trekked through a dense forest with a canopy so thick it blotted out the sun. Even though Erianna's keen ishlanian eyes allowed her to see clearly through the gloom, the underbrush and frequent trunks blocked her line of sight. She lit up her skin for Zelnor's benefit, but the teal glow hardly staved off the walls of darkness on either side.

Mundane sounds were more unsettling in this still, damp air. The birdsong echoed strangely. The crack of a twig under her foot felt like a bone snapping. Together it formed an eerie endless night, suspending all sense of time.

Of course it's ominous. It leads to Torrin. But somehow, the path was worse than the last time she walked it…

Erianna tried to chase away the memories with conversation, but the half-elf had practically turned mute since they'd met. Zelnor had had plenty to say when she'd hated Erianna, but ever since they'd agreed to act cordially, Zelnor had gone unnervingly silent. *Probably trying to keep all her insults to herself.*

Still, Erianna had never been the type to give up.

"Let's play a word game," she suggested.

"Let's not," Zelnor said.

Of course, the bearded woman would act disinterested. Erianna had never met anyone more against having fun.

Erianna decided to start the game by herself. She was confident she could get Zelnor to play: the smart-mouth wouldn't be able to resist the chance to one-up her. And even if she didn't join in, at least it would fill this Liscuntia-damned silence.

"It's a simple game. One person says a word, the other needs to find a rhyme," Erianna explained. "Whoever can't think of a rhyme or uses a word that doesn't match, has to pick the next one."

"I told you I'm not playing," Zelnor said.

"I'm refreshing *myself* on the rules," Erianna said.

The half-elf sighed and gestured to her, as if to say, carry on then. Erianna cleared her throat and began.

"Fish, wish, dish, miss—"

"Miss doesn't rhyme," Zelnor interrupted.

"It's a slant rhyme," Erianna said.

"Do slant rhymes count?"

"They do if everyone playing the game agrees to them."

"Then I say they don't count."

"Well, then … I've lost that round and it's your turn," Erianna said.

Ha! She had successfully tricked Zelnor into playing. Erianna wiggled her shoulders in a little dance at her victory. She knew how to dance "properly," but proper was never any fun, and right now they both needed a bit of fun.

Zelnor snorted at Erianna's uncoordinated dance, but when Erianna turned toward her traveling companion, she already wore a scowl again. Even so, the half-elf reluctantly agreed to play, and the two bandied words back and forth. After a fierce round, Zelnor tried to use the word *thwap*.

"You can't use a sound as a word," Erianna said triumphantly.

"That wasn't in the rules," Zelnor grumbled.

"I forgot that part, didn't I?" Erianna said. "Would you like to start over?"

"No, I couldn't think of another word anyway, so you won," Zelnor sighed.

"Let's call it a tie instead," Erianna suggested with a half-smile.

"Sure." Zelnor shrugged.

Zelnor was actually a good sport when it came to competitions. Not something Erianna had expected, considering how spiteful she'd acted when they first met. Maybe she had something against thieves? *A bit hypocritical, coming from a thief.* Erianna still wanted to hear how she'd stolen the ring. It wasn't as though she would judge

Zelnor; Erianna wanted to know how she had found herself in this predicament, and more importantly, who *exactly* she had pissed off.

But Zelnor was guarded—easily one of the least trusting people Erianna had ever met. After spending a little over a day with her, Erianna had decided that the only reason she'd been able to steal from Zelnor was because she'd been so flustered by the bard's attention. Embarrassment was the half-elf's only weakness. Maybe if Erianna opened up to her first, Zelnor would at least be willing to hold a light conversation.

"Sometimes I play these games to loosen up before performances. They help with nerves," Erianna offered.

"You don't seem like the type to get nerves," Zelnor said.

Only when I'm doing something I hate, Erianna thought bitterly.

"Everyone gets nerves, don't they?" she said.

"Then…why do you do it?" Zelnor asked.

Their talk was rapidly exiting "casual topics territory" and veering straight into "mind your own business," but it was a fair question. Gods only knew Erianna wanted to stop singing. She wasn't sure why she felt the need to continue. Maybe because it was easy. She'd built up enough of a reputation that she could at least guarantee she'd never go hungry.

"It's a way to make coin at the moment." She shrugged.

Erianna expected Zelnor to press her on the subject, but the half-elf surprised her.

"I can understand that," Zelnor said, and added, "You have a nice voice, by the way."

The praise, as genuine as it had been, felt hollow. It was the first compliment that the Zelnor had given her, and Erianna wished it had been about *any* other aspect of her. *A nice voice.* That nice voice was a curse. At least, she'd started earning gold for herself now, but it still didn't feel right. It never would.

"All right. So, I won last round. Our next word is life," Erianna announced, a little too cheerfully.

"Strife," Zelnor said.

"Kni—"

The bard felt the tip of a blade against her armor. She leaped backward and spun toward her attacker. The cloaked figure clutched a dagger in its unnaturally pale, bloated hand. Its skin was stretched too tightly across its neck and jaw. Its blank, black mask had been fused to its face.

A vocarii. It had been years since Erianna had last faced one of the Broken Claim's assassins. *Thorns' unspoken name! How did they find me?*

Without taking her eyes off her attacker, Erianna pulled her knife out of her boot and raced forward. But before she even reached the vocarii, a bolt of lightning flew past her shoulder.

Erianna whirled, looking for the source, and found… *Zelnor?* The half-elf's arms crackled with energy. Her white hair whipped around her face, and her eyes glowed with a faint white light. It was like looking at someone in the center of a storm. No, someone who *was* a storm.

Erianna tripped over a root, falling to the ground with a *thud*. Another bolt of lightning jumped into the cloaked figure. Convulsions wracked its body, and Zelnor only stopped when it had stilled. The glow in her eyes faded.

"Z-Zelnor…" Erianna said.

The half-elf looked just as shaken as Erianna felt.

"I'm sorry! I'm so sorry! They attacked you. I had to—Oh no, oh gods."

Her hands started trembling. Erianna followed her eyeline but didn't see anything. Erianna scrambled away, her heart racing. What in the Seven Afterworlds was going on? How had Zelnor taken out a vocarii? Had the lightning actually killed it?

Glancing nervously at Zelnor one last time, she darted toward the body.

Erianna patted the body down, checking for items, documents, anything to identify the person. Nothing. Just the dagger it had threatened her with. She checked its shoulders, its clavicle, its upper arms, all the usual spots. Its skin had that odd tacky feeling that only the dead could manage. A few patches of flesh had gotten a chance to rot before this one had been created. It was a disgusting process, but she persevered. Vocarii were rarely created by accident, but it was always possible. She had to be sure.

Finally, she found what she was looking for: a tattoo of a dead spider on its palm. *Shit.* They really had found her. At least, the monster was well and truly dead.

What was that blast of lightning Zelnor had summoned? It wasn't Torrin's power. The dragon gave people the power of farsight and teleportation, which Erianna had been careful not to tell Zelnor, so the other woman wouldn't be tempted to use it. The bard had never heard of anyone controlling lightning before. Even if Torrin did have some hidden power that Erianna hadn't known about, Zelnor had cast the spell so easily. She had only just gotten her pact. Could she have grasped the basics of pact magic that quickly? It was possible, but Zelnor was clearly hiding something.

Had Plindurin sent her too? No, that was unlikely. Zelnor wouldn't have killed that vocarii if she worked for the Claim, and she certainly wouldn't seem so upset about the whole thing. The bearded woman's brows were pinched.

"Are you—?" Erianna started.

"No!" Zelnor shouted.

"What is it?"

Erianna took a couple steps closer to the mage, closing the

distance between them.

"Stop! Stay back. I… No, no, no, no!"

The half-elf's eyes darted around.

"Zelnor! Calm down!"

She grabbed Zelnor's shoulder, and suddenly, Erianna flew upwards. She screwed her eyes shut, barely clinging to whatever was in front of her. Her stomach felt like it was in her throat.

But almost as soon as it had started, it stopped. Slowly, she opened her eyes.

Erianna screamed. She was *very* far away from the ground! The treetops were a few dozen feet below her. A low-hanging gray cloud floated past. She was standing on some kind of high ledge. Had Zelnor teleported her up here? Where *was* here?

"ERIANNA."

The sound of her own name rattled her bones. The platform shook. She held onto the ground beneath her. It was…fabric. Dusty, dirty fabric. She turned and saw a massive beard next to her. She noticed for the first time that each strand was tipped in gold.

Erianna was on Zelnor's shoulder. The bearded mage had grown larger than a castle!

"What in Thorns' unspeakable, bloody name happened to you?" Erianna shouted.

"WELL—" Zelnor said.

Her voice nearly knocked Erianna off again.

"Please talk softer!" Erianna yelled.

"Sorry!" she whispered, and her volume went from deafening to just loud. "I'll explain later! Where's Torrin?"

Zelnor tried to turn her head to face Erianna, but it caused her cloak to shift—moving Erianna dangerously to the edge of her shoulder.

"Let me stand on your hand!" Erianna ordered.

Zelnor obediently held her right palm up to her shoulder, and

Erianna stepped into it. Erianna was no bigger than a doll in the mage's giant hand. Erianna noticed that the pact gem hadn't grown with Zelnor—it looked like a small green and blue freckle.

The half-elf brought Erianna close to her large face, her breath blowing Erianna's hair into an unkempt rat's nest.

"Keep heading east!" Erianna yelled.

"WHICH—" Zelnor spoke in her booming voice, before she remembered to whisper. "Which way is east?"

Erianna had always had a knack for knowing cardinal directions, but it didn't take a genius to find east from this height. Being bad at directions was one thing, but Zelnor must have been absolutely hopeless. They were right next to the eastern coast of Alaspinor.

"Head toward the *OCEAN!*" Erianna shouted.

With Zelnor's long strides, they reached the beach just as night fell. The giant mage leaned down and carefully set Erianna onto the ground. Zelnor shrunk right after she lowered her to the sand. Erianna wondered whether the mage had dismissed the spell or if it was just excellent timing.

"Before we go any farther, you need to tell me what in Liscuntia's name *that* was," Erianna said.

"I'm…not sure," Zelnor said.

Of all the times to lie. They were *way* past minding each other's business. Erianna could have fallen to her death! She deserved an explanation.

"Not sure?" Erianna said.

"It's the truth!" Zelnor insisted. "I don't know where this magic came from or what it is."

"Do you at least know how it works?"

"It just happens. It's an instinct, like regular magic. But its abilities are unlimited. It does pretty much whatever I want it to…mostly," Zelnor said.

"That's incredible! I've never heard of anything like that before," Erianna said.

"That's the problem," Zelnor grumbled.

"Think of all the things you could do with it!"

Erianna couldn't even count the number of dangerous situations she could have avoided with that kind of power. And unlike a pact, this magic wasn't tethered to that conniving dragon.

"I can't control it," Zelnor said.

"You could learn!"

"From *who?*" Zelnor asked.

"You could train yourself. Practice. That's how everyone gets better," Erianna said.

"You don't understand. There's a price," Zelnor said. "Every spell I cast comes with a second spell."

"You get to cast two spells at a time. That hardly seems much of a price," Erianna scoffed.

She had only seen one other type of magic practiced, the only magic in Alaspinor: light magic. She'd seen the power abused—stretched far beyond its original purpose—and even those who practiced it with benevolent intent still suffered the consequences. Light magic destroyed people, and Zelnor was worried about casting two spells instead of one?

Zelnor spoke slowly, anger building behind her words.

"I just want to get rid of it. It is a curse," she said.

"I'm sure that's…inconvenient," Erianna said, trying to reason with the mage, "but with some training—"

"It's a curse!" Zelnor shouted.

"All right. Fine. I apologize!"

Far be it from Erianna to disagree with an all-powerful mage. Frankly, after dealing with the Broken Claim, she didn't have the energy to start an argument.

"Do you know who attacked us?" Zelnor asked. "I saw you checking the body."

"No clue," she lied.

If Zelnor didn't already know about the Broken Claim, then Erianna certainly wasn't going to tell her. Getting involved with them was worse than a death sentence.

After an uncomfortable silence, Erianna stretched out her back and headed toward the water.

"Where are you going?" Zelnor asked.

"To see Torrin," Erianna said.

Torrin's lair, for whatever reason, lay beneath the waves of the Ethnarian Ocean. As an ishlanian, Erianna could breathe underwater. As a half-elf, Zelnor could not.

It shouldn't be a problem though—they wouldn't have to go especially far to reach him. He wanted mortals to make deals with him, after all.

"You can swim, right?" Erianna asked.

Zelnor wore the same hapless look she had when Erianna had told her to go east. Erianna sighed.

"Then can you cast a spell to breathe underwater?" Erianna asked.

"Do I have to?" Zelnor asked.

"Well, drowning would also get rid of the pact," Erianna replied. "And I suppose it would fix your magic problem too."

"What happened to 'putting aside hostility'?" Zelnor asked.

Erianna pinched the bridge of her nose and took a deep breath. When she looked up again, she had managed to force a more pleasant look back onto her face.

"I'm sorry. I'm just not looking forward to this," Erianna said.

She glared at the gently lapping waves. She couldn't believe she was going back to Torrin. At least it was a pleasant swim there. *Just a fun swim to an evil, giant reptile.* What had she gotten herself into?

Chapter Four
The Dragon's Lair

Zelnor waded into the ocean. The frigid water sent a chill up her spine. She had just cast a spell and could not believe that she was already about to cast another one. And with someone so close by at that.

"Hurry up!" Erianna called.

The ishlanian was already treading water a few feet away. She wouldn't wait for Zelnor much longer. With the ocean about her shoulders, Zelnor formed a small sphere of air beneath the surface and jammed her head into it. As always, the six white lights appeared, hovering just a few feet away from her. The way they wavered and shimmered with the refraction of the water was almost enchanting… If only they didn't spell literal doom for herself and everyone around her.

Zelnor focused on the dots, willing them to stay where they were, as she followed Erianna into the sea.

I'm sure this will go well.

In the same way a snake's body curls in a horizontal motion to slither across the ground, Erianna weaved through the ocean. She flowed as smoothly as waves lapping against the shore. A soft teal glow surrounded her, lighting the path ahead for Zelnor.

Zelnor was grateful for that glow, otherwise she would have lost the ishlanian immediately. No matter how hard the half-elf flailed, she barely moved at all, and she rapidly realized the futility of it. She should've turned herself into a fish. Water breathing alone wasn't cutting it. Even if the mage had been able to swim—which she definitely couldn't—maintaining the spell and keeping away the dots left her no energy to direct toward the Alvetchian effort that was *swimming*.

Erianna must have noticed Zelnor's absence, because she spun around in a little somersault and slid effortlessly back through the water to Zelnor. The ishlanian's gills fluttered. She clasped her hand, and Zelnor begrudgingly allowed Erianna to tow her along. The ishlanian continued her graceful descent through the water, pulling Zelnor along like a piece of driftwood.

Erianna made swimming look easy. In fact, she made *everything* look easy. She had no trouble talking to people, and she knew which way east was—as though it were so obvious. Erianna always had to rub it in Zelnor's face, didn't she? Zelnor was tempted to wrestle her hand out of the other woman's grip. They were rapidly approaching an underwater cave, and Zelnor knew she could make it on her own. If she let go now, maybe she could get to Torrin's lair with at least *some* of her dignity intact.

Something shimmered out of the corner of Zelnor's eye: the constellation had closed in while she wasn't paying attention. She had to warn Erianna. She tapped her arm, but Erianna didn't understand.

The white dots slammed into Zelnor, and a new tuft of gold and white fur sprouted at the base of her spine. The mage yelled, but the sound didn't make it past her little bubble.

Zelnor's vision went black.

At first, she thought she'd gone unconscious, but she was still very awake. She gasped and breathed in saltwater. She'd dropped the spell. This was bad, very bad. She was going to drown!

Zelnor felt a blast of cool air on her face. She coughed, spitting water from her mouth. Luckily, she hadn't inhaled much, and after a couple violent coughs, she started breathing normally again.

Zelnor gripped the ishlanian's arm tightly, worried that she would let go and set Zelnor adrift.

"What happened?" Erianna asked.

She was on Zelnor's left side, her arm still looped around Zelnor's middle.

"Nothing," Zelnor rasped.

It was a stupid lie; Zelnor knew that. It would become painfully obvious what had happened the moment she tried to move without the bard's help. But Erianna would make the whole thing into a joke, and that was the last thing Zelnor needed right now. It was bad enough that she'd lost control *and* lost her sight. She could've gotten Erianna killed (thank Felsha'kor she hadn't), but in some ways, this was almost worse.

Zelnor was a liability. As soon as Erianna realized that, she would abandon her and leave Zelnor trapped alone in total darkness. If she wanted even the slimmest chance of survival, she had to fool Erianna until the second spell wore off. Hopefully, it wouldn't take too long…

Erianna dragged Zelnor to a rocky shore. Zelnor clambered out and awkwardly shifted position so that she sat with her legs partially in the water. She heard footsteps walking away, presumably Erianna's.

"Hold on. I…need to rest," Zelnor said.

Her voice echoed loudly. They must have made it to the cave, then. It seemed like it was somewhat large based on how far away her voice sounded after she spoke.

"Rest? I carried you the entire way here." Erianna laughed, little titters trickling out from the sound as though a group of Eriannas had chuckled behind her.

"I just need a moment," Zelnor said.

She heard footsteps coming back toward her. She grabbed her hood and pulled it over her head, hoping to shield her eyes. She couldn't be sure whether they had changed.

Erianna spoke just behind Zelnor: "You're not…*afraid,* are you?"

Zelnor could hear the smile in her voice. Did this bard take nothing seriously? She was so childish.

"Afraid? Of a dragon? Why would anyone be afraid of a dragon?" Zelnor asked.

"Good. I was worried," Erianna said.

Zelnor heard a soft slap to her right and felt something land on her shoulder. She instinctively turned toward the sound, but realized it was just Erianna's hand. Zelnor swallowed and pulled the hood down farther.

"I'll be with you the entire time. And it's not as though you need protecting. Really, there's no reason to—" Erianna gasped.

Zelnor's hood was yanked back. She moved to cover her eyes, but it was too late. She felt two hands forcibly turning her head.

"What happened to your eyes?" Erianna exclaimed.

Zelnor tried to shrink away, but the ishlanian's grip was impressive.

"Oh. Is something…wrong with them?"

"You don't know?"

Erianna inhaled sharply. Zelnor felt the bard's fingers pressing into her skin, as she turned her head again.

"Fine! I'm blind. Happy? That stupid spell, my stupid curse." Zelnor dissolved into angry muttering. "If you had just waited a couple minutes—"

"When you made that bubble, your second spell made you *blind?*" Erianna asked.

"Having a second spell doesn't seem so good now, does it? Now, would you let go of my face?" Zelnor asked.

Erianna's hands disappeared.

"Sorry. Are you going to be all right?"

"I should be. It always wears off," Zelnor said.

"How long will it take?" Erianna asked.

"Do you have somewhere to be?" Zelnor snapped.

"Well, I'm not *entirely* comfortable spending several days right next to a dragon," Erianna said. "You do realize the sooner we finish here, the better, don't you?"

"Obviously, I want to leave, but I told you, I just don't know!"

As the last sounds of Zelnor's voice dissipated across the cave, the two fell silent. Everything about this situation was completely absurd. Zelnor was just a short distance away from an actual dragon, and she'd gone blind in the presence of not just a stranger, but a thief. She was just *begging* to get taken advantage of.

Usually, Zelnor recovered from her curse's side effects fairly quickly but…what if this one really did last days? Or weeks? How would she survive?

"I'll lead you," Erianna said.

"What?" Zelnor asked.

"Not being able to see will be a blessing, trust me. Whatever you're imagining when you think of Torrin, the real thing is much worse," Erianna said.

Zelnor felt a hand clasp hers as the ishlanian pulled her up.

"Fine," Zelnor agreed, "but only if you describe everything you see."

"I won't describe Torrin," Erianna said firmly.

The bard *would* refuse to describe the most interesting thing in the cave. Zelnor stumbled over the uneven rock, and they slowed, so she could keep her footing. She smelled the salt from the ocean behind them. Her heavy, waterlogged clothes clung uncomfortably to her skin, but luckily, the warm breeze whistling past them kept the cold at bay.

"We're in a cave," Erianna said. "It's dark, and the ceiling is dripping seawater."

"Riveting," Zelnor said. "You should be a poet."

"You asked for a description, not a sonnet," Erianna replied.

Zelnor's shoulder brushed against the wall, and she reached out to steady herself. She explored the rock next to her with her fingertips, surprised to find deep jagged trenches carved into the stone. The carvings were at least three times as wide as her palms.

"What are these?" Zelnor asked.

"Claw marks," Erianna said.

"They're huge…"

Zelnor faltered, and Erianna tugged her forward, urging her to continue walking.

"Well, they were made by a dragon," Erianna said. "Stay close to me."

Erianna yanked Zelnor toward her. Zelnor bit back a comment about not needing to be babied. After all, she couldn't see, so in all honesty, she *did* need looking after. Erianna had to catch Zelnor several more times throughout the walk; all while she narrated their mundane surroundings.

Finally, Erianna tightened her grip on Zelnor's hand, keeping her from continuing forward.

"We're here," she said.

A soft rumbling filled what sounded like an enormous cavern. The heat reached a temperature that could rival midday in Kialma'keer. Zelnor's hair flew away from her face. The subtle breeze had grown into a wind that rushed forward and retracted rhythmically in a steady push and pull that reminded Zelnor of the ocean. Whenever the wind receded, it left a slight chill in the air.

"He's here?" Zelnor asked.

"He is," Erianna replied bitterly.

Zelnor cleared her throat.

"Torrin. Esteemed dragon. We would like an audience with you," she requested, careful to keep her tone polite and respectful. "In regards to the matter of—"

"Take back your godsdammed scale!" Erianna shouted.

"What are you doing?" Zelnor hissed.

"Getting to the point."

"Erianna. You are just as courteous as I remember."

Zelnor heard the deep, haughty voice telepathically. The feeling of having someone else in her head sent chills down her spine. She couldn't help but wonder what kind of creature had this much power. She imagined a giant beast leaning over them with rows and rows of teeth. The thought paralyzed her. She heard the dragon shift, its movement sending rocks clattering.

"This does not concern you, ishlanian," the dragon said. *"We have no business. Zelnor, on the other hand…"*

How did the dragon already know her name?

"I know much about you, little Fragmentum. For instance, I know why you have sought me out. You wish to break your pact, do you not? Are you sure that's wise?"

"I'm sorry, but I—I have enough problems already," she said.

"You don't yet know what I am offering. It's rare for such good fortune to come along."

"Good fortune?" Erianna scoffed.

"What's a fragmentum?" Zelnor asked. "Do you know something about my magic?"

"The Fragmenta Aeternum Patris-Matri. An exceptionally rare bless-ing from a time beyond mortal histories. I know a great deal about 'your magic.' However, I only share my knowledge with those I deem worthy."

"Just take the scale back," Erianna said.

"How can I prove I'm worthy?" Zelnor asked.

"Become my emissary, and I will reward you with answers."

Erianna tugged Zelnor closer. "Don't trust him. He could be lying."

"I already trusted one liar," Zelnor said.

Zelnor felt the other woman's hand fall away.

"I've never lied to you," Erianna replied.

Erianna couldn't possibly understand how much Torrin's meant to Zelnor. This dragon was the first person—or, more accurately, the first creature—to know anything about elemental magic. If she ever hoped rid herself of these awful abilities, she needed more in-formation. The cost of that information didn't matter. At this point, Zelnor had already sacrificed everything worthwhile in her life. She had nothing left to lose. And regardless, this deal was none of Erianna's business.

"And, as far we know, neither has Torrin," Zelnor said, before addressing the dragon again. "What would I have to do? I won't...I won't kill anyone for you, but other than that—"

"Kill? No. I have no desire to harm anyone. I want you to find some-one. Speak with him and ascertain his intentions."

"That can't be all you want. You have plenty of followers al-ready," Erianna spat.

"Mistrustful ishlanian. Do you still begrudge me for my actions, years ago? I was not the one who made the choice. Christine approached me."

Erianna didn't reply, and Zelnor wished she could see her face. Who was Christine? What had happened to her? Erianna had allud-ed to knowing someone with a pact before, but the dragon made it sound *much* more personal than just "some drunk she'd met once."

Why hadn't Erianna told Zelnor about this other person? Christine's story could've helped her understand Torrin, or at least give her some idea what she was walking into.

Zelnor had known Erianna was hiding something, but she hadn't expected her to withhold such crucial information. She should've expected as much. It was better to get her information from the source anyway; although, Erianna had brought up a decent point.

"Why me?" Zelnor asked Torrin. "Why do you need *me* to talk to him?"

"You are uniquely qualified."

"That didn't answer the question," Erianna said.

"If you would remain silent for even one moment."

A low growl subsided almost as quickly as it surfaced. The wind pulled sharply away and stilled for a moment, before rushing back again.

"There is an elf, a self-proclaimed High Mage. He purports to possess the same abilities as Zelnor."

Zelnor felt a flutter of excitement. There was another mage like her!

"I fear he seeks disastrous ends. I must know his plans. I have sent others, but he will only welcome one he considers an equal. Arrogant creature."

"You're calling someone else arrogant?" Erianna muttered.

The rocks in the cave shifted again, and the air around them got hotter.

"I hope your brutish companion will not be accompanying you. Her impatience and lack of decorum will hinder your success in diplomatic matters."

"Maybe I will go with Zelnor," Erianna said. "There's nothing you can do to stop me."

"Very well." The words curled in Zelnor's mind. She could feel the smile in them. *"By all means, join the little Fragmentum in Nirdeem."*

Zelnor cursed her lack of sight. The mage felt a tension in the air. There was a hidden meaning behind Torrin's words, but without reading her expression, Zelnor wasn't sure how the dragon had silenced Erianna. Was she angry? Afraid? Zelnor was clueless to the context. Yet another reminder to get rid of this accursed magic as soon as possible.

As for Torrin's deal, there was no real downside. This agreement was beneficial for both of them. She would get a chance to meet someone else with elemental magic, and afterwards, Torrin would tell her more about her powers. Between this High Mage and the dragon, Zelnor would learn more than she had in years of research.

"I'll be your emissary," Zelnor said.

"Zelnor! You don't know what he'll ask next!" Erianna cried.

"Cruel ishlanian, assuming the worst of me. I only wish to uphold the work of the First Dragons and keep the world in balance. All my actions serve mortals as much as myself. Often more so."

Erianna grumbled but didn't say anything else.

"Hold out your hands, Zelnor. I would give you a symbol of my good faith."

Zelnor didn't feel especially keen to reach out toward a dragon, but Torrin might take offense if she didn't. She held out her cupped palms. Something smooth and circular landed in her hands. She ran her fingers across it and realized it was a medallion.

"A trinket. From an age long past, created by a race of mortals long gone from this world. It allows you to breathe water as your companion does, so you may reach my abode with ease."

Zelnor put on the necklace and tucked it under her shirt. She had read somewhere that magic could be stored in objects, but only the most skilled mages could master the technique. The medallion contained a water-breathing spell—maybe even the same spell she had used to get into the dragon's lair—which meant this "ancient, lost race" had mastered elemental magic. This amulet *proved* that Torrin had the answers she needed.

"Thank you," Zelnor said earnestly.

"Head south to the mountains. Find the High Mage. Tell me his goals, and the lengths he is willing to go to achieve them."

When the two emerged back onto the shore, Erianna set Zelnor down and wandered a few paces down the beach. Things had somehow gone even worse than she had expected. That bastard Torrin. The condescending lizard had tricked Zelnor like it was nothing. He spouted a few obvious lies, and the mage fell for every single one. *Dragons just want to "serve mortals." Serve, my ass!* Dragons obviously thought they were above mortals and felt no remorse or sympathy for them.

Erianna poured the water out of her boots and set them next to her. Her feet felt like ice in the frosty air of the Bitter Season. Even in its last month, the season's chill still clung to the land, unwilling to let go and finally give way to the blessed warmth that dawned with the next year. The sky was nearly pitch black. Parenus provided a feeble white light, barely enough to call a crescent, and the smaller blue moon, Cytho, wasn't visible at all.

Erianna had thought she could protect Zelnor from Torrin; instead, it was happening all over again. Ever since Erianna got involved, she had only made Zelnor's life worse.

But what else was Erianna supposed to do? If she had left Zelnor alone, the mage would've sold the gem to some other sap, even more clueless than she was. Although, it was hard to imagine the ring ending up with a bigger idiot than Zelnor. The mage had no idea the trouble she had just willingly agreed to.

But then, with her strange magic, maybe Zelnor was used to trouble. At least, the white cataracts had finally disappeared. Thank the gods for small mercies. The half-elf narrowed her clear amber eyes at Erianna.

"Why are you still here?" Zelnor asked.

"That is an odd way of saying 'thank you,'" Erianna said.

Zelnor huffed, but surprisingly, her next words sounded genuine.

"Thank you, Erianna. For leading me to Torrin. Finally finding someone who can help me, it's… Really, thank you."

Zelnor smiled. She actually *smiled*. It was the first time Erianna had seen the bearded woman do anything other than scowl or roll her eyes. If Zelnor really was happy with her choice, then maybe it had worked out for the best. Maybe Torrin really did want to help Zelnor, as long as it benefited him at the same time. A powerful, fully in-control mage at his disposal could only be an asset. But Erianna couldn't shake the feeling this mission was some sort of trap; a mysterious mage who was just like Zelnor, a quest that only *she* could accomplish—it all sounded too contrived for Erianna's liking. And this mage just so happened to be the High Mage of Nirdeem? A powerful political figure who lived in the *one* place that Erianna couldn't go?

"And thank you, for getting me here," Zelnor continued. "Good luck, I guess. And goodbye."

Zelnor raised her hand up awkwardly and held it for a moment, before swiveling on her heel and heading back into the forest. Erianna joined her, matching her strides.

Zelnor slowed to a halt.

"Wha—What are you doing?" she asked.

"I'm going with you," Erianna decided.

"Just because Torrin said that you shouldn't, doesn't—"

"You couldn't even find the ocean when we were right next to it, and you were gigantic," Erianna said. "With your navigational skills, you'll end up on a different continent."

"I think I can find the Reindune Mountains," Zelnor replied evenly. "They're the only mountains on this side of the continent. Hard to miss. Besides, I've been there before."

Zelnor patted Erianna's shoulder and walked past her.

"You're walking north," Erianna said.

Zelnor stopped, standing stock-still, then turned on her heel and strode in the opposite direction. Erianna jogged after her.

"Listen, I'm heading south anyway," Erianna lied. "Let's just travel together for a little while."

Zelnor started walking faster, but Erianna matched her pace.

"We're not traveling together!" the half-elf said, breaking into a run.

"Why not?" Erianna demanded, racing after.

For Liscuntia's sake. She only wanted to help. Why was Zelnor making it so damn difficult?

"It's dangerous!" Zelnor shouted.

Erianna jumped in front of her, forcing her to skid to a stop. Erianna put both hands on the bearded woman's shoulders, holding her in place, and looked directly into her eyes. Erianna expected anger or frustration, but instead she saw…fear.

"Everything in Alaspinor is dangerous," Erianna said.

"What happens when…when I cast a spell, and the second one lights you on fire?"

"It's Alaspinor. It'll probably be raining," Erianna said. "If it isn't, I'll jump into a well."

"You could die! Don't you care?" Zelnor asked.

Of course I care! Erianna cared more than Zelnor could possibly know. She should just let the mage go on this reckless journey alone and continue about her business. Getting anywhere near Nirdeem was absolute madness. It would easily be the stupidest thing she'd ever done.

But to be frank, Erianna didn't think Zelnor could handle the trip on her own. The poor fool was wandering right into a trap, and that was exactly what Torrin wanted. If she joined Zelnor, she might be able to keep her from becoming another one of the dragon's victims. After all the trouble Erianna had caused, she owed Zelnor that much.

"Apparently not," Erianna sighed. "Let's make camp and leave in the morning. It's a long trip."

Zelnor tried to argue, but Erianna ignored her. Erianna just set her large bag, still sopping wet, against a tree and started clearing out space for a fire. They would need one to dry their things. Zelnor muttered something about gathering firewood, and by the time the half-elf returned, Erianna had a small blaze going.

Erianna curled up on her bedroll and stared blankly into the embers. She couldn't close her eyes without seeing blood, hearing screams, feeling hands on her. Erianna sat up again, tucking her head between her knees. She would be fine. As long as she didn't set foot in that godsforsaken city, she would be *fine*.

Chapter Five
Haunted Halls

The road to the Reindune Mountains curved through the countryside. The tall grass rippled in the cold wind. As it picked up, Erianna's lavender hair fluttered behind her. The chatty bard had stopped talking. Zelnor had thought it only a momentary pause, but that moment had stretched into several until it turned into a deafening silence. Zelnor waited for Erianna to start another conversation, but instead, the bard just stared at her.

Quiet was fine. Zelnor always traveled in silence. After all, she was always alone, so she had no problem with quiet. And she had no problem with the bard's blue-gray eyes scrutinizing her every move.

Gods, Zelnor needed to say *something*, but she had no idea where to start. Her nomadic way of life and shabby appearance led most to misidentify her as a beggar and ignore her, and for the most part, she appreciated that. It made her life significantly easier, but since traveling with Erianna, she realized that her social skills were a little… lacking. She hadn't been forced to strike up a proper conversation with anyone in two years.

Vel'erma! Has it really been two years? No wonder this was so diffi-cult. Zelnor hadn't realized how much Erianna carried their conver-sations until the woman went silent. Granted, their chats often ended in *arguments*, but still better than this stifling awkward tension.

"So…how far away is Nirdeem?" Zelnor asked.

"Three more weeks at this pace," Erianna said.

The bard looked expectantly toward her, as though waiting for another conversation prompt.

Why did I ask such a simple question? But what else was Zelnor supposed to ask? Was it too soon to ask personal questions? Zelnor still wanted to know about this Christine and her relationship with Torrin, but now that Erianna was traveling with Zelnor, the wrong question could make things even more uncomfortable between them. How would she even bring it up? Did she just ask or should she ease into it? *Ugh. Ease into it?* Oh, sure, Zelnor was *great* at that. She was well known for her tact.

Zelnor shuffled her feet through the dirt, creating little puffs of dust on the road. Without thinking, she started humming an old Kialma'keeran lullaby under her breath. Her mother used to sing it to her whenever Zelnor got nervous. It was a song about a foolish man who asked for gold instead of water, but Zelnor had forgotten the lyrics.

Erianna started singing the words as Zelnor reached the last verse. Zelnor stopped humming and just listened, captivated by the ishlanian's voice.

"Drink deep of greed, gold lost in golden sand," Erianna sang. "Sate thirst for coin but die a hollow man."

"You know the song?" Zelnor asked. Her voice felt stiff and alien, after the beautiful impromptu performance.

"I've met a couple people from the desert. One of them taught it to me," Erianna said.

"I forgot how morbid the song is," Zelnor said.

"It is pretty dark," Erianna agreed.

The ishlanian put her hands behind her back and rolled on the balls of her feet.

"You finally found something to talk about," she said. "I'm impressed. I thought we'd be walking in silence forever."

Zelnor turned slowly toward the bard and saw the flippant smile on her face. Erianna was teasing her. She'd been quiet *on purpose*.

"So, you're from Kialma'keer, then?" the ishlanian asked.

"I am. Not. Talking. To you," Zelnor grumbled.

"Oh, come on. You've been giving me nothing but one-word answers. I was only teasing," Erianna said. "I promise I won't do it again, *if* you answer my question."

"I'm from a small town, near the northern border," Zelnor said. "Kezeek Mesa."

"I didn't know Kialma'keer had towns," Erianna said.

"It doesn't have many. There's the city Bokest al'Bar, of course. And a few other villages on some of the bigger mesas. The largest one is on the other side of Felsha'kor Canyon, but it's cut off from the rest of the desert."

Some Kialma'keerans called that town the "hidden village." While it wasn't actually *hidden*, per se, the lack of contact with the kunari who lived there naturally fostered a sense of mystery about the place.

"What's Kezeek Mesa like?" Erianna asked.

Zelnor hadn't thought about her home in a while, but she described it for the ishlanian.

Only about a dozen yards off the ground, Kezeek Mesa stood on what could hardly be called a mesa at all, but it was still the tallest landmark for miles. The empty desert stretched endlessly in every direction around it. A few wells dotted the town, filled by a system of underground caves. The only entrance cave on the surface was marked with a small rock. She had enjoyed playing there as a child, despite warnings from the adults and the mildly disturbing folk songs. She still remembered lounging on the cool rocks to escape the summer heat and avoid her chores.

And there was so much more Zelnor didn't tell Erianna. How the days of her childhood had moved agonizingly slowly from hour to hour. The boring afternoons spent fetching water, cooking, helping barricade the town from small predators, fixing houses; always working to finish an endless list of busy work—all crucial to the upkeep of a small settlement, her mother constantly assured her. The only interesting part of Zelnor's day was listening to the stories from the refugees in the shelter, and playing with her best friend, Heeden, of course.

Every day, she had hoped for an adventure, for something more than repetitive, meaningless work. She had jealously watched her father come and go, exploring beyond the dry heat and long days of her youth. She begged him to take her every time he left. He always refused, and she always nursed her grudge against him for about a week, before missing him took precedence.

Now, though… Now, Zelnor pined for those slow, easy days. Everything she did was in the hopes of one day getting back to them, though it would never be the same without Heeden. But even if it was just a pale imitation of the home she'd so desperately wanted to escape from, it would be enough.

"So, what about your home?" Zelnor asked. She instantly regretted bringing up the bard's home as she watched Erianna's face sour.

"I don't really have a home."

Zelnor tapped a hand against her knee, searching for another topic. Clouds filtered the sunlight into a dim gray. The sky had darkened over the course of the day, and Zelnor felt giddy despite herself. Although rain was a little inconvenient when traveling, she enjoyed the feeling of the cool water cascading down around her. It was far from novel, after a decade in Alaspinor, but growing up in the scorching desert heat had permanently endeared her to rain.

"Looks like it'll rain soon," Zelnor said absently.

She winced. She might be out of practice, but even she knew that bringing up the weather was a hallmark of someone trying and failing to hold up their end of the conversation. Luckily, Erianna took pity on her.

"It does…" Erianna said. "We might need to find shelter soon."

"Can't we just keep going?" Zelnor asked. She often continued through storms. In fact, she preferred it. It made it far less likely to run into other travelers, and everything looked prettier in the rain.

"You're serious? Traveling in the rain is miserable. And it's almost impossible to navigate," Erianna said.

"I do it all the time," Zelnor said.

"I'm beginning to see why you're always lost," Erianna said.

"If we stop *every* time it rains, we'll never make it. It rains constantly here. I can count the sunny days I've seen on one hand," Zelnor said.

"You're exaggerating!" Erianna argued. "It's pleasant during the Warm Season, sunny most of the time."

"It still rains practically every day the rest of the year."

"Not nearly as much as you seem to think," Erianna snapped.

"It must take you *years* to get from one town to the next." Zelnor rolled her eyes.

"At least, *I* won't be sick when I arrive!"

"That's a myth! I've never gotten sick from rain. It's just water, for Vel'erma's sake! That's the stupidest—"

"Hold on," Erianna said.

"What?" Zelnor asked.

"Are we really arguing about the weather?" Erianna asked with a half-smile.

"Oh. Um…" Zelnor grimaced. "Yeah. We are."

Erianna shook her head with a sigh.

"Can we go a month without killing each other?" she joked.

"You're the one who wanted to travel with me," Zelnor said.

"All right. Let's compromise." Erianna clapped her hands together. "We keep going *only* if we can see. Otherwise, we take shelter. Fair?"

"I can agree to that," Zelnor said.

They continued until, inevitably, the precipitation started tumbling down. Erianna flinched when the first drops of water hit her face. For someone who claimed to know Alaspinor well, she wasn't very well-acclimated to its climate.

"Don't ishlanians like water?" Zelnor asked wryly.

"Aren't half-elves supposed to be charming?" Erianna shot back.

Zelnor had walked right into that one. She was about as far from that particular stereotype as a half-elf could get, and she couldn't blame it on her elemental magic either. Between her mother, a pragmatic elf of few words, and her father, an eccentric human academic of big words, awkwardness ran in the family.

"And I do like water," Erianna added. "Just not—" The light, misting became a torrential downpour. "Rain," she finished with a pout.

The two took refuge in the forest just off the path, though calling the collection of trees a *forest* was a bit generous. It covered a large area, but the trunks were well-spaced and only gathered in small clusters like a collection of groves. Still, it provided better cover than the farmlands and empty fields on the other side. She could see clear to the Alvetch River across them.

Erianna complained again when another drop of water hit her eye. She threw her oversized bag off her back and huddled under the base of the nearest tree, squeezing the water out of her hair. She leaned against its trunk and a torrent of rainwater fell from its branches. Her skin flared bright teal, and Zelnor had to stifle her laughter.

"Couldn't your magic make us a shelter or something?" Erianna asked.

"You want me to use my incredibly dangerous abilities…to keep you dry?"

"To keep *us* dry." Erianna smiled hopefully, but Zelnor shook her head. "Never mind. We'll just sit here and get soaked, then."

"How far is the nearest town?"

"Too far," Erianna grumbled.

Zelnor walked over to the nearest tree and started scaling its trunk. Her foot slipped, and she tumbled back down to the damp grass with a muffled *thump*. Rummaging through her satchel, she took out her cooking knife and lodged it in the tree. She circled her legs around the trunk, pried out the blade, and stuck it as high as she could reach. She managed to haul herself up about an inch. With her strength, it should only take her an hour. Or two.

"What are you doing?" Erianna asked.

"Climbing," Zelnor said.

"Is that what you call it?"

Zelnor refused to acknowledge the snide remark with a response. She wrenched the knife back out again, but before she could pierce the bark, she slid back down to the grass.

"*Why* are you climbing?" Erianna asked.

"To get a better view," Zelnor said.

"Huh. Not a bad idea," Erianna said.

The bard leaped to the lowest branch and launched herself up the tree at an impossible speed. In seconds, she had disappeared in its leaves. Zelnor slipped back down, wrenching her knife out of the trunk as she went. She stuffed the blade back into her bag.

"I'd be good at climbing too, if I were as tall as her," Zelnor griped to no one in particular.

A few minutes later, Erianna dropped back down. She was completely drenched, but she was beaming, glowing brightly in the gloom. Zelnor wondered what caused her skin to glow like that. So far, it had lit up when she was angry and happy, and sometimes, when it was just dark. *Does she have control over it or not?*

"Great news," Erianna said. "I found a castle!"

"A castle? Here?" Zelnor asked.

All the castles in Alaspinor were much farther north. Most of them were in the Court of Kings and Queens. She'd heard of a couple near Goldhaven, but she had never heard of any in the middle of the countryside. She couldn't imagine a noble comfortable living amid farmlands and small villages. Prevator Apalandis looked disgusted at even the mere thought of dirt sullying her opulent clothes.

"That's odd," Zelnor said.

"It is. A little," Erianna admitted. "But it's the perfect place."

Zelnor's eyes widened at the lunatic ishlanian. *The perfect place?* No prevator, no noble for that matter, would ever willingly take in strangers like themselves. Surely, she couldn't be implying they should stay there.

"The perfect place for…?"

Zelnor waited for the ishlanian to explain, to say anything other than—

"Taking shelter." Erianna smiled easily, saying the exact thing that Zelnor had somehow known she would say.

"Have you ever *met* a prevator or a noble?" she asked.

"No… Not exactly," Erianna said.

"Well, I have, once. And there's no way they'll let two dirty travelers stay in their *castle.*"

"Speak for yourself. I'm plenty clean."

"Oh, I'm sorry, your highness. I guess I'll wait outside, then." Zelnor pursed her lips and plopped down on the grass, resting her back against a tree. "Have fun."

"We're both going. There's a good chance that the occupants are gone right now. No one would even dream of taking a vacation in this miserable weather. They'll never know if we pop in to get out of the rain."

"And if they *are* home?" Zelnor furrowed her brows. The last thing she wanted was to get in even more trouble with high profile people.

"I happen to be an ishlanian songstress."

Erianna threw her hair over her shoulder, but the matted waves got stuck in her fingers. She scowled, taking a moment to detangle it.

"And?" Zelnor prompted.

Erianna rolled her eyes, as though her meaning were obvious.

"Ishlanians are *rare* in Alaspinor. Ones with my talent, even rarer."

"So humble," Zelnor said.

"My *point,*" Erianna said, "still stands. I can charm them with my voice, and they'll grant us refuge for a few hours."

"That really works?" Zelnor said.

"Well, it worked on you," Erianna replied smugly.

Zelnor kept her face neutral. If Erianna noticed the way the comment made her stomach flip, the bard would never drop it.

"Whatever," Zelnor said. "There's still no way they'll let *me* in."

"They will…" Erianna dug through her bag, smiling when she found what she wanted. "…if you're wearing these."

The bard tossed Zelnor two tightly wrapped balls of fabric. Zelnor unrolled the thick, black bundle and discovered tight leather pants and a waistcoat. The last article was a flowy white blouse.

"You think if I look fancy, they'll let me in?" she asked.

"I think they'll let you in if you're my attendant."

Erianna shimmied out of her leather cuirass and made a little twirling motion with her pointer finger. Zelnor immediately turned around. When Erianna said she could turn back, the ishlanian had slipped into a lacy black dress. The bard shoved her drenched clothes into a dark, cloth bag. Did she always put wet clothes in bags? *And she thinks I smell?*

"I'll dry them later," Erianna said. "Now, put yours on."

Zelnor eyed the outfit with disdain. It looked uncomfortable and flashy and everything she emphatically wasn't.

"Do I really have to change? I'm supposed to be a servant anyway," she said.

"You'll be an attendant. They won't let you in dressed like that." Erianna lifted one of the loose, frayed sleeves of Zelnor's tunic. "Frankly, I'm surprised these haven't fallen apart already."

"I don't think your clothes will fit me."

"Why not? We're about the same size."

Zelnor looked down at her small chest and then at Erianna's larger one. She *really* didn't want to wear the other woman's clothes. The shirt was going to be baggy in the most awkward way. Erianna noticed the look and snorted.

"You don't have to worry about *that,*" Erianna said.

Zelnor looked skeptically down at the outfit.

"They'll look good on," Erianna insisted. "The blouse is supposed to be loose, and the waistcoat is tight on me."

"Everything you wear is tight on you," Zelnor grumbled.

"Noticed that, did you?" Erianna teased.

Zelnor ignored the bard's pointed question, glaring at her until she turned around. Annoyingly, Erianna had been right. She fit much better into the waistcoat than she'd expected, and the pants were close enough to her size; although, they were much looser on her than they would be on Erianna. Zelnor had to admit, she did look more like someone who would accompany a traveling bard. She slung her threadbare gray travel cloak back onto her shoulders, spitefully dulling the effect of the fancy clothes.

Erianna clapped when she saw the outfit, and Zelnor pulled her cloak tighter about her.

"How does it feel to change clothes for the first time in your entire life?" Erianna asked with a smirk. "Was it a harrowing ordeal?"

Zelnor chucked her smelly clothes at the bard. Erianna yelped as the damp outfit struck her in the face. She coughed in disgust, balling up the musky clothes and stuffing them into her laundry bag.

"How long has it been since you washed those?"

"I don't know," Zelnor said. "A week or two maybe?"

Erianna sniffed the air and grimaced, like she could still smell the mage's clothes. *Always so dramatic.*

The forest thickened around the castle, offering them some cover from the rain but also hiding the building until they had almost reached it. Zelnor could immediately see why the ishlanian had assumed the estate abandoned. The stone edifice was so worn it had grown lopsided on one side. Moss and vines crawled up the walls, and one of the large wooden doors hung partially off its hinges. As they neared the entrance, the dirt path transitioned into a gray stone walkway with a few glaringly different, mismatched replacements.

No self-respecting noble would set foot near this place, but something about it bothered Zelnor. The path was bordered by manicured hedges with not a single twig out of place. The box hedges came up to chest height and occasionally curved upward into archways, beyond which she saw gardens full of roses blooming in all colors, alongside other flowers native to Alaspinor. The plants looked well-tended and healthy, but the fountains, baths with vicious beasts immortalized in pristine marble, had run dry.

It was a disquieting contradiction. Someone was taking care of the grounds, but since no one guarded the entrance, that person obviously didn't live in the castle. Farmers and villagers had no love for nobility…so who had taken care of these flowers? Who owned this ruined castle? Would a prevator really let their home fall into such disrepair?

Erianna clearly didn't share Zelnor's reluctance. She marched right up to the imposing wooden doors and knocked. The three solid *thuds* hadn't even faded, before the bard shoved the door open.

"What did I say? Free lodgings," Erianna said.

"Which means I didn't have to wear these silly things," Zelnor said.

"Oh, come now, you look nice," Erianna argued cheerfully. "You're handsome when you're not covered in grime."

Zelnor ignored the half-compliment and moved past her into the building.

A musty, stale smell hung in the static air. Candles lit the otherwise dark hall; only the second floor appeared to have windows. Situated too far apart, the flames only partially filled the space, leaving stretches of almost complete darkness between them. Even the somewhat dim light of the overcast day seemed blinding as it spilled in from the wide doorway.

"If it's abandoned, then why are there candles lit?" Zelnor muttered to herself.

The tattered red carpet exposed patches of the weathered stone floor. Dusty suits of armor lined the walls at regular intervals. They left the large door open behind them. Zelnor told herself it was only to supplement the feeble lighting in the room, but she knew it was also a quick escape route. One they were traveling farther and farther away from…

Zelnor glanced back toward the entrance every few seconds. Each time she looked back, she half-expected the door to slam closed behind them, but it remained open—a constant reminder that they could leave at any time.

"You know," Erianna mused, "this reminds me of a creepy story I heard."

"Why would you say that *now?*" Zelnor hissed.

"You have to admit it feels like one. The main character wanders in, the candles are mysteriously lit, but no one is home. No way to know what creatures lurk in the dark…"

"That's exactly what we're doing," Zelnor gritted out.

"Well. Those are just stories," Erianna chuckled.

Zelnor crossed her arms against a sudden chill. "Obviously."

Erianna's head darted around. Her skin flared a bright teal, lighting up the space.

"You're not scared, are you?" Zelnor asked.

"No," Erianna said. "Just providing some light. You're welcome."

Huh, so she can control it. Well, provided she wasn't lying.

The castle was smaller than Zelnor expected, with only two floors and two towers. They peeked into a kitchen, the servants' quarters, and a small armory with a meagre stock of weapons. They didn't find any people, but luckily, no ghosts either.

As they wandered farther, the rain pounded against the castle. Its steady yet erratic beat filled the vacant hallways and spacious rooms. Zelnor wasn't willing to stay here until they'd investigated every room. Someone had to have lit those candles, and she did not want to get ambushed. She didn't believe in ghosts, but there could be criminals holed up somewhere in here.

They crept up the stairs to the second floor. *Clang!* Something metal fell, followed by a frantic skittering.

Zelnor and Erianna froze.

"That was a rat…" Zelnor said. "Right?"

"Maybe we should go back downstairs," Erianna suggested.

"You can, but I'm staying," Zelnor said.

"Well, I'm not going to split off from you now. That really is what would happen in a ghost story," Erianna said.

They found mostly bedrooms, still well-furnished and brimming with the possessions of previous occupants. Luxurious silken bedsheets, gold jewelry packed away in boxes, extravagant portraits lining the walls, all providing the impression that nobles still lived here.

And yet everything held a thick layer of dust. None of it had been used for decades, if not longer. Shouldn't opportunistic traders, lawless bandits, or even the previous residents have picked the place clean? The farther in they got, the more unsettled Zelnor felt.

Wind whistled down the passage as they stepped back into the hallway. They'd checked every room, save for the small blue door in the center of the second story. There were spots of a slightly lighter shade in the door's paint job—touchups after it had first been hung—but it still looked as dusty and disused as the rest. The hinges creaked loudly. Something about this particular room felt especially ominous, as though a sinister secret waited behind it.

Gods, I sound just like a character in a horror novel.

But beyond the door waited something far from the imagined horrors Zelnor had been so afraid of. She lit up with giddy excitement.

"Books!" Zelnor exclaimed.

This room was absolutely filled with books, and the uneven spines poking out from the shelves indicated at least one additional layer behind the visible ones. The bookcases were pressed so tightly together that the blue flowered wallpaper, peeling and yellowed and covered in dust, was barely visible through the cracks. Zelnor headed directly to the bookshelves on the far wall, bracketing an unevenly cut stone window.

Erianna stumbled behind her, almost tripping over even more stacks on the floor.

"Books," she grumbled.

Rain plodded against the walls outside and a gust blustered through the window, catching Zelnor's hood and pushing it away from her face. She ran her fingers along the titles on the books' spines, unbothered by the adverse conditions.

"There goes all your caution. At least the place is empty." Erianna sighed. "Now, I wonder if there's any fiction."

Zelnor skimmed through the thick tomes. They were all technical books and research studies with lengthy titles like *Animal Regeneration: Renewable Food Source* or *Animal Abuse; A cross-section of unethical farming practices in Alaspinor*. Finally, she found a book that interested her—*Reaching into the Body: A study on abusive practices of light magic* by Emric Veloria. Zelnor didn't recognize the tome. It had been a while since she'd found a magic theory book that she hadn't already read. She flipped it open, skimming the pages and seeing a few technical terms she was familiar with and some that were completely foreign to her. She smiled, elated at the prospect of diving into this brand-new book.

She had originally started researching magic theory to find a connection between the magic other mortals practiced and her elemental magic. She had never found anything helpful in them, but at some point, she'd started reading them for fun. The wide variety of applications and intricacies of light magic fascinated her, and she always enjoyed what scant information she could find on the foreign practice of shadow magic. Her study of magic theory had developed into an admittedly time-consuming hobby, but it was a nice respite from worrying about her own unstable, incomprehensible magic.

Zelnor saw a few armchairs nestled in the corner of the study, near Erianna. Well-upholstered with navy cloth, the chairs looked dusty but luxurious. As she brushed the seat off, she noticed a shape behind it—a little cloud of smoke. The fireplace was unlit. How had smoke gotten into the castle?

Zelnor reached toward the cloud. The smoke writhed around her fingers, like it was avoiding them. This smoke was *alive*. She backed into Erianna, knocking the bard into a bookshelf.

"Liscuntia's sins! You startled me," Erianna said.

"There's something there," Zelnor muttered.

"There's no need to jump at shadows," Erianna said. "We've looked through the whole castle. There's no one else… Oh gods."

The small puff of smoke grew until it formed a humanoid shape. Erianna's skin flared bright teal, and she brandished her knife. Zelnor had never heard of a creature made of smoke. She didn't want to believe in ghosts, but this thing couldn't be anything else. She grabbed her own knife out of her bag, as the mist coalesced into a young boy, no more than ten or eleven, floating above the chair.

The boy's downturned eyes made his gaze appear melancholic, despite the small smile that his face seemed to naturally settle into. His appearance, although unkempt, indicated a noble status. His long, jet-black hair, woven into an intricate plait resting between his shoulder blades, his silk pants, and his neatly pressed blue doublet implied excellent care and attention from likely several attendants; however, the smudges of dirt smeared across his dark skin and the wild wisps pulled from his braid showed how little he cared for his appearance.

Erianna relaxed. She slipped her knife back into her boot and glared at Zelnor like *she* was the crazy one. Zelnor reluctantly lowered her arm. Daggers wouldn't do much against a ghost any-way. Thankfully, that wasn't her only weapon. One wrong move and she would learn whether or not elemental magic worked on ghosts.

"He's a child," Erianna whispered.

"A ghost child," Zelnor hissed back.

The ghost boy stared at the two of them with wide, owlish eyes.

"Why do you glow? No, I mean *how* are you glowing? I thought only—but if it's not—What does it mean?" the ghost asked.

His eyes darted between them.

"I'm an ishlanian. That's what we do," Erianna said, and then, her voice lowered imperceptibly, softening in a way Zelnor hadn't heard before. "What's your name?"

"That isn't what I—" He stopped when he registered her question. "Oh. I'm Lyle! Um, Lyle Veloria of the Simrelius Line."

The ghost was nothing like Prevator Apalandis. He had intro-duced himself with the long title of a noble, but shared none of the prevator's confidence. Zelnor assumed that the ghost had been taught from a young age to carry himself with a gravitas suited to his lineage, but it seemed like none of it had sunk in.

"I'm Erianna," the ishlanian said. "And the grumpy one with the beard is Zelnor."

Zelnor shushed her. They had no idea what this creature want-ed, or what it could do with their names. The last thing they need-ed was to give it more information. Of course, Erianna ignored her.

"Do you live here by yourself?" Erianna asked the first question that most adults would have asked a child, a *living* one.

"For now," Lyle said. "But my parents will come back soon. And the servants too!"

"And how long have they been gone?" the ishlanian prompted.

"A long time," he said.

"I bet you're the one keeping the candles lit, huh?" Erianna asked.

Lyle nodded.

"What about the gardens?" Zelnor asked warily.

The child beamed, and the smile lit up his eyes, washing away any illusion of sadness.

"They look good, don't they? Mom said to stay inside, but now that the gardeners are gone, I've started taking care of it! It's been fun. I really miss everyone, though." His happy expression fell, and he hunched his shoulders. "Don't tell my mom…please."

"I won't, I promise. And he won't either," Erianna said, referring to Zelnor.

Zelnor buried the little twinge of happiness she felt when the bard remembered to address her as "he" around a stranger. Any points Erianna earned for conscientiousness were immediately lost when she decided to trust a ghost.

Erianna beckoned Zelnor out of the room. She flashed a fleeting smile at the ghost, assuring him that they would return, before shutting the peeling blue door behind them.

"Something terrible happened in here, and I don't think his family are returning anytime soon," Erianna said. "We need to find a way to help him."

"Absolutely not. The only ghosts I've heard of are violent ones," Zelnor argued.

"Does he seem violent to you?" Erianna asked.

"They don't start that way, but things always get worse."

No one talked about ghosts in Kialma'keer, and Zelnor still remembered how terrified she had been when she heard her first ghost story. An elderly woman was found facing the wall, sobbing. A teen walked up to the distraught woman. They raised a hand to comfort her, and she turned around. Her empty eye sockets bled, and she screamed before vanishing. Zelnor hadn't slept for a week after that—finally, comforting herself with the knowledge that those scary stories were just the product of local superstition.

"Have you ever *seen* one? Or only heard stories?" Erianna asked.

"I do my best to avoid the living," Zelnor said. "Why would I want anything to do with the dead?"

"Lyle is stuck here alone, and you're suggesting we just abandon him because you're *scared,*" Erianna retorted.

"If you're so friendly with ghosts, then why were you so worried about coming in here?" Zelnor snapped.

"Oh, I don't know: bandits, criminals, thugs," Erianna replied. "We're straying from the point! There's got to be something we can do. Who knows how long he's waited here? What if his parents are dead? We can't just leave him."

Zelnor imagined being stuck in this old castle, waiting years for people who might never come back. That had to be hard, especially for someone so young. Maybe they could free him before his spirit twisted into something ugly. If they helped the ghost move on, they could keep him from hurting anyone else.

"We should banish him," she said.

Every village in Alaspinor had someone capable of spirit banishment. Healers habitually practiced the light magic spell during funerals and when moving a family into their new home.

Zelnor had observed the practice. It seemed simple enough—frustratingly simple, in fact. She had read enough books to know how to do it in theory, but truthfully, she'd never successfully cast light magic before, though she had tried several times; the ability to heal would have been useful considering how frequently she found herself in danger.

"We don't know where they go when that happens," Erianna said. "We can't do that to him."

There was one other spell. A rumor that Zelnor had heard people talking about in taverns. She'd never read about it in any books and didn't believe in spirits at the time, so she had dismissed it as yet another ghost story. They would need to track down more information first, delaying their trip and prolonging their time together, but Zelnor just knew that Erianna wouldn't let the matter go until they tried *something*.

"I've heard of a light magic spell that's supposed to put spirits back in their bodies," Zelnor said.

Erianna's face went uncharacteristically still. She gripped the hem of her dress tightly.

"You're talking about the Rite of Vocarii," she said.

"So, you know it? Does that mean you know how to cast it?" Zelnor asked.

"You'd kill yourself trying," the bard said, "and Lyle wouldn't come back the same, if he came back at all."

Zelnor wondered why no one ever mentioned that part. With a cost that high, it was a wonder anyone considered using the spell at all.

"Well, I doubt I would've been able to cast it anyway," she said.

"That's for the best, trust me," Erianna said grimly.

The bard had an abundance of knowledge about light magic for someone who hated it so vehemently. She knew about the practical applications of that type of magic, as opposed to just the theory of it. Had she been a healer once? Another topic that Zelnor was determined to revisit after they'd dealt with their ghost problem.

"What do you suggest, then?" Zelnor asked. "Because I don't know anything else other than banishment."

"I..." Erianna hesitated. "I know of *one* thing."

The abandoned castle would've been the perfect hideout for the Broken Claim, but thankfully, Erianna had seen no trace of them. Just when she'd finally thought she could relax, though, they had found a different problem. She couldn't in good conscience leave a child trapped and alone. He had already been deserted by everyone he'd ever known.

What sort of people left their own child behind? What terrible situation had his parents put him in that he had died so young? Had Lyle been killed? Maybe the boy had died of an illness, and his parents couldn't bear to stay where they had lost him.

Inadvertent or not, they had still abandoned him. She refused to do the same.

"There's a light magic spell that binds a spirit to an object," Erianna told Zelnor.

It was one of the few good memories she had of her father—teaching her that light magic spell. The sub-something? Although he'd called it a ritual, not a spell, and he'd told it to her while drunk, which didn't especially inspire confidence…

Ritual or spell, whatever it was, it wasn't especially complicated. She just needed to focus on an object important to the ghost and imagine a thin strand tethering him to it. It was so simple that even she should be able to cast it.

"So, you want to attach him to something…and then what?" Zelnor asked.

"Talk to him? Help him move on, I suppose. Or at least keep him company," Erianna said.

"You want to take a ghost with us?" Zelnor balked.

"With *me*. You'll only have suffer our presence for three more weeks, at most."

"You're not coming into Nirdeem with me?" Zelnor asked.

The bearded woman's tone was careful, but the meaning behind her words was obvious. Erianna smirked. Oh, she had not expected *this*.

"Do I sense a hint of disappointment?" Erianna leaned forward into Zelnor's space and whispered, "Are you going to miss me?"

"No. I was just—" Zelnor took a step back. "Wondering how long you were going to follow me like a lost puppy."

"If anyone here is a lost puppy, it's you. You're the one who needs to be led."

"Can't you just come back later, and do this by yourself?" Zelnor asked.

"Are you really afraid of traveling with a child?" Erianna asked.

"He's not a child! He's a ghost. What if he attacks us?"

Erianna had known the mage was ornery at times, but she hadn't imagined that Zelnor could be this heartless. She would make this child wait weeks here, alone, and for what? Because she expected a twelve-year-old boy to hurt them? Caution was one thing, but this pushed past prudence and into lunacy.

"He won't!" Erianna said. "For Liscuntia's sake, you're more powerful than anyone I've ever met, and he is a *child.*"

"My magic might not even work on ghosts. And you need to stop trying to make me use it. You have no idea how much it's cost me!"

"And you have no idea what it's like to be young and alone and know that *no one* gives a shit about you!" Erianna yelled.

Zelnor frowned. Erianna's words had stunned her into silence. Erianna could almost laugh. She had finally convinced the mage to shut up, and it was because she had revealed a little taste of just how pathetic she really was. Gods, what was wrong with her?

"I'm sorry," a voice said behind them.

Lyle had passed through the wall and joined them. With his feet on the ground, he looked human. Just a regular child watching arguing adults with misplaced guilt. Erianna's heart ached.

"I didn't mean to make you two fight," Lyle said.

"You didn't, sweetie. It's not your fault We fight all the time," Erianna said.

She crouched down and put a hand on Lyle's shoulder, wincing when it passed right through.

"But I heard you talking about me," he said.

"How much did you hear?" Erianna asked.

"Um… Well…" Lyle winced. "All of it. I *promise* I won't hurt you. I just really want to leave the castle. It's empty and quiet, and I miss my parents. I want to see them. Even if they can't see me."

"It's all right, Lyle. I'll help you find them. I promise," Erianna said.

The ghost had probably spent years in this castle. A few more weeks wouldn't make much of a difference. A small sacrifice to keep harmony between Zelnor and herself. But how could Erianna tell this sad boy they were leaving him, even if only temporarily?

"What do you need?" Zelnor asked.

Erianna turned around to face the half-elf. Just moments ago, Zelnor had hated the boy, had been vehemently against helping him. She had changed her mind so quickly that it almost made Erianna dizzy. It seemed Zelnor did have a heart.

"An object," Erianna said. "Something significant to Lyle. And…"

Was there some other component to the spell she wasn't thinking of? No, she remembered it being simple. Just the object and her intent. Most of the work was in the magic itself.

"That's it," Erianna said, addressing Lyle. "Is there anything special to you here? A toy you loved or a favorite book?"

"Well," Lyle considered her question. "When I was alive—"

"Wait," Zelnor interrupted. "You know that you're…"

"I heard you call me a ghost," Lyle said.

"Oh… Oh Lyle," Erianna said. "I'm so—"

Lyle giggled, and Erianna chuckled when she realized he'd been teasing them. The two of them were going to get along very well.

"I knew already. I've always known," he said. "Anyway, what I liked most was definitely the garden. But a flower probably wouldn't work, right?"

"We need something more permanent," Erianna said.

"Hmm… Oh! There's a statue in the garden!" he exclaimed.

Zelnor groaned behind them, and Erianna had a feeling she knew what the mage was upset about. How would they bring a *statue* along with them? Erianna's bag was large, but she certainly couldn't fit an entire sculpture in it.

"We have a small shrine to Thermoren on the grounds," Lyle continued. "The statue has been in my family for generations. My oldest brother would pray to it with me sometimes. Before he left with everyone else."

The figurines in traditional prayer shrines in Alaspinor only reached half a foot at most. They could easily carry one. There was something fitting about binding a ghost to an image of Thermoren, too. Death's Attendant—the god of funeral rites and nourishing flame, the symbol of rebirth from the ashes of tragedy—seemed a fitting choice for a ghost who had died so young.

"We'll go downstairs and get it," Erianna said. "Just wait here."

Erianna and Zelnor started to walk down the hallway. Lyle's hand shot out toward Erianna to stop her, but it passed right through. He gazed at her, imploring her not to go.

"Zelnor, would you get it? I think I'd like to stay here."

"Sure, I guess. What does the statue look like?" Zelnor asked.

"You don't know what Thermoren looks like?" Erianna asked incredulously. "How have you never seen him before?"

"I told you. I didn't grow up here," Zelnor said. "I've heard the name a couple of times, but that's it."

"He's the god of *death*. How have you never encountered a shrine to him? There's one in every graveyard," Erianna said.

"I have no reason to visit graveyards," Zelnor said. "I know a *goddess* of death, Felsha'kor. But I'm assuming I'm not looking for a golden, fiery bird?"

"No, definitely not," Erianna said. "Strong warrior. Strapping. Holding a sword—one hand gripping the hilt, blade resting in the other."

Zelnor darted down the stairs, while Erianna ushered the ghost back into the study. Now that she thought about it, Thermoren was an odd choice for a noble family's shrine. Then again, what did she know? She'd never met a prevator before.

There was a rumble in the distance, followed by a flash of light. The rain fell harder than ever, with no signs of stopping. Part of her felt relieved not to be out in it. Although she felt a little guilty sending the mage out alone into the downpour, how could she ignore Lyle's pitiful eyes? He clearly hadn't wanted to be left alone for even one moment. Erianna was happy that she wouldn't have to leave him here for the few weeks it would take to journey to Nirdeem.

Lyle curled up in the same navy chair he'd first appeared behind. He put his fingers in his mouth and started chewing on his nails. It was amazing how lifelike he looked. If not for his still chest and the way he drifted when he moved, she wouldn't have guessed he was a ghost. Erianna sat in the chair next to him, and the boy looked over at her with a frown.

"What if…" Lyle curled up a little tighter. "What if my parents come back while I'm gone?"

Erianna considered the idea for a moment. Although it was possible, she doubted they would return. The place hadn't seen another living mortal in a while, based on all the dust. It seemed unlikely they would search for their missing son in their own home. If they were searching for him at all.

"Why don't we leave a note telling them that you've left and you're safe?" Erianna suggested, more for the ghost's peace of mind than anything.

"How will they find me?" Lyle asked.

"Let's tell them to leave us a letter in Bimblebarrow, and if we don't find them, we'll check there," she said.

"All right! That sounds good," he said. "Do you think…they'll be able to see me?"

Erianna hadn't seen many ghosts herself, or at least, she didn't think she had. Her last was a beautiful woman she'd spoken with at a boutique in Goldhaven. No one else had acknowledged the woman's presence. Still, that didn't mean they couldn't see her. It wouldn't be uncommon in such a large city for strangers to pass by without a greeting, and ghosts looked so similar to the living that it was possible people just couldn't tell the difference. She hadn't seen the living and the dead interact enough to know for sure either way.

"I don't know," Erianna answered.

"Yeah… That makes sense."

"But I'll pass along anything you want to say to them, so don't worry too much, all right?" Erianna reached out to grab his hand, before she remembered she couldn't and decided to lay it comfortingly on the arm of his chair instead.

"Can we write the letter, while we wait?" Lyle suggested.

"Of course," she said.

Lyle guided her to one of the bedrooms they'd seen earlier. Apparently, the room next door was his. It was elegantly furnished, similar to the rest of the castle, but there were a few touches that made it obvious that this room belonged to Lyle. It was a wonder she hadn't noticed how different it was from the others. It was messier, with dirt tracked across the floor and a few books strewn about. The bed was rumpled and unmade. The walls were lined with framed flowers and plants—dried, pressed, and preserved—and landscape paintings. A vase with fresh roses sat on the writing desk tucked in the corner.

Lyle dictated a long, heartfelt message explaining how much he missed and loved his parents, and how he hoped to see them soon. He outlined the two travelers' arrival at the castle, giving a full, physical description of Erianna. He also started describing Zelnor, and Erianna didn't have the heart to explain that the mage wouldn't be traveling with them.

Erianna paused in her dictation.

"Do you want to tell them what happened to you?" she prompted gently. "How you died?"

"I don't remember," Lyle said.

"Oh." Erianna wasn't sure whether that was normal or not. She brushed the thought aside and continued writing.

Lyle told them about the object he was bound to and had Erianna provide brief descriptions of both Bimblebarrow and *The Violent Temptress*. The two ended the letter by promising that Lyle would find his parents one day. He told her to add a postscript saying that he'd included a sketch of his two traveling companions.

Erianna paused. A spot of ink dripped down and stained the parchment. "I'm…not an excellent artist. But I'll do my best."

"Oh, I'll do it!" Lyle offered.

"You can draw?" Erianna asked.

"Well, yeah. Of course," Lyle replied. "My parents made sure I could draw. It's important for conducting experiments and writing studies."

Erianna decided not to tell Lyle that she'd been more surprised over his ability to draw as a ghost, not his having learned to draw as a mortal.

Lyle reached out, and the quill started moving on its own, filling in minute details and shading with precision. In an absurdly short time, he had produced a detailed sketch of them that not only depicted their likenesses but also their essence. Erianna's inked duplicate eyed Zelnor with a sly smile.

"Impressive," Erianna said.

"It's really nothing," Lyle said. She imagined that if he could have, he would have blushed. "I've had some extra practice, since I died."

"You don't have to be so modest. You've really captured Zelnor's grumpiness."

Erianna tucked the sketch behind the letter and folded them together into an envelope. She wrote "Mother and Father," per Lyle's request, on the outside and left it on the desk.

"Thanks for helping. I've got really bad handwriting," Lyle said.

"Of course. Feel better?" Erianna asked.

Lyle nodded, and the two returned to the library. As they waited for Zelnor, Erianna's mind drifted back to the spell. She still couldn't shake the nagging sense that there was a component missing… She was probably just nervous about casting light magic. She wasn't exactly eager to take up the horrid practice again, but if she could help Lyle, then it would be worth it.

Zelnor walked back down to the first floor, the pounding rain muffling her footsteps. She heard a crash of thunder. Even she didn't want to be out in this downpour.

The castle entrance was still open, water spilling in and drenching the edge of the red carpet. Reflecting on it now, it seemed a little paranoid to keep the door open behind them, but in fairness, there really *was* a ghost haunting Castle Veloria, so her suspicions weren't entirely unfounded. She pulled up the hood of her traveling cloak before plunging outside.

Freezing water immediately soaked through her outerwear, sinking into her bones, and the wind bit her face. Zelnor loved the rain, but weather this intense helped her understand why everyone else hated it. As she traipsed through the garden, mud gushed into the holes on the sides of her boots where the seams had ripped from overuse. She wished Erianna had lent her a new pair of shoes too. Although, the bard probably would've gotten mad at her for dirtying them.

Zelnor trudged through the thick sludge of the garden paths, passing the widest variety of plants she'd ever seen in Alaspinor. Every path led to the shrine to Thermoren. Small and unassuming, the shrine consisted of only the statue on a pedestal, bracketed by two planters filled with freshly cut white and red roses. She hadn't expected the shrine to look so simple. The small figure, which she assumed must be Thermoren, had broad shoulders and full armor, his head exposed. He clasped a sword hilt in his left hand and rested the flat of the blade in his right palm, just as Erianna had described.

Zelnor reached for the statue, but her hand hovered just before she grazed the immortalized god. Removing a god from their shine was bad luck in Alaspinoran culture. Lyle hadn't seemed concerned about that superstition. Maybe it'd skipped the younger generation? Or maybe nobles just didn't care about respecting the gods. She wouldn't be surprised.

Zelnor snatched the statue. She was already cursed. What else could the gods do to her? It felt much lighter than she expected, most likely hollow.

The force of the raindrops pummeled the petals in the garden and assaulted the thin material covering her head. She broke into a sprint, attempting to leap over a tall rosebush to reach the door that much faster. Her boot caught on a mess of thorns, and she plummeted face down into the mud.

Wet earth went up her nose and into her mouth. She righted herself and spluttered, wincing at the disgusting taste and snuffling to remove the sod that had invaded her sinuses. Walking the remaining steps to the entrance, she closed the doors and attempted to brush the mud off. Still soaking and a bit sticky from the liquid dirt clinging to her now ruined new clothes, she snorted and wondered half-heartedly if bad luck curses were just as real as ghosts. She ascended the stairs carefully, concerned she might trip and tumble back down them.

In the study, Erianna had curled up in a chair, her back to the door. The ghost had moved across the room, warming himself in front of a fire. His braid slipped from his back over his shoulder as he leaned forward. He looked eerily lifelike, like a boy enjoying the heat from the hearth. Could ghosts even feel the cold?

Zelnor hesitated. This was her last chance to back out and refuse to indulge the bard's insane desire to take a ghost along with them. Zelnor could pretend the statue had gone missing. Erianna stirred, while the mage was debating. *Too late.* Zelnor handed her the statue of Thermoren.

To Zelnor's surprise, Erianna didn't comment on the mud. She just took the figure and placed it on the floor, sliding down to sit next to it. Zelnor joined her. She was fascinated, despite herself. Apart from some occasional healing and the one banishment, Zelnor had never seen light magic performed.

Erianna beckoned Lyle over to her, and the two sat across from each other. She picked up the statue and took a deep breath.

"Ready?" Erianna asked Lyle.

Zelnor almost thought she heard the bard's voice shaking slightly, but Lyle didn't seem to notice. He just nodded.

Erianna clasped her hands around the statue, as though she were praying. She squeezed her eyes shut and golden threads of light sputtered around the figure. She shuddered and mumbled something. Zelnor wondered if it was related to the spell, or if the bard was simply talking to herself.

Strands of light wrapped around Erianna's fingers. Their bright gold illuminated the entire room. The threads snaked toward Lyle, tangling around his wrists and ankles. The golden threads tightened. It looked painful.

The light around Erianna's hands intensified and grew until it entangled her arms. The light dragged Lyle closer to her, and Erianna drooped, as she struggled to hold herself upright. She'd said the spell was easy. It shouldn't be draining her energy so quickly!

Lyle's form flickered. The golden light fizzled. It sparked a couple of *pops* before disappearing completely. Erianna cried out, crumpling forward.

Chapter Six
Fading Memories

Zelnor turned Erianna over onto her back. She didn't know anything about medicine, and couldn't even cast the most basic light spell. The bard was so still. Was she *dead?* Lyle hovered over her shoulder, his silent presence like an ominous portent.

Zelnor shooed the ghost away and forced herself to calm down. There were ways even a non-healer could check for signs of life. She placed her hand on Erianna's stomach and waited a moment.

Zelnor's hand rose slowly and fell again. Erianna was breathing. Zelnor felt like an idiot for not noticing before. The bard groaned and sat up.

"What happened?" Zelnor asked.

"I'm fine," Erianna said.

Her voice was devoid of emotion; her gaze unfocused. From what Zelnor had read, it was normal for light magic to drain your spirit, leaving healers feeling hollowed out and exhausted—it was why they could only see a certain number of people per day—but this reaction was by far the worst Zelnor had ever seen. After a healer finished, they seemed a bit subdued, sure, but Erianna was acting vacant, like nothing existed behind her eyes.

Erianna mumbled something, before curling back up into a ball. Zelnor wasn't sure what healers normally did to take care of themselves after a taxing light spell. Maybe some sleep would help her recover.

A blanket flew past Zelnor, and she saw Lyle directing it with his hands. The blanket draped itself over Erianna. Lyle swayed unsteadily in the air, before lowering himself to the ground.

Ghosts could interact with objects in the physical world, like blankets…or knives. *What a comforting thought.*

"Is that some kind of magic?" she asked.

If Zelnor could understand ghosts, then maybe she'd be able to combat them. Better to find out now than when the boy dropped a rock on their heads or flung flaming coals at them. But the ghost turned his owlish, hazel eyes to the mage and shrugged his shoulders. Of course, it wouldn't be that easy.

"I'm not sure. If I focus, I can move things. I do it all the time, but…for some reason, it's not as easy as it should be. I feel so sleepy."

Lyle shrunk into a little whisp of smoke again. At least that told Zelnor something: ghosts could run out of energy, just like the living. How long did she have until he rematerialized? Did he sleep for the same length of time they did? Either way, they shouldn't let their guard down, *especially* when they were sleeping. Thankfully, she and Erianna usually took turns keeping watch at night anyway. They could easily keep an eye on Lyle at the same time.

Of course, once Erianna went off on her own, the ghost would have plenty of opportunities to hurt her, but that was hardly Zelnor's fault. After all, Erianna had been the one so desperate to take the ghost along. She would have to deal with the consequences.

Erianna slept deeply, her chest moving in slow, full breaths. She looked peaceful like this but also vulnerable. The sleeping ghost had drifted over, a little wisp above her—so small, yet so dangerous. *How can she be so reckless?* Even if she was right and not all ghosts were evil, Erianna had no guarantees that this one wouldn't turn on her.

Zelnor turned away from them. Who cared if a stranger wanted to gamble with their own life? There wasn't anything Zelnor could do about it. In just a few weeks, it wouldn't matter anymore.

Zelnor went back to browsing the shelves, stuffing a few more books into her bag. Like the previous shelf, she noticed that many of the books centered around light magic and all of them were highly technical—not a single book about etiquette, making money, or fairy tales. Most of the books in the library also heavily emphasized morality. Zelnor had only met one noble, but what few rumors she'd heard made these books seem severely out of character for the upper echelons of Alaspinor. She wondered what kind of people the Veloria family were.

By the time she finished, her satchel was so full that the strain on the seams threatened to rip the entire bag apart. She tried, as a rule, to keep her belongings to a minimum, but she'd never seen so many interesting books in one place. Besides, no one else was using these books. Leaving them to gather dust in the castle would be a waste.

Thankfully, space wasn't a concern anymore. Zelnor dragged Erianna's oversized bag to the center of the room, grunting with the effort. It was *much* heavier than it looked. How did Erianna carry it all day? She had swung it onto her back that morning like it was nothing. Well, that meant Erianna definitely wouldn't notice if it was just a little bit heavier. Zelnor tossed the largest books into the bag, keeping one aside to read.

She curled up in a chair across the room, propping the tome open in her lap, but her eyes drifted back to the ishlanian. The gray light made her look overly pale. Lyle had propped up the warrior statue at her feet. Thermoren, Death's Many-Faced Attendant, watched Erianna with empty eyes.

It's like a burial. A peal of thunder exploded from just overhead, and bright light filled the room, throwing everything into sharp relief. Zelnor jumped reflexively, but the blinding white passed almost as soon as it appeared.

Erianna shifted in her sleep, moving her neck into an awkward angle. Zelnor tossed her book aside and grabbed a pillow, shoving it under the ishlanian's head. Erianna wasn't dead. She was just asleep. Zelnor threw herself back into the armchair and squinted at the pages through the dim candlelight. Erianna would wake up soon.

When Lyle finally recovered, both the bearded half-elf and the ishlanian woman were asleep. Daylight streamed in from the arched window. A large puddle underneath it sparkled in the morning light. The rain tended to pool there, ever since the glass had broken. Normally, he didn't care, but he hoped the water hadn't gotten on Erianna.

The teal woman had been sleeping for a long time… It had been a while since Lyle had been alive, but he didn't remember ever sleeping so long. Maybe ishlanians needed to sleep longer than humans? Or maybe Lyle's parents were just much stricter about waking up on time?

Lyle hoped that was all it was, because there wasn't much he could do for her. Something had happened to him. Usually, he had enough energy to tend to the many gardens and still practice a bit of drawing without any trouble, but after just lifting a blanket—something that should've taken very little energy—he'd suddenly felt exhausted.

That weird light magic spell must have made him a little tired.

That was probably it. Lyle would go down to the gardens outside, as usual, and tend to them. Everything would go back to normal.

The ghost floated confidently out the door. He suddenly stopped. He felt a strange sensation, like a string tied around his chest was holding him back. He backed up and raced forward, only for the same pull to stop him again. For some reason, he couldn't cross that point. Every time he tried, it felt like he had gotten the wind knocked out of him. He couldn't even breathe anymore! There shouldn't be any wind to knock out.

Something was trapping him here. His eyes landed on the statue of Thermoren. There was a white light mixed with the golden one around it. It was the same white light that had surrounded Lyle his entire afterlife.

He had assumed that white light around him was just something that all ghosts had, but after meeting Zelnor, he had realized his theory probably wasn't right. Zelnor had the same white glow around him that Lyle did, except Zelnor's glow was even brighter. Lyle had assumed that Zelnor was a ghost at first, but then the half-elf had started picking up books with his hands. Zelnor also had this pretty little swirl of green and blue light around his right wrist for some reason.

It was really weird, actually. Lyle had never seen that white light on any living mortal. Though, to be fair, he also hadn't seen that many living people in general. And he hadn't seen any other ghosts at all, so maybe he didn't have the best "sample size," as one of his uncles liked to say.

Adding to Lyle's confusion, Erianna also glowed. She always had a faint gray light around her, so dim that it was difficult to spot in the daylight. He had also seen her glow teal in her sleep. Although, he was sure that was something different. The white and the gray light, even the blue and green one coming from Zelnor, had this warmth to them? Or maybe not warmth exactly, but they felt almost... alive?

The teal glow didn't feel like that.

The ghost turned his attention back to the statue of Thermoren. He felt a connection to it. Like it was…

"A tether?" Lyle said out loud.

His energy had gotten tied up with the statue, so now he was stuck to that instead of his home. Erianna had said the spell would connect him to an object, but this felt more like a horse tied to a hitching post. Lyle glared at Thermoren. It was the first time he'd ever been angry at a statue.

Lyle concentrated and lifted the statue up. It took more energy than he expected, so he set it down just outside the door—only a few steps away from the boundary that he'd been unable to cross earlier. He steeled himself and floated forward. He passed over the statue without any problem but only drifted down a few stairs before the tether prevented him from moving farther. There was no way he could carry the statue all the way out to the gardens, which meant he'd have to wake one of the living people. He really hoped they weren't angry at him for it.

Lyle floated back to Erianna. The ishlanian had been asleep for much longer than the half-elf, so it made sense to ask her first. Plus, the teal woman seemed really nice and didn't randomly hate him.

Lyle placed his hand on her shoulder to shake her awake. It passed right through. Of course it did. What had he thought would happen?

"Excuse me," Lyle said.

Erianna didn't budge a muscle.

"Hello?" he said. "Erianna!"

Lyle heard a gasp and a loud *thump* behind him. The half-elven man had fallen out of his chair. His white hair stuck up in all directions and his expression was dark. Zelnor obviously wasn't a morning person.

"What are you doing?" Zelnor asked.

"I was trying to wake Erianna?" Lyle said.

"She's still not awake?" Zelnor asked.

Zelnor's dark look deepened as he rushed over to Erianna. The man rested a hand against the teal woman's stomach and waited. The half-elf was really worried that she hadn't woken up yet. He muttered something under his breath and started stroking his white beard.

"What did you want with her?" Zelnor asked.

"I can't go far away from the statue. And I just," Lyle stammered, "I want to go outside…to see the gardens."

Lyle smiled pleasantly, like his mother had taught him. Anyone could be won over with kindness and persistence! Even really, really, *really* scary people.

Zelnor looked back down at Erianna again, and his white hair shifted, so that Lyle couldn't see his face. The half-elf brushed away some of the dried mud caked on his pants and strode out of the room. He picked up the statue as he left, slipping it into his satchel, and Lyle hurried after him. The statue would start dragging him if he fell behind.

The two passed by room after room, and Lyle realized he couldn't remember which family members they belonged to. Yesterday, he could have named every single cousin, all his aunts and uncles, *and* what fields they studied. Now he could only name two thirds of them. Maybe even less. He felt a sinking dread.

At least, he still recognized the room nestled near the bottom of the stairs. It had belonged to his favorite aunt. Aunt Amari always brought seeds whenever she returned from her trips to Goldhaven. She'd taught him how to keep his gardening tools from rusting.

They finally emerged from the castle and into the daylight. Lyle saw the sun shining, but he couldn't feel its warmth on his face or the cool morning air. He didn't understand. It wasn't the same as when he was alive, but he used to feel it a little! Had the spell really taken this from him too?

He tried not to let it bother him. He should focus on the fact that he was outside, and soon, he would explore the fresh green grass and beautiful rolling hills of Alaspinor, going further from his home than he ever had before. That was what mattered.

The two passed through the arches into the garden, and Lyle rushed over to his rose bushes as soon as he was able. The garden had always been his favorite place. There was something satisfying about gardening: working with plants to bring out the best in them, nurturing them until they grew into something beautiful.

His mother had understood it, spending hours tending to the plants with him, while his siblings studied indoors. She had told Lyle stories about her own mother's fascination with gardening and how she'd named all her daughters after flowers. Lyle's grandmother had been the one to plant the roses that the two of them loved so much. His mother and grandmother would've been proud that Lyle was still taking such good care of the family's garden.

Lyle had always wondered why the rest of his family insisted he study all day instead. Hopefully, he could ask them when he saw them again. *If I see them again.*

Lyle reached toward the flowers, but he faltered. He would need help to tend to these gardens. If only moving a blanket or moving a little figurine exhausted him, then he doubted he'd do more than tend to a few plants before he needed to rest again. He turned toward the half-elven man next to him with a hopeful smile.

"Would you help me in the gardens?" Lyle asked. "Well, I guess I mean, will you take care of the plants for me?"

"Why?" Zelnor asked.

"Because the flowers are important to me. Very important to me," Lyle said.

"You're planning on leaving. They're going to die anyway."

"Well, I guess you're right. But I still want to take care of them. One last time."

"I don't know anything about gardening," Zelnor admitted.

"That's all right! I can help with that," Lyle said.

Zelnor grumbled, but as Lyle expected, the half-elf quickly lost himself in the task. Lyle watched the man wistfully. He missed the soothing, repetitive work of watering and weeding. Using his ghost power had never been the same, and now, he couldn't even do that. Still, Lyle was happy to see the tension finally leak out of Zelnor's body as he worked his way across the expansive grounds. The half-elf needed this more than Lyle did anyway.

Even with Lyle's guidance, Zelnor wasn't the *best* gardener. At one point, Lyle stepped in to prune a bush when the half-elf completely botched it, cutting off several beautiful blooms. Other than that, Zelnor finished the job fairly well—as well as someone so obviously new to gardening could. There were things that Lyle would have done differently, but with his limited ability, he didn't have much choice other than to rely on the grumpy half-elf and be grateful for his help.

The mist cleared away and the sun shone almost directly above them by the time they finished. Zelnor plopped down into the mud. At this point, he was completely covered in it. He didn't seem to mind, though. The silence between them felt less hostile than before, and Lyle hoped he had managed to convince Zelnor to trust him, at least a little.

Lyle gazed into the dense forest that had surrounded him his entire life. He had spent so many days playing in the branches and running through this maze of plants. Their house was always so full and loud, but the gardens had always been quiet. He missed the noise, the arguments, even the admonishments for getting his clothes all dirty. Since he'd woken up this morning, his memories of the castle and his family had started fading, but that only made him even more determined to hold on to them.

Lyle still remembered reaching up to tug at his mother's dress, hiding behind her when a simple debate among his siblings developed into a loud argument. Her warm smile always made him feel just a little calmer. He still saw her as clearly as he had when he was alive. He could almost feel his father's hand on his shoulder, could see his steady gaze.

He missed them.

"Thank you," Lyle said. "The flowers, they remind me of my mother and my aunt."

"You're—" The half-elf paused, his face unreadable. "You're welcome."

Lyle felt like Zelnor still didn't like him. Lyle missed Erianna. He really hoped that the spell hadn't been too much for her.

"Is she going to be all right?" Lyle asked.

"She'll be fine," Zelnor said.

"Can we go check on her?" Lyle asked.

"I was already planning on it."

Zelnor looked back toward the castle. Between his bright white glow, stark white hair, and the sun shining on him, it was difficult for Lyle to look directly at the half-elf. Zelnor picked himself up and held a hand out to Lyle, before retracting it in embarrassment.

He tried to help me up! Maybe he's warming up to me! Lyle smiled up at him, but Zelnor had already turned away.

Lyle took one last look at the garden as they went back inside. What if he forgot his family entirely? What if staying in the castle was the only way he could remember?

Even if that was true, he didn't think he could force himself to stay any longer. Spending every day doing nothing but waiting was unbearable. Besides, his parents were somewhere beyond those rolling hills in the distance. If he found them, then he wouldn't have to worry about forgetting them.

The two found Erianna with her back against the wall. Zelnor laid a hand on her shoulder, but she didn't react. Her eyes were open, but it was almost like she was still asleep. For the next few minutes, Lyle and Zelnor tried to help her. They tried to get her to speak or move or do *anything*. She was acting so…empty. Lyle had never seen anyone like this before.

Zelnor slung the teal woman's large backpack onto his shoulders, staggering under its weight. He had to grab Erianna's hand and drag her out of the library. She shuffled listlessly behind her friend. It was scary, seeing the kind woman suddenly so quiet.

Chapter Seven
Trust Issues

Zelnor slung Erianna's arm over her shoulder, as the bard shifted from one foot to the other in what could only generously be called walking. Their progress was slow. Ever since she'd cast that light spell on Lyle, Erianna had been stuck in this semi-comatose state.

Erianna sagged into Zelnor, putting all her weight onto Zelnor's weak arms. *Not again.* This was why she stayed so close to the bard. The woman couldn't manage more than a couple of hours travel before needing another rest.

Lyle hovered a few feet off the ground behind them, peering over their shoulders. Part of Zelnor felt for Lyle—a ghost child implied something unimaginably tragic—but that didn't mean they could let their guard down around him. They had no idea how long he'd haunted that castle. Based on the dust, the place had stood untouched for at least a decade. Years of solitude had a way of wearing on even the soundest of minds. Isolation to that degree broke people.

The ghost needed to be monitored at all times until Zelnor had gauged his mental state. She had stayed awake the past two nights until her eyes burned. By the second night, she knew she couldn't sustain it, but she still cursed herself for letting sleep take her. She awoke, gods knew how many hours later, expecting the worst, but thankfully, the bard slumbered unharmed. The ghost hadn't slit their throats—this time.

Zelnor pulled Erianna toward the edge of the road. Between the tall ishlanian in her arms and the large pack on her back, it was a nearly impossible task. The weight lifted: Lyle was using his telekinesis to help carry Erianna. As soon as they set her down in a small grove, he curled into a little ball of smoke.

Despite how exhausting he found it, Lyle insisted on helping every time Erianna collapsed. Zelnor hadn't seen any reason to refuse. When he turned into a wisp, he lost all awareness of his surroundings, and she didn't have to worry about him.

Zelnor couldn't keep watching the ghost by herself. She needed Erianna to wake up and help her take care of the mess that she had gotten them into, but she doubted Erianna's stupor would fade on its own. It didn't seem to be getting worse, but considering Erianna couldn't even walk properly, Zelnor wasn't sure it *could* get worse. There were no towns for miles, which meant no healers for miles. She would have to figure this out herself.

Zelnor slipped Erianna's ridiculously large backpack off and rolled her aching shoulders. She rooted around, sifting through several dresses until she found one of the tomes she'd nabbed from Castle Veloria about light magic abuse in Alaspinor. She prayed it would have something about mitigating the detrimental aftereffects of light magic.

After a cursory glance at the table of contents, she found a promising section and settled in, her back resting against the rough bark of a tree trunk. A knobby root poked into her thigh. She was thankful for it. It was the only thing keeping her from nodding off, now that she'd finally sat down.

Even so, it was difficult to concentrate. Her eyes focused and unfocused. The words swam together. The text kept veering so far off-topic that the she hardly knew what she was reading anymore, and thanks to all her backtracking, chapters that would normally take ten minutes to read took well over an hour.

Erianna stirred next to her, and Zelnor glanced up from her book. The ghost was awake too, and he hovered over her. He held his hand just above Erianna's shoulder, as though to comfort her. Despite herself, Zelnor smiled at the gesture.

She tried to think of something, *anything* to say, but she just couldn't force out another empty platitude. Erianna's eyes looked so dead. Finally, Zelnor decided to go back to her research. It was the only way she could help now, and gods knew she needed all of her dwindling attention for it.

The bard mumbled something, and Zelnor immediately snapped the book shut and tossed it aside. For the first time in *three days,* Erianna had spoken. Surely, that meant she was finally getting better. Zelnor leaned in closer to hear her.

"— useless," Erianna mumbled.

Of course that was the first thing Erianna would say. Zelnor might not be functioning with her usual efficiency, but her suboptimal was better than most people's exceptional. Zelnor was a lot of things, but she was *not* useless. If she was good at anything, it was research. Erianna would regret critiquing her skills.

Zelnor went back to the book with a renewed fire, and finally found a footnote that mentioned an old remedy: a tea made from chamomile, mint, and opeli leaves that eased the symptoms of light magic. To think, all this time, the solution was tea. Erianna had made tea a few times while they traveled. She probably had most of the ingredients with her.

Zelnor searched until she produced a pouch filled with wilted herbs organized into neat bundles. Among them she recognized chamomile and mint, but unsurprisingly, the little bag didn't have opeli leaves. The white and blue plant was used in many remedies, but it was rare. Still, it was native to Alaspinor, and their group had passed a farm just up the road. The people there might know where to find some. It was worth trying, at least.

Zelnor hesitated. She couldn't carry Erianna all the way back, but she couldn't leave her alone either. Criminals would see her as an easy mark. She was in no shape to defend herself. She needed someone to stay behind and watch over her.

Lyle was the only choice. It would take half an hour at most to get back to that farm. The ghost liked Erianna. It was obvious he cared about her, and he had already passed up a few opportunities to harm them… This was a tremendously stupid idea, but she couldn't think of a better one.

Zelnor tucked the statue of Thermoren into Erianna's belt. The bard hadn't changed clothes in three full days now and hadn't complained about that fact, either. It was almost more worrying than her listlessness.

Zelnor started a small fire to keep Erianna warm and chase away the surrounding mist. The smoke would hardly be visible on a day like this, so she figured it was safe enough. Finally, steeling herself, she packed up the two bags, slinging her own on her shoulder and Erianna's onto her back, and placed a blanket over the sleeping ishlanian. Hopefully, once she had taken all of their stuff, Erianna would be an unappealing target to criminals.

Zelnor leveled the ghost with a serious look.

"Lyle," she said.

"Yes?" he asked.

"If anyone comes, can you scare them away?" Zelnor said.

"I'll protect her. You can trust me." Lyle nodded firmly.

Can I? It wasn't too late to change her mind… What was the alternative, though? She couldn't continue on like this.

With one last anxious glance at the ghost and the ishlanian, Zelnor jogged through the tall grass, weaving around the sparse trees that surrounded the little grove they'd settled in. The sun was sinking toward the horizon, tinting the pale grass orange. This part of Alaspinor was a never-ending plain stretching in every direction.

Zelnor spotted a farm in the distance. Picking up the pace, she reached the cottage and small barn. A farmer reached for a bundle of herbs hanging on the front porch. When the woman saw the mage, she froze. Her silver-blue eyes trained intently on Zelnor. A second later, she tugged the hood of her gray cloak lower and yanked the herbs down.

The woman wore a high-collared, black tunic. Her crooked nose sat a bit too far left on her head, and her skin was a pallid white, lined in deep wrinkles. Although difficult to discern with her weathered face, the stranger surely wasn't over forty. Her hair, a fluffy bob of unevenly cut, vibrant red strands, showed only a few, scant signs of gray.

The herbs gripped in the stranger's hand were white with blue veins running along the backs of the leaves. Opeli leaves. Somehow, the farmer had the rare plant, already dried and perfect for brewing tea.

"Could I have some of those?" Zelnor asked. "I don't have enough coin, but I could do some chores in exchange maybe?"

The stranger thrust the bundle of dried leaves forward.

"I've extra. Take the lot of them," the redhead said.

Her voice was gravelly from disuse and thick with a lilting accent Zelnor couldn't place. Her voice sounded familiar. Zelnor must have met someone in the shelter who'd hailed from the same country as this woman.

Zelnor dug around in her bag for some coin, but the stranger shook her head. She pressed the herbs into Zelnor's hand.

For free? The opeli plant was so rare. The woman could easily get a dozen gold coins for them. Zelnor had a hard time believing that the stranger would really just give them away. She probably didn't know their value. Literacy wasn't exactly high in Alaspinor, so it wasn't that unreasonable. Or maybe she couldn't find a way to get them to the nearest town safely. Still, something about this situation felt wrong…and it frustrated her that she couldn't figure out what. It was like her mind was swimming in molasses.

Zelnor couldn't waste time puzzling over this stranger's generosity. The longer she was away, the greater the chance someone might stumble upon the clearing where Erianna was resting. And gods only knew what would happen if she were discovered by bandits in that state. The mage was entrusting the bard's life to a *ghost*.

"Thank you," Zelnor said.

She felt the stranger's eyes on her as she walked away.

What was it about the farmer that bothered Zelnor so much? Her clothes had been simple, her skin weathered as though she worked in the sun. There wasn't anything obviously out of place about her. It was a little unusual for a farmer to wear black, but she might have just returned from a funeral. And yet, a gnawing feeling that something was off had settled in the back of Zelnor's mind, and she couldn't seem to shake it.

The closer she got to Erianna, though, the more the ishlanian occupied her mind instead. Zelnor burst back into the clearing, expecting the worst. But everything was as she'd left it.

Erianna was still curled into a ball, sound asleep, with Lyle watching over her. An hour completely alone with the catatonic bard, and the ghost hadn't tried anything nefarious. In fact, he'd set a pot filled with water on the small fire. He must've read the book she'd left open, and when he'd figured out what Zelnor was planning, his first reaction had been to help.

The water was already bubbling. Zelnor quickly shredded mint and chamomile and tossed them into the pot, before it boiled over. She leaned over to skim the recipe again. The opeli leaves were needed partway through, and she dutifully began pulling the white and blue leaves apart.

"Is there anything I can do?" Lyle asked.

"No, I've got it," Zelnor replied.

"Oh. All right," the ghost said.

He sounded so dejected. The ghost had been so attentive since Erianna had fallen into her semi-conscious state. He'd always tried his best to help two perfect strangers, one of whom clearly mistrusted him.

"I'm sorry," Zelnor said, "about the past few days."

"That's all right. You're really worried about your friend."

Zelnor and the bard were hardly friends, but she didn't correct the ghost. Instead, she beckoned Lyle over to her, and he studied her movements with fascination. It was as if he'd never seen someone make tea before. *Well, he is a noble.*

Zelnor explained the process as she worked. He paid close attention and even asked a couple of questions. *A diligent student.* He stared at the tea as she poured it into a metal cup, and a thought occurred to the mage.

"Can you eat or drink?" Zelnor asked.

"No," Lyle replied. "Sometimes I want food, especially when you're eating. But I never *actually* feel hungry…"

Zelnor hoped that her question hadn't been too insensitive. She'd only just made amends with Lyle, and she was already making a mess of it. Now that they were actually talking, she remembered how painfully bad she was at it. Apparently, she would never be a people person, whether they were living or dead.

Zelnor brought the steaming cup over to Erianna. It took a few minutes of encouragement to get the ishlanian to sit up, and even upright, she still curled forward, as though a weight dragged her back toward the ground. Zelnor had already done this several times for Erianna. It reminded her of helping her mother tend to the refugees—getting them to drink in small sips of water after days lost in the desert.

Zelnor guided the cup toward Erianna's mouth, gently holding her head, expecting to have to coax her to drink it. Surprisingly, Erianna acted on her own, lifting the cup the rest of the way and sipping the warm liquid.

Erianna had felt as though she were lost in a fog, drowning in pockets of memories and thoughts that swirled in and out of focus. A deep exhaustion seeped into every nook and cranny. Everything had felt hazy and heavy. Someone had forced her to take one step after another, when all she'd wanted to do was crumble under the feeling. Succumb to it.

But then, she'd started waking up again. The chilly night air brushed against her back as a fire warmed her front, lighting the little grove in an orange glow. Nocturnal birds crooned to each other. Sounds and sights came back to her, and it had all started with the bitter taste of overbrewed tea, followed by the intense, cool flavor of dusk mint.

She felt warm liquid flowing down her face in a small stream. *Did I spill my tea?* She pressed her hand against her cheek and realized they were tears.

Useless. She heard the word in her head. It was her word, her thought, but somehow it sounded just like her mother. *Useless.*

The tears flowed faster. Lyle tried to hold her in his ethereal arms. She choked. She was acting pathetic. Stupid. *Why can't I pull myself together?* Lyle was too young to see someone falling apart this way. But they just wouldn't stop.

And then Erianna saw Zelnor, standing over her with a frown and a pinched brow. Erianna tried to wipe the tears away. She hid her face, but the mage was annoyingly persistent, always coming back into view.

If only Erianna's mother hadn't forced her to learn light magic, then she wouldn't be a sniveling, disgusting heap of a woman.

"It's all her fault," Erianna said.

"What! *My* fault?" Zelnor scowled. "What did I do?"

The green and blue gem in Zelnor's wrist sparkled in the firelight. Maybe it *was* her fault. This mess was all thanks to her stupid pact with that monster. Erianna had been fine before. Making consistent coin, enjoying herself, always staying one step ahead of danger. Everything had been fine until Zelnor showed up.

But is it really her fault? No, it was Erianna's. All of this was Erianna's fault. Zelnor hadn't really done anything. The mage was an idiot, sure, but Erianna could have just left her to deal with it on her own. She'd chosen to get involved, and for what?

Did Erianna really think that she could help Zelnor? Erianna would lose the half-elf, just like she'd lost Christine—a slave to a reptilian tyrant, forced to give up her life serving him. Even if Erianna *had* managed to free Zelnor from her pact with Torrin, it wouldn't change the past. Erianna couldn't take back what she'd done. She would never be anything other than a selfish, awful brat. And now she was bawling like an infant. Pathetic. Now everyone else finally saw how worthless she was.

I'm nothing but a liability. A burden. Deadweight.

Zelnor wanted to be mad at Erianna, but the ishlanian looked so pitiful. Even when she'd blamed Zelnor, her voice had trembled, breaking on every word. Zelnor reached out a hand toward her, but stopped and crossed her arms instead.

How was she supposed to comfort Erianna, when it was apparently Zelnor's fault she was upset? Zelnor sat down next to the ishlanian. When Erianna recovered (*if* she recovered), she was getting an earful from the mage. They barely knew each other, and it had been Erianna's choice to cast that light spell.

More importantly, it seemed like Erianna was getting even worse. Was this how it always progressed? Or maybe the tea…? Oh, Thorns' bloody name! It was the tea, wasn't it? It had to be. She'd started sobbing right after she drank it.

Erianna's head fell onto Zelnor's shoulder. Her skin glowed softly. This close, Zelnor could see her eyes were swollen and shut. She had cried so hard that she had fallen asleep.

"What did she mean?" Lyle asked.

Zelnor explained why Erianna had referred to a bearded half-elf as "she," and the pronouns she preferred and when to use them. She could hardly believe that she'd explained her situation to two strangers now.

"Oh, all right. I'll keep that in mind," Lyle said. "But actually, I meant about it being your fault?"

"It's nothing," Zelnor snapped. "She's just upset."

"Well, all right. I hope… I hope she gets better soon."

Lyle looked down at Erianna, looking ready to cry himself. The bard's head felt heavy on Zelnor's shoulder. What if Erianna never recovered? Zelnor had never seen anyone cry so much, and she'd met war refugees. Everything she knew, the book she'd been reading, all of it told her that Erianna would've been fine, if Zelnor had just been patient. Instead, she'd ruined everything.

There had to be a solution. Some way to fix Erianna. *I'll find a town. Pay for a healer, somehow.* Zelnor just needed to find a professional. She could still help Erianna…right?

Exhaustion weighed heavily on Zelnor. Screw-up or not, she couldn't keep her eyes open any longer. Before she could drift off though, a breeze whistled through the trees. Having the ishlanian next to her helped, but it was still freezing out here.

Zelnor stretched forward, twisting her body and reaching for the cloak she'd discarded earlier. No matter how she contorted herself, it was always just out of reach. She couldn't get to it without jostling Erianna.

Just when she had resigned herself to a chilly, unpleasant slumber, the cloak floated upward and draped itself over the two of them like a blanket. Zelnor looked up to see Lyle's tentative, sweet smile.

"Goodnight," the ghost said.

Zelnor had been wrong about the tea—so painfully wrong—and she had been wrong about Lyle too. Maybe even wrong about ghosts in general. If they were like this one, they couldn't be nearly as dangerous as she'd heard. She felt better knowing Lyle was there to watch over them.

Zelnor thought again about the strange woman dressed in gray and black who'd given her the opeli leaves. Suddenly, she realized why she hadn't trusted the "farmer": not a speck of dirt on any of her garments or under her nails. A farmer who worked with the soil would always be at least a little dirty. They couldn't afford not to work, even on the same day as a funeral.

Had those even been opeli leaves at all? The stranger had hidden her face and given away an incredibly valuable herb for free. It all made sense now. The woman had tricked Zelnor. *Felsha'kor's flames! I'm such an idiot!*

Chapter Eight
Faceless

"**W**AKE UP!" Lyle shouted.

The ghost had heard something in the dark. Whatever it was, it was close. And it was coming for them.

Zelnor bolted upright, knocking Erianna to the ground. The ishlanian muttered something and huddled closer to the fire, going back to sleep. Zelnor scratched her head, making her already messy white hair stand up in all directions.

Lyle tried to explain, but in his rush the words kept getting all jumbled.

"I can't understand you," Zelnor interrupted him. "Take a breath. Actually, can you breathe? Never mind, just speak slowly."

Lyle couldn't really breathe. So instead, he forced himself to carefully say each individual word.

"There was a rustling from behind the trees," he said.

Zelnor leaped to her feet. She pointed toward the direction Lyle indicated and mouthed: *This way?* Lyle nodded, and Zelnor grabbed one of their spare logs, holding it above the fire until it caught and emitted a soft glow. Lyle tilted his head. The half-elf glowed so brightly with that white light. If she needed to bring a torch, then she must not be able to see the blinding glow around herself.

Zelnor crept into the darkness. Lyle floated next to her, scanning the tree line. A breeze whispered through the trees.

The half-elf pulled her cloak tighter around her with one arm. She rocked on the balls of her feet, suddenly lunging forward and looking around the corner.

There was nothing there. Lyle knew he should feel relieved by that, but not knowing what he'd heard made it feel even scarier. His home had felt impenetrable. He couldn't remember anyone entering since he'd died, except for Zelnor and Erianna.

Zelnor relaxed, holding the torch loosely at her side.

"I think you heard an animal. Maybe a bird?" she said.

It hadn't sounded like a bird. But it was dark, and everything sounded scarier in the quiet. Maybe he was making a big deal out of nothing…

"Sorry for waking you," Lyle said.

"It's fine." Zelnor sighed.

The two returned to their little camp, and Zelnor dropped another log onto the fire, causing it to flare up again.

Erianna shivered in her fitful sleep. Zelnor dug around in the large backpack and piled a few dresses and a cloak on top of the ish-lanian. Lyle wondered how long the two had known each other. They seemed pretty close.

Zelnor stared into the darkness one last time, before she picked up the cloak she'd discarded and dropped down next to Erianna. Lyle watched the half-elf fall back to sleep. He floated around the clearing again, but couldn't see anything in the dark. The feeble white glow he emitted wasn't nearly enough.

Zelnor was probably right. It was just his imagination. He had heard a little bunny or maybe a fox. But he couldn't shake the feeling that something was out there…watching them.

What if it killed his friends? Or took the statue of Thermoren? Lyle needed to make sure they were safe. But what could he even do? He already felt a little tired from lifting the cloak onto Erianna and Zelnor earlier. How was he supposed to protect them when he could only lift a couple light things and see weird glowing?

Actually, there was one other thing Lyle could do. He knew how to make the glow around himself brighter. There weren't that many trees. If he could light up the clearing, then the attackers (or bunnies) wouldn't have anywhere to hide.

Lyle focused intently on his hands. His body—if you could call it a body—had started feeling different after he'd died. It was like he was always moving, spinning around and around even when he was standing still. It made him think of putting a stick in a pond and moving it in circles until he created a little vortex. He pictured the movement getting faster and faster, until he glowed so brightly that it was almost like daylight.

The bright white light illuminated every corner. Lyle felt his eyes start to drift shut. He forced them open again. He could sleep in a moment. He just needed to be sure, absolutely *sure*, that they were alone. He explored the clearing one last time, but no one was there. It must've been an animal he heard after all.

Lyle heard more rustling. He swiveled around and saw two tall silhouettes. There *was* someone watching them. The ghost's glow retracted when he lost focus.

Lyle had to warn his friends.

"Zelnor," he muttered.

He was so tired. His form was getting weaker… He struggled against his weariness, begging his body to stay awake for just a few more seconds. He had just made friends—he couldn't lose them already—but no matter how hard he tried, his voice got softer and softer, until Lyle curled up into smoke.

A yelp woke Zelnor, and she heard the hiss of something large dragging across the dirt. Still half asleep and reacting on instinct, her hand darted out and caught something before it moved too far away. A violent jerk nearly pried it from Zelnor's grip, and a flare of bright teal light chased away her grogginess.

Zelnor was locked in a tug of war with a cloaked figure. She desperately tried to keep ahold of Erianna's leg, but she could feel the bard slipping away.

Six dots appeared around Zelnor, and in an instant, her fists were encased in brown, smooth rocks. Her grip was unbreakable now. She easily tore Erianna away from the attacker and scrambled to her feet.

Zelnor might not look like it, but she could hold her own in a fight. You couldn't grow up traveling through Alaspinor without learning how to throw a punch. And with rock gauntlets? The poor bastard didn't stand a chance.

The figure brandished a knife.

"Bringing a knife to a fist fight? Tacky," Zelnor quipped.

The rocks shot up her arm, allowing Zelnor to block the blade. She grabbed his arm with her other hand and yanked him forward onto her fist.

CRACK! Pure stone slammed into the figure's chest. Zelnor winced at the audible crunch as her attacker crumpled into the dirt. Oh gods, what had she done? She had killed another person. Oh gods, oh gods. Felsha'kor save her.

The assailant rose back to his feet, wiping the blood from his chin. He heaved, struggling to breathe through his broken ribs.

What kind of person could sustain a blow like that and still stand up again?

She didn't have time to think about it. Her attacker was already on the offensive again. The would-be kidnapper lifted his knife above Zelnor's head and swiped downwards.

She raised her arm to guard her face. But with a flick of his wrist, he moved the blade down instead and went for her stomach. He had tricked her by pretending to make a clumsy strike. Zelnor moved the stones to cover her abdomen just in time, and the man lodged his blade into the rocks instead.

"What the—?" the assailant growled in a deep voice.

The man tugged desperately at his knife. Zelnor shoved her shoulder into him, and he stumbled at the impact.

She pulled the knife out of her rock-covered stomach and took a swing at him.

The kidnapper dodged. The firelight reflected against something smooth and black under his hood. Zelnor lunged again, but the man turned and ran back into the trees, away from their camp.

Zelnor released her stony armor. The constellation of dots had closed in around her—dangerously close. She would need to take care of them, right away.

"I'll be right back," Zelnor said.

Erianna didn't respond.

Zelnor whirled around. A second person in a dark cloak had grabbed Erianna. The kidnapper had one hand clasped over her mouth to stifle her cries, and the other under her arm as he dragged her into the forest.

Zelnor started forward, but the constellation floating around her stopped her in her tracks. She needed to cast the dots' spell before she got too close to Erianna.

Zelnor let the constellation crash into her. A burst of hair sprouted on her ankle and power rippled over her body. Thank the gods there were no explosions or lightning strikes; instead, her nails grew into long, spindly claws. With these, she could free Erianna, if she hurried.

But Erianna didn't need Zelnor's help. Erianna pulled a knife from her boot and slashed at the masked man's throat. She shoved her attacker off, escaping through brute strength, and scrambled to her feet.

Blood clung to the man's neck, congealing around the gaping hole. His arms went rigid at his sides, but otherwise, he didn't react to the injury.

What in Thorns' bloody, unspoken name was this thing?

It lunged for Erianna again, and she ducked behind Zelnor. Zelnor raised her shaking hands, brandishing her new claws.

It stumbled toward them, blood pouring from its neck. Zelnor swiped at the air between them. It didn't even flinch.

Her thin claws looked flimsy compared to the menacing figure with blood soaking its cloak.

Zelnor slashed at its stomach and more blood seeped out. It kept advancing. She slashed again. She had to wear it down. She readied her hands for another strike, but the claws retracted. The second spell had already faded.

What shitty timing. They should just run, right? There was no way to fight this thing, but it didn't seem fast. Maybe they could get away.

"Erianna! We need—"

Erianna tackled Zelnor to the ground as a column of heat and light exploded next to them. With a start, Zelnor realized that the ishlanian had thrown alcohol onto the fire.

The kidnapper was wreathed in flames. It hadn't moved, hadn't even *tried* to get out of the way or put out the fire. It didn't even scream. A sickly-sweet smell mingled with the smoke.

"We have to move!" Erianna shouted.

The bard was suddenly standing above Zelnor. *When did she get up…?* she wondered in a daze.

Erianna hauled Zelnor to her feet, both of their bags already strapped to the ishlanian, and dragged Zelnor away. Zelnor stumbled after her, still hazy with shock.

By the time they stopped, the fire was just a light in the distance. Zelnor stared at it. Fire only knew how to consume. Fire destroyed everything. It was going to happen again.

"I have to put it out," Zelnor said.

A teal hand caught her arm. Erianna's face was pale. Her nails dug so deeply into Zelnor's arm that she could feel them through her tunic. She had never seen Erianna this tense, but she wasn't looking at Zelnor. Her eyes were locked on the fire.

"Don't get any closer," Erianna said.

"It's going to spread," the mage said.

"Alaspinor is damp, and it's still the rainiest season. It'll go out on its own."

"But—!"

"Don't go near it! It could still be alive," Erianna said.

"I don't care!" Zelnor shouted.

Erianna was so surprised that she let go, and Zelnor raced back toward their campsite. She heard the bard calling after her, but she ignored her. Zelnor refused to let anyone else get hurt in a fire that she could prevent. But when the mage returned it was just like Erianna had said—the flames had already run their course, leaving a ring of black and a charred corpse behind.

Zelnor warily eyed the body of their mysterious assailant. The disgusting, sweet smell still lingered in the air. She wanted nothing more than just to pack up and avoid thinking about this ever again, but she'd been attacked by these cloaked figures twice now. The more they knew about them, the better.

The thing that had attacked them was burned beyond recognition. Anything it might have been carrying had been incinerated, which was supremely unhelpful when it came to identifying who or what had sent it. Even its facial features were nothing but a flat, smooth black. A little too smooth, actually. It didn't look like it had been burned, more like…an absence? Like its face had been sliced off. Or maybe its face had never existed in the first place?

Zelnor was being ridiculous. There was a rational explanation for that strange way its "face" shimmered in the bright blueish-white moonslight.

Zelnor reached her hand toward the strange oval of smooth black. Suddenly, the body moved! She gasped and scrambled backward. Erianna had grabbed the body's leg and started hauling it away. It left a trail through the charred dirt.

"It's not sanitary," Erianna said simply.

Zelnor tried to object, but she had already disappeared into the trees. Zelnor had half a mind to pack up and go, but Erianna still had her satchel. Zelnor would rather not leave without it. Even if she could, whenever she tried to get up her legs started shaking.

It had all been too much. In just under two weeks, she'd been attacked by mysterious cloaked assailants *twice*, made a deal with a dragon, and started traveling with a ghost. Her unique magic made her life perilous and unpredictable, of course, but even for her all of this was absolutely insane. And it had all started after she met that bard.

As if summoned, Erianna emerged back into the clearing, her hands covered in soot and her clothes caked in mud. She didn't meet Zelnor's gaze and didn't explain either. The ishlanian slid her backpack off and removed Zelnor's satchel, setting the smaller bag next to its owner. Her movements were stiff and halting.

Slowly, Erianna took the statue of Thermoren out of her belt and slipped it into the main pouch of her large bag. Lyle, still just a wisp, hovered next to the backpack. He had slept through the entire conflict.

Zelnor had known traveling with another person was a bad idea. The bad-luck bard and unstable mage were a disastrous pair. Zelnor needed to end this before one of them got seriously hurt.

Just as Zelnor started to voice her thoughts, Erianna plopped down in front of her. The ishlanian finally looked directly into Zelnor's eyes, and the words died in her throat, replaced by the uneasy clenching of her stomach. Erianna's icy gray-blue eyes glinted in the light of the nearly full moons.

"I'm sorry," Erianna said.

A strange feeling bubbled up in Zelnor at the inexplicable apology. The embers that had formally been their campfire had died out, and she couldn't make out the ishlanian's expression in the dim light. Her voice sounded cold, resigned. Why did it feel more like a goodbye than an apology?

"For what?" Zelnor asked.

"Does it matter?" Erianna asked.

"Yes. It does," Zelnor insisted stubbornly.

She wasn't sure why she cared. Maybe it was curiosity, or maybe she was just being contrary, but she still wanted to know.

"You want a *list?* Fine! Well, there's—This!" Erianna said.

She grabbed Zelnor's right wrist, her fingers covering the gem imbedded there.

"And of course, you having to take care of me like I was a child for the past few days," Erianna continued. "And…and…"

Erianna's grip around Zelnor's wrist loosened. Her skin glowed, allowing Zelnor to finally see her face. Her mouth was set in a deep frown. Her eyes were downcast.

In a way, the pact *had* been Erianna's fault—at least partially. Zelnor would never have met Torrin without Erianna. The mage would never have even known where to go, and by now, someone else would have the ring. Without Erianna, Zelnor might have finally lost hope. As petrifying as being connected to a dragon was, it was the first clue that she had ever gotten about her unique brand of magic, and ultimately, it was Zelnor who had decided it was worth allying with Torrin.

"Apology accepted," Zelnor said.

"What?" Erianna asked.

"Something wrong with your hearing?" Zelnor quipped.

"No," Erianna said. "I *heard* you."

Zelnor smirked, thinking how good it felt to finally be the person who teased instead a victim of it. Erianna glared at her, but that only made Zelnor grin wider.

"Then…did you not want forgiveness?" she asked. "Isn't that why people usually apologize?"

Erianna scowled at her for a moment, before breaking into bright, clear laughter. It was the first time Zelnor had heard her laugh since Castle Veloria. *I missed it.*

Where had that thought come from? Zelnor hadn't missed the bard's constant teasing and mocking. *Definitely not.* She was just relieved she wouldn't have to take care of the woman, and thankful that Erianna finally seemed like her strong, capable self again.

"You seem better," Zelnor said.

"I am…finally," Erianna agreed. "I don't do well with light magic."

"You might've mentioned that a few days ago, *before* you cast a light magic spell," Zelnor half-joked.

"I don't expect you to understand," Erianna said, "but Lyle is worth it."

"You say that, but you didn't take care of someone practically comatose," Zelnor said.

Erianna winced, and Zelnor felt a pang of guilt. Her words came out harsher than she had intended.

"You were right about Lyle, though," Zelnor said. "He doesn't seem as dangerous as I thought."

"Hold on. Did you just say that *I* was right?" Erianna asked. "Could you repeat that one more time?"

Gods, Zelnor hated this woman. Not two seconds into her recovery, and Erianna was already mocking her again. Just for that, the annoying bard was going to take first watch.

"Come ooooon. You may as well practice. You'll be saying that a lot from now on, after all," Erianna sing-songed.

As she lay down, Zelnor watched the ishlanian's glow fade, shrouding their camp in darkness. She had almost asked Erianna to stop traveling with her, and yet somehow, the two of them had sidestepped the issue once again.

Traveling together was the practical choice. Zelnor needed a guide, and Erianna was her only option. The bard was a means to an end, just one not-all-that helpful person on her journey. Zelnor needed her, but only temporarily.

The bard hummed a lilting tune that Zelnor didn't recognize, and she found herself drifting off to sleep a little faster than usual.

Chapter Nine
Desperate Times

Erianna's naturally cheery disposition returned, and she felt relieved that things were going back to normal—or at least, her new normal, traveling with this strange half-elf. The atmosphere had somewhat shifted between the two of them. Erianna wondered if her embarrassing behavior during the aftereffects of the light magic spell had caused it.

With their time together dwindling, it wasn't worth worrying over. One more week or so and they would arrive at the border between Alaspinor and Nirdeem. They would reach it soon, very soon, and then Erianna would free herself of her obligation to Zelnor. It was the best recompense Erianna could reasonably offer, and once she had, she could wash her hands of the strange mage, and their business would finally be done.

Still, the closer they got to the border, the more uneasy Erianna felt. *Of course I'm uneasy, going near Nirdeem again.* Her discomfort had nothing to do with their impending separation.

Getting close to Nirdeem was more dangerous than ever.

Something had gotten the Broken Claim's attention. They had tracked her well enough to attack twice. It had been a long time since they had caught up with her, and only one thing had changed recently. While Erianna didn't want to blame Zelnor, she couldn't deny the giant half-elf suddenly appearing had likely led them in her direction.

Erianna had made sure their little group steered clear of major settlements, and she was confident she'd left their pursuers no trail to follow. Intimately acquainted with every little back road and un-marked path, Erianna had long-since learned how to disappear from the Claim's sights. And thanks to her efforts, their journey had been blissfully uneventful.

It was nice, not having to sing in taverns for a while. As the week wore on and bled into the next, she bounded along the path, chat-ting with Lyle and teasing Zelnor—leading to a bandy of words that the mage almost always lost and leaving Erianna with a smug, self-satisfied victory. Things were good.

Well, they *were* good, right up until breakfast.

Zelnor turned expectantly toward her.

"Food," the mage demanded.

Erianna chuckled. The half-elf really was grumpy in the morn-ing, and easily confused apparently. Erianna didn't have the food. They'd eaten the last bit of bread and dried fruit she carried last night.

"You're the one carrying it," Erianna said.

"No. I'm not," Zelnor replied.

Zelnor opened her empty bag and gestured to it emphatically. Zelnor didn't have food either. This never happened when Erianna traveled on her own. Why hadn't one of them kept better track?

"You're out of food?" Lyle asked. "What are you going to do?"

There was only one thing they *could* do. Erianna pulled a map from her bag. They were close to a placed called Vespar. She didn't recognize the name, but it was the closest town big enough to have a market.

Erianna would rather avoid the place. The Broken Claim flocked to populated areas, which already made the rather large town a risk; considering how close Vespar was to Nirdeem, there was an uncomfortably high chance that its members were offering the Claim's "services" there. But as long as they kept the trip short, they should be able to avoid detection. If she hid her easily identifiable hair and skin, Erianna could slip through the crowds relatively unnoticed. She should get her gold out now though, so they could leave the place as soon as possible.

"Looks like there's a town nearby. We can stock up there," Erianna said.

The bard stowed her map and shoved her hands into the side pouches of her large backpack. She maneuvered her hands through her many belongings until she found her coin purse and...oh. *Oh shit.*

"Well." Erianna clicked her tongue. "That's bad."

"What is it?" Lyle asked.

"We're out of gold...and silver. Aaand...copper," Erianna said.

Of course, she didn't have any coin. How could she have forgotten? The whole reason she tried to steal that ring from Zelnor in the first place had been because she'd been running low on gold.

"You're saying we have *nothing?*" Zelnor asked.

"Well, we have whatever you have," Erianna said.

"We have nothing," Zelnor said.

The half-elf didn't even bother checking her bag. And what had Erianna expected, really? The half-elf had made it abundantly clear that she was currently lacking when it came to funds.

"How do you usually earn coin?" Erianna asked.

"Odd jobs, farmhand work, painting fences…"

"Well," Erianna said, "I'm sure someone needs—"

"Why don't you just sing?" Zelnor interrupted. "It'd be a lot faster, and a day's work would only get us a handful of copper. With my condition, I'd rather not spend days in town doing chores for people."

"Your condition?" Lyle asked.

The mage shrugged, unwilling to explain herself to the boy.

How could Zelnor use her "condition" as an excuse? Surely, a couple of days wouldn't be that big a problem. Even if she did cast something, as far as Erianna had seen, the mage's second spells were mostly harmless.

Unfortunately, Zelnor was right that Erianna could make much more than a few coppers in a fraction of the time. The logic behind the mage's suggestion made it that much harder to turn it down. Not that Erianna didn't have an excellent reason to avoid singing there; if she performed in Vespar, she chanced her pursuers getting one step closer to finding her. But to make that point, she would need to admit that those assassins were there for *her*. Erianna had successfully sidestepped telling Zelnor about the Broken Claim, and with so little time left together, she'd prefer to keep it that way.

Oh Liscuntia, she couldn't think of a reason to disagree.

"Just a short performance," Erianna said.

It was a risk—and a stupid one at that—but as long as they left as soon as possible and kept moving, Erianna would get away with it. After she dropped Zelnor off at Nirdeem, Erianna would run north again. By the time the Broken Claim investigated the rumors of an ishlanian singer in Vespar, Erianna would be nowhere near the place. Perhaps it would even be enough to throw them completely off her trail again, redirecting their search to southern Alaspinor. The situation could even work in her favor…

That sort of wishful thinking was dangerous. Erianna would settle for not getting cornered by them for the third time in as many weeks.

After Zelnor asked Erianna to sing, the bard had gone noticeably quiet. Her steps seemed heavier, her posture sagged. Zelnor belatedly recalled Erianna mentioning stage fright once, and guilt settled in the base of her stomach.

But Erianna had to sing; the last thing either of them wanted was to extend their trip by multiple days.

"So, where are we going?" Lyle asked Erianna.

"Vespar," Erianna answered.

"What's it like?" Lyle asked.

"Not sure," Erianna said. "Never been."

"I haven't either," Lyle said ruefully. "I haven't really been… anywhere."

"I've been there," Zelnor said.

Lyle turned to the mage with a rapt expression, waiting expectantly for her description, and Erianna folded up her map, also turning her full attention to Zelnor. Zelnor did her best to shake off her habitual morning grumpiness, which had only intensified upon learning that they had no food or gold. Partly as a distraction and partly due to Lyle's intense curiosity, Zelnor started telling the ghost, and by extension the bard, everything she knew about Vespar.

Vespar had been her first stop after passing through Nirdeem. Despite only visiting once, she'd read a good deal about it. With simple dirt roads, a limited library, and a small tavern, it was easy to overlook, but it was still a fairly large town—significantly bigger than any of the other settlements in the area.

Despite its size, very little of the town's income came from merchants passing through on their way to Goldhaven. The bandits on the main roads posed a high risk to their valuable cargo. Most merchants traveled through Alaspinor as quickly as possible, only stopping when absolutely necessary. Only a severely underprepared trader would resupply in Vespar, given its proximity to Nirdeem.

As a result, the small southern town drew most of its prosperity from its robust market. With Bimblebarrow a perilous two-week journey, local farmers sold their excess crops to Vespar, growing their produce market until it was larger than the town's population could need and becoming the source of most of its wealth.

A long and overly detailed way of saying that Vespar was the ideal place to shore up your supplies. Small enough and filled with modest folk, such that nothing was overpriced, but still diverse and plentiful enough that, if one had the coin, one could easily get everything needed for even the longest journey. After all, it was the largest market in southern Alaspinor.

"That's lucky!" Lyle exclaimed. "It's the perfect place for you two to get more food."

"You sound like you swallowed a guidebook," Erianna said. "How do you know so much about Alaspinor anyway?"

"I've been traveling here for a long time," Zelnor said.

"So have I. But I don't know nearly as much about these towns and their politics and specialties," Erianna said.

"Maybe I just pay more attention than you," Zelnor said.

"Or maybe you're a know-it-all," Erianna retorted.

"Maybe I do know it all. I do seem to know everything."

"You don't know everything," Erianna said.

She pulled on a pair of gloves and gathered her lavender hair under the hood of her cloak. Her smile suddenly seemed just the slightest bit false. Zelnor wondered what the bard had meant by that.

"We're here!" Lyle exclaimed, flying as far forward as his tether allowed.

Vespar was the same lively market that Zelnor remembered. The group passed through stall after stall of fresh seasonal crops. There were even some dried meats. If only they had the coin now—passing by all this food made Zelnor's stomach scream. Sadly, they had to walk past all of it and straight to *The Bottomless Tankard.*

The tavern was plain, constructed with the same pale, beige wood commonly used across Alaspinor. Little knicks and cuts pockmarked the tables, and the floor was scuffed from years of chairs scraping against its surface. A couple of barrels were tucked next to a limited selection of whiskeys. Brightly colored pennants had been strung across the middle of the room and an arrangement of green and orange gourds was displayed next to the door. Zelnor wondered if there had been a festival in Vespar recently.

Erianna spoke with the owner in hushed tones, leaving Zelnor to impatiently await the coin that would pay for their next few meals. The bard was surely paid in advance? She hadn't stopped to collect anything at *The Violent Temptress,* so that must mean the owner would pass her some gold, and they could finally eat.

"How do you think it's going?" Lyle whispered.

Zelnor almost replied immediately but hesitated. She wasn't sure how many people could actually see ghosts. The few people they'd passed had looked right through him. If she talked to him, and people couldn't see him, they'd think that she had lost her mind. For the moment, the tavern was empty—save a drunk in the corner who'd likely been sleeping there since the night before—but once Erianna started singing, Zelnor knew that would change.

"We'll see soon," Zelnor said. "But Lyle…"

The ghost tilted his head. His wide, downturned eyes and open features reminded Zelnor of a sad puppy. She tried to phrase her next statement as kindly as possible. Lyle's downcast expression was almost *physically* painful.

"While we're in towns," Zelnor said, "or around people who can't see you… We, might, maybe—"

"I shouldn't talk. Right?" the ghost said.

"Sorry. It's just…"

"It's all right," Lyle said. "We'll be leaving soon. And I can listen, at least. It's better than nothing."

And there it was. The dejected face of someone preparing to be ignored. Zelnor stewed in guilty silence until Erianna returned a few minutes later. Zelnor noticed, with dismay, that she wasn't carrying any gold.

"Well. Some bad and good news," Erianna said.

"Bad news first," Zelnor requested, bracing for it.

"Bad news is…" Erianna said. "Mr. Whittlebon can't afford to hire me."

That left helping around town as their only option. Zelnor's mind started immediately working through possibilities. She needed to find an errand that required as little contact as possible. A delivery maybe? No, they never went particularly well. Maybe they could hunt something and sell it? If Erianna did the actual selling, then that would be a viable option.

"The good news is," Erianna continued, "I've managed to work out another arrangement."

Zelnor remembered the circumstances under which the two had met. Knowing Erianna, this "arrangement" probably involved something dubious. She hadn't seemed particularly interested in looting Castle Veloria, so maybe only desperate times had pushed her to steal from Zelnor. That said, the woman hadn't seemed especially remorseful. Zelnor didn't care all that much, but given that she'd caught the woman with relative ease, the last thing they needed was to get kicked out of the tavern.

Erianna eyed her coldly.

"Liscuntia only knows what sort of illicit deal you're picturing," she said. "I don't just sleep with anyone for a hot meal and a pretty coin. I'm not a harlot."

Why had Erianna assumed—? When had Zelnor ever said—? She tried to say something, but the mortification was like rocks weighing down her tongue.

Erianna flushed, her cheeks turning a faint purple. "So, you didn't mean—? Most people… M-My mistake. Then, what were you referring to? Actually, never mind."

"Should I ask what a harlot is?" Lyle asked.

"No!" they said at the same time.

After another excruciating moment, Erianna continued.

"The owner wants more publicity for his tavern. He agreed to give us a free meal, and I can pass a collection plate around after my performance."

"A free meal?" Zelnor asked.

"I can't tell if you're more excited about the food or the cost," Erianna commented dryly.

"Not all of us are used to getting handouts," Zelnor said.

"Handouts?" Erianna glowed brightly. "I'm working for it. I'm trading a valuable service for food. *Your* food. It's more than you're willing to do."

"You're right. Thanks," Zelnor said.

Of course Erianna would treat Zelnor's curse cavalierly. She had never even tried to understand. Zelnor turned on her heel and left Erianna for the bar. Mr. Whittlebon worked a rag across its surface. The grizzled human man, just on the other side of his thirties, took a couple minutes to notice her. Nothing Zelnor wasn't already used to, and she didn't particularly mind a moment to herself to cool down, after getting worked up yet again by that hot-tempered bard.

"What can I get ya?" Mr. Whittlebon asked.

"I'm with the, um, singer," Zelnor said.

"That right?" the man asked.

More and more these past couple of weeks, Zelnor was running into new problems with her appearance. Of course, this man wouldn't believe that an elegant songstress would willingly travel with someone like Zelnor. Clearly, he hadn't seen the two talking moments ago. Or maybe he had. Maybe he'd seen their spat and assumed Zelnor was just trying to capitalize on the bard's presence after picking a fight with the woman.

"I'll just…wait for her to join me, then," Zelnor said.

"As you like," Mr. Whittlebon replied, his tone not nearly as ambivalent as his words.

The man went back to cleaning the bar top, and Zelnor was forced to wait for Erianna to join her. The bard wandered over a few minutes later—after making several strange sounds with her throat that Zelnor presumed had some relation to singing. Whatever it was, the sounds were the perfect excuse not to talk.

The ishlanian did pause long enough to acknowledge Zelnor's status as her "attendant," and Zelnor took a bit of pride in the astonishment on the owner's face when he learned the scruffy half-elf had not, in fact, lied about knowing the bard.

Erianna bolted down her food at a breakneck pace, her eyes snapping to the door every time it opened. She probably wanted to finish her food before the midday crowd descended on Vespar's only tavern, but her agitation seemed like more than a harried rush to eat or stage fright.

Maybe she had angered someone in this town and didn't want

them to find her? Or maybe it really was just her nerves getting the better of her.

Regardless of her reasoning, Erianna was right to rush. In less than half an hour, villagers and farmers had packed into the tavern. The bard sprinted off to the other end of the room to capitalize on the influx of customers. Despite the sudden crowd, no one took the seat she'd occupied.

Mr. Whittlebon frowned at Zelnor, and she fixed her attention back on her half-finished food. *Thunk.* A tankard appeared next to her plate.

"On the house," the owner said.

Zelnor nodded in thanks, taking the offered ale for the apology it was.

"James!" A farmer called the owner's name from the other side of the bar, and the man rushed off to fill other cups.

Erianna began her performance. The bard's clear, beautiful song soothed Zelnor's anger, teasing it out of her and replacing it with a breathlessness anticipation. Erianna's voice was so enchanting, it made the mage wonder if there was actual magic in it.

This time, with her full attention on Erianna, Zelnor saw what she'd missed during the singer's first performance: her dancing.

Although, dancing seemed too crude a word to describe it. Graceful as a curling trickle of water flowing from a cup, but also fast and precise. It was mesmerizing.

Zelnor chided herself for getting so easily taken with the bard. She shouldn't forget how obnoxious this woman was. She was *insufferable.* She might be an admittedly talented performer, but that didn't excuse her abysmal personality.

Zelnor turned back toward the counter, refusing to let the bard see her interested. She polished off her food just as Erianna finished her final song and circulated around the room, her plate rapidly filling with coins.

A stranger practically flung herself into the seat next to Zelnor's. The woman had wispy blond hair, so dark it was almost brown, and cut so short that it floated around her, as if blown about by a constant wind. Her face was covered in freckles and sun spots, and even in the soft candlelight her cheeks had a ruddiness to them. *She's probably a local.*

"Jamey," the woman whispered.

Mr. Whittlebon immediately stopped his conversation with a patron and moved to speak with the new woman at the bar instead.

The bartender's urgency caught Zelnor's attention, and she turned an ear toward their conversation, her curiosity piqued.

"Milly," the owner said. "You've not been round for… I don't rightly know how long. I've been meaning to stop by."

"So you heard?" Milly asked.

"Your mam was a good woman," James said.

"They tried hard to save her. But…" Milly trailed off.

James took the blond's hands.

"Melody," the man's voice grew gentler. "They… Well, they did all they could, but no one would blame ya for resenting them. Just a bit."

"It's my da that's the problem. He's fallin' apart! He hasn't left the room with her…her…" She inhaled sharply, and the owner squeezed her hands. "He won't even let us bury her."

"And your brother? Isn't he helping?" James asked.

"He worries me even more. That's why I came here," she said.

"He ain't encouraging your da to continue mourning? He must miss her dearly, but…"

"No…nothing o' that sort. Bryn's been meetin' with a strange man," Milly said. "Talking to him only at night, when he thinks I'm asleep."

"A tryst?" James asked. "Wouldn't be the worst thing for him, I s'pose. Though the timing—"

"It's not that… Not from the way they talk," Milly said. "The man unsettles me. Never shows his face, always wearin' a black mask."

CRASH!

Erianna scrambled to pick up an assortment of coins. She had dropped the plate and scattered its contents all over the ground. Her skin glowed bright teal.

"Let me help ya," Milly said.

The young woman stooped next to the bard.

"I'm fine!" Erianna said. The bard closed her eyes, and when she opened them, she was smiling easily, but her skin was still glowing. "My hand slipped. I've almost got it up."

Erianna scooped the last of the currency into a pouch from her backpack—which she had picked up again sometime during her rounds—and straightened.

"Well, it's time we leave. Thank you, Mr. Whittlebon."

"'Course. Hope to have you again," the owner said.

"Of course." Erianna smiled.

Erianna put her hood up and turned to Zelnor, grabbing her arm with a viselike grip.

"We'll be going now," Erianna said amicably to the owner.

The bard hauled Zelnor out of the tavern and back to the market, weaving through the stalls and only stopping briefly to purchase what they needed. Zelnor tried to talk to her, to ask what in the Seven Afterworlds was going on, but the bard ignored every attempt.

It wasn't until they were fully out of the town that Erianna ceased her harried flurry of movement and seemed to relax again.

"Why did we leave so fast? Is everything all right?" Lyle asked.

"Everything's fine. We just don't want to waste too much time," Erianna said. "Sooner we arrive, the better."

The closer they got to Nirdeem, the more skittish Erianna seemed to become. She had also gotten upset when Torrin mentioned the city-state. Given her sticky fingers and the fact that she refused to go into the city, the ishlanian had probably stolen something from the wrong person and wanted to avoid the authorities there. Now that Zelnor thought about it, who exactly *were* the authorities in that country?

Most of what Zelnor knew about Nirdeem was from a history book she'd read recently. It touched on the founding of the city-state and how it gained its independence. Its origin was fascinating. Centuries ago, the space had stood empty, nothing but a large valley in the Reindune Mountains with a massive lake. A group of wealthy merchants from Goldhaven had seen potential in the land and secured funds from the Five to harvest ore from the mountains.

The merchants had used their gold to carefully shape the lake into two rivers that ran along the edges of the valley and into the land beyond it. The mining operation required a town to provide shelter and a few parcels of farmland to sustain the workers, both of which were swiftly granted. The project was a success, providing ore to not only the Five but evolving into the largest supplier of precious metals in all of Tularien. Eventually, the small town had grown into a large city-state and established their independence by holding their supply of ores hostage until the Five agreed to cede the land to them.

Though certainly interesting, the book hadn't given much insight into Nirdeem's current justice system, and her visit to the city hadn't been much help either in that regard. When she had first passed through, she and Heeden had been children, and it didn't take long before they learned there was almost nothing more conspicuous than a nine-year-old and a twelve-year-old running around the nicer districts unchaperoned. So, they had moved quickly, leaving the city-state, before they had the chance to really explore it.

Although brief, her first visit to the city had been nothing short of exhilarating. Those first impressions had mostly faded now, but the few memories she still had remained vibrant in her mind: buildings far larger than the ones in her childhood; some homes so gaudy that they hurt to look at, while others seemed moments from collapse; people of all kinds, some kind to children, others menacing. More than anything, she remembered the excitement of it all and the wonder that she'd felt drinking in the atmosphere of a culture so different. It was the farthest the two of them had ever been from home.

I should never have let him come with me.

The Reindune Mountains grew larger by the day. Soon Erianna would decide she'd gone close enough, and she would leave too, taking Lyle with her. Zelnor would enter the city of Nirdeem alone, returning to it for the first time in a decade. She had mixed feelings about it, but she couldn't deny her excitement at the prospect of finally finding some answers.

Chapter Ten
Old Scars

Erianna stoked the fire, watching sparks drift up toward the stars. A nightmare had woken her before her turn on watch. She had thoroughly startled Zelnor and an exhausted, flickering Lyle. The mage had stared at her as though she were The Lord of Thorns Themself. After a brief chat—far briefer than Erianna would have preferred—Zelnor bedded down and the ghost soon followed.

Erianna rarely dreamed, but over the last month, she had dreamed about her past every night. These nightmares had plagued her ever since she started traveling with the mage, and they had only worsened since passing the first wall and traveling through Nirdeem's farmlands. She had tried to delay their group, picking up food at a small village, but the detour had hardly taken any time at all. Now that they were less than a day away from Nirdeem City, unpleasant dreams were the least of her worries.

Still, this one had shaken her. Erianna was a little girl again, at one of Plindurin's monthly scale removals. In the dream, the woman's features shifted and blurred. Only a couple defining features persisted through the haze: that sickening smile of hers, and the long, diagonal scar that split her face in half.

Plindurin pulled out one of the last navy scales from Erianna's clavicle. Blood barely trickled down her narrow shoulder, before bright golden threads coiled from her mother's fingers to close the wound. Fresh purple-pink arches marred Erianna's teal skin.

Erianna glanced at Porter, her eyes pleading, *begging* him to help her. He avoided her gaze. He was younger then, wearing a serving uniform and still attempting to fix his perpetually messy hair. He stayed by the door, ensuring they wouldn't be interrupted by unwanted visitors. At least, that's what Plindurin had claimed at the time. Erianna later learned that she had forced him to watch as a punishment—for what, Erianna still wasn't sure.

Even back then, she could tell that Porter was terrified of her mother. Everyone was.

Plindurin ignored the look between her daughter and Porter. She twirled the golden earrings hanging from her rounded, human ears. As she considered her daughter, a smile curled on her lips, like the last smoke of an extinguished candle. It was nothing like the large, gaudy grins she flashed the rich patrons. This was a *genuine* smile.

When Plindurin plucked the last scale, Erianna yelped. Porter winced at the girl's soft cry but quickly looked away, clasping a hand over his mouth.

"The scales grow back slower every year. Tonight might be the last time we need to remove them," Plindurin said wistfully.

Plindurin pulled her daughter's sparkly purple dress up to cover the scars again. The pale purple almost matched Erianna's hair. Her dresses were always exquisite—worth more than a family living on edge of the Slums should be able to afford. Even then, she had known that most of their wealth came from the worst, most despicable places.

But she didn't care. These pretty little outfits were one of the only comforts she found in that cold place.

"These…" Plindurin muttered, examining Erianna's neck. "So ugly."

Erianna's mother grabbed her chin and tilted her head upward, running her fingers along the little ishlanian's gills. Erianna flinched away, and the woman placed a hand on her shoulder. Glowing golden magic seized Erianna's muscles, locking her in place.

Plindurin tutted, pinching one of the frills tightly. The little girl screwed her eyes shut and held her breath, sure the woman would rip them out too.

After a few excruciating seconds, her mother let go. She couldn't rip out Erianna's gills. If the ishlanian survived, the wound could leave a large and ugly scar across her neck. As long as Erianna struggled to master light magic, she was only as good as her beauty and her voice.

The little ishlanian had a remarkably mature voice for someone her age, hitting notes with precise accuracy and an evocative clarity. Everyone in Nirdeem came to see her, turning *The Spiral Cup* into a thriving business.

Less than an hour after the removal, a horde of patrons descended on the tavern. Those with the misfortune of standing next to the walls found themselves jammed in between the stone and their neighbors' shoulder. The crowd packed into the room, trapping those in the center amid a sea of bodies. People grumbled and bickered, clamoring toward the stage.

The mood escalated, as a burly kunari shoved a human trying to weasel his way through the mass. Shouts rose from the throng and a brawl broke out.

Erianna peered out nervously, as she did every night—dreading getting up in front of them. Plindurin watched her daughter neutrally, but the woman's eyes were cold—warning her not to avoid the one responsibility she held here. Erianna did as she was told.

Amid the chaos, the little ishlanian kicked her leg up, trying to climb up onto the tall stage. She angled herself into a number of awkward and unladylike positions, once almost ripping her long dress, until she finally managed to clamber onto the platform. She didn't introduce herself or smile. She just sang.

Her voice filled every corner of the room, silencing the disharmony in the stuffy bar. Everyone's eyes fixed on her at once. Erianna wilted under the attention, but seeing her mother's face in her peripheral vision, the girl held her arms stiffly at her sides and straightened her back. The last note of her performance lingered long after she stopped singing, resonating and rippling through the crowd.

The audience watched her with awe, but also with…now Erianna would call it *hunger*. As soon as the show ended, the little girl hopped off the raised stage and darted to a storage closet in the staff area. She huddled underneath a shelf filled with extra whiskey bottles, listening for the swift clacking of her mother's tall shoes.

The door opened a crack, and Erianna cowered away from it until she recognized the familiar silhouette. Porter placed a lit oil lamp next to them on the floor, far enough away that neither of them would knock it over. The flickering yellow light exaggerated the dark circles and subtle wrinkles already starting to develop on the young man's face. He had a simple leather book tucked under his arm—a collection of Gealtalmhn folktales.

"Have you ever heard the tale of Anya and the Winter Star's Light?" he asked.

Erianna shook her head, making Porter chuckle. He knew she was lying. Of course, she'd heard the story before—it was her favorite—but she always wanted to hear it again.

Porter hadn't even finished the story before they heard Plindurin calling their names. Somehow, her soft voice rang with a deafening clarity. The young man shivered. He closed the book with a snap, stowing it behind the bottles on the shelf, and led the little ishlanian girl back to her mother.

The scars had faded after ten years, but Erianna had given up hope of them disappearing completely. So, she hid them. She had specifically commissioned her leather armor with a wide strip to cover the little arches, and when she disrobed, she kept her partners far too distracted to notice a few little marks. On some days, she could even pretend they weren't there at all.

Erianna placed a hand over her clavicle. Some days were better than others.

Lyle marveled at the castles and marble Judgment buildings tall enough to be seen above the wall surrounding Nirdeem City. He tipped his head back to stare at the vast mountains on either side of the valley. Erianna could almost picture the city through the ghost's eyes: grand, majestic, and exciting. She could almost forget how it felt to be trapped inside it.

A suffocating feeling arose in Erianna's chest. She tapped a simple rhythm on her leg and forced herself to pay attention to her companions before it overtook her. Zelnor was watching Lyle with a fond smile, as he flitted around in front of them. The ghost pointed to the giant waterfall tumbling from the western mountain.

"What is that?" Lyle asked.

"That's a waterfall," the half-elf said, and when Lyle tilted his head, she continued, "It's water that, well…falls over the side of a cliff."

"Wow." Erianna clapped slowly. "Almost like reading a dictionary."

"I'd like to hear you explain it," Zelnor said.

"Me? How could I explain it better? Water. Falling. What more is there to say?"

Lyle ignored their bickering. He held out a finger and traced the two rivers that flanked both sides of the second wall. The wide rivers stopped just short of the gate, flowing into the farmlands and curling off in the distance. Eventually, they joined the ocean.

Erianna wasn't usually one for remembering dull facts—and she considered history and politics some of the dullest—but seeing the city again reminded her of conversations she'd overheard when she was young. It was impossible not to pick up a thing or two, considering the types of patrons who frequented The Spiral Cup.

Despite being the world's smallest nation, Nirdeem held vast political power. It maintained neutrality and housed its own formidable standing army in the mountains to ward off potential power plays from either bordering country. Not that there *were* any power plays. No, Nirdeem had an army so that it would feel powerful, and its authorities reveled in that. The Judges cared more about their country's dominance over the other nations than the quality of life of their own citizens.

But no matter how much the Judges liked to pretend otherwise, they held no real authority in the city. The ones who actually controlled Nirdeem resided in its dark underbelly, in the corners of the city that upstanding folk would prefer to forget. Speaking of which… it was long past time to turn back.

The North Gate loomed over her. She hid her teal hands and arms within the folds of her tawny cloak. Her eyes darted toward every person they passed, waiting anxiously to feel that telltale twitch on her leg. She should have turned around, long, long ago.

Zelnor could find her own way. The place was literally within sight. Practically only a few more steps, and they would enter the main city. Even Zelnor wasn't *that* bad at directions.

Yet, here Erianna was, still traveling with the half-elf. She pulled her hood further down and did her best to stay calm. If she started glowing now, there would be no question of her identity, and she couldn't risk word spreading to the wrong person. The Broken Claim had eyes everywhere in Nirdeem. She was about to wish the mage well with a goodbye and good luck, but Zelnor spoke first.

"So," Zelnor said. "What do you know about the city?"

"Nothing," Erianna lied.

"Really?" The mage raised an eyebrow. "I got the feeling you visited it at least once."

"Aren't you supposed to know everything already, know-it-all?"

Zelnor glowered at her and stomped farther ahead. Lyle opened his mouth, like he wanted to say something to Erianna, but closed it again. He glanced between them before he zipped up to talk to the mage instead.

Typical. Zelnor had thought that ghosts were evil murderers and hadn't even wanted him to exist, let alone come with them, and now Lyle liked Zelnor better than her. Well, if Lyle wanted to remain with the mage, Erianna wouldn't stop him. Either way, she couldn't stay any longer.

"Hold on a minute, would you?" she called.

The mage circled back, eyeing Erianna with an uncomfortably genuine concern.

"Do we need to stop for a while?" Zelnor asked. "You look a little...awful."

"Thanks," Erianna said.

"That's not what she meant," Lyle said.

"I know. It's just a headache," Erianna said dismissively.

"Are you sure?" Zelnor asked. "That you're all right, I mean?"

"I've taken you far enough. I—" Looking at Zelnor made Erianna's throat dry up, so she turned to the ghost instead. "Do you still want to go with me? Or would you rather stay with Zelnor?"

"I…" Lyle hesitantly looked between them. "Do you really have to go, Erianna?"

Erianna started to feel an actual headache form.

"I do," she said, "but if you want to see the city, I'm sure Zelnor can take you."

Erianna looked to the half-elf for confirmation. Zelnor frowned, staring for a moment, before she nodded.

"Of course I want to see it. But…will I see you again?" Lyle asked.

"I doubt it," Erianna said.

"Are you sure you don't want to come into the city?" Zelnor asked quietly.

"Why? Are you going to miss me?" Erianna teased half-heartedly.

"No. I just—! I might get lost," Zelnor said.

"Sure." Erianna smirked. "It's not like the city is literally right behind you or anything."

"I meant *inside* the city, asshole."

"Oooh! Right. Of course." Erianna pursed her lips to keep from laughing. "But no, I can't stay. So, Lyle. Who would you rather go with?"

"Well…I guess I'll stay with Erianna," Lyle said.

He tried to hide it, but his hesitation was obvious.

"You don't have to," Erianna said. "I won't be hurt if you choose Zelnor."

"No… I—I think my parents are still in Alaspinor," he said. "But I was hoping that—"

Before the ghost could finish, a burly woman knocked into Zelnor.

"Watch where you walk, old man," the muscly woman said. "Wouldn't wanna bump into the wrong person."

The woman sneered, moments away from making a huge mistake.

This thug had no idea what a powerful mage the half-elf was. Though, considering how reluctant Zelnor was to use her powers, Erianna doubted she'd get the pleasure of seeing the inconsiderate stranger knocked on her ass. Erianna would have to deescalate this herself. *Liscuntia, I hope Zelnor doesn't get into* too *much trouble without me.*

Erianna approached the brute with a smile. A few honeyed words would smooth this situation over. The muscles in Erianna's thigh spasmed. Her blood ran cold. *Shit.* She hoped to the gods she was wrong, but there it was, displayed prominently, almost proudly, on the woman's bicep: a tattoo of a dead spider, on its back with legs curled close to its body. The spider's legs twitched violently, and the broad-shouldered woman's gaze snapped toward Erianna.

"It's *you,*" the woman said.

There was no time to think. They had to run.

Erianna grabbed Zelnor's hand and took off at a full sprint, her lavender hair flying out behind her. She heard the woman yelling behind them. If the woman had any doubts about her identity, they were gone now.

Erianna pulled Zelnor through the gates of the second wall, past shouting guards, and through a twisting maze of alleys and side streets. Finally, she stopped, leaning against a wall and taking heaving, shaky breaths.

"What's wrong? Why were we running?" Lyle asked.

"Was she—" Zelnor started breathlessly. "Do you owe her gold? Did you steal from her?"

Erianna started to tell a plausible lie to account for her skittish behavior, then she realized what she'd done. She had run into Nirdeem City, straight into the heart of the Broken Claim's power. She might as well have handed herself over to them.

"Liscuntia's tits," Erianna hissed through gritted teeth. "I'm screwed."

Chapter Eleven
Lightning's Wake

"Piscuntia's… what?" Lyle asked.

Zelnor flushed at Erianna's particularly obscene profanity and moved to cover Lyle's ears, before she remembered she literally couldn't. She had momentarily forgotten that he was a ghost.

"So? Was I right?" Zelnor changed the subject.

Erianna frowned. "About what?"

"You owing that person gold."

Zelnor had to be right. Erianna was obviously avoiding this city. That burly, rude woman must be the one that the ishlanian had stolen from.

"No, I don't owe her gold. I don't even know her."

"Then why did we run away from her *and* those guards?" Zelnor asked.

"That's—! Could you please just give me a minute?" Erianna clutched her temples, her face pinched with pain.

"No, you're not getting out of this. We deserve to know,"

Zelnor insisted.

Lyle put his hand on Zelnor's shoulder, but it passed right though. He looked sadly at his own hand.

"She has a headache, remember? We should let her rest," Lyle said.

"She can rest after she tells us what's going on!"

Lyle stuck out his bottom lip, making himself look utterly pitiful. *Ugh.* As if Zelnor could possibly say no to that face.

"Fine," Zelnor said. "One minute. Then, you tell us everything."

She walked to the edge of the alley they were hiding in—because Erianna was definitely hiding from *someone*—and took a moment to admire the city. Booths, tents, and market stalls lined the thoroughfare just beyond the gate. Zelnor basked in the bright colors and chaotic clamor.

It was a little overwhelming but exciting too. Kezeek Mesa had been so small, and the towns in Alaspinor weren't exactly gigantic, so this was only the second time she'd been in the middle of such a lively place. She loved reading about cities, fascinated by their commerce and politics, but she definitely preferred seeing them firsthand.

An eclectic mix of red, baked clay buildings that reminded her of Kezeek Mesa mingled with the solid stone buildings that she'd become accustomed to while traveling through Alaspinor. If she craned her neck, Zelnor could see the tops of castles peeking over the roofs. They were scaled down to fit, barely, within the confines of the city's wall and squeezed together so tightly that they almost touched their neighbors. Between gaps in the buildings, she could just spot the pristine, white marble buildings in the city's center, where Nirdeem's government ruled over the small city-state.

Just beyond the alley, a cacophony of voices struggled to triumph over each other, as merchants hawked a variety of wares: beads, silks, furs, linens, shells, *everything*. People of all walks of life and of all races were conducting business here or making their way somewhere else: a half-kunari man in ful'prakta haggled with a merchant over rare ores; an elven woman in a slick, neatly pressed dress headed to the center of town; a couple of human children screamed and chased each other between the stalls.

Zelnor was a little surprised to see such a large assortment of people. Though she supposed it made sense. From what she'd read, once the city's founders had split the valley's lake into two rivers, the bustling settlement had attracted a large collection of people. Farmers drawn in by the promise of free land and people tired of the harsh desert in Kialma'keer found refuge in Nirdeem—a country perfectly situated between the two nations and yet independent from both.

How could the Five have possibly given up this place? The Reindune Mountains formed a natural border between Alaspinor and Kialma'keer, leaving Nirdeem perfectly situated in the valley between them. Belonging to neither nation, the small country had put itself in a unique and powerful position to serve as an important focal point for trade. It was nigh-on impossible to bring goods over the mountains, so any trade done by land had to pass through Nirdeem.

Ceding control of that valley had to be the most foolish thing the Five had ever done. And for what, a bit of gold? A delayed shipment of bronze? Did the Five just not care about politics? Did the current Five regret their predecessors' decisions? Did the nobles even realize just how much they'd given up?

Someone brushed against Zelnor, and she startled out of her reverie. Her elemental magic fluttered in the pit of her stomach. One slip-up and she might level the entire district. She took a deep breath. As long as she stayed calm, that wouldn't happen. It had only been a couple weeks since her last spell. She had time before her magic got out of control. *Hopefully.*

She decided that she had given Erianna more than enough time to compose herself. Any longer and the bard might just run away again. When Zelnor returned, she almost thought Erianna *had* run away; she hardly recognized the woman.

Erianna had wrapped a dark blue scarf several times around her head and tied it tightly, leaving only a narrow slit to see though. She'd put on a long-sleeved gray tunic, far more modest than her usual fare, and had pulled the hood of her tawny cloak over her head. Thick, light gray woolen mittens covered both hands. She looked ready for a bitter snowstorm.

Zelnor struggled to keep her laughter at bay. Erianna just looked so out of place.

"Shut up!" Erianna snapped.

While Zelnor couldn't see her expression, she glowed faintly—something Zelnor had realized signified embarrassment or, more commonly, anger. Even so, she just couldn't hold herself back anymore.

"What are you *wearing?*" Zelnor asked through her laughter.

"It's brisk," Erianna said.

"It's not even raining."

"Well, I'm cold."

Erianna pushed past Zelnor to the end of alleyway, scanning the street.

"Oh, horseshit. You're hiding!" Zelnor scoffed.

"That's none of your business," Erianna said. "I don't know when or why you suddenly got so nosy. I don't have to explain mysel—"

Erianna gasped and sprinted into the main thoroughfare.

"Oh no you don't! We're not done," Zelnor growled, chasing after her.

The ishlanian was difficult to follow. She weaved nimbly through the crowd while Zelnor bumbled, shoved, and staggered into the throng of people. She managed to keep up with Erianna, but only barely—pursing her through winding cobbled streets and away from the bustling marketplace.

Erianna stopped at a small adobe building, and Zelnor ducked in after her. Despite its simple exterior, almost every chair had a person in it. Zelnor took in the adobe counter, the polished oak tables, and the mural of a desert spring painted across the back wall. The display cases were filled every baked good she could imagine: cupcakes piled high with frosting, glazed cakes, pies, pastries, and other desserts she didn't recognize.

Erianna joined the long line in front of the counter. A short elven woman in her mid-twenties smiled at them when they reached the front. Why had the bard so desperately needed to visit a bakery? Zelnor turned to Lyle for his theory as to her strange behavior.

"Maybe she just really wanted some chocolate?" Lyle suggested.

Zelnor snickered, but neither Erianna nor the worker seemed to notice.

"Welcome to The Oasis!" the young woman said.

"I'm looking for a man," Erianna replied.

"Well…there are plenty of men here, but I don't think they're what you're looking for," the woman said. "I'd try Dahlia's if you want companionship."

"No, Juniper—" Erianna pulled the scarf away from her mouth, revealing her face. "I'm looking for a *mutual* acquaintance."

Juniper's eyes widened almost imperceptibly.

"Of course, you're here to pick up your order," she said.

"I'm not here for dessert," Erianna hissed.

"Don't worry. It's already paid for," Juniper said, adding, "by a friend of Anya's."

The words sounded innocuous enough, but based on Erianna's reaction, they must have some significance that Zelnor didn't understand.

"Thank you," Erianna said.

The bard pulled her scarf back over her face. Juniper placed a slice of light brown cake with a dark purple glaze onto a plate and handed it to Erianna.

"Who is Anya?" Zelnor demanded. "What is going on?"

"Shh. I'll explain, just *be quiet,*" Erianna muttered.

The ishlanian guided Zelnor over to a table in the corner that had just opened up. Erianna chose a seat with her back to the wall, eyeing the other patrons warily. The two women who had been sitting there—dressed in elegant gowns, adorned with jewels—whispered to each other and glanced nervously at Erianna and Zelnor. Zelnor glared at them and they scurried away.

"Well?" she asked.

Erianna scanned the room one last time before she pulled down the scarf, so her voice wouldn't be muffled. "Fine. I'll admit I've made a few enemies here, and I wasn't planning on coming back."

"I figured as much," Zelnor said. "What did you do?"

Erianna ran her fingers around the edge of her plate.

"What I had to," she finally said.

"That's not an answer," Zelnor said.

"It is an answer, just not one you like," Erianna insisted.

"It is not. Answers should…answer things!" Zelnor said.

"Articulate as always," Erianna replied.

"Erianna…" Zelnor growled.

"Here, why don't you have some?" the bard asked.

Erianna pushed the plate toward Zelnor.

"You won't distract me with cake. I'm not a child." Zelnor glanced awkwardly at the ghost. "No offense, Lyle."

"I'm not a kid, either!" he said.

"Sure," Zelnor said. "Anyway. I don't want cake. I want an explanation."

"Just try it. Octillo's desserts are *legendary,* some people travel from other continents for them," Erianna said. "Come on. You know you want to."

"I already told you. I don't want it." Zelnor's stomach rumbled loudly.

"Really?" Erianna asked.

The bard waggled the fork in front of Zelnor's face. Zelnor snatched the utensil and stabbed into the slice in front of her.

"As if a single slice of cake could—"

As soon as she tasted it, her annoyance evaporated. Cloves, cinnamon, and black pepper spiked across her tongue, mellowed by the sweet date glaze. She detected a welcome hint of lemon, not present in the traditional recipe. It was the spice cake that her mom always made for her birthday. A pleasant wave of nostalgia washed over her.

"I've had partners who didn't please me as much as that cake pleases you," Erianna said.

"*What?* No, I'm not—it just reminds me of—Never mind! Stop deflecting and tell us who's after you," Zelnor said.

"We barely know each other. Why should I?" Erianna asked.

"Because you promised," Zelnor said.

"I don't recall saying the words, 'I promise,' at any point."

"Do you really want to argue semantics with me?"

"I can't tell you," Erianna said. Zelnor started to argue, but the bard held up a finger and continued, "Even knowing about them is dangerous."

"I can handle myself," Zelnor said.

"You don't understand. They aren't just thieves or mercenaries. They're…" Erianna fiddled with the hem of her scarf.

"You're afraid of them," Zelnor realized.

"Everyone is."

They lapsed into silence, and Zelnor continued eating the spice cake, taking great pains not to make any untoward sounds. That explained why Erianna had been so uncomfortable around Nirdeem. The people after her were more than just irate victims of her petty theft. What had Erianna done to anger people like that?

"Why'd you run in here in such a hurry? Were they after you again?" Lyle asked.

"Actually, I saw an old friend. I followed him here," Erianna said.

"Is he here? Can we meet him?" Lyle perked up.

"No, it seems like we just missed him." Erianna put a hand over her pocket. "I have a feeling that we'll be meeting up later, though. You can meet him then."

"So, does that mean you're staying in the city?" Zelnor asked.

"It seems like it," Erianna said. "For a little while, at least. I'll know more once I've…checked on something."

"You are really secretive, Erianna. And vague," Zelnor grumbled.

Erianna stole Zelnor's fork and started eating her cake.

"I prefer the term discreet. And speaking of, call me Anya, while we're in Nirdeem."

"Who in the Seven Afterworlds is Anya? A sister? Cousin?" Zelnor tugged at her beard. "A girlfriend?"

"I don't have a girlfriend," Erianna assured her, and added with a smirk, "At the moment, at least."

"I'm sure they're lining up around the corner, as we speak," Zelnor said. "But who is Anya?"

Erianna shrugged and took a few more bites of the spice cake.

"This cake is really good. Nothing that would make me moan, but maybe I just have a bit more experience than—"

Zelnor stole the fork back.

"Eri—I mean *Anya*. Answer the damn question," she said.

"You're no fun," Erianna said. "Anya is no one. A fairytale character."

"Oh. It's an alias, then?" Zelnor asked.

"Obviously. Thought you would've put that together by now,

know-it-all," Erianna teased.

"Stupid bard with your stupid secrets, stupid code names," Zelnor grumbled.

"Finish your cake."

Zelnor stopped mid-bite, stared at her, and continued at an excruciating pace, chewing each bite deliberately.

"Very mature," Erianna said.

"I don't know what you're talking about," Zelnor said.

The bard scowled and pulled her scarf back over her mouth and nose.

"At this rate, I'll meet up with my friend sometime next *year*," she said, voice muffled.

Zelnor smiled innocently as she slowly lifted the fork up to her mouth again.

After what felt like several hours of watching Zelnor eat, Erianna and the half-elf finally left The Oasis. As much as the delay annoyed her, the expressions Zelnor had made when Erianna had commented on her shockingly lurid moans were well worth the mage's act of petty revenge. Erianna would miss her banter with Zelnor, but sadly, their extended time together was just a (rather unfortunate) accident. Now that they were in the city, they would be going their separate ways, as discussed.

Erianna turned her attention toward the note Juniper had slipped beneath her plate. The bard had hidden it in her pocket, but she couldn't check it in the crowded restaurant. You never knew who might be watching, and more importantly, you never knew where people's loyalties lay. Erianna had already taken more than enough risks for a lifetime.

Erianna ducked into a hidden nook near the bakery, taking Lyle with her, and was surprised to see Zelnor following.

"What are you doing?" Erianna asked.

"What do you mean?" Zelnor replied.

"Aren't you supposed to find the High Mage?"

"I thought…" Zelnor shrunk. "I thought we were both going. Sorry. I don't—That was stupid."

"Oh! Well, just." Erianna turned away from her. "Just give me a moment."

Erianna pulled the scrap of paper out of her pocket. Lyle and Zelnor leaned over her shoulder to read it. She nudged Zelnor away, but the mage only looped around and peeked at it from her other side instead. *I suppose it's nothing she doesn't already know.*

The note was short: "Anya—Meet me underneath the moons' shadow in the lightning's wake."

Erianna recognized a few code words that she and Porter had used in the past. "Underneath moons' shadow" meant the hour when the moons were directly overhead: midnight. The second half was unfamiliar. She'd never been good at riddles.

"Lightning's wake," Erianna read aloud. "Any ideas?"

"I think he's referring to the Mistress of Storms… Maybe her temple?" Zelnor suggested. "How many are there here?"

"Three." Erianna ticked them off on her fingers. "One in the Courts, of course. There's a very small one—more of a shrine really—in the Copper District. And a ruined one, in the Slums."

"It's the ruined one. He says in its 'wake,' which implies Delaith abandoned it. Or he could be referring to the ceremony after a funeral. Either way, it's definitely that one."

Erianna would admit she was impressed. For all her teasing about Zelnor being a know-at-all, the mage really was smart. Not that Erianna would ever tell her. Zelnor hardly needed the ego boost.

"Your *friend,*" Zelnor said the word as though it tasted sour, "should be there."

"You don't have to be jealous," Erianna laughed. "He's like an older brother to me."

"I'm not jealous," Zelnor said.

Zelnor was almost too easy to mess with. She smirked, leaning her head close to Zelnor.

"Of course not. But I'm just saying," Erianna whispered, "I'd understand if you were."

"I'm not," the mage said, shoving her head away.

"All right, sure," Erianna said. "Not jealous."

"She seemed a little jealous," Lyle stage-whispered.

"Lyle!" Zelnor squeaked.

Erianna and Lyle burst out laughing. It took the two a while to get ahold of themselves again. Several snooty looking people glared at Erianna as they passed, but she ignored them, basking in the half-elf's flustered annoyance. Finally, Lyle turned his wide, pleading eyes on Erianna.

"Can we travel together a little longer?" he asked.

His lip started quivering. She crumbled almost immediately under his pitiful stare.

"Well." Erianna glanced at Zelnor. "That's not entirely up to me."

"I don't see why we can't stay together for one more day," Zelnor said.

"YES!" Lyle cheered.

"Only! If...*Anya* wants to," Zelnor said.

"Sure. Why not?" Erianna cleared her suddenly dry throat.

"You have a while until your meeting, right?" Zelnor asked. "We should find the High Mage first."

"All right, let's find the bastard."

One more day, then. Erianna was already in the Broken Claim's den, and she needed to stay in the city long enough to meet Porter anyway. What harm was there in spending one more day with the entertaining half-elf? Besides, she would rather Zelnor didn't visit the High Mage alone. The man had refused to work with the Claim, which meant he was either highly moral or he held opposing yet equally vile interests. If the High Mage matched even a fraction of the rumors about him, then it was surely the latter.

Chapter Twelve
The High Mage

Zelnor took a deep breath. The street was packed with well-dressed people, all in a hurry to get somewhere else. The frowning, focused faces were more than a little unnerving. Flashes of gold and finely woven fabric screamed that she didn't belong. Normally, Zelnor would let Erianna handle these situations, but the bard had already taken a few steps back, pulling her scarf higher over her face. It seemed she wasn't planning on helping. *Fantastic.* Well, one of these very busy people had to know where she could find the High Mage.

It took a while to find anyone willing to speak to her. Even when they did stop, Zelnor would open her mouth only to utter a quiet apology and scuttle away. She was considering giving up, when finally, a kunari woman took pity on her and Zelnor managed to get the question out. According to the woman, the High Mage lived in the tallest castle in someplace called the Diamond District.

Zelnor returned to Erianna, more than a little annoyed.

"Thanks for all the assistance," Zelnor said.

"I'm in hiding," Erianna said. "I can't exactly stop people in the street."

"Excuses," Zelnor grumbled. "So, do you know where the Diamond District is?"

Erianna pointed just a few yards away from them, to a tall, stone wall with a few castles peeking over it. Lyle gasped, and Zelnor nearly gasped herself. She'd never seen so much precious metal in one place. A golden gate with spiraling bars blocked the way to the Diamond District. The crushed jewels inlaid at the foot of the gate sparkled.

A bored-looking man guarded the entrance. Looking past the guard, Zelnor could tell exactly which castle the High Mage owned. Even though she could only see the towers, the architecture was too peculiar to belong to anyone else.

The High Mage's towers bulged in odd places, and one tower was noticeably taller than the other. Zelnor marveled at the way they both seemed to defy nature itself, curling toward each other at an impossible angle. The two towers had long iron spirals sticking out of the top, crossed over each other like swords. Veins of bright red jewels ran through the stone in random patterns, reminding Zelnor of a broken vase that someone had tried to piece back together with paste. A castle like this one couldn't exist without powerful magic.

The castle looked exactly like a place someone with mystical, one-of-a-kind powers would live. This High Mage really was like her!

Only one obstacle stood between her and answers: this wall. There were several small buildings posted regularly atop it, with ar-mored men pacing between them. Guard towers. Erianna must have agreed, because she stopped the group just short of the expansive barricade and pulled them to the side.

"This country really likes walls," Zelnor said.

"Understatement," Erianna said.

"So, what're we gonna do?" Lyle asked. "I can pass right through the wall, but you two—"

"Erianna's welcome to try," Zelnor said.

"You'd like that, wouldn't you?" Erianna huffed.

"I would. I really would." She smirked. "But maybe we should just head through the gate?"

Erianna scowled at the suggestion. She clearly didn't agree, but instead of arguing, she stared at the wall. Was she planning to tear out each individual brick? Zelnor ignored the bard's theatrics and started toward the entrance, but Erianna caught her arm.

"I think it would be better if we took an…alternate route," Erianna said.

"What kind of 'alternate route'?" Zelnor asked.

"It shouldn't be in use right now," Erianna mumbled to herself. "But we should still be quiet, just in case."

"Well, *that* sounds safe," Zelnor said. "This is something illegal, isn't it?"

Erianna just shrugged. *Yup. Definitely illegal.*

"Isn't there any other way?" Lyle asked.

"You need a mountain of paperwork to get permission to enter legitimately. Paperwork that we don't have," the bard explained.

It had never occurred to Zelnor that she might need documentation. She'd never run into a situation like that in Kialma'keer or Alaspinor, and it certainly hadn't come up last time she visited Nirdeem. Still, there had to be a way to get in through the proper channels.

"All right. Who do we talk to?" Zelnor asked.

"Trust me, it's not an option," Erianna said. "It takes months *and* you need high-placed connections or a vast fortune."

"If you don't have permission to enter, then how do you know all this?" Zelnor asked.

"I watched my—" Erianna cut herself off. "I watched someone get the proper clearance once."

Someone? Whoever they were, it was obvious this person had been close to Erianna. Did that mean she used to live here? Or maybe she had been friends with someone from the Diamond District. Based on her tone, it didn't seem like Erianna and this person were on good terms anymore. It hinted at the bard's complicated situation in Nirdeem, stoking Zelnor's curiosity even further. She was determined to uncover the full story later.

For the moment, though, Zelnor was more concerned with getting into the Diamond District. She was vehemently against sneaking in. The castles in this district were the definition of opulent excess, exactly the sort of people she wanted to avoid making enemies of. That said, if the choice came down to keeping Torrin waiting for months while they attempted to get in properly—potentially alienating herself from the only hope she had of ridding herself of elemental magic—or pissing off a few rich people, Zelnor knew which she'd prefer.

"Fine. We'll try the shady way," Zelnor said.

Erianna led their group to the place where the Diamond District wall met the outer wall of the city. She pointed out a narrow gap between them. It was obscured by shadow and hidden behind a pile of crates marked with a dead spider—nigh-on impossible to spot unless you knew exactly where to look.

"I never thought I'd come back here," the bard said.

"To Nirdeem?" Zelnor asked.

Erianna's eyebrows shot up. She probably hadn't meant for anyone to hear her.

"Well, yes but also no. Never mind." She turned away. "We should go, while the guard isn't looking."

Erianna wedged herself into the gap in the wall. She made an uncomfortable grunt and mumbled something about it being easier the last time, and Zelnor slipped in after her. The total darkness reminded her of the spell that had blinded her before visiting Torrin. She could still feel his searing breath on her face, the way his movements shook the cave. Her heart skipped a beat at the memory. Zelnor almost asked Erianna to light up the passage with her teal glow, but they might as well scream: "Hello we're breaking into this very nice district. Don't mind us!"

They shimmied along the dark passage, and Zelnor ran her hands against the wall as she went. She took careful steps and prayed she wouldn't stumble over anything. It was much longer than she had expected. Based on the width of the Diamond District's wall, they should've already passed through and into daylight again.

"Erianna—" Zelnor started.

The bard shushed her. "Not now."

Erianna seemed abnormally tense, and Zelnor suspected this tunnel was not as abandoned as the woman had implied. Zelnor continued running her hand along the rough stone until it shifted to wood. She stopped and grasped around until she found a handle.

"There's a door here," Zelnor whispered.

"Don't touch it!" Erianna hissed.

"Are we in someone's house?" Zelnor asked.

"Shh!"

What in Kalkor's Divine Punishment was this idiot thinking? They couldn't just go trapsing through someone's house, especially not a rich person's house! Zelnor would be arrested in two seconds flat.

"We have to get out of here!" Zelnor whisper-shouted. "What if they're home? What if they report us to the guard?"

"I can check to see if anyone's here," Lyle suggested.

"Stop it, you two." Erianna glowed brightly. "We're almost out.

Be quiet or we'll get caught."

"Why would you bring us in here in the first place? You're going to get us killed," Zelnor growled under her breath.

"You have to trust me," Erianna said.

"Why should we?" Zelnor retorted in a whisper.

"Because you already have. You came in here with me, now let me get you out."

At this point, Zelnor had no way of knowing how far they'd gone through the passage. If she turned around now, it might take even longer to get back. So Zelnor bit her tongue and kept following the ishlanian. The progress was a lot faster with a light source. Even through all the layers she was wearing, Erianna put off enough light to rival a torch. Zelnor wasn't sure whether the woman was producing light to help them, or if she was simply furious enough that she couldn't help it.

Finally, the group emerged through a crack on the other side. Zelnor had never been more relieved to leave anywhere in her life. What was that place? Why was there a hole leading directly through it? How had the owners never noticed?

Sunlight glistened off the castles around them. With so many precious metals incorporated into every stone and archway, Zelnor could hardly see a few feet down the gilded cobblestone road. Who put gold in a road anyway? Sure, it looked pretty, but it also seemed like a hazard. How many accidents had happened on this road because a cart driver couldn't see?

"We need to get away from here," Erianna said.

She crouched low to the ground and stalked forward. Gods, could Erianna look more suspicious? Zelnor distanced herself from the bard. No sense in them both getting caught.

"What are you doing? Get down," Erianna hissed.

Erianna tugged on Zelnor's arm. A single yank on her sleeve

pulled Zelnor to her knees, reminding her just how strong Erianna was. The bard could probably scoop her up and carry her if she wanted. Erianna had toned arms but not nearly enough muscle to account for that kind of strength. How was she so strong anyway? Zelnor just knew that, if she asked the question, Erianna would find a way to turn it into an inappropriate joke.

"Why are we sneaking?" Zelnor asked instead. "We're already inside."

"You think they don't have patrols?" Erianna retorted. "Guards pacing around, looking for people who don't belong?"

"We stick out even more if we're skulking around," Zelnor pointed out.

She found that blending in attracted far less attention. Between Erianna's eccentric outfit and their suspicious behavior, the two stuck out worse than a horse inside a tavern.

"Well, we can't just walk down the street," Erianna said. "They'll know we don't belong. We don't have pins."

Pins? Erianna hadn't mentioned any pins before. Zelnor glanced at the ghost, but he shrugged, just as lost.

"They're symbols that you belong in this district, hard to fake and even harder to obtain legally," Erianna explained. "Remember the paperwork I mentioned?"

They had no chance of slipping through the Diamond District unnoticed. It had been a long time since Zelnor had tried to sneak around. Not since she was a little girl pilfering an extra helping of dessert. And her raggedy clothes would draw even more attention in an upscale place like this. How had she not thought of that? How could she even suggest just walking down the street?

"We're going to need a little luck, but we'll make it," Erianna assured her.

"I know!" Zelnor snapped, embarrassed her worry was so obvious.

The three crouched behind the large buildings, making their way forward. Lyle offered to scout ahead, but Erianna rejected the idea. They would have no way of knowing who could and couldn't see him until it was too late.

Erianna traveled in front, leading the group. Zelnor watched the ishlanian slip between the shadows. She blended in seamlessly with them, alert to even the slightest noise. The silent movements were all the more impressive with the unwieldy backpack still strapped securely to her back. Zelnor had always thought of the bard as a flashy attention-seeker, but she had to admit that Erianna was more adept at sneaking than she'd expected.

Erianna stopped suddenly, and Zelnor crashed into her backpack. The teal woman pitched forward into an ornate flowerpot, shattering it on the ground and scattering dirt everywhere. Gods, Zelnor had jinxed them.

"Come out!" a guard shouted.

Heavy boots plodded toward their hiding spot. They needed a distraction. Zelnor glanced across the way and saw a tired-looking woman carrying a tall stack of wrapped packages.

Zelnor held out her hand and willed her magic through it. She pulled up a chunk of cobblestone and the woman tripped, yelping and sending her boxes sprawling all over the walkway. The guard spun around to help her collect them.

Erianna, Zelnor, and Lyle darted across the street and safely behind a castle. The guard checked their previous hiding place, then started to investigate an area in the opposite direction. He had only gone a short distance when Zelnor saw six white dots forming a circle around her.

Don't panic. Don't panic. Stop panicking! Vel'erma, how could Zelnor have been so stupid? She shouldn't have used her magic. Even if she didn't get everyone here killed, what if the second spell was something big and flashy? It would be like a beacon telling the guard exactly where they'd gone.

Zelnor started crawling away, but Erianna grabbed her foot. The bard shook her head vehemently and inclined her head toward the guard. Zelnor tried to pull her leg away, but the ishlanian held fast. Her grip was too strong.

"Let go," Zelnor hissed.

But Erianna didn't. What in the Afterworlds? Erianna *knew* what would happen next. Zelnor needed to get away. She had to get some distance before—

Too late. The dots sank into Zelnor. They were done for.

Zelnor waited.

But nothing happened, and the guard finally walked away. His footsteps receded as he continued his patrol. *Thank Vel'erma!* Her second spell rarely ended up so subtle.

Lyle gaped at her. This was the first time he had seen her cast a spell, and the first time he'd seen the aftermath of her powers. Zelnor smiled, trying to assure him that she was fine, but it did nothing to soothe him. She could only imagine what sort of horrific thing had happened to her face to illicit that response.

Zelnor looked down to assess the damage. Her hands had turned dark purple. Knowing her luck, she would bet the rest of her skin had turned purple, too. Now she was even *more* noticeable. An inconvenient second spell, but hardly the worst one she had experienced. She just hoped it would wear off before they met the High Mage.

Lyle was still staring. He looked a little freaked out. It might not be the best time, but Zelnor needed to explain, at least briefly. She tried to tell him that this was "normal" for her, but as soon as she tried to speak, a stream of water poured out of her mouth.

What in Thorns' bloody name?

Lyle gasped. He frantically moved to try to help but clearly didn't know how.

"Zelnor's fine. She does that sometimes," Erianna reassured the ghost.

Zelnor snapped her jaw shut again and clasped a hand over her mouth—a *purple* hand. She was most certainly not fine! In all ten years with this curse, Zelnor had never had two adverse effects. Whenever she cast a spell, no matter how big, there was always one additional spell once those six dots hit her. One spell. Just one. How was this happening? Was her curse getting worse?

"Oh…all right," Lyle stammered. "So, Zelnor has magic with weird dots that make crazy stuff happen?"

"Dots? I don't know about any dots, but yes, she has magic. It gets a little out of hand sometimes, but it's fine, really." Erianna tugged at Zelnor's arm. "Now, come on."

Oh gods, please let there be another explanation. It can't *be getting worse!*

What if…it was one spell? It was just a spell that turned people purple and put water in their mouths. It was *one* spell with *two* effects. That had to be it. Now that she thought about it, it made sense. *Nothing to worry about,* she told herself. *It's not getting worse.*

The High Mage's castle looked even gaudier up close, and yet, Zelnor and Lyle gazed at the structure with undisguised wonder. The castle was opulent and undeniably bizarre, but it hardly deserved that much admiration. Erianna had no love for obscene displays of wealth like this one—it reminded her of the insufferable, arrogant fools her mother had wrapped around her finger.

Although, part of Erianna understood why they were so enamored. The castle was unique. The same veins of blood red gems that crisscrossed along the two towers spiraled through the front of the building. On either side of the door, long lines of red gems extended from floor to roof. Spirals of those same red veins broke off from the main ones at irregular intervals, creating a design reminiscent of two giant, magical plants on either side of the doorway. The doors themselves were equally resplendent, crafted from silver and outlined in iron. The entrance was massive, easily double Erianna's height.

Erianna might have begrudgingly admitted the design was a little pleasing, if it weren't for the towers. The way they bulged and curled toward each other with those spiraling iron protrusions on the ends, covered in those dark red veins… She just couldn't help but compare them to something else. She valiantly attempted to hold back herself back, but it was useless.

"They look—" A sharp laugh burst out of her. "They look like weirdly shaped dicks."

Erianna doubled over, unable to contain herself any longer. Zelnor glared at her, but the effect was ruined by the half-elf's bright red cheeks. Zelnor spluttered indignantly, which only made the situation even *funnier*, and just as Erianna started to regain control of herself, she lost it again. It felt good to find something to laugh about. Ever since they'd snuck through The Spider's Nest, she had felt something crawling under her skin.

Erianna noticed Lyle out of the corner of her eye. The ghost examined the towers, a small frown forming on his face. Liscuntia, she had forgotten they were traveling with a child.

"Anyway," Erianna said. "Let's go inside!"

"You have a dirty mind," Zelnor grumbled.

Zelnor's solid thuds barely sounded like light taps on the thick silver doors, yet improbably, they opened the moment her knuckles touched them. Almost as though the High Mage were expecting them. *That's not suspicious at all.*

Based on everything Erianna had seen so far, the High Mage was likely the pretentious prick she expected. She only hoped that was all he was, because Zelnor and Lyle were both too taken in by the splendor to question the man's motives. They had left Erianna to act as the sensible one. Gods, she hated being the sensible one.

The large doors opened into a foyer more than twice the size of The Spiral Cup. A huge chandelier held candles sputtering with deep red flames, bathing the room in a crimson glow. A narrow, silver carpet led to a grand central staircase, branching off in two different directions—presumably toward the dick towers. Several silver doors, much smaller than the main entryway, lined the walls.

The most striking thing in the room was the High Mage himself. An elven man around their age descended the central staircase and greeted them with an annoyingly smug smile.

The High Mage had platinum blond hair, cropped close on the sides of his head and long on the top. It drifted weightlessly in the air above him, as though rippling with a gentle ocean current. An ethereal, ruby mist smoked from the corners of his hazel eyes. His white, billowy tunic, embroidered with small dark red jewels, was tucked into a pair of tight, shimmering silver pants. He wore a cloak of deep crimson that fluttered in an imaginary wind.

Of course his outfit matches his house. Erianna didn't know whether to find that level of coordination obnoxious or impressive. Her expectations had been exceeded. This showy, ostentatious asshat somehow outmatched all the other self-entitled bastards who lived here.

The elven man continued down the stairs at a leisurely pace. He spoke softly, yet the three easily heard him.

"Welcome, Zelnor." His voice was smooth and melodic. "We meet at last. Come closer. I don't bite."

Lyle shot forward as soon as The High Mage reached the bottom of the staircase, and Zelnor followed in awed, halting steps. The High Mage took her hand and kissed it. She responded with a strangled squeak.

"I am High Mage Devlin Devereux," the elf said. "The greatest sorcerer in the city of Nirdeem and the world's foremost practitioner of elemental magic, expert in all things arcane. And"—he winked at Zelnor, leaning closer—"Nirdeem's not-so-secret weapon."

Devlin Devereaux was one of the only powerful players in Nirdeem who the Broken Claim didn't have in their pocket. The gaudy elf was well-liked among Nirdeem's elite, and an integral part of the Judges' harshest sentence. The criminals sent to the High Mage vanished for the duration of their punishment—completely cut off from the outside world. They all returned home broken and haunted. No one knew what Devlin did with them.

Erianna stepped in between Zelnor and the High Mage. The elf was only an inch or two shorter than her, but she made use of her slight height advantage. They would not be swayed by any of his alleged charms.

"I am—"

"Erianna, I know," Devlin said. "Zelnor's superfluous traveling companion."

"Superfluous!" Erianna voice cracked slightly.

"It means unnecessary," Devlin said.

"I know what it means! Your—" Erianna's voice cracked again, and she cleared her throat. "The only thing 'superfluous' was your explanation."

The High Mage put a hand to his chest.

"My apologies. I only meant to emphasize Zelnor's *vast* power. I'm sure your talents are"—he chuckled—"greatly appreciated. What is a journey without musical accompaniment?"

Erianna fumed, too angry to respond. Her skin glowed bright teal through her carefully wrapped clothes.

"Erianna is really good with directions," Lyle argued. "We never would've got this far without her!"

"She's been a great guide," Zelnor agreed.

The mage rarely complimented her, and it had sounded so genuine, too, but Erianna wished Zelnor would take the situation more seriously. She shouldn't immediately trust the man just because he had a similar skillset. Erianna expected more from Zelnor than to fall prey to Devlin's blatant manipulation.

"I'm sure she has," Devlin said. "But aren't there other matters you want to discuss, Zelnor?"

"Yes, definitely!" the mage said.

"How do you know their names?" Lyle asked.

At least someone was cautious. Unfortunately, Zelnor was a lost cause.

"Follow me," the High Mage said, ignoring Lyle's question. "We'll take tea in the West Tower while we talk."

Devlin flicked his wrist, and the front doors slammed shut. He spun with a dramatic flourish and ascended the stairs in deliberate, annoyingly graceful steps. The last thing Erianna wanted to do was have tea with this asshole, but she couldn't, in good conscience, leave Zelnor alone with him.

Lyle waved a hand to catch Erianna's attention. He pointed to the High Mage, crossing his eyes and sticking out his tongue. Erianna snorted. *I suppose I can endure this a little longer.*

Erianna followed the two mages up the left staircase. The stone steps were laid out in a surprisingly straightforward path. The tower's odd shape should have created a tilting, lurching stairway, but instead, it merely turned in a steady upward spiral—like any other castle tower would.

"Darling, you can remove that ridiculous disguise," the High Mage told Erianna. "My castle is protected from unwanted intruders and wandering eyes. No one will see you here."

Erianna pulled the hood of her cloak further down. As though she would ever take his word for it. In fact, she hoped Devlin wasn't telling the truth. Gods only knew what he might do to them away from prying eyes. Not that he'd get the chance, not while she was around.

"Must be easy to dispose of your enemies, then," Erianna said.

Devlin chuckled, the sound crisp and derisive.

"If I wanted you killed, I wouldn't do it in my own home," he said. "It's not an especially intelligent suggestion."

"So, you've considered it," Erianna accused.

"Everyone has enemies," Devlin replied lightly, "but I find more civil ways to deal with them."

Erianna gritted her teeth, ready to refute him with a scathing reply, but Zelnor glanced pleadingly over her shoulder. Erianna bit her tongue. *He isn't worth it.*

They passed a few silver doors before Devlin stopped and waved his hand, causing the one in front of them to open. He ushered them inside and the door shut behind them. The parlor was decorated in the Alaspinoran style, featuring a round mahogany table draped in dark red lace with three plush dining chairs. Bejeweled sconces bathed the little drawing room in the same disquieting crimson as the rest of the castle; however, a crackling fire on the opposite side of the room filled it with a comforting orange glow, mitigating some of the red light's ominous ambiance.

The room only had four paintings—all landscapes, each radically different from each other. Devlin's attention to detail in the way he coordinated his clothes with his house made Erianna wonder if there was some connection between these places.

One was a painting of The Old Barrows in central Alaspinor

and another a painting of the Weareely Marshes at the far northern end of Eltun. Both places were Alaspinoran, but she couldn't think of anything else that linked them. The third painting showed a blizzard so fierce it almost looked like a blank canvas. That location had to be somewhere in either Gealtalmh or the Reindune Mountains. Nowhere else snowed like that.

If all the paintings weren't of Alaspinor, then what was it? Was he trying to represent different climates? No, that would be far too pedestrian for someone with such a flair for the dramatic. Perhaps he'd been to all these places, and it was just another extension of his vanity?

"Cozy, isn't it?" Devlin asked Zelnor.

The bearded woman ignored his question. Instead, she stared intently at the last painting. This particular landscape depicted somewhere in Kialma'keer. It captured an eternity of endless dunes tapering off into the distance. A cloud of dust bloomed at the far edge of the desert's horizon. The only thing of note was in the foreground: a jagged, pockmarked hunk of sandstone with a narrow gap in the center—an opening into unknown depths. The entrance was barely visible, hidden by the angle of the sun. It was hardly the most interesting painting in the High Mage's collection, though Erianna would admit she was curious where that opening led.

"Have you been to all these places?" Zelnor asked.

Devlin waved his hand, and the silver teapot on the table poured steaming tea into three waiting cups. With another gesture, the cups floated in the air and landed gently in front of each chair.

"Only some of them." Devlin's gaze lingered on the same picture.

The High Mage lowered himself into the chair across from Zelnor, and Lyle plopped down into the remaining seat. The ghost sniffed the tea. Would the High Mage try to poison them? He had made a fuss about not killing someone in his own home, but his emphatic denial only made Erianna more suspicious.

"Please have a seat," Devlin said.

The man gestured to the chair Lyle was *already sitting in.*

All this time, Erianna had assumed that Devlin was ignoring Lyle, but now it was glaringly obvious that the High Mage couldn't see him. Surely, someone able to practice elemental magic should be able to see ghosts. Was Zelnor more powerful than him, or did this "High Mage" not have any real magic at all? Were his showy levitations and his "mystical" appearance all just a trick?

The High Mage, unaware of Erianna's realization, shrugged at her silence and turned his attention back to Zelnor. The mage hadn't noticed anything amiss with the elf's statement. It was possible that not all elemental mages could see ghosts, but something still felt wrong here. Devlin Devereux was lying to them. The moment Erianna had set eyes on him, something about the man had struck her as false.

"I'll come straight to the point." Devlin sipped his tea. "I assume you're here about your powers? Our gift is rather rare. You must have questions."

"So many!" Zelnor exclaimed.

The elf flashed a half-smile and gestured for Zelnor to continue.

"How many of us are there?" she asked.

"To my knowledge, you and I are the only ones," Devlin replied. "But I am not omnipotent. There may, of course, be others I've yet to meet. On a different continent, perhaps."

"How did you get your powers?"

"I was born with them," the alleged High Mage answered. "And yourself?"

"They appeared…when I was nine," Zelnor said.

"Interesting. Any idea what might have triggered them?"

Zelnor hesitated.

"If the experience was too confusing or private, I could ask the ishlanian to leave," Devlin prompted.

Erianna's skin flared teal. "I've known Zelnor longer than you have."

"Yes, but some things are better shared with those with the appropriate…aptitude for them," he replied. "Someone so ordinary could never understand."

"Trust is formed on more than just 'aptitude,'" Erianna said.

"It's got nothing to do with trust," Zelnor cut in, curling her hands around her teacup. "It happened right after my dad died."

Erianna took a step forward. Zelnor had never talked about her family before.

"Oh, shit. Zelnor…" she said. "I—"

"I'm so sorry," Devlin interrupted, placing a hand on Zelnor's arm. "It's a trade no child would make, love for power, but … at least you've made the best of it."

"Actually, I don't want these powers," Zelnor said.

Devlin flinched and retracted his hand.

"Don't want them?" he asked. "But your gift is one of a kind."

"I've been trying to get rid of them," Zelnor admitted.

A flash caught Erianna's eye. The glint of something metal moving rapidly under the table. A *weapon*. Erianna lunged forward and grabbed Devlin's wrist.

The High Mage tilted his head. A small smile curled over his lips. Something glimmered in his eyes for just a moment, before he regained his composure.

"He has a knife," Erianna said.

"Do I?" he asked.

Erianna looked down at his hand. It was empty. *How* could it be empty? Devlin held up his other hand. There was nothing in that one either—just a small cut between his fingers.

"I have no intention of harming the only other elemental

mage I've ever met. What would possess me to do such a thing?" Devlin asked.

Does he really think he can play games with me?

"Under your cloak!" Erianna demanded.

"See for yourself," Devlin said.

Erianna flung the red fabric aside. Still nothing. Nothing in his lap, strapped to his hip or up his sleeves. She saw no point searching under his tight pants. Any weapon *there* would be obvious. His shoes were no more than slippers, crafted from a fine, blood-red silk: no space to hide a knife there either.

"Would you like me to disrobe, as well?" Devlin asked.

Erianna tightened her grip on his wrist. *What in Liscuntia's name did I see?* Was it only a trick of the light? No, he was far too smug for that. He must have had some sort of hidden compartment, and now he was using it to make her look like a fool.

"How do we know you have the same powers Zelnor does?"

"He's been levitating things since we got here," Zelnor said. "Last I checked, light and shadow mages can't lift things without picking them up. With their *hands.*"

"What if it's not magic at all?" Erianna accused.

"Then how is he doing all this?" Zelnor asked.

"I can make things float," Lyle argued.

"You think he has a personal ghost that we can't see," Zelnor said.

When put like that it sounded…implausible, but Erianna wasn't willing to give up just yet.

"He could be a performer," she insisted. "It could all be sleight of hand."

"I took you for a skeptic the moment I met you, Erianna," Devlin tutted. "I suppose you want proof?"

Erianna scoffed, glowing even brighter.

"You're saying you have something that proves you're capable of more than basic parlor tricks?" she asked.

"I do. And I am happy to accommodate you. Provided you return my hand and stop blinding me," he answered.

Erianna dimmed her glow and reluctantly released the elf's wrist. The High Mage took Zelnor's hand.

"Might I ask, is your skin normally this shade of rich plum?" Devlin smiled, as though he already knew the answer.

"No, it happened because of my powers," Zelnor said. "It hasn't faded yet."

"Allow me to assist you, then," Devlin said.

Beginning at the point of contact where the High Mage's hand grasped hers, a wave of tan spread up her body like a river carving through dense purple earth. Within moments, her skin had turned back to its natural hue.

Zelnor held her hands up and stared at them incredulously. Devlin turned to Erianna, another infuriating smirk spreading across his lips.

"Satisfied?" the High Mage asked.

Erianna most certainly wasn't, but she couldn't think of any other objections. Zelnor had turned purple before they had even entered the castle. Even Lyle looked convinced. Devlin's powers were, apparently, legitimate.

"How did you do that? You had no second spell. No adverse effects. Your magic is completely under control!" Zelnor marveled.

"Well ..." Devlin said. "In all honesty, I am nowhere near as powerful as you. Controlling elemental magic is much simpler when you have less."

"That's not possible. You're—Look at you. At this castle!" Zelnor insisted.

"I'm hardly weak, but the elemental magic I sense running through you could rival *gods*."

Devlin smiled and squeezed Zelnor's hands.

"Gods …?" Zelnor breathed. "That's—it's even worse than I thought. No wonder I'm so dangerous."

"Ah … Now I understand your enmity toward our magic," Devlin said. "It's noble to want to keep others from harm, but you don't have to get rid of your magic to accomplish that goal. You just need to harness it."

Zelnor pulled her hands away.

"I tried living with it," she said. "And I paid a heavy price."

The High Mage thought for a moment, and then the red haze drifting from his eyes sparkled. He retrieved a map of Eltun and the surrounding Ethnarian Ocean from a chest in the corner. With a wave of his hand, the teapot and cups disappeared in a puff of red smoke, and he spread the map across the table. Another flick of his wrist and a quill and inkwell floated over.

"There may be a way to reduce your power," the High Mage said.

Devlin drew three marks on the map: one in the marshes of northwestern Alaspinor, one in central western Alaspinor, and the last in the Reindune Mountains, east of Nirdeem.

"Our power comes from pools of white mist. There are more than three, but these are the ones I know of. Although there is one other …"

Devlin drew a large circle in the Ethnarian Ocean, off the eastern Alaspinoran coast, and stabbed the spot with the quill.

"Somewhere in this area," he said. "Unfortunately, every ship that has gotten close has sunk."

"Then how do you know it's there?" Erianna challenged.

"The legend surrounding the place proves it beyond doubt. Just like the others."

"Wait. My powers, *our* elemental magic, comes from pools?" Zelnor asked. "How? Why? What are they?"

"I don't know. I've pieced together frustratingly little. Forgotten legends of great four-armed beings wielding unimaginable power. The first true gods, shaping the world and sharing their gifts through artifacts they imbued with elemental magic.

"No mortal in recorded history has possessed that same power," Devlin said. "Until … us. And it all relates to these pools."

"You can put magic into objects?" Erianna asked.

"Yes, yes, of course. How do you think the healers create their restorative tonics? It takes a highly skilled mage, but it's not uncommon." Devlin waved his hand dismissively. "Now artifacts, on the other hand, are rare. Made even rarer by the dragons that hoard them. Zelnor's medallion is a perfect example."

"You know about Torrin?" Zelnor's eyes widened.

"You aren't the first ones he's sent," Devlin said. "He doesn't like what he can't spy on."

The elf locked eyes with Zelnor, his gaze startlingly intense.

"But that's not important, right now," he said. "You need to seal these pools. It won't rid you of your magic completely, but it will weaken it."

"I'll be able to control it?" Zelnor asked.

"Yes. And your life will be infinitely easer," Devlin said.

The High Mage's solution sounded too easy to Erianna. She might believe that Devlin was an elemental mage, but that didn't mean he wasn't also a self-serving asshole. Definitely not the type to help others without an ulterior motive of his own.

"Closing these pools will weaken you too," Erianna said. "Why would you want that?"

The red haze around the High Mage's eyes shifted, obscuring his eyes for a moment before it moved away again. He fixed Erianna with an appreciative smile.

"A fair and intelligent question, Erianna," Devlin praised. "Don't worry about me. I have plenty of power already. It's a small price to help the only other elemental mage in existence."

"I wasn't worried," Erianna said. "The less power you have, the better."

"Glad we understand each other," he replied. He rolled up the map and handed it to Zelnor, then flicked his wrist and the tea set returned. "Now that that's settled, let's finish our tea. I want to hear all about your travels."

Erianna refused to sit down—with Lyle at the table, there wasn't an open seat anyway—but this time she took the cup the High Mage offered her. She sipped it gingerly. The blend was smooth and, to her surprise, still warm. It was the most expensive tea Erianna had ever tasted, and yet it left a bitter aftertaste.

Chapter Thirteen
Two Halves

Zelnor adjusted the symbol pinned to her tunic—a curved silver tower with three red gems embedded in it. The brooch was the High Mage's symbol. Devlin had told them that the jewelry represented an official acknowledgement from the High Mage himself and gave them permission to wander freely in and out of the Diamond District, which would be very helpful during their next visit.

Devlin had even given Erianna one. *Shocking, considering how poorly they got along.* Although, to be fair, it was Erianna's fault for always picking fights with the High Mage. For some reason, the bard had taken an instant dislike to him.

Zelnor would admit that Devlin was a trifle arrogant, but he was a powerful elemental mage, in absolute control of his abilities. If anything, that gave him the right to be arrogant, didn't it? And more importantly, he had been incredibly helpful *and* forthcoming; yet despite all that, the bard still didn't trust the extraordinary elf. She'd barely said a word over tea, and she was practically marching them out of the district.

"Where are we going?" Lyle asked.

The ghost flew in front of Erianna, and the ishlanian stopped abruptly to avoid walking right through him. She ducked around him, continuing forward.

"Out of the Diamond District," Erianna said.

"We just got permission to be here," Zelnor said. "Don't you wanna look around?"

"I've seen more than enough, thank you," Erianna replied.

Zelnor jogged forward and grabbed Erianna's arm, forcing her to stop again.

"What is your problem?" Zelnor asked. "You were a dick to Devlin, and now you can't wait to get out of the one place your enemies won't find you?"

"The one place they can't find me?" Erianna scoffed. "I'm no safer here than anywhere else."

"You're kidding, right?" Zelnor asked. "This place has roving guards and a giant wall separating it from everywhere else. It requires special permission to even enter."

"Do you think we're the only ones who know about the gap in the wall?"

Zelnor's hand fell away. Erianna made a good point. If the three of them had managed to sneak in, then obviously someone else could do the same.

The teal woman met the rest of Lyle and Zelnor's questions with silence. They followed Erianna back into the Gold District. She led them aimlessly through the streets, tacking turns seemingly at random. Once the castles were well behind them, she finally slowed down.

"You're not really going to do what he says, are you?" Erianna asked.

Her face was impossible to read behind its coverings, but her tense shoulders and crossed arms conveyed her annoyance well enough.

"Why shouldn't I?" Zelnor asked.

"Because people like him always have an agenda," Erianna said.

"People like him." Zelnor scowled. "You mean mages? People with *magic?* You're saying no one with elemental magic would ever use it to help others?"

"No, I mean people with power, people who live in that district, in this city! They don't care about anyone but themselves."

"Devlin is different," Zelnor insisted.

Muffled teal light radiated from behind the layers of fabric wrapped around Erianna. She put her hands on Zelnor's shoulders.

"Devlin is *worse*. He has power *and* magic. Don't you understand how dangerous a combination that is? Just tell Torrin what you learned and forget about Devlin," Erianna said.

"Oh, so now you trust dragons?" Zelnor asked.

"At least Torrin didn't hide what he really wanted from you," Erianna said. "So, yes. I trust dragons more than some insidious, conniving—"

"Stop it!" Zelnor shouted. "Devlin is the only one who understands my powers. Do you have any idea how long I've—"

"You're so desperate for someone to tell you what to do that you're letting some charlatan use you!"

"He is *not* a charlatan!"

"GUYS!" Lyle screamed.

"WHAT?" the two women shouted in unison.

"I…wanted to check out that toy store," Lyle said. "If that's all right?"

The ghost curled away from them with a meek look on his face. This argument had gone far beyond their usual spats. It wasn't Zelnor's fault. Erianna had, like always, blown the situation out of proportion, but Zelnor had risen to the bait instead of letting the bard's comments pass. Now poor Lyle was caught in the middle.

"Sure. I mean, we have some time until your meeting, right?" Zelnor asked Erianna.

The bard nodded. The glow from her skin had faded.

"It's not for a while. Of course we can go," she said.

Lyle slowly perked up again. He led them to a store so unique that Zelnor was shocked she hadn't noticed it when they first passed by. Seshvin's Toy Emporium was printed in bold, neat letters above the *door. The hand-painted s*ign looked almost bland against the whimsical blues, reds, and yellows that covered the shop. Even among the shining, overly opulent buildings of the Gold District, the store still managed to stand out.

Instead of one large display window, several small circular windows with green tinted glass showed off toys, some familiar and some strange. Zelnor saw a model ship and a set of building blocks—stacked to look like a castle—but also a game with oddly shaped pieces. In the lowest window, a small stuffed cathmal with a hand-knitted hide looked out at her with little button eyes. The little feline desert mount reminded her of those from back home.

The inside was so cluttered it bordered on dangerous. Stacks of children's books and board games formed a perilous maze. As Zelnor neared one of the towering piles, it shivered, threatening to tip. If someone got buried underneath one of those stacks, it might take days to find them—if they were found at all. At least the store smelled all right, which meant that no unlucky customers had been forced to take up permanent residence in the Toy Emporium. *Well, at least not recently…*

Zelnor edged away from the stacks and to the nearby shelves. They were so stuffed that it was difficult to make out any one individual toy. Removing one without causing several more to topple out would be almost impossible. How did anyone find anything in here?

Despite the haphazard shelving, the toys were well cared for. There were no rips in the dolls' clothes and not a single scratch on the model wooden carriage balanced between two perpendicular shelves. The shop also had an incredible variety. More toys than Zelnor had seen in her entire lifetime: stuffed rabbits and wolves, games she'd played and some she hadn't, hundreds of books, model castles and ships, and undoubtedly more hidden behind those.

Miniature rails built near the ceiling ran around the entire shop, high enough that an errant train wouldn't knock anything over. Lyle levitated a toy minecart onto the start of the tracks. The little cart zipped down them the instant the ghost let go. He flew alongside it.

Zelnor smiled, watching Lyle enjoy himself for the first time since they'd met. She should buy him a toy. She wanted him to have something to remember her after she left. She just needed to find the shopkeeper.

Zelnor spotted someone with an armful of painted wooden animals and ships blocking their face. They stumbled, and she steadied them, keeping the toys from tumbling out of their hands.

"Thank you!" a muffled voice cried. "I'll help you as soon as I finish with this."

Zelnor helped them place the enormous stack of toys into every spare nook and cranny they could find. When the two had finally dealt with the toys, she managed to get a good look at the shopkeeper. They were ishlanian, but they looked nothing like Erianna.

This ishlanian's face was sharp and angular, the opposite of the bard's rounded features. The shopkeeper's ears were longer than Erianna's, too, although both had the same slight downward curve. Their skin's hue was jade instead of the bard's teal, and unlike Erianna, the shopkeeper had scales: a single, large patch of emerald scales that covered the left half of their face and trailed down their neck, disappearing underneath their loose shirt. The most striking difference was the eyes. The shopkeeper's eyes were pure black. No sclera or irises or pupils, just black.

There were still a few similarities, though. The two ishlanians both had gills. And the shopkeeper was only a little taller than Erianna, towering over Zelnor by at least a foot, just like the bard did. They were both unmistakably ishlanian, just in very different ways.

The shopkeeper pulled at their seaweed green, corkscrew-curl hair, trying and failing to remove the drying streaks of blue and white paint. They accidentally smudged more wet paint across their cheek in the process. Finally, they gave up and pulled their hair into a short, unruly ponytail.

"Thanks again for your help! I'm Seshvin Zlesh."

"Zelnor," she replied.

The shopkeeper offered a glistening, paint-covered hand, and Zelnor awkwardly debated whether she should take it. Seshvin looked down at their palm and winced, doing their best to wipe it off. Their apron and pants were covered with multicolored stains. Seshvin even smelled like paint. Zelnor got the feeling this happened often.

"Nice to meet you. How can I help?" they asked.

Lyle had stopped following the minecart and wandered to the far end of the aisle. He hovered near the top shelf, sticking his head in to see the toys in the back. How was Zelnor supposed to explain that she needed a toy for a dead child?

The shopkeeper followed her line of sight.

"Ah. You want something for the boy over there, right?" Seshvin asked.

"You can see him?" Zelnor asked.

"Of course," Seshvin said. "All ishlanians can, or at least, everyone in Ishahnan can."

"Really?" Zelnor asked.

"Oh, I guess most people don't know," Seshvin said. "Ishahnans are taught, and expected, to guide spirits to the afterlife. My family mostly worked with children gone before their time. Or, well, I—I guess they still do."

Why hadn't Erianna mentioned any of this? Was her duty as a ghostly guide the reason she had been so insistent that they take Lyle with them? How much of her ishlanian heritage did she know? Had she emigrated to Eltun, or did she grow up here?

"Anyway!" Seshvin clapped their hands together. "I'm gonna go talk to your friend."

The shopkeeper made their way carefully through the stacks—by some miracle managing to avoid toppling anything—before arriving at the shelf Lyle was inside. He had gone so far into the display only his legs were visible.

"Hey there! I'm Seshvin, but you can call me Sesh. What's your name?"

The ghost pulled himself out and floated down next to the shop owner.

"I'm Lyle!" he said. "And you can call me…Lyle."

The young noble didn't seem at all surprised that Seshvin could see him. Then again, Lyle hadn't seemed surprised that Zelnor or Erianna could see him, either. Did he have some way of knowing who could and couldn't see him?

"Alright, Lyle. Would you enjoy…reading an exciting story?" Seshvin asked.

"Eh, I kinda like reading…I guess."

Lyle drifted up until he was lounging on his side.

"Not interested in reading, huh. How about a pirate ship?"

"Mm…maybe?" Lyle said.

"Wait! I know!" Seshvin exclaimed.

The shop owner jogged to one of the ever-teetering stacks at the end of the aisle and removed a plain, leatherbound box with impressive precision. They raced back again and showed it to Lyle. The boy's eyes lit up.

"What is *that?*" Lyle asked.

Zelnor wandered over to join Erianna, watching the ghost fawn over the board game.

"This is my recreation of Checkmates," Seshvin said.

He handed the box to Lyle, and it fell right through the ghost's outstretched hands and onto the floor. Seshvin's eyes widened.

"You're clearly—But then why aren't you...? Huh," they said.

The shopkeeper frowned and muttered something under their breath. Their skin started glowing a faint jade green.

"Can't what?" Erianna asked.

"Nothing," Seshvin said. "Let me tell you more about the game."

The shopkeeper eased the lid off, revealing a wooden board folded into quarters and three pouches filled with tokens.

"It's an ishlanian game that's easy to learn but takes some strategy to master. There're only three types of tokens, and they each do different things. I remember really liking it as a kid. Well, I liked it when I won, at least." Seshvin laughed.

Lyle arched his back and stretched onto his toes, until he started hovering a few feet off the ground. He peered into the box and glanced at Zelnor and Erianna with a hopeful smile. Lyle's excitement was absolutely adorable.

"How much?" Erianna asked.

The ishlanian rummaged around, retrieving a coin purse out of her massive bag. Zelnor wondered how Erianna had managed to get through the entire store without that unwieldy backpack knocking something over.

"Free of charge. It's..." Seshvin smiled sadly. "It's been a long time since I talked to a ghost. I hope you enjoy it."

"Thank you," Erianna and Zelnor said in unison.

Zelnor flushed and grabbed the game from Seshvin, packing it carefully into her satchel, nestling it between a book about light magic and their water supply. When she looked up again, Lyle quickly looked away. She could tell he wanted to play it now.

"Did you play this game when you were young, Eria—" Lyle stopped abruptly. "I mean, Anya?"

Seshvin's attention snapped toward Erianna.

"Are you an ishlanian?" they asked. "I hope you don't mind, but what district are you from? There are so few of us in Nirdeem. I really thought I'd met everyone."

"No, I'm not! I uh—I just," Erianna stuttered.

Her skin started glowing teal, and Seshvin's eyes widened in recognition.

"Wait. Are you…?"

Erianna snatched Zelnor's hand and raced out of the Emporium and down the street.

Erianna pulled Zelnor along behind her at a breakneck pace. She had never seen Seshvin before, but they had *certainly* recognized her. Of course they had. She was famous all over Nirdeem. Her mother had made sure of it. Erianna had thought disguising herself would be enough, but clearly that hadn't worked. If that shopkeeper told the Broken Claim where she'd been…

Idiot! You absolute MORON! Why hadn't she just waited outside?

Shockingly, Zelnor didn't complain at all, so Erianna let go, trusting the mage to follow her. She cut straight through The Judgments, weaving around tall, marble buildings until they emerged at the edge of the Slums.

Erianna hadn't meant to come here, not specifically. Her feet had just moved on their own. The echo of some long-dormant instinct had surfaced, borne from years of sneaking out of The Spiral Cup and escaping here. The Slums had always been a haven for her. Most of the clients from her mother's tavern wouldn't be caught dead there.

The homes in the Slums were cobbled together from jagged pieces of stone in several discordant colors and shapes. All their building materials came from the mines, useless stone that needed to be removed to get at the more precious minerals. It had always looked a little rundown, but the people were kind and hardworking and had never once gotten Erianna in trouble.

"Anya…I'm so sorry," Lyle said. "It's my fault we had to leave, isn't it? It's because I almost said your real name, right?"

It hadn't been Lyle's fault, at all. Erianna had given herself away when she started glowing. She got the feeling Lyle would still find a way to feel guilty over it, though. Thankfully, she knew just how to cheer him up.

"Actually, I wanted to show you something. That's why we left so fast," she lied. "I wanted to get here before nightfall."

"Really?" Lyle asked.

He could obviously see the distraction for what it was. Erianna was, once again, impressed with his skepticism. He was much wiser than she had been at his age.

"Yes, *really*. I swear," she insisted. "You'll love it."

"And what is it exactly you wanted to show us?" Zelnor asked.

"It's a surprise." Erianna winked.

"Of course it is," Zelnor said.

A steady *whoosh* filled the district, growing louder the farther into the Slums the group traveled. Soon, the *whoosh* transformed into a bellowing *roar*—the persistent noise of the giant waterfall raging nearby, so tall and wide that it could be seen from anywhere in the city. Although most residents had acclimated to the sound, Erianna knew it got on some people's nerves. She found the noise soothing. She'd grown up close to the Slums, and it had taken her a long time to feel comfortable sleeping without that constant *whoosh*.

Finally, they reached the back of the Slums. The outer wall that was supposed to protect this district from the river outside had crumbled a long time ago. The Judges had ordered a few attempts to fix it back in the day, but the repairs would inevitably crumble just a couple of years after they were made, unable to stand against the powerful waterfall. It might have lasted longer if not for the shoddy materials and underpaid, uninvested construction workers. Stemming the mountain river would dry up the river surrounding the city—a natural moat that formed an extra layer of defense—and the breach in the wall was inaccessible from the outside at this angle. So, the Judges had just given up.

The hole in the wall had been a permanent fixture here for nearly a century, and the river flowed freely into the Slums. The residents had taken advantage of this fact, creating a small lake. The community here used it for chores and play alike, and it was just as common to see children splashing about in it as it was to see people washing their clothes.

"I learned to swim here," Erianna said.

Lyle hesitated, frowning at the water.

"What's wrong?" Erianna asked.

She had expected Lyle to be at least a little excited. Maybe she was the only one who liked the water.

"Uh, well, I…never learned how to swim," the ghost admitted.

"Lyle," Erianna laughed. "You're—well…I don't think you'll drown."

"Oh," Lyle said. "Oh. You're right!"

He sped toward the lake, halting only when he reached the end of his tether. He raced back to her, floating up and down in an excited bounce.

"Hurry, Anya! Hurry! Let's go!"

"Hold on," Erianna said. "Give me a moment to get changed."

Lyle waited impatiently around the corner while Erianna ducked behind a house and stripped down to her undergarments: a thin-strapped undertunic fitted around her waist and a pair of loose pants cropped at mid-thigh. She bundled up her dress and stuffed it in her bag, hiding it in a nook between two houses. Finally, she removed her knife from its sheath, refashioning it to hold the statue of Thermoren instead. After tugging on the statue a few times to ensure it was secure, she turned back toward Zelnor.

The mage had joined her a few minutes into the process, waiting with her back turned. Why bother coming if she was just going to turn around? It wasn't like Erianna cared who saw her undressing; she was about to walk out in her undergarments, after all. They weren't even particularly revealing—at least, no more so than her dress had been.

Erianna crept toward Zelnor's back and leaned over her shoulder.

"I'm done," she whispered.

Zelnor jumped backward and whirled around. The mage's eyes roved over Erianna instinctually, before she realized what she'd done. She quickly looked away.

"S-Sorry!" Zelnor said.

"I understand," Erianna said. "You won't be able to get nearly so good a look at me while we're swimming."

"I wasn't planning—" Zelnor's voice cracked, and she cleared her throat. "I wasn't planning on swimming. I don't want to… you know."

Zelnor gestured vaguely to her clothes.

"Just swim in your clothes, then." Erianna replied.

"They'll get wet," Zelnor said.

"They'll dry," Erianna said.

"I can't swim," Zelnor insisted.

"Yes, I know. The way you flailed around when we were swimming to Torrin's lair made that pretty obvious," Erianna said. "But now is the perfect time to learn. You can't drown either, remember?"

Erianna flicked the medallion around Zelnor's neck. The mage opened her mouth a few times and then closed it, obviously trying to come up with another reason.

"Enough excuses," Erianna chastised. "When was the last time you did something fun? Come on."

Zelnor caught Erianna's arm. She let the bearded woman pull her back behind the house, even though escaping her grip would've been laughably easy. Zelnor's hand lingered on Erianna's wrist, and the mage's eyes flicked down to Erianna's clavicle. Zelnor stared at her raised, pale blue scars.

"Those people after you, did they…?" Zelnor trailed off.

Erianna stiffened, waiting for the half-elf to ask about the marks.

"You should put your cloak back on, before someone recognizes you," Zelnor said instead.

"Oooh, so *now* you care about my safety. Right after I ask you to swim. Convenient timing," Erianna said.

Zelnor's frown only deepened. Erianna's strained joke clearly had little effect on her.

"I'm serious," Zelnor hissed. "You've been in a disguise all day. Is it really safe for you to go out there, like this? You're pretty recognizable."

Erianna hadn't expected Zelnor to care. After today, the mage wouldn't have to worry about Erianna's pursuers. Was she really that worried about assailants showing up in their last few hours together? Or was it possible that Zelnor was genuinely concerned about her?

The thought made Erianna's chest tight.

"All I heard was you calling me pretty," Erianna said.

Zelnor suddenly pulled her closer. Erianna stammered. This was rather forward for the half-elf. Erianna enjoyed teasing her, of course, but Zelnor tended to change the subject whenever things got too serious. Erianna's flirting was always done jokingly for that very reason. Not that Erianna wasn't interested in her…

Zelnor pushed her away again, just as suddenly, and Erianna followed the mage's gaze. A kunari man disappeared around the corner. So, the mage had only pulled her closer to hide her from the stranger.

Erianna felt oddly disappointed. She wouldn't have minded a brief tryst before they parted. On the other hand, it seemed Zelnor really did care about Erianna's safety; her eyes darted around, scanning the area and angling herself to block the ishlanian from view. It was almost sweet. Unnecessary, but sweet.

"I'll be fine," Erianna said. "People here look out for each other. No one will say anything unless someone who works for them happens to show up."

"And if you're wrong? If someone tells them you're here?" Zelnor asked.

"They won't," Erianna said.

"You can't guarantee that!" Zelnor insisted stubbornly.

"My risk. My choice," Erianna snapped.

Zelnor opened her mouth, then shut it again in a thin, grim line. She ran her hands through her beard.

"You're right. It's not my problem," Zelnor agreed.

"Can we go swimming now?" Lyle asked.

Gods, how long had the ghost been there? From the looks of it, probably long enough to overhear most of their argument. Again. Zelnor just couldn't manage even a few moments of peace without immediately finding something to criticize.

"Of course," Erianna told Lyle.

"I'll watch your stuff," Zelnor said.

Erianna had never heard a phrase so helpful spoken so bitterly.

"Thank you," she replied.

Zelnor snatched Erianna's backpack from its hiding spot, stumbling a little under its weight. Erianna didn't help her. Instead, she stomped over to the lake with Lyle. Every so often the ghost glanced between them, worrying at his lower lip.

"Don't pay Zelnor any mind," Erianna said. "Today will be the last time we see her."

Out of the corner of her eye, Erianna saw Zelnor flinch, and Erianna smiled smugly at her reaction. It was strange. Erianna wasn't an especially antagonistic person, or at least she hadn't thought she was, but sometimes Zelnor just *irked* her. Erianna had never met anyone so petty. Their impending separation was obviously for the best.

Lyle flew into the lake and dived beneath the surface, bursting back up again and moving through it as though it were air. The moment Erianna plunged into the water all her cares melted away. Swimming would always be worth the risk. Almost all her best memories were tied to this lake: secret outings with Porter and stolen moments of reprieve away from Plindurin. The last day she'd spent with her father… Well, that memory was not quite so happy as the others.

Lyle used his powers to splash some water into her face.

"Lyle, how could you?" she gasped. "This means war!"

Erianna chased him all over the lake, trying to splash him, but he always managed to dodge out of the way. Finally, she managed to fake him out, aiming one way, only to turn with lightning speed and splash him with her other hand. The water passed right through him.

"I guess I'll never actually know what it feels like to be splashed." Lyle said.

Dammit. Erianna had meant to cheer him up, not remind him of his limitations.

"You're right!" she said. "You're an absolute *cheater!* I can't believe you're using your powers to keep from getting wet. How am I supposed to win?"

She made sure Lyle saw her smiling, so he knew she was teasing, and the child flashed her a small grin in return.

"I guess it is kind of like a…special talent?" he asked.

"Unfair is what it is," Erianna said.

"Maybe a little," Lyle said.

"Still, even with your talents, I bet I could beat you in a race," Erianna said. "No one has ever beat me yet."

"Really?" Lyle asked.

"Nope. Not a one."

The ghost narrowed his eyes.

"THREETWOONE GO!" he shouted.

Lyle sped off at top speed.

"Hey! You cheater!" Erianna called after him.

The two did a lap around the lake, Erianna always just a few paces behind Lyle. Truthfully, she could've beaten him. He was fast, but no one outraced Erianna in the water, not even a ghost. Unfortunately, it wasn't even a fair competition—the tether wouldn't have let the two get far apart. But most importantly, she wanted Lyle to win. He deserved it.

"I did it!" Lyle shouted, after finishing just inches ahead of her.

"I guess you're the new champion," Erianna said.

"I'm King of the Lake!"

"Would you like to play another game, your Majesty?" Erianna asked.

"Yeah! Uh—I mean, yes, my loyal knight."

Lyle straightened, trying to look regal, and Erianna bowed so low her face smacked the water.

"I am at your command," she replied.

The two played until the sun disappeared and a chill settled into the water. The lake was deserted by the time the two finished, with the chores done and the children taken home for dinner. Erianna's undergarments had gained several pounds of water weight, and her lavender hair lay limp and plastered to her face, but her lacking presentation didn't bother her—nothing could wipe her wide grin away.

Erianna stumbled awkwardly back to Zelnor, shivering as wind blew her soaked garments against her skin. The half-elf quickly looked down at an open book in her lap.

"Have fun?" she asked.

"We did," Erianna said. "Almost as much fun as you had watching us."

"I wasn't watching you. I was reading."

Erianna had seen the half-elf staring at them. It was too far to see her face, but Zelnor had clearly not been reading.

"In the dark?" Erianna challenged.

Zelnor snapped the book shut and tucked it into her satchel, bolting back to her feet. She shoved Erianna's bag into her arms.

"Your giant backpack," Zelnor said.

"Thank you." Erianna chuckled.

"Whatever," Zelnor said. "Get dressed so we can go."

Erianna set the backpack on the ground and plopped down next to it. She smiled sweetly up at Zelnor.

"Are you really going to miss your own meeting, just to spite me?" Zelnor asked.

"Maaaaybe," Erianna hummed.

Zelnor flopped down next to her.

"Petty," she muttered.

Erianna pointed to the moons, barely risen.

"I'm only joking. We have until midnight," Erianna said. "Besides, my undergarments need to dry anyway. Or as much as they can in this season."

Erianna passed a wrapped parcel of dried meat and fruit to Zelnor. The half-elf grunted in lieu of a response. Lyle shot Erianna a look that clearly said, *fix it,* and flew back to the edge of the water, diving into the lake.

It was hardly Erianna's fault that Zelnor excelled at making herself miserable. The bearded woman had chosen to miss out on a fun day of swimming to sulk on the sidelines for hours. But still…Lyle was probably right. No sense in their last few hours together being uncomfortable. They didn't have to part on bad terms.

"Ask me a question, and I'll answer it," Erianna said.

She scooted closer, so she wouldn't need to yell over the roaring waterfall. She wouldn't apologize for her choices, but she *was* willing to present a peace offering. In their short time together, she'd learned that knowledge was the one thing Zelnor couldn't resist.

"Any question?" Zelnor asked.

"Anything besides who's chasing me. Or these." Erianna pointed to her scars.

"All right," Zelnor agreed, and after a moment's consideration, she asked, "Why do you look so different from Seshvin?"

Erianna's skin flared briefly with surprise. Of all the questions, she hadn't expected Zelnor to ask that.

"Sorry," Zelnor said. "That sounds bad. I didn't mean—It's just, I've never met another ishlanian, and I don't know a lot about them, and I wondered if there were different races of ishlanians, I guess? Felsha'kor, I'm so sorry."

"I don't mind! But I can't really answer the question. I haven't met many ishlanians. I'm actually half-ishlanian, half-human. Most people don't know the difference, so I'm often mistaken for a full ishlanian and…I tend to think of myself as one. Besides, it's not worth correcting people."

"I can understand that," Zelnor said. "Which parent is which?"

Erianna pursed her lips. "My mother is human."

"I'm guessing you two don't have a very good relationship?" Zelnor probed.

"I said *one* question. You've already asked two."

"They're follow-up questions. You can't tell me that you didn't expect—" Zelnor sighed. "Fine, how about this? You ask me two questions, then you answer mine."

Erianna did not want to talk about her mother, of all people. But she had been wondering about something since the day they'd met. Tonight was her last chance to ask.

"It's about the beard," Erianna said. "How did you grow one? Where did it come from?"

"Well, to answer your first question," Zelnor started.

"Oh no you don't! Those are one question. *One*," Erianna interrupted. "Don't cheat me out of my second one."

"At least let me answer first. Vel'erma's pages!" Zelnor said.

That was exactly what she was going to do. For someone so quiet, the half-elf was unexpectedly shrewd with words sometimes.

"Anyway," Zelnor continued, "every time I cast a spell, this white fur grows on my body, and for a while, it kept growing on my chin, until I had…this."

"Why does it happen?" Erianna asked.

"I don't know. Sometimes I worry that—Never mind. I'm not gonna count that question."

"Thank you for that," Erianna said. "I guess my second question is does it bother you?"

"The beard?" Zelnor asked. "Not really. I mean, it's warm and soft, and it gets pretty cold in Alaspinor, so it's really useful. I used to have to pull my scarf over my face, but now—"

"That's not what I meant. I was talking about people mistaking you for an old man."

"Oh! No, that doesn't bother me. I…"

Zelnor scratched at her beard, keeping her eyes fixed on the ground.

"I guess it's a little weird," she muttered, "but I like it when people mistake me for a man."

"Oh. Then, does it bother you when I refer to you as 'she'?"

"Actually, I'm fine with that too. I'm fine with either." Zelnor smiled, but the expression faltered. "I guess that makes me *really* weird."

"I don't think you're weird," Erianna said. "Although my skin glows, I have gills, and I'm taller than every woman I've ever met, so I suppose I'm not the best person to ask."

"Ha… Yeah." Zelnor smirked. "You're *way* weirder than I am."

"Shut up," Erianna said.

Erianna stuck out her tongue, and the half-elf laughed. As they lapsed into a brief silence to eat their food, Erianna looked out over the dark waters. The moons shimmered on the lake, two separate halves facing the same direction. The tiny blue Cytho huddled close to the large silver Parenus. Two halves that didn't fit together, but still remained at each other's side.

The water rippled in the breeze, causing the moons' reflection to flicker before settling again. Erianna could almost imagine that Lyle caused those ripples, poking his head up out of the water. In moments like these, the city seemed almost peaceful, comforting.

"So, what about your mom?" Zelnor asked.

Erianna's mother…the sole reason that she could never find peace anywhere. If only that witch of a woman would leave her alone.

"We don't get along," Erianna said. "She tried to raise a puppet and didn't take it well when I decided to cut my strings."

"She lives here, doesn't she?" Zelnor asked. "In the city."

Erianna flared brightly, chasing away the darkness with a sudden explosion of teal. *How in Liscuntia's name did Zelnor guess that?* She suppressed the light a moment later, but it was too late. Her reaction had answered for her.

"I'm sorry. It's my fault you're here," Zelnor said.

Erianna combed her fingers through her damp lavender locks.

"It is what it is. At least I'll get a chance to see Porter again."

"Why all the secrecy, anyway? A riddle? A meeting at midnight? It's all a little…"

"Cloak and dagger?" Erianna suggested.

"I was going to say excessive," Zelnor said.

"Well, you can never be too careful when people are chasing you," Erianna said. *Especially when those people are the Broken Claim.*

"Is Porter…dangerous?" Zelnor asked.

"No, he's not. Not at all," Erianna said.

Porter wasn't dangerous, but there was a chance that her mother would have him followed, now that she knew her rebellious daughter was finally back in the city… But he had always been careful. Her mother was the type to set traps, Porter knew that. He would make sure he wasn't followed. This wasn't the first time they'd hidden from her.

Erianna shivered.

Zelnor tossed Erianna's tawny cloak over her shoulders and gestured to the dress and corset Erianna had been wearing earlier, now folded in a neat pile. At some point, Lyle had stopped playing in the water and come back to sit with them. When had he returned? And when had Zelnor gotten Erianna's clothes out? Erianna must have been lost in her own thoughts. It was so unlike her…

"We should go," Zelnor said.

"Just give me a moment to get dressed," Erianna said.

Zelnor immediately spun around. Erianna would never understand the mage. Why would she want privacy to put her clothes back on? Still chuckling, she strung her corset and slipped her flowy, pale pink dress over her head. She paused for a moment, gripping her leather cuirass so tightly her knuckles paled. Porter wouldn't let himself be followed. He wouldn't.

"Erianna?" Zelnor said.

Her two companions were staring with matching frowns. Erianna beamed at them, but it didn't seem to ease their concerns.

"Almost done," she said lightly.

She fitted the cuirass snugly over her torso. Whatever her old friend wanted, she knew it had to be important—he wouldn't have contacted her otherwise. *Everything is going to be fine.* She would meet Porter, get out of this Thorns-damned city, and never, ever come back.

Chapter Fourteen
Eyes in the Dark

Though Zelnor would never admit it to Erianna, she'd enjoyed watching the ishlanian chase the ghost around the lake. She was annoyingly cheerful and smiled often, but even so, those couple of hours were the happiest Zelnor had ever seen her. It made Zelnor feel strangely warm—a feeling that she hadn't hated as much as she thought she would.

But all that joy was gone now. Erianna flinched at the faintest sound, turned at the slightest movement. She scanned every shadow. She had sounded so confident earlier, so sure that she was one step ahead of the people after her, but it was clearly all for show.

Zelnor's mind drifted back to the scars all over Erianna's shoulder. Zelnor suspected the old injuries had come from the ones chasing the bard. Whoever these people were, they'd hurt her before. Erianna was strong enough to fight off a dozen attackers at a time, but somehow these people had gotten the better of her.

Zelnor had a feeling they were heading straight into a trap, but by Felsha'kor's Eternal Flame, she desperately hoped she was wrong.

The volatile nature of her magic made her abilities no better than a candle next to a powder keg. Sure, she'd gotten lucky the past few times. That didn't mean her luck would last forever. What if she accidentally hurt Erianna instead of their attackers? Zelnor couldn't go through that again, but without her elemental magic, she was practically useless.

The lamps in the Slums were poorly maintained. The candles inside some of them had burned down to the width of a single copper, but even in the dim flickering light, Zelnor could see the gem in her wrist sparkling. The dragon's scale shifted from sapphire to emerald and back again.

Pact magic surely wouldn't have the same side effects as her own, but unfortunately, it wasn't an option. Using Torrin's magic for the first time, *tonight* of all nights, would already be a terrible idea, but coupled with the fact that she was planning on betraying Torrin…any attempts at using *that* power would blow up in her face. Maybe literally.

She shuddered at the thought of betraying a dragon. Even the memory of Torrin's searing breath set her legs trembling, but she had no choice. She wasn't going to tell Torrin about the High Mage. She couldn't do that to Devlin, considering how much he'd helped her, and once Torrin realized she'd disobeyed him, he wasn't going to be happy. An unhappy dragon in charge of her magic sounded like the worst idea she had ever had.

And yet, Zelnor could feel the power coming from it. A core of magic centered in her wrist, separated from her own elemental magic but also oddly similar. Why was that? Were elemental magic and pact magic related? Maybe that was what Torrin had wanted to tell her.

Not that it mattered anymore. That door was long closed, even if the dragon didn't know it yet. Besides, that hum of green and blue magic might feel familiar, but its power was nothing compared to the storm of elemental magic she kept at bay on a daily basis.

That's it! Just because Zelnor couldn't use pact magic directly didn't meant she couldn't find some other use for it. Maybe she could drain some magic from the pact to make her own more stable. She still wasn't sure her magic was compatible with Torrin's, or if the dragon would even allow it, but if it did work…Zelnor could help Erianna *and* she'd have a short-term solution to the unpredictability of her magic.

This idea was almost as stupid as just using pact magic, but Zelnor had to try. *Gods, that bard is a terrible influence on me.*

Zelnor held the gem at eye level and coaxed her own magic to the scale. Luckily, it was fairly easy to control, given how recently she'd cast a spell. She hesitated, stopping her magic right before it reached that ball of pact magic coiled in her wrist.

There was a strange tension between the two energies, an intense urge to combine. Zelnor would have found the feeling fascinating, if it wasn't so concerning. She got the feeling that this combination would definitely result in an even worse side effect than usual. A small headache bloomed at her temples as she strained to keep the two of them apart.

Zelnor's foot caught on an uneven patch in the road. Her face headed straight toward the cobblestone.

A hand on Zelnor's shoulder caught her mid-tumble: Erianna had turned at the last moment and stopped her from faceplanting. She squeezed Zelnor's shoulder, before letting her hand fall away. Zelnor couldn't help but feel like Erianna was judging her. She wished she could see her face.

Zelnor felt her magic rush into the dragon scale. The gem glowed sapphire. Her stomach flip-flopped. Her body fizzled with energy. Pins and needles prickled across her skin.

In that one split second before everything went to shit, Zelnor had just enough time to think what an idiot she was.

Erianna could only watch as a dark sapphire mist surrounded Zelnor. Veins of bright white light fractured the billowing cloud, mirrored by the cracks of glowing white growing in her eyes. The white spread through her like a sickness. In seconds, it enveloped her completely.

And then, Zelnor was gone.

"ZELNOR!" Lyle yelled. The ghost searched frantically, going as far as his tether would allow.

It happened again. Erianna wanted to think that Zelnor had just run away or turned invisible, that the display had something to do with Zelnor's strange magic, but she knew better. The scale had *glowed.* It had to be the pact, but the cracks in the mist didn't look right. It wasn't the way Erianna remembered it. That dragon had done something to Zelnor. The bard's skin flared brightly as she thought of the reptile's smug face.

"Torrin," Erianna growled under her breath.

This was what that vile dragon did. He tempted people with promises of power, used them, and disposed of them like pawns. He moved on without another thought of those he'd sacrificed in service of his massive manipulation. *Not this time.* Erianna wouldn't allow Torrin take another life, especially Zelnor's.

"Erianna?" Lyle said.

"She's fine. We'll find her," Erianna said. "Everything is fine."

"Then… Then why are you crying?"

Erianna put a hand to her own cheek, scoffing when she felt tears there. No. No, absolutely not. She wasn't sad. She was *angry.*

That dragon. That Thorns-damned dragon and his sick games. She wiped the water off her face in a few vicious swipes.

"I'm not crying," she said.

Erianna continued down the street, dragging the ghost after her. They were almost there. She was going to meet Porter, and then she would go straight back to Torrin and he was going to make things right. He would bring Zelnor back. If he tried to get out of it again, the overconfident reptile wouldn't live to regret the choice.

The Slum's Temple to Delaith was easily the most modest temple in all of Nirdeem, even before it fell to ruin. Like all buildings in the Slums, it was constructed from the miner's leftovers, rocks of different types and sizes. They had been smoothed down in an attempt to appease the tumultuous goddess, but the temple had been doomed from the start. The place of worship had been built on an incline, and as a result, the left wing of the building had collapsed inward during a particularly bad flood. The rubble had obliterated the simple wooden pews inside, littering the interior with bits of splintered wood and chunks of heavy rock.

From this angle, Erianna and Lyle couldn't see inside. She considered the possibility that she might be walking directly into an ambush, but she strode through the open doors anyway, ignoring her instincts. She didn't care anymore.

Erianna picked her way over the pile of debris in front of the entrance. A figure stood at the pulpit on the opposite side of the temple. His messy black hair, peppered with gray, and the hunch to his shoulders, the slight tremble of his right hand that could only be stilled by clasping it with the other... It was Porter!

Erianna barreled forward. Tripping and nearly tumbling to her knees, she righted herself and finally reached Porter, throwing herself into his arms. He stumbled backward with a soft *oof* before he wrapped his arms around her back.

As Erianna hugged him, she felt her breathing slow, and the fierce teal glow that hadn't dimmed since Zelnor disappeared finally faded. Gods, she'd missed Porter. It had been too long.

He held her at arm's length to look up at her, his eyes shimmering in the moonslight.

"You've grown even taller," the man said.

"Maybe you've just gotten shorter," Erianna said.

"Maybe I have." Porter chuckled.

Her old friend's stare turned uncomfortably perceptive.

"What's wrong?" he asked.

"Nothing," Erianna lied.

He frowned, but didn't push the issue.

"Anyway, Porter, this is—"

Erianna started to introduce Lyle, before she realized that they didn't know if Porter could see ghosts. Lyle waved a hand in front of Porter's face, and the man stared through it, not even blinking. Lyle mumbled something about keeping watch around the area and drifted away.

"Never mind," Erianna said. "More importantly. The note. Why did you want—"

"—to meet?" he finished. "I know it's dangerous. But there were things I wanted to give you before…"

Porter looked over Erianna's shoulder. Erianna turned and peered into the darkness, but she didn't see anyone.

"Nothing. It's—It's nothing," Porter said. "I'm just a paranoid old man."

"You're sure you weren't followed?" Erianna asked.

"I was careful. I just pray that I was careful enough," Porter said. "Regardless, I can't be away long. Here."

Porter handed her a familiar, leatherbound storybook.

"The book of Gealtalmhn fairytales," Erianna said.

"It was always supposed to be a gift for you. I held onto it, so Plindurin wouldn't take it. Your—*Someone* very important asked me to give it to you, years ago. I should've gotten it to you sooner."

Erianna flipped absently through the pages, tracing her fingers along an illustration of a young girl collapsed in a snowy forest.

"Thank you," she whispered.

Porter reached down and pulled something out of his boot, placing it on top of the open book. It was a dagger. Its bright, well-polished silver hilt curled into a wave collapsing in on itself, a pearl set at its center. She held the blade up in the moonslight, using her other hand to snap the book shut and tuck it into her backpack.

The small weapon was stowed in an iron sheath, far simpler in design than the delicate dagger. It was obviously a replacement for whatever fancy scabbard the blade had come with initially. Erianna unsheathed the dagger and saw opals inlaid into the silver blade at even intervals. She started to ask Porter why he'd given her such an ornate weapon—she already had a much more functional one— when she finally recognized it.

"This was my father's," Erianna said.

"Yes, and it's the key to finding him again," Porter said.

Erianna's head snapped back up.

"I don't know how he got it back to me without Plindurin noticing," Porter continued.

Erianna glared at the weapon. Her father *would* send her some fancy, useless dagger. It was just like him.

"Erianna, please. Give him the opportunity to explain, to apologize. He had no choice," Porter said.

"He did have a choice. He chose himself," Erianna spat.

The rubble shifted with a loud clatter. Erianna looked up and saw shadows darting through the darkness. There were eyes on them. Eyes everywhere. How had she not noticed them sooner?

Lyle flew back toward them.

"It's those black-cloaked people!" he shouted.

"They're here," Erianna said to Porter.

"You need to run," Porter whispered.

Erianna stared at the man who'd raised her, the man who was more family to her than her own blood. He was asking her to leave him behind. They would punish him, torture him in ways that would shock the god of cruelty Himself. Kalkor's Fury paled in comparison to the Broken Claim's.

"Go," Porter repeated.

Erianna wanted to argue, but the dark expression on her old friend's face left no room for debate. He would die protecting her if she didn't leave now. So, she turned away from him. And she ran.

As Erianna careened out the door, she burst through a crowd of people in blank masks and dark cloaks. Her skin glowed like a beacon in the night. It didn't matter anymore. The Broken Claim had found her.

Erianna raced in the opposite direction. She needed to reach the South Gate. The Claim wouldn't send the vocarii into the desert—their corpse puppets couldn't survive in intense heat—and the living members were forbidden from crossing into Kialma'keer. Plindurin wasn't above breaking her own rules, but no one would dare violate them without her permission. Crossing the southern border would at least give Erianna a head start.

Torches flickered in the dark streets. They disappeared and reappeared behind buildings, as more Claim members circled around to join the hunt.

Erianna gripped the silver dagger tightly. It would be close, but she was fast, faster than anyone in the Claim. She could outrun her pursuers.

Torches appeared ahead of her. They were trying to cut her off.

Godsdammit, she should've expected this. She could fight them off, but she'd lose precious time. And while she had more than enough strength to handle two dozen Claim members, if she had to fight more than a handful of vocarii, she was screwed.

Erianna swerved around the new group. *Not far now.* Just a few more turns and then it was a straight shot out. She could hear footsteps on all sides. Someone dashed out of the shadows, grabbing her backpack. The motion set her off balance as two other figures lunged at her.

Suddenly, the three Claim members flew backward. It was Lyle! The ghost had used his abilities to push them away.

Erianna sprinted forward with a burst of speed. She was so close. The South Gate was within reach. She could just see the top of it.

She rounded the last corner, and the South Gate came fully into view. An army of blank masks were lined up in front of the exit. They had been waiting for her.

For Liscuntia's sake! Why had Erianna come back to Nirdeem? She was an idiot to think she could avoid the Broken Claim here, of all places. The city where their leader lived. The place where the foul organization had started.

One of the figures stepped away from the group, sauntering up to Erianna. Even with his face covered, she recognized one of the Claim's most dangerous members. Plindurin never used his name, but he often watched her "sessions" in The Spider's Nest. She called him the Observer.

The man placed a cold steel blade against her neck. The crowd looked on with their blank, expressionless masks.

Erianna couldn't fight them all off, even with Lyle's help. It was over. They would take her back and make sure she never escaped again. But she wasn't going to make it easy for them.

Erianna pulled away. The knife scraped across her neck. She

kicked the Observer between his legs, and the man collapsed into a groaning, pitiful heap. She leaped backward, unsheathing the silver dagger and brandishing it at the remaining Broken Claim members.

Even with their masks on, she could feel their incredulous stares. They knew that she wouldn't win a fight against all of them. Someone twice as skilled as Erianna wouldn't be able to take on so many. She couldn't do this; even with her unnatural strength, she didn't stand a chance. In less than a minute, the other group would catch up, and Erianna would be surrounded.

Blood trickled onto Erianna's shoulder. Her neck stung, but the wound didn't hurt nearly as much as the thought of going back. Nothing was worse than becoming her mother's puppet again. No options. No life. No hope.

Erianna had had enough. Enough of manipulators like Torrin and Plindurin. Of all the people who tried to take advantage of her. Of everyone constantly trying to tear her down, to mold her, to use her. People who took away the few things she had left to care about.

"Step. Aside," Erianna growled.

A thick, ebony shadow flowed out of her palms, winding up her arms. Her breath caught in her throat. *What in Thorns' bloody name is this?*

She flicked her wrists, trying to dislodge the shadows, but they shot forward instead. The darkness latched onto the crowd of Broken Claim members. They screamed, in almost perfect unison, and gripped at their own faces. Some of them even threw off their masks. The vocarii waited for orders that weren't coming.

Erianna didn't waste a moment. She rushed past them into the harsh Kialma'keeran desert, their anguished cries fading behind her.

Chapter Fifteen
The Endless Dunes

Erianna kept running, her feet struggling against the sand. She ran until her calves burned and dry air forced her to take ragged, labored breaths. It felt like hours passed before she finally slowed and plopped down behind a tall sand dune. Lyle huddled next to her, curled up tightly to avoid being seen; Erianna was too tired to point out that they likely couldn't see him anyway.

She strained her ears. They could be sneaking between the dunes even now. It was night, and with it came cool temperatures and the cover of darkness. It was unlikely: The vocarii could only pursue her until the sun rose again, after all, and it was too soon for the living members to have gotten permission to follow. She hoped.

"Lyle," Erianna whispered. "Could you…?"

Erianna gestured to the top of the dune they hid behind, and the ghost nodded. He floated upward and peeked over the edge. Erianna didn't dare move.

"I think they're gone," Lyle said. "I don't see any lights…"

"No movement either?" Erianna asked.

He popped back up again and returned a moment later, shaking his head. Erianna pressed her back into the mountain of sand behind her. It seemed like they were letting her go. For now. They probably didn't think it was worth sending the vocarii into the desert. Or maybe they were still too injured to give orders.

What had happened them, anyway? Those living shadows, and the way the Claim members had just…collapsed, it was odd. She'd never seen anything like it before.

"What are we going to do now?" Lyle asked.

Erianna dug her hands into the dune. *Great question. I've got no Thorns-damned idea!* But she couldn't say that to a child. Not after everything he'd just seen. The edges of his form flickered slightly with exhaustion, and the little noble hugged his arms so tightly around himself that she was afraid he would collapse. Lyle was obviously looking to her for direction. Gods, she hated being the responsible adult.

"We go back to Torrin and find out what happened to Zelnor," Erianna said, with as much confidence as she could muster.

"All right… Not sure who this Torrin person is, but if he can help, then that's good. So, where is he, exactly?" Lyle asked.

Oh no. The ghost had inadvertently pointed out a major flaw in their plan.

"Torrin is a dragon, and Zelnor's pact with him is why she disappeared," Erianna explained. "His lair is…in Alaspinor."

"Is that a problem?"

"Well…"

It was a *big* problem, actually. They needed to go back the way they came, and the quickest way to Alaspinor was through Nirdeem, but she was never going back to that city. That really only left two options: climbing over the Reindune Mountains or sailing up the continent on the Ethnarian Ocean.

The mountains would be faster and cheaper. Although, the path would be difficult and even getting that close to the city felt like a risk. Even so, it still seemed like the best option, if they had the supplies for it.

Erianna pulled her backpack off and rummaged through its contents. She delicately placed the storybook in the sand and tossed the silver dagger on top of it. She removed her dresses and found there was more than enough bread and dried meat, along with books about light magic (when had Zelnor put those there?) and her map of Alaspinor. When she'd emptied her backpack completely, she realized there was something missing. Something *very* important.

"Water," Erianna said. "Zelnor was carrying the water."

"You don't have any water?" Lyle asked.

"Nope." She laughed sharply. "Well, shit."

No water. She was in the desert, and she had no godsdamned water. And to make matters worse, her map only showed Alaspinor. The map that the High Mage had given Zelnor, the one of Eltun? That was also still with the half-elf. So, no water, no map, and no going back. Wonderful.

"But! What are you gonna do?" Lyle stuck his head in her empty backpack, searching in vain and reemerging even more upset. "Without water, you'll—"

"It's fine," Erianna said. "I'll think of something. I always do."

Water…water. How could she get more without going back to Nirdeem? Think. *Think.* There had to be somewhere she could go. Some kind of town or…

A town! That was it. How could she have forgotten?

"Zelnor's hometown!" Erianna exclaimed. "She said it was close to the border. It's called…something Mesa? They'll definitely have water."

It was one of the first things the mage had told Erianna, back when they had only just met. Unfortunately, Erianna didn't know exactly where to go. It's not like Zelnor had given directions, but it was a start.

"We'll head there tomorrow," Erianna said.

The ghost started to say something but hesitated.

"What is it?" Erianna prompted.

"Your neck. Is it all right? Does it hurt?" the ghost asked.

Erianna's hand shot toward the wound on her neck. She'd completely forgotten it was there. The blood had stopped, but now that he mentioned it, the wound still stung. Luckily, it was close enough to her jaw that it hadn't reached her gills. Though, given how shallow the wound was, that was likely no accident. It had been more a warning than a threat.

The scratch would probably heal on its own. Hopefully, anyway… And even if it didn't, she couldn't risk light magic. She couldn't afford to lose herself like that again, not when there was a chance the Broken Claim might follow her here. Besides, she'd used up all her bandages. She would have to wait to treat it until they reached the town.

"Don't worry about it," Erianna said. "Just rest for now."

After a long pause, Lyle nodded and curled up into a little puff of smoke. He hovered close by, almost as if he were trying to comfort her. Running her hands over her face, she fell back into the sand and stared up at the stars.

Erianna had made a real mess of things this time. The Broken Claim had almost caught her, and she knew that Porter would pay the price for her escape… He was strong. And her mother knew how much she cared about him, so she wouldn't hurt him, right? At least, not without healing him again afterwards.

Gods, she was an awful person. Why hadn't she asked Porter to come with her? Why had she just *left him behind?*

Her eyes darted toward the ornate dagger. She had no interest in seeing her father again. Did the asshole really think he could just wander back into her life whenever he pleased?

Erianna hurled the dagger into the bottom of her bag. She would sell it the first chance she got. Let someone else find the bastard.

She shook out one of her rumpled dresses and began packing everything into her bag again. Her hand stilled on the leatherbound book, pulling it into her lap. Today was the first time she'd ever held it. Porter always guarded it, hiding it whenever anyone got close. He had read it to her and showed her the pictures, but it had always been their secret.

Gently, Erianna opened the cover. To her surprise, it had an inscription.

"To Midnight," she read aloud. "May your future be free from shadow."

Midnight... What a strange pet name.

Erianna had no idea what it meant, but Porter definitely hadn't written it. She would recognize his handwriting. She'd seen it often enough, when he was teaching her to write. He had mentioned that this book had been a gift to her, and it was obviously not a gift from her mother. But if not her, then who? Honestly, Erianna wasn't sure this gift was even meant for her. No one she knew called her Midnight.

Erianna wished Porter had gotten the chance to give her more of an explanation. Why give her this book now? Who was the gift-giver to her? And how was a knife supposed to lead her to her father, anyway? Erianna huffed and flopped back down onto the sand. None of it made any sense. Maybe Porter had finally cracked under the pressure. Considering all that time spent under her mother's thumb, it wasn't impossible... The thought pained her.

"I'll deal with it tomorrow," Erianna mumbled. "I'll deal with all of it...tomorrow."

Erianna awoke from a dreamless, peaceful sleep. The first rest in a full month that hadn't come with a nightmare about her past. *So, Celrelborain has finally taken pity on me,* she thought wryly. A small mercy, considering that she'd somehow gotten drenched in sweat.

Based on the sun's position, it couldn't have been more than an hour or two into the morning, but the heat was already unbearable. Erianna sat up and shifted uncomfortably, trying to get rid of the sand that had somehow found its way into every little divot and gap in her garments and stuck to her skin. Finally, she gave up. It was never coming out again.

The sand must have gotten into the cut on her neck too. It was already swollen. She touched a finger to the wound and winced at the little shock of pain. *This is going to be a very long day.*

"Good morning," Lyle said.

"Morning," Erianna replied. "Been up for a while?"

"Uh…" He scratched the back of his head. "A little while."

Erianna chuckled. He'd probably been awake for hours.

"Well, let's get going, then."

Erianna jumped to her feet and slung her bag onto her back. Regrettably, she didn't see any mesas nearby, but she hadn't really expected to. If the town were that close, she would've spotted it last night. She would just have to pick a direction and hope for the best.

Erianna closed her eyes and clasped her hands together. *Please, Ireeshnem. Please let me pick the right direction.* She wasn't usually much for praying, especially not to that particular goddess, but they could use all the luck they could get.

When she opened her eyes again, she'd decided. South. They

were going to head directly south. And then, if they were fortunate, they would spot the town, and they could change course accordingly.

Erianna started walking with confidence, but soon her steady gait became more of a trudge. The sand made every step feel as though she was wading through syrup. As the sun crawled from morning to afternoon, its bright light bore down on her, and beads of sweat dripped into her eyes. A searing wind blew grains of sand into her mouth. She spluttered, sticking out her tongue.

Erianna plopped onto the ground for a rest and a quick meal. The salt-cured meat stung the inside of her cheeks. Her throat was raw with thirst.

The journey only got worse from there. Her head started throbbing and her mouth felt drier than parchment. The scratch on her neck burned, and at some point, it had started bleeding again. And through all of it, there was the heat. The intolerable, inescapable fire was cooking her alive.

Lyle floated next to her, moving his legs as though he were walking. It might have been convincing too, if it weren't for the fact that he glided through the sand without any resistance. Every so often, the ghost glanced at her, started to say something, stopped, and looked away again. This little pattern went on for a few minutes, before Erianna finally halted in her tracks and turned to him.

"What?" she asked flatly.

"I—" Lyle frowned. "I just thought that maybe…you should take a break?"

Erianna rubbed her fingers against her temples.

"I'm all right. We're almost there. I don't need one."

"But—"

"I said I'm fine!" she snapped.

The desert swam around her. Was it the heat that caused everything to ripple like that? Everything started spinning. Her heart pounded loudly, a rapid drumbeat that echoed in her head. It was making her headache much worse. Why did her head hurt so badly?

Erianna fell to her knees. It was all spinning too fast. She just felt so tired and *thirsty*. She needed to rest. Just for a moment. She'd get up again…in just a few minutes…

Lyle was about to insist Erianna rest when she suddenly collapsed. Was she taking a break? No, it was too sudden. She must have passed out. Was it the wound or the lack of water?

"Erianna?" Lyle said. "Erianna!"

She wasn't responding. Something was definitely wrong. Her lips were dry, and her shoulders and face were both slightly purple. At least, she still had that faint gray glow around her. That was a good sign, right? That had to mean she was still alive.

The ishlanian groaned and muttered about water.

Plants have water. Lyle searched frantically around them. If he could just find a plant, *any* plant that he knew, maybe he could get some. But all he saw were dry, twiggy looking bushes and spiky plants. Somehow, he doubted that either of them had any water in them.

"Even if I could find a plant, how would I get the water out?"

Lyle smacked the sand with his hand. It remained undisturbed. He *hated* being a ghost sometimes. He was so helpless. All he could do was lift things, and not even for very long.

But that was something, right? Erianna had said they were close to Kezeek Mesa. He didn't know what a mesa looked like, but he would recognize a town when he saw it, and at this point, any town would do. He just needed to drag her to someone who could help.

Lyle nodded to himself. He held out his hands and focused, watching his friend slowly lift a couple inches off the ground. He towed her forward at an agonizing pace. She was so much heavier than anything he'd lifted since he'd gotten his new limitations.

He hauled her a few more feet before the edges of his hands started to flicker and distort. *No! Not yet.* They needed to get farther. She had said they were almost there. He couldn't give up now.

Lyle's eyelids drooped, and his body started to fade.

No, no…

Erianna's body thudded back to the ground. Lyle held his hands out, trying to lift her up again, but he could barely keep his eyes open.

"H-Help," Lyle cried weakly, even though he knew no one could hear him.

He saw someone crest the dune. For a moment, just one blissful moment, his heart leaped into his throat. Someone had really come to save them! But then he saw the backlit, cloaked figure rushing toward them, just like those evil people who were chasing them in Nirdeem. They'd finally caught up.

In a burst of energy, Lyle reached out his hands and lifted Erianna again. He couldn't get her fully off the ground, so he dragged her through the sand instead. He pulled her behind a dune and covered the ishlanian in sand. He couldn't let them find her. He hoped it was enough.

His form flickered, and he fell asleep.

Chapter Sixteen
Shelter

Erianna dreamed of something cool against her lips, just the smallest sip of what she so desperately craved, but she was barely able to drink a drop before it was removed again. Through her squinted eyes, she saw the blurry outline of an elf, with golden skin sparkling in a shaft of sunlight. She heard soft footfalls and a muffled *click* as the tall woman retreated from the room. Erianna tried to call after her, but she could hardly manage a croak.

Groggily, Erianna flipped over again and drifted back to sleep. *Back to sleep?* Could you fall asleep in dreams? The thought faded with her consciousness.

Erianna awoke again in a dimly lit room. Her hands immediately darted to her neck. It hurt more than before, but it stung of alcohol now. Someone had cleaned it and wrapped it securely in bandages. The bed beneath her bowed, a simple cot made from a tanned hide with a single, rather lumpy, pillow.

As she sat up, she saw a crowded desk, filled with objects, with a very important one in the center: a pitcher of water. Her throat suddenly felt very dry. She lunged for it, but her hand stopped mid-way when a note in bold letters caught her eye.

DRINK SLOWLY OR YOU'LL GET SICK it said in tidy, square handwriting. Erianna scowled at the note but did as it asked, pouring the water into the glass next to it and taking careful sips. It was maddening, not drinking it all in one gulp, so she cast about for a distraction, settling on exploring the little room.

She turned up the oil lamp, throwing everything else on the desk into sharp relief. A place for the pitcher and cup had been carved through a wide variety of items, so numerous that a few of them had spilled over onto the floor. The room's owner had accumulated an eclectic collection of rocks, crystals, and stones of all shapes, sizes, and colors; various strangely shaped sticks; and other assorted bits and bobs: shards from pots, bottles, and even little carved figures.

Across the room from the bed, a small stack of thin and well-maintained books was tucked neatly in the corner. Based on the bright colors, prominent pictures, and length, she would guess they were intended for a child. A child's room, then? Perhaps the son or daughter of whoever rescued her.

Erianna's backpack rested against the door, a small wisp of smoke floating just above it. She set her glass aside as it occurred to her that her supposed "savior" may very well have robbed her. She rifled through her bag. She counted her coins: the exact amount she'd had before. Everything else was where it belonged, too. Frankly, she really didn't have much worth stealing in the first place.

But that didn't mean she could trust this person yet. The Broken Claim wanted her, so she would probably fetch a hefty ransom—far more than the measly change in her coin purse. She might be a prisoner instead of a guest. She tried the door: it was unlocked. Well, that was a good sign, at least.

It's a shame that Lyle is sleeping. He might have seen what happened.

Erianna wandered into the next room. The main living area had a few chairs gathered near a cooking hearth and a dining area near a freestanding cabinet on the other side. It was a small and unexceptional house. Unexceptional but for the gigantic portrait on the wall. It seemed so out of place in the rustic home that it was impossible for the eyes not to be immediately drawn to it.

Almost as tall as the wall itself, the painting was of a family: a human man, an elven woman, and a child, even younger than Lyle. The elf stood with her back straight and a stern expression on her face. She was easily the tallest figure in the painting, at least a few inches taller than the man. She had hardened hazel eyes, a square jaw, and a narrow, angular nose—the antithesis of femininity. Her long, chestnut hair was pulled together into a severe bun that transitioned into a long ponytail down her back. Her skin had a peculiar golden glisten to it.

The young girl standing between her parents inherited very little from her mother: skin a few shades darker, amber eyes, and considerably less pointed, half-elven ears. The only resemblance to her mother lay in the chestnut hair, braided simply and practically, and the matching scowl. Erianna chuckled, imagining the young girl asking over and over to go back out and play.

But it was the father in the portrait who really caught Erianna's attention. The man looked exactly like Zelnor. He had her round, amber eyes, wide nose, and narrow face. His shoulder-length hair was unbound except for a single braid in front. The braid was even on the same side as the mage's!

But it wasn't Zelnor.

The man's face had wrinkles and lines that hers didn't. His skin was darker, his hair jet black with only a few hints of white. And as a human, obviously, his ears were rounded where they should come to slight point. But the biggest difference: he was absolutely beaming, his arm wrapped tightly around his pouting daughter's shoulder. He looked just a moment away from bursting into laughter. Erianna had never seen Zelnor with a look of such unadulterated joy on her face.

How was it such an uncanny likeness? Why did this man look so very much like Zelnor? Erianna reached out her hand, fingertips just barely brushing the smooth canvas. She had a sneaking suspicion that this man might be...

"Kezok," said a sharp voice behind her.

Erianna gasped and stepped away from the painting. When she turned, she saw the elven woman from the picture: long, graying chestnut hair, tall, and much more intimidating in person.

"S-Sorry?" Erianna stuttered, not sure what else to say.

"That's my husband, Kezok Fahra'keen," the woman repeated.

The elf pushed past her. She put a rabbit carcass on a small table and started skinning it. Erianna's attention drifted back to the painting. She couldn't get over how...similar the two looked. It was like staring at Zelnor's double.

"I'd love to meet him," Erianna said.

"He passed away. Years ago," the woman said. "Go to the cabinet, get me the red-brown powder."

Gods, Erianna was an idiot. She had just learned that Zelnor's father had passed away. That is, if this man really was Zelnor's father. The elven woman cleared her throat, and the bard moved across the room to get the spice she'd asked for. There were, as it turned out, several different spices that all looked reddish-brown, and after bringing the wrong one twice, the elf got what she wanted herself.

"Cut these," the elf ordered. "You do know how to cut?"

The stern woman held some kind of pale gourd. She eyed Erianna with skepticism, and the bard snatched the vegetable from her.

"Of course," Erianna said.

The two worked side-by-side in silence for a while. The woman only spoke to give Erianna more tasks. She was brusque and straight-forward, but after Erianna completed a few steps successfully, the elf's tone softened ever so slightly. As Erianna stirred a stew in a large pot, she tried again.

"My name is Erianna," she said.

"Keep an even motion," the elven woman said as she corrected her stirring technique.

"Thank you for saving me," Erianna persisted.

Erianna adjusted her grip on the spoon and continued stirring. She thought they would lapse into silence again, but the woman paused her work, wiping her hands on a towel.

"Someone left you on my doorstep," the elf said. "If I'd found you, I would have been tempted to leave you. Wandering alone with no protective gear and no water, so close to a vaal'akkar den. And an ishlanian, no less."

Erianna was about to ask what in Liscuntia's name a "vaal'akkar" was when the last part of the woman's statement sunk in.

"What does my being ishlanian have to do with anything?"

"Sun sensitivity and tendency toward dehydration," the woman said.

Erianna hadn't known that ishlanians were sensitive to sunlight. It would explain why the heat felt so overwhelming, and why her father had never left The Spiral Cup during the day. She had never had any issues with heat before, but then again, Alaspinor was cool and damp even during the Warm Season.

"I'm only half-ishlanian," Erianna argued.

"You still obviously have *some* sensitivity to the sun. I've never seen anyone get dehydrated so rapidly," the elf said. "Although, the Daeyarus's flower likely accelerated your dehydration."

"Daeyarus's flower..." Erianna repeated.

That explained her wound's rapid deterioration, and the ensuing sluggishness. She should have realized sooner. Only Plindurin's most trusted human agents had access to it, and the toxin was a favorite of the Observer. She'd watched him pull in deserters, nearly delirious with exhaustion, stumbling over their own feet.

"A poison. It's a common tactic of the Broken Claim's when pursuing someone."

How does she know that?

"But I don't have anything to do with them," Erianna lied.

The elf gestured toward Erianna's leg.

"I saw your tattoo. I needed to ensure that there weren't any other poisoned wounds before I treated you. I apologize for invading your privacy," she said.

Erianna paled, her skin emitting a dim glow. There were many scars on her body that she would prefer stay hidden but none more than that Thorns-damned tattoo. She'd tried cutting, burning, even acid, but it was still there. It would *always* be there.

"Refugees from the Claim will always have a place here," the elf said.

"Thank you," Erianna whispered.

The elven woman nodded, spooning the stew into two bowls and setting them on the table. Erianna slid into the seat across from the woman who might or might not be Zelnor's mother. To say that it felt awkward would be grossly understating it, but she was starving.

The stew smelled amazing and tasted even better. It was well seasoned, with a spiciness that built at the back of the throat, perfectly countered by the soft vegetables and the sweet fruit on the side. Erianna hadn't expected something that looked so drab to have so much flavor, but she found herself completely devouring it, abandoning any semblance of conversation beyond a muffled "thank you."

Erianna pushed the bowl aside and considered her next move. It had been at least two days. Plindurin had certainly sent a legion of living Claim members by now. Erianna would have a difficult time evading them long enough to make it to the Reindune Mountains. Even if she made it there, the temperature was low enough for the vocarii to follow her as well. She'd have no hope of escaping Plindurin then. Erianna had to travel through the desert and journey back by ship. But would Zelnor last that long? What had Torrin done with her?

Things had been so much simpler when avoiding the Claim was Erianna's only concern.

"Do you have anything to drink?" Erianna asked.

"You have a drink already," the elf said. She gestured to the partially filled water glass next to Erianna's empty bowl.

"Nothing stronger?"

"You've just recovered," the woman said.

"Please… It's been a long day," Erianna said.

The elven woman rose from her chair and retrieved a large green bottle from the cabinet. Erianna had seen it when she'd gone on her fruitless mission for that "red-brown" spice, but she had assumed it was some kind of syrup or sauce. It seemed just a touch too viscous to be anything alcoholic. Apparently, she'd been wrong. The woman pulled out a glass and uncorked the bottle. Immediately, the room filled with a sweet, heady fragrance. She tipped the bottle and filled the cup a quarter of the way with the thick, auburn liquid.

"Not having any?" Erianna asked.

"Some things cannot be forgotten, no matter how strong the liquor," the woman said.

Maybe it wouldn't erase Erianna's problems or her painful memories, but at the very least, she could gain a reprieve from them.

"Won't stop me from trying," Erianna said.

She grabbed the bottle and filled her glass the rest of the way up. The elven woman's eyes widened.

"Duur'een wine is *very* strong. I would not recommend starting with so much," she advised.

"I may not look it, but this is hardly my first time drinking," Erianna said.

The elven woman frowned and inhaled sharply. She opened her mouth only to snap it shut again.

"It is your choice," she said.

Erianna lifted her glass.

"Thank you for everything, Mrs. Fahra'keen."

The woman shook her head. "It's Lia. I have no family name, and I don't use my husband's."

"Oh. All right. Well, to you, Lia."

Erianna raised her glass and turned it nearly vertical, downing the contents all at once. It burned all the way down and left the taste of sweet smoke lingering on her tongue.

Erianna's head pounded, almost worse than when she'd been lost in the desert. She clutched a green, glass bottle tightly in her hand. It was smaller than the bottle that she'd finished the night before but otherwise identical. Had she been considering drinking more, even in her near unconscious stupor? Probably. That sounded like her.

She shut her eyes against the aggressive brightness streaming in from the window. It had been quite some time since her memory had gone fuzzy from the joys of alcohol, and it was time to play her least favorite game: what on Tularien had she done and said last night?

From what she could recall, her behavior had been fairly tame. No belting out songs or dancing on tables, just a long, if overly honest, chat with her host. Lia had mentioned she ran a shelter, and told Erianna about a heavily scarred woman that she had taken in once. Somone had lost her daughter, but Erianna couldn't remember if it was the scarred woman or Lia.

At some point, Erianna had regaled Lia with her visit to Nirdeem. That memory was a bit clearer. She'd described the haughty High Mage, their trip to the lake in the Slums, and then…she'd mentioned Zelnor.

"Oh shit."

Erianna had cried in front of Lia. The moment she had uttered Zelnor's name, she had started *bawling*. She had sobbed for…minutes? Hours? She wasn't sure. Liscuntia, she hadn't cried that much in her entire life, not even as a child. And gods only knew she'd had plenty to cry about back then.

"Are you all right?" Lyle asked.

Erianna startled. She hadn't noticed the ghost there in the corner. Gods, she hoped that he hadn't been around to see her make a fool of herself. How was she going to face Lia now? Maybe Erianna could slip away without the elf noticing.

Knock, knock, knock. Three firm raps on the door crushed that fledgling hope.

Erianna was never, ever praying to Ireeshnem again. She'd never had worse luck than over these last two days. *Goddess of Luck my ass. Nothing more than a sailor's superstition.*

Reluctantly, she opened the door to an impatient Lia waiting on the other side. The elf's eyes darted toward the duur'een wine she was still holding, and she hastily hid the bottle behind her back. With a look of deep disappointment, Lia shoved a white bundle at Erianna.

"Get changed," Lia said.

After delivering the order, the woman turned on her heel and left.

Lyle followed her into the next room to give Erianna some privacy.

The cotton shirt and baggy pants fit loosely and covered every scrap of skin from her collarbone to her ankles. She frowned as she examined herself in a full-length mirror. It was the least attractive outfit she'd ever worn. Erianna was tempted to take it right off again, but she didn't. This unflattering garb was likely part of the "protective gear" Lia had mentioned before dinner. Well, that or some kind of diabolical punishment for overindulging last night.

Her eyes widened at the last garment. *Oh gods, that hat.* Now Erianna was certain these clothes were a punishment. It was a floppy, pale blue thing with white cotton sewn around three-quarters of it, forming a little screen. It would provide shade…at a very high cost. The hat almost made the outfit look good by comparison.

Glumly, she collected the extra shirts and pants Lia had given her, along with the green bottle and the pink dress she'd been wearing the past couple of days. She sniffed her dress and her face crumpled reflexively. Musty. She would need to add it to her laundry, though Liscuntia only knew when she'd find enough water to clean it again. Erianna went to put the dress away and paused. Her bag was missing.

"Where has it gone?" Erianna asked herself.

Lyle popped his head through the wall.

"Lia moved it," he said.

"She hasn't looked through my things, has she?" Erianna asked.

"Nope. She's putting things in."

Lia had set the large backpack on the table and was just fastening the latches as Erianna entered. Lia lifted several flasks, sloshing with water, and affixed them to the side of the bag. Erianna watched her secure no less than ten of them before she was satisfied.

"Do I really need that much?" Erianna asked.

"It's double what you need," Lia said, "which is already double what a human would. However, considering possible accidents or delays and the amount needed to care for your neck, it's still crucial to ration it well and take frequent stops to refill."

Lia didn't have much faith in her, if she thought that Erianna would get lost enough to use ten flasks of water. *She must think I'm an absolute moron after my behavior last night.*

Lia left to grab something, and Erianna slipped the green glass bottle into her backpack. She had a feeling she would need it later, when her mind inevitably reminded her of this embarrassing visit. Thankfully, Lia didn't strike Erianna as much of a drinker, so she likely wouldn't miss one small bottle.

Lia returned, moving Erianna's bag and spreading a map of Kialma'keer across the table. The parchment was already covered in circles and x's.

"The x's are water." The woman pointed. "Underground caves and oases. The canteens I gave you are enough to get between them, even if you lose your way. But it will only last so long."

"Got it," Erianna said, adding quickly, "and before you ask, I can read a map. I promise."

Lia brought her quill in a sweeping line, tracing a route through the x's and carefully bypassing the circles on the map.

"Follow this line as closely as possible. Avoid the circles. They are vaal'akkar territories. Be especially careful here."

Lia pointed to three circles that almost perfectly filled the gap between the mountains and Felsha'kor Canyon. She wrote "Vaal'akkars' Wrath" across the belt of circles. The Path passed through the tiniest sliver of space between two of them.

"What's a vaal'akkar?" Erianna asked.

"It means beasts of life," Lia replied.

"But what are they?" Erianna persisted.

"They are death," Lia said.

"If they're *death*, then why are they called 'life' beasts?" Lyle asked.

Erianna repeated Lyle's question, along with several of her own. What did they look like? Where had they come from? What made these creatures so dangerous? Were the vaal'akkar the reason the Broken Claim was forbidden from entering the desert?

"They are killers. That is all that matters," Lia said. "Fascination with them will do you no favors. And yes, to my understanding, the beasts are responsible for the Claim's law."

"Is there any recourse against them?" Erianna asked.

Lia hesitated. Her hand hovered over a pouch tied to her belt. Finally, she handed Erianna an opaque brown vial. Erianna reached for the stopper, but Lia clicked her tongue.

"Open it *only* when a vaal'akkar is within sight, and throw it as far away as possible," Lia instructed. "It might give you time to get away. I can spare only one. Pray you don't need to use it."

Giving Erianna a mysterious vial and telling her not to open it seemed needlessly cruel. She was sorely tempted to open it immediately, out of spite, but at Lyle's expectant stare, she just dumped the little bottle into her pack.

"I'd prefer you travel with someone else. Traveling in the desert alone is imprudent, even for those who know the Path. I could send Nabir with you?" Lia offered.

Erianna glanced at Lyle, hovering over the table and squinting at the map. He gave her a solemn nod and two thumbs up.

"I think I'll be fine," Erianna said.

Lia furrowed her brow but didn't comment. Instead, she left the house, beckoning Erianna after her with a sharp nod. Lyle rushed out the door after her, eager to see whatever other boons the woman would grant them.

Erianna blew the last lines of ink dry, stowing the map in an outer pouch. Maybe their fortunes were turning around. She was lucky that some kind soul had dropped them off here and even luckier that Lia had taken her in. Despite the woman's abrupt, tight-lipped speech, she really seemed to care.

Erianna slung her bag onto her back. It weighed twice as much with all the extra water, but the difference was negligible for her. She paused, turning to face the painting. The man who bore a striking resemblance to Zelnor gazed at Erianna with his permanent grin.

"I'll find you, Zelnor," she said. "I promise."

And with that, Erianna forced herself to turn away, plunging into the harsh sunlight and nearly running straight into a very strange beast. It stood with its back to her.

Lyle flitted around the creature before finally reaching out to pet it. He pouted when his hand went straight through.

The animal was clearly meant to carry them across the desert, but it was much larger than a horse and looked nothing like one. Even facing away from her, she saw the tall, black horns that curled toward its hump. Its *hump*. She'd never seen an animal like it.

Lia covered the large hump on its back with a tan blanket, before moving to secure something on the other side of it. The creature's chest was the width and shape of a massive barrel, and its muscular legs pronated outward with bent elbows and webbed feet. It was so low to the ground that Erianna had thought it was laying down at first.

She smoothed her hand over the animal's short, gray fur. To her surprise, it started purring. And when it turned its head, she saw a feline face: muzzle, whiskers, and contented yellow eyes slipping closed.

Lia held its reins. Her skin shimmered in the daylight with the faintest golden sheen.

"The cathmal's name is Eli," Lia said. "He moves at the same pace of a healthy young mortal but requires less supplies and rest, so utilize him properly. Give him some of the food I packed and water every two weeks. He can travel for a few days straight after eating, if you find yourself in an emergency."

Lia helped Erianna up onto the cathmal's back.

"I've already fed and watered him. Head south toward the tallest rock. Do not stray from the Path."

"I won't. I'm a great navigator," Erianna assured her.

"Your dressing will need to be changed in a couple days," Lia continued, barely acknowledging the response. "I packed bandages and *medicinal* alcohol. I assume you can take care of your own wound. If you leave it, it will fester."

"I know how to treat it," Erianna said.

Lia nodded. Erianna held out her hands for the reins, but the woman hesitated, clutching them tightly. Erianna smiled, trying to show Lia that she would be fine, that she didn't need to fret over her. Erianna could handle herself, and the elf had more than prepared her for the journey.

Lia looked down at her hands.

"Erianna, I…" Her voice dropped to a whisper. "I hope you find her."

Before Erianna could respond, the stern woman turned and marched back into her house without so much as a goodbye. It was the first time anything had shown through her unflappable exterior. If Lia really was Zelnor's mother, why not say something or ask directly about her daughter? Were the two on bad terms? That would be surprising, considering how kind Lia was. Erianna scratched Eli, and the beast wiggled its stubby tail, purring happily.

"Shall we go?" Erianna asked Lyle.

Lyle only nodded, more focused on trying (and failing) to get the cathmal's attention.

Erianna dug her heels into the cathmal's flanks, and Eli waddled forward with an endearingly wide gait, his torso swaying back and forth in an almost slithering motion. She felt the hairs stand on the back of her neck and looked over her shoulder.

Nothing but empty desert. The living members of the Broken Claim hadn't caught up with her. Not yet. She tightened her hold on the reins.

Chapter Seventeen
Unknown Depths

The first landmark was obvious, even without Lia's map. A green dot on the tan horizon that Erianna and Lyle could see within a week of southeastward travel. They continued to see it in the distance, but it never seemed any closer, no matter how far they went. Erianna might have thought it an illusion or trick, but after nearly another week of trekking across the dunes, they finally arrived.

"Whooooa," Lyle gasped.

Moons' Dance Oasis was filled with bright green trees and underbrush; even the sand looked more vibrant here. A breeze rustled through the tall trees. It seemed almost magical, a small pocket of life in a barren wasteland. Two large, crescent-shaped springs were the centerpiece to the mystical scene, a smaller one tucked inside a bigger one. They reminded Erianna of the moons at the end of each month, when Cytho moved to the center of its sister Parenus. *Must be why they call it Moons' Dance.*

People shuffled in and out of the many tents set up around the Oasis. Kialma'keerans and even a few from Nirdeem gathered water from the springs or enjoyed a quiet meal in the cooler air. Erianna nodded amicably to the nearby travelers. A few of them returned the gesture, but most just stared. Erianna was used to the feeling of eyes on her, unique and talented as she was, but the strangers' gazes felt more pointed than usual.

Maybe because she was an ishlanian in the desert. Or perhaps it was her clothes. Ugly, baggy, and ill-fitting. She wasn't supposed to look like this. She took a shaky breath. *Just ignore them,* she coached herself. She would need to get used to this crowd's judgmental gaze. She and Lyle had already decided to stay the night.

Erianna refilled their empty flasks and directed Eli toward the outskirts of the oasis. Reds, oranges, and yellows filled the sky as the sun dipped behind a distant dune. She unfurled her bedroll and settled onto it.

The hairs stood up at the back of her neck, and a creeping sensation prickled down her spine. Her head darted to the left. At that precise moment, a woman with a crooked nose and bright red hair turned her head in the other direction. Erianna narrowed her eyes and watched the human for a while. The traveler bundled her dark gray cloak around her shoulders, leaning closer to her fire. She kept to herself, not looking over again.

Erianna doubted the woman was a threat. A Broken Claim member would have confronted her already. The stranger was probably just curious. Erianna was an ishlanian in the desert, after all. It was unusual.

Ever since they'd left, Erianna hadn't been able shake the feeling that she was being watched, even when there wasn't anyone around for miles. Vigilance was all well and good, but this feeling veered too close to paranoia for her liking. They had kept a good pace. She hadn't given the Broken Claim any chance of catching up. She couldn't let her fear numb her senses to actual threats later down the line.

"You all right?" Lyle asked.

"I'm fi—" Erianna almost snapped, before she caught herself.

The ghost had been asking her that constantly. Ever since they had left Nirdeem, he was always asking her if she was all right. And he *kept* asking it, no matter how many times Erianna insisted she was fine. She had eventually snapped at him (which she still felt incredibly guilty over), stopping him from inquiring needlessly about her mental state for a time… But now the question was back, and Erianna was too tired to deal with it.

"How are *you?*" Erianna redirected the ghost's question, hoping to distract him.

"Me?" Lyle asked.

"It's only fair."

"I'm worried about Zelnor," he admitted.

The ghost floated down to sit next to Erianna and braced his hands on his intangible knees, staring into his lap.

"I know you said that we'll find her. But…what if she's gone? What if she's dead?"

A young palm tree bowed low to the water as a large-eared animal skittered to the top of its narrow trunk. The creature leaned over and lapped its small tongue through the water, heedless of its precarious position.

What if Zelnor is dead?

Impossible. Torrin was clever. A manipulator like him would never take such a powerful playing piece off the board. Zelnor had to be alive.

But did Erianna really believe there was no chance that the dragon had killed the half-elf? She wouldn't be surprised to learn that Torrin could just vaporize pact-users on a whim. Was it really a coincidence that Zelnor had disappeared mere hours after she'd chosen to betray him? They might already be too late…

"It wouldn't be *so* bad if she died. You would have someone to spend time with," Erianna said.

Lyle's kind features hardened. His eyes sharpened with something that neared hatred. Erianna flinched. The joke had slipped out before she could think better of it.

"Being a ghost is awful," Lyle said. "You can't feel anything. Not the breeze or water. All your other senses are dull. And no one can see you. You're so…so alone."

"Lyle, you're not alone." Erianna's hand hovered over his.

"But Zelnor will be!" Lyle shot upward and turned his back to her. "We can't let this happen to her. I don't want her to die!"

Erianna jumped up and moved in front of Lyle, meeting his eyes to show him she was completely serious.

"Zelnor won't die," Erianna said.

"Do you promise?" he asked.

Lyle stared up at her, and his owlish eyes almost seemed to shine in the fading light. Could ghosts cry?

"I promise," Erianna said. "I promise we'll save her. Whatever it takes."

She stared out at the oasis as she tucked herself into her bedroll. She had made a promise she wasn't sure she could keep, to a child who had already lost everything. She turned over, facing away from the ghost.

Erianna unwrapped the bandages around her neck. As she unwound the last layer, she had to peel the cloth from her skin. The slight tackiness of her injury was reflected in the splotchy yellow stains on the bandages. At least it had finally stopped bleeding.

Erianna had never had a wound heal this poorly before. Granted, the cuts and bruises she had gotten when she was young never had to heal naturally, but she'd been in her fair share of scraps as an adult. A shallow cut like this one shouldn't take over a month to close up. She could partially blame the poison. Daeyarus's flower was famously difficult to remove, traces of it staying in the body weeks after taking the antidote. Erianna supposed it didn't help that she had forgotten to change her bandage those first few nights, nor that grains of sand blew into the injury whenever she took the bandage off.

But taking care of a little cut could hardly be her first concern. With Zelnor facing an unknown fate, could Erianna really be blamed for neglecting something so small? And then, there was the Broken Claim. The fact that Erianna hadn't caught sight of them yet was almost more nerve-wracking than their presence.

Sometimes, just as Erianna awoke in the early morning, she felt the creeping sensation of eyes on her even, though a thorough sweep of their surroundings showed nothing on the horizon. They couldn't have followed this far. Without knowledge of the Path, the vaal'akkar had surely taken care of them by now. More likely, her nerves had tricked her senses.

Unless the Claim could make themselves invisible. A scary thought. She shuddered to think what Plindurin would do with that sort of power.

Erianna cleaned and rewrapped the wound. She set as little water as she could get away with into a pot to boil the soiled bandages. Lia had seemed overly concerned, giving Erianna so many canteens, but now she was grateful for the elven woman's caution. They weren't dangerously low on water yet, but she had used more than she'd expected to.

Erianna brushed the sand before her into a relatively flat space and unrolled Lia's map. Lyle, who'd been watching her change her dressings with poorly disguised worry, flew closer to stare at the map over her shoulder.

"Halfway to Bokest al'Bar," Erianna said.

"So, we're around…?" Lyle's finger hovered over the map.

"Here," she said.

Erianna tapped on a spot less than a mile away from Vaal'akkars' Wrath. Their territories were broad. At the speed Eli traveled, it would take four full days to cross the belt. Erianna had been thinking about this part of their journey for a while. If a vaal'akkar wandered to the edge of its territory at an inopportune moment, they were doomed. There wasn't enough cover to hide from the beasts, and Erianna was not eager to test the last resort Lia had given them. Safe passage through the vaal'akkars' territories would come down to a matter of luck.

Erianna had a plan to pass Vaal'akkars' Wrath, though—one she was sure Lyle wouldn't approve of. It wasn't without its risks, but it could turn the odds in their favor. Ireeshnem willing.

Lyle and Eli slowed to a halt. The sun had set well over an hour ago. Erianna slid off the cathmal's back, and the other two waited for her to set up camp. But she didn't stop. Instead, Lyle felt an unexpected tug at his tether as Erianna hiked her backpack higher on her shoulders and trudged onwards.

"Where are you going?" Lyle asked, flitting next to her.

"Bokest al'Bar," Erianna replied lightly, as though she hadn't disrupted their entire routine.

"That's not what I meant," he said.

Lyle flew in front of her, and Erianna changed course just in time to avoid passing through him. He blocked her path again, making her route as difficult as he could, until she finally answered his unspoken question.

"We're not stopping until we pass through Vaal'akkars' Wrath," Erianna finally said. "The less time we spend here, the less likely we are to run into a vaal'akkar."

Lyle was so shocked that he froze. The statue pulled him forward again as Erianna continued, determined to make the worst decision possible. How could she keep going? It was definitely going to take more than just a day and a night to get through this place. Erianna couldn't possibly stay up that long.

"Don't you trust me?" Lyle asked.

For the first time, Erianna actually paused to look at him.

"Of course," she said.

"I can warn you if they get close," the ghost said.

"I know, Lyle, but by the time you see them, it'll be too late," Erianna said.

It stung, but he knew she was right. He kept watch for their group, but he wasn't much use beyond that. He could barely lift a couple of blankets without needing to rest. He couldn't even help Erianna find Zelnor. What could he possibly do to fend off a monster?

But that didn't make what Erianna was doing any better. She'd make herself sick! And her cut was still looking pretty bad. She needed rest.

"What about Eli?" Lyle said. "Even if you can go for days straight, he can't."

"He'll be all right," Erianna insisted. "Remember, Lia said after cathmal's eat, they can travel for several days at a time."

No matter what arguments Lyle made, Erianna refused to budge. Lyle wished that one of his relatives were here. Academics loved arguing, whereas he had always been bad at it. Maybe Zelnor might have been able to convince the bard? Despite how often they fought, Erianna really seemed to care about Zelnor's opinion.

But no one else was with them, so Lyle could only let himself get dragged along, helpless to prevent what was clearly a terrible decision.

The first night was mostly fine. Erianna seemed in better spirits than usual, telling Lyle Gealtalmhn fairytales about desperate people making terrible choices. They were dark, sometimes even a little scary, but he liked hearing them. He had hoped that she would be okay, that maybe she could deal with the loss of sleep better than he'd expected, but by daybreak she started getting very grumpy, snapping at him whenever he said, well, pretty much anything.

Eventually Lyle stopped trying to make conversation and paid attention to their surroundings instead. The sand stretched on seemingly without end, only broken up by the occasional scruffy shrub or pointy plant. In the distance, he saw a large cluster of mesas, peeking over the Reindune Mountains. The rocks huddled so tightly together that they'd formed one giant mesa. He could just barely make out a few specks that he thought might be a village on top.

At the start of the second night, things somehow got even worse. Erianna bounded through the sand, singing at the top of her lungs, and after about an hour of that strange jubilance, the teal woman could barely move her legs at all. At one point, Erianna was sure she'd seen Zelnor. She ran up to an empty space of desert, waving her hands through thin air. It took Lyle a really long time to convince her that Zelnor wasn't a ghost.

Now, Erianna leaned heavily on Eli. The cathmal bristled at the added weight, unhappy about their endless trek, but not nearly in such poor shape as the ishlanian. She could barely keep her eyes open as she shuffled listlessly through the sand. Lyle had had enough. He couldn't watch his friend do this to herself anymore.

"Erianna," Lyle said.

The bard blinked blearily at him, pushing herself off the cathmal.

"What?" she muttered.

"You need to sleep," he said.

"Sleep? But we're so close."

"Isn't that why you should stop?" Lyle argued. "A few more hours won't really matter."

"Fine," Erianna groaned.

The bard collapsed, hurling her backpack at the ground. The pack burst open and spilled its contents across the sand. Dresses unfurled, the map fluttered into a nearby dune, and the storybook and silver dagger skidded away. Erianna surveyed the carnage, picking through her belongings and emerging with a small green bottle and a little vial.

"I'd forgotten about these," she said.

Erianna toyed with the vial's stopper, slipping a nail under the seal.

"Lia told you not to open it," Lyle warned.

The bard considered his words for scarcely a second, before, *pop*. She broke the seal. *NO!* How was she more of a child than he was?

Erianna swirled the liquid around, bringing it up to her noise. She recoiled. She stuck the vial into the sand and scooted away from it. As annoyed as Lyle was at her blatant disregard for Lia's warning, he couldn't help his own curiosity.

"What does it smell like?" Lyle asked.

"Blood," Erianna said.

Why would Lia give them blood? If the vaal'akkar hated the smell of blood, then why would they kill people in the first place? Lyle flew over to the vial and inhaled deeply. Flowers, rich oils, and peppermint. The fragrance was familiar and much stronger than he'd expected. After his death, scents had become distant. Faint. Maybe he'd known someone who'd used it, and some of what he was smelling was just his memory filling in the gaps? Regardless, the liquid smelled nothing like blood. Erianna really wasn't well…

Erianna tossed the green bottle between her hands. She muttered something about drinking it, and Lyle couldn't suppress his horror at the prospect. Dealing with the sleep-deprived bard was already harder than babysitting his youngest cousins, he couldn't imagine how much worse Erianna would get while drunk. Thermoren's grace, couldn't she just go to sleep?

"Oh fine," Erianna sighed. "I'll stick it into my secret corset pocket. For later."

The bard tucked the bottle under her clothes—which was a huge relief—but she still wouldn't settle. She slumped forward and jerked back up again in a rhythmic motion, fighting against her drowsiness. Just when Lyle was considering reading her a bedtime story, Erianna's eyes sharpened with a startling clarity. She scrambled to her feet and stared at something over Lyle's shoulder.

"Zelnor?" Erianna said.

Eli hissed and skittered away. *Oh no! Where is he going?* Things just kept getting worse! Lyle couldn't leave Erianna alone, not when she was so vulnerable. Maybe, if he could calm Erianna down, they could look for Eli before the cathmal got too far.

Lyle steeled himself for what would likely be another argument with the bard. He just knew she wouldn't budge until he proved that what she was seeing wasn't real. Lyle turned to fly in the direction that she saw "Zelnor," and froze.

There was a figure in the near distance. The desert blurred behind them, like someone had rubbed their hand through a wet oil painting. The harder Lyle looked at it, the more his head reeled. A pinprick white light flickered inside it, and it disappeared.

Was *Lyle* hallucinating now?

Erianna breathed out a little puff of white air, as the temperature dropped. Lyle shivered. He was cold. Ghosts didn't feel the cold.

The figure appeared again, right in front of them. It stood no taller than Erianna, with four arms and thick white fur. It was noseless and eyeless. Its long, cow-like ears were torn nearly to shreds.

"A vaal'akkar," Lyle whispered.

The chill bit into Lyle's cheeks. Everything swam around the creature. It stayed so still that Lyle wondered if he was dreaming. This couldn't be real.

Erianna wasn't moving, either. The quickened mist of her shallow breathing had stopped. Her eyes stayed placid and unblinking. The bard's lips were stuck in that half-hopeful smile she'd worn when she'd thought this *thing* was Zelnor.

With a grinding sound, the vaal'akkar extended one of its upper arms. A symbol glowed bright white on its wrist—a dot with five spirals. More dots flickered to life higher on the creature's arm. The light curled toward them, forming another symbol. Then another and another, until a series of interconnected runes covered the creature's arm. Its eye sockets filled with swirling white magic.

Erianna's long, lavender hair drifted above her head. Her feet left the sand.

Rocks grew over the vaal'akkar's hand, forming sharp claws. It sunk them into Erianna's shoulder and tugged her closer. The bard didn't even flinch.

The vaal'akkar opened its mouth with the horrible grinding of bone against bone.

Lyle threw out his hands, directing all of his force at the creature. *Crrrr. Crrr.* Its legs creaked with each stumbling step backward. It had barely moved, but it was just enough to get its claw out of Erianna.

He gritted his teeth. Lyle blinked out of existence for a moment, before flickering back to consciousness. He couldn't hold the monster much longer.

If they were going to escape, Erianna needed to grab the statue and get out of here, *now*. But she was still affixed in the air. She waited for her death with that relieved, expectant expression. There had to be some way to break the vaal'akkar's hold on her.

Lyle's eyes landed on the vial. A few moments were all they needed. He knocked it over, dislodging the loose stopper and dumping a colorful liquid all over the sand. The creature vanished and reappeared next to it, releasing Erianna.

As soon as Erianna's feet connected with the ground, she took off running without looking back. She left the statue of Thermoren behind. She left *Lyle* behind!

He started to call out to her, but the words died.

Erianna had vanished.

The vaal'akkar must have done something to her! But the monster was rocking back and forth, still obsessed with the liquid seeping into the sand. Lyle felt just as paralyzed as Erianna had been. Thanks to his tether, he couldn't go more than a few feet away from the creature. All he could do was stay still and hope that, without a living body to devour, the beast would wander away.

Criiick. The vaal'akkar turned its head. The white energy in its sockets had gone out. It stared directly at Lyle. The monster could see him.

Lyle wanted to disappear. He wanted to close his eyes and will himself into a little wisp. He had so little energy left, it would be so easy. But he couldn't. He couldn't sleep knowing that he wouldn't wake up again. He couldn't tear his eyes away from the vaal'akkar's empty gaze.

The gashes in Erianna's shoulder throbbed, soaking her ful'prakta in blood. She needed somewhere to hide. Shadows curled up her legs and around her neck, diffusing across her body. It was like a piece of the monster clung to her, no matter how far she ran. She needed to get away.

Her um'prakta flew off her head. She glanced over her shoulder. She could see two still figures facing each other. Why wasn't the vaal'akkar following her?

The ground slid beneath Erianna, sending her skidding down the steep edge of a dune. Her boot caught on something buried in the sand. She pitched forward and slammed her shoulder into a rock. Erianna crumpled in a heap on the ground.

She forced herself up again. Any second the monster would come after her. Injured prey was the easiest to kill. She couldn't run much farther in this condition. It probably knew that. This was exactly what the beast had intended.

Erianna had to get out of its line of sight. She ran her hand along the jagged, pockmarked hunk of sandstone she'd hit, hoping to find a small crack to huddle in. Instead, her hand plunged into thin air. The narrow gap in the rock hid a cave.

Erianna dove in. The cave was pitch black, but as an ishlanian, she had always been able to rely on her ability to see in the dark. She braced herself against jagged walls, hurtling down the sinuous, curving tunnels.

Her momentum nearly flung her into a wall. It was a fork in the path. She picked the direction that led farther down. Anything to get her away from the surface. Away from that monster.

At each branch, Erianna continued picking the deeper paths—all of which happened to have strange kunari drawings etched on the walls around them.

Even as she distanced herself from the vaal'akkar, her chest clenched. A deep foreboding gripped her.

Finally, Erianna burst into a large cavern. The air was stagnant. *Plip, plip, plip.* Water dropped off spikes of stone hanging from the ceiling. A matching one grew up from the floor to meet it, always in pairs, one above and one below. They reminded her of teeth.

Erianna had the nagging feeling she'd forgotten something... *Lyle.* Gods, Lyle! She'd left the ghost behind. She needed to go back. She needed to save him from that monster.

The floor of the cave changed from dark gray to a pristine white marble. Sunlight from a high window illuminated the room in a glittering, soft yellow. The chill from the white marble chair bit into Erianna's back, seeping through the thin silk dress she wore. A heavy iron scent stung her nostrils. Reddish brown stained the marble chair's arms and legs. Pools of dried blood flaked on the floor beneath her mother's shoes.

Plindurin laid her hand loosely on Erianna's wrist. The woman's fingers curled, as cold as the corpses she controlled. Bright threads of light flowed from her fingertips, braiding themselves together until they formed a golden weave that wound tightly around Erianna's limbs. Erianna was paralyzed—helpless before the cold, empty gaze of a monster.

A rock poked into Erianna's back where she had slumped against the cave wall. The scratchy canvass of her ful'prakta chafed against the claw marks in her shoulder. It took Erianna several breathless gasps to understand that she wasn't actually in The Spider's Nest.

The vision had been so vivid. Erianna trembled. She didn't know whether she'd fallen asleep for a moment or hallucinated, but she would not get lost in that memory. Not again.

The bard pulled the small bottle of duur'een wine out of the hidden pocket in her corset. She popped the cork off and drained the bottle. As the thick, sweet liquor burned her throat, the ache in her shoulder dulled. The strong alcohol sent a pleasant buzz down her spine, and that familiar fuzziness overtook her mind.

But it wasn't enough. She could still see Lyle facing down the vaal'akkar as she sprinted away. Ghost and monster, both still as death itself. Hunter and prey frozen in a fragile tableau.

Erianna and Lyle had traveled together for months now. He had watched over her during their long trek through the desert. Lyle had saved her from the vaal'akkar. He cared about her. He *trusted* her.

But Erianna still couldn't go back. That thing would paralyze her. She had to stay here, hidden and safe. She had no choice.

"He did have a choice. He chose himself."

Erianna remembered the words she had told Porter before she'd fled the ruined temple of Delaith. She had admonished her father, seconds before leaving her oldest friend to face the Broken Claim's punishment alone.

Her father had chosen to leave her, just like Erianna had chosen to leave Porter. To push away Christine. To abandon Lyle.

Erianna was no better than her worthless father.

Pitiful, strangled sounds wrenched themselves from her chest. She desperately wanted to stop the wretched weeping, but the harder she tried, the faster the tears streamed down her face. Even after her tears dried up, she continued in heaving, waterless sobs.

When Erianna finished, she felt hollow and disgusting. The tears had dried into a salty sediment that clung to her cheeks. Her throat was raw. Her skin glowed a dim teal. The buzz of alcohol didn't feel nearly so pleasant anymore. She wanted desperately to sleep, but she couldn't.

Erianna saw a pool at the far end of the cavern. The water would soothe her throat, and she could splash a little on her face while she was at it. If she rinsed off the remnants of her pathetic display, maybe she could forget it entirely.

Erianna collected the empty wine bottle and its stopper as she staggered over to the little pond. The pool's surface was shrouded in a white mist that almost seemed to glow, but it was just a reflection of her own light. She leaned over the water, bringing the bottle closer. She hesitated. Her fingers tightened, turning her knuckles baby blue.

It doesn't want me here. The thought came so suddenly, so unexpectedly that she wondered if the pool had somehow spoken to her. That was insane. Water didn't want things, and it certainly couldn't speak in people's minds.

Erianna dipped the bottle beneath the wispy white layer. The container grew heavier as liquid flowed inside. A tingling ran up her skin where her arm was submerged. *Just the cold.* But the longer she lingered, the surer she became: the liquid wasn't just cold. It felt alive, prickling with that buzzing fizzle of a limb that couldn't wake up.

This wasn't water. This was something else, and she really didn't want to find out what. But before Erianna could withdraw her hand, fingers brushed against hers.

Erianna shrieked. She yanked her arm out of the pool and scrambled backward. She clutched the full bottle against her chest. Even in her haste to escape, she hadn't spilled a single drop.

Erianna waited a minute. Two. Her eyes fixed on the pool's mist-covered surface. She prepared for a beast to spring from its depths, a vaal'akkar to burst forth or a vocarii to clamber out.

Nothing emerged.

Erianna started to wonder whether the entire encounter could be attributed to alcohol-soaked, sleepless hallucinations. Surely she'd imagined the tingling up her arm, the hand in the water.

But what if she hadn't? The fingers had twitched. If someone really was in there, then they were still alive. Erianna hadn't gone back for Lyle or Porter, and she had lost Christine forever, but maybe, if she acted now, she could save *somebody*.

Erianna stuck the stopper in the bottle and stuffed it back in her hidden pocket. She crawled toward the pool again. Should she really be doing this? It could be anything down there. Or worse, maybe it was nothing at all. Maybe she would pitch forward and drown in a shallow pool while she searched for a hallucination. That would be incredibly embarrassing. Wouldn't it be better just to sit back and let the lingering effect of her buzz wash over her?

No, it was too late to back out. For gods' sake, she had sobbed for hours like a pathetic, sniveling baby. She needed to do something to redeem herself; otherwise, she'd never be able to face herself again.

Erianna plunged her arm back into the "water." The prickling shot up her arm with a new intensity. She rooted around in it, searching for the hand again. She delved in deeper until she was up to her shoulder. It turned out the pool wasn't so shallow, after all.

Just when it seemed hopeless, Erianna found it: four fingers and a thumb. She submerged her other arm, feeling around nearby and hooking her arm under the person's shoulder. She leaned back to pull them out, expecting the liquid to weigh its victim down, but she met no resistance from the pool.

The person came flying up. Erianna fell backward as someone landed on top of her, knocking the wind out of her.

Instinctively, Erianna curled her arms around them and shimmied away from the water's edge. She righted herself and adjusted the person in her arms. Finally, she saw their face.

"Zelnor?" Erianna breathed.

Erianna could hardly believe it. Zelnor was clutched in her arms. If Erianna couldn't feel the woman's steady breathing against her, she would've thought it another hallucination. But this was real. By the Liquid Vixen, what was Zelnor doing at the bottom of a magical pool in Kialma'keer?

"Zelnor," Erianna repeated.

Erianna slapped the other woman's cheek. Zelnor was out cold. Her beard felt so soft. Surprisingly so. Erianna wanted to touch it again. She wanted to run her hands through it.

Gods, Erianna was far too drunk for this. She rose with Zelnor still neatly tucked in her arms and collapsed against the opposite wall—as far from that strange liquid as possible. She nestled the half-elf against her and curled forward, resting her chin atop Zelnor's white hair. As she finally drifted off, Erianna realized that *this* was the warmth she craved.

Chapter Eighteen
One of a Kind

Zelnor could only see white. *Murderer.* An infinite void of pure white that stretched in every direction. *Unworthy.* She felt it pressing in around her.

The whispers were deafening, all-consuming. Crushing her, suspending her in place. Her body stood out jarringly against the unnatural background. Her fingers buzzed with barely contained energy.

Amari. Bright white fissures crawled up her legs. She could see the light through her clothing. *Lyle.* It burned as they carved a bone-deep path through her flesh, tearing her apart. *Tarnished legacy.*

The void pinned Zelnor's arms to her sides, preventing her from covering her ears. *Failure. Go. Vile creature. Feilra.* The whispers surrounded her. Inescapable. Dizzy with anger, sadness, and fear.

Ravastiors. Let me go. Unworthy.

Bryn, please. Zelnor tried to focus on a single voice, but the mass overwhelmed her. *Come home. Don't trust them.*

The voices bled together, until the discordant echoes formed one single word, repeated over and over in infinite voices: *Death.*

I'm not dead! she thought desperately. She could still feel her heart pounding against her chest. She was still alive. But as the cracks crept closer, her conviction slipped just a little further away. The cacophony suffocated her.

"I need to escape."

Her own words were lost in the din, but she clung tightly to them. Her elemental magic pulsed in time with her heart. She could feel the power expanding, trying to burst violently out of her stomach with a determination it had never shown before. She let go. There wasn't anything to lose here.

Magic sprung from her fingertips, and a stream of rainbow light flew from her into the void. It broke apart into millions of little spots of color drifting through the blank abyss.

A red dot floated close by. She struggled against the weight around her, reaching toward it. The red light grew into the silhouette of a tiny dragon, curling around her index finger. The creature touched a claw to her skin and *pop:* the dragon exploded into hundreds of silhouettes—humans, elves, and ishlanians. The little figures swam through the void around her before drifting away and melting back into pinpricks of colored light.

Death. Promise. Peace.

The voices plunged into her ears like daggers. Louder and louder. The pressure tried to force her arm back to her side. Searing agony locked her legs in place. The cracks had reached her upper thighs.

The dots were the answer. They were trying to tell her something. Her *magic* was trying to tell her something. She could feel it humming all around her. It didn't want her here. It assured her that it wasn't time yet. It wanted to help her. If only she could quiet the voices long enough to hear it.

A dark purple light darted toward her. It split into six purple dots and a silver thread shot between them, drawing a line with two curling spirals, like ram's horns. They collapsed back together into a purple silhouette with four arms.

Zelnor closed her fist around the purple figure. *Please help me,* she thought as loudly as she could over the voices chanting death.

For two weeks Zelnor and Heeden had slept on the ground, unable to scrape together enough silver for even the shoddiest inn. It was the worst Bitter Season they had seen in eight years. The air hung heavy with water until it inevitably poured down in frigid, unrelenting sheets. Blankets of morning fog burrowed into every scrap of fabric, from their bedrolls to their cloaks, so no matter how many layers they placed between themselves and the cold, it always found a way to seep in.

Camping was far from ideal in these conditions, but what choice did they have? Work had been scarce and charity even scarcer. So when they finally found someone willing to take them in for just a copper, Heeden had actually wept, overdramatic as always. Though, in all honesty, Zelnor had nearly cried herself. To the two teens, the humble barn was more luxurious than a castle in the Court of Kings and Queens.

Zelnor raced into the barn, barely stopping herself before she crashed into a pile of unpacked hay. Her best friend lingered behind. Heeden had been strangely quiet the last few days, and when she'd pressed him, he'd only said he had a bad feeling about the direction Zelnor was leading them. His lack of faith was completely unfounded. She'd never been more sure they were going the right way in her entire life. She could feel something calling her, a deep, inviting pull that she couldn't explain.

Heeden joined her, staring pensively at the ground. Too serious. She shoved him into the pile of hay. His head popped out a moment later, little pieces of hay sticking out of his thick, unruly black hair. Instead of smoothing it, he ruffled his hair so that it covered his dark, pockmarked face. Zelnor flopped down in front of him. He shoved her aside, crawling out and nudging her with his shoulder.

As they looked out at the torrents of rain, Zelnor inexplicably thought of her home for the first time in years. She had no clue why the rainy countryside reminded her of it, but nonetheless she thought of her room, cluttered with rocks and artifacts—some from her dad, others from her own little expeditions. Her mother always nagged her to clean up the mess and had even rearranged her room a few times, throwing out her daughter's treasures. They'd gotten into more than a few fights over it, but somehow, Zelnor was always the one who ended up apologizing.

Zelnor's stomach twisted, and she felt a buzzing on her fingertips. Pins and needles. She'd felt them all day yesterday, too. Normally she hated that feeling, but in this languid atmosphere, the prickling made her feel all warm and bubbly, like a sudden boost of confidence and strength was surging over her. She hadn't felt this safe, this happy since she was home in her little town, getting into all sorts of trouble while she waited for her dad to visit.

"This place sort of reminds me of the time we stole Eli and found that cave," Zelnor mused.

She wasn't exactly sure *why* the barn reminded her of the cavern deep in Kialma'keer, but before she could ponder it further, her stomach groaned, turning her attention to more important matters: food. Before showing them the barn, the generous woman had handed Zelnor a bag with freshly baked bread, two apples, and a sealed jug of water. The meal was definitely worth more than a single copper, but Zelnor certainly wasn't complaining.

Zelnor searched for a place to unpack the feast, and her gaze landed on some hay bales pushed together, adorned with candles. Their faint yellow-orange glow was a beacon in the dim barn. She took a seat at the makeshift table and tucked in. Heeden joined her, biting into a slightly overripe apple and staining his clothes irreparably in the process.

"Do you miss it?" Zelnor asked.

"What? The cave?" Heeden asked.

"No! Home," Zelnor said.

"Are you thinking of going back? I'm sure Lia would be thrilled. Imagine." Heeden put a hand over his chest and flopped backward. "The triumphant return of her child, after all these years. The tearful reunion when she *finally* recognizes you."

"Mom didn't even cry at Dad's funeral," Zelnor said.

"Never underestimate the power of a tearful reunion. It melts hearts faster than a cathmal cub," Heeden joked.

Zelnor ran her fingers through the fur on her face.

"What *would* Mom think?" she asked.

Heeden raised his eyebrows at the question. Zelnor was honestly shocked herself. *Where did that come from?* Since when did she care what her mother thought?

She tugged at her patchy beard, wincing when she pulled a bit harder than she meant to. Heeden nudged her arm away and put his hand firmly on her shoulder.

"She'd be happy to see you," he said.

Zelnor shook her head.

"After everything I've done, everything *she's* done…it's too late."

"If you just talked to her about it—"

"I've got nothing to say to her."

Zelnor tried to focus on the food, but she couldn't stop thinking about her mom, about her home, and the harder she tried to purge it from her mind, the stronger the images seemed to get.

As the candlelight flickered, Heeden fixed her with an appraising gaze.

"What?" Zelnor asked.

"You can't let it go, can you?" he said.

"I'm fine."

"Really?"

Heeden stared at her, resting his chin in his palm. She glared back at him, but eventually she cracked, like she always did.

"Do you really think we can go home?" she asked.

The two of them had dedicated every day to finding a way to control Zelnor's elemental magic. They'd scoured town libraries, perused bookshops, even asked locals, but as far as Zelnor could tell, she was the only one in all of Tularien with this curse. How in Thorns' bloody, unspoken name was she supposed to control her powers if no one had ever even heard of them? Her current "solution" was to wait as long as she could between uses and try to get away from others when she couldn't hold it in anymore.

What if this became her life? She liked learning about magic, she liked traveling around Alaspinor, but this was never what she'd pictured for herself. How many years would she need to sacrifice to find an answer? What if she never found one? She had wasted so much time already.

"Do you want to go home?" Heeden asked.

"Kind of..." Zelnor admitted. "Is that irresponsible?"

Heeden hummed. His eyes glazed over as he stared into the flames nearing their end. They only had half an hour at most before the candles would start to gutter. The rain had finally stopped, and its absence somehow made Heeden's pause all the more nerve-wracking.

"I don't think so," he finally said. "Honestly, I don't think your magic is that bad. A little unpredictable, but you've gotten a lot better at controlling it."

"Heeden, I lit you on fire," Zelnor said.

"That was years ago, and besides, it was a small fire. It takes more than that to get rid of me." He laughed.

"I wish you'd stop joking about it, for once," she muttered.

Zelnor hugged herself tightly, standing up. Heeden lunged forward to keep her from leaving, and suddenly, bright flames erupted between them.

For a disorienting moment, Zelnor thought that *she* had caused the fire, but then she saw a glint of something metal in a pool of rapidly melting wax. Heeden had knocked the candles onto the hay.

"Zelnor!" he shouted.

By the time Zelnor snapped out of her trance, the fire had leaped from the haybales to the walls. Scorching heat surrounded them on all sides. The wooden walls charred black as flames licked even higher, converging above them like a blazing orange sky.

Thick gray smoke filled the air. Zelnor coughed reflexively, tears in her eyes. Her lungs burned with every breath. They ran for the exit. *CRACK!* The roof caved in, sending fire raining down in front of them. Debris blocked their path.

Zelnor searched frantically for another exit. THUD! A beam fell, narrowly missing Heeden. *Godsdammit!* There was no way around it, she had to use magic.

The moment she thought it, her magic leaped inside her. A cool, tingling sensation instantly spread across her palms, as an enormous stream of water gushed from her hands. She stumbled, almost swept off her feet by the sheer force of it. She spun in a slow circle, arms outstretched, dousing the flames.

Zelnor kept her eyes fixed on the six dots hovering just a foot away from her. They were brighter than usual and vibrated with an intensity she'd never seen before. It took most of her concentration just to keep them at bay.

By the time the last trickles of water faded away, the fire had been reduced to embers. Zelnor looked down at her hands in wonder. Her magic was much stronger than she remembered. Was it permanent, or did her powers get a boost in emergencies? It wasn't something she'd noticed before …

The dots sped toward her, while she was distracted, and she willed them backward again. Their vibration intensified, almost like they were angry with her. By Vel'erma's all-knowing wisdom, why did those dots always appear? Why couldn't they just fade away after she finished her spell?

It's going to be all right, she told herself. *Don't panic. Don't panic.*

Zelnor's skin still felt warm. She hadn't suffered any burns, but she felt so strange. Her palms still tingled with pins and needles. Her magic swirled inside her, desperate to get out. Usually, it calmed down for a while after she cast a spell. What was different this time?

The six dots hovered ominously around her. They waited for a moment's hesitation, a chance to slip past her defenses. She scanned the countryside. She needed to find a good spot away from Heeden and the farm, preferably far away from anything flammable.

Her eyes landed on the ruins surrounding them, the only remnants of the kind farmer's livelihood, and her heart sank. Was this the woman's reward for her kindness? Zelnor didn't deserve her help.

Heeden crumpled to the ground, retching. *He must've inhaled too much smoke!* She rushed to her best friend's side, completely forgetting about the dots. The little white pinpricks of light surged into her, as she touched Heeden's shoulder.

Zelnor withdrew her hand, but it was too late. Heeden was gone. She'd vaporized him completely. No ashes, no burned clothes, just … nothing. Nothing was left. Another clump of white fur sprouted on her chin.

Zelnor froze—still on her knees, hand outstretched. Only the crackling and shifting of lingering embers cut through the absolute silence.

A blot of white bled through the sky, consuming the scenery around her. This hadn't happened the first time. It was a tear in the memory. The void was returning.

A flicker of purple light appeared where Heeden had stood, like a bolt of frozen lightning. The light widened into a figure. It grew four arms and long bovine ears.

The creature extended a hand. Zelnor grasped it.

Erianna awoke in an exhausted, pain-induced haze. She felt like someone had carved her head out from the inside. The throbbing in her shoulder had spread to her upper arm. This pain … It was the golden threads. She was still trapped in The Spider's Nest!

Erianna felt someone shift against her. Zelnor was cradled between her arms. Erianna calmed her racing heart. She wasn't with Plindurin anymore. That was only a nightmare. They were at the bottom of a cave somewhere in the Kialma'keeran desert.

The mage's warmth was an oddly comforting sensation, soothing her remaining terror and easing the tightness in Erianna's chest. It was almost enough to lull her back sleep. Unfortunately, she couldn't drift off knowing that Zelnor might wake up before her and discover them in such a compromising position. Not only was it far too intimate, but it was also wholly inappropriate. Zelnor had not agreed to be spooned, and the fact that Erianna had done so without asking was as wrong as it was mortifying.

Erianna disentangled herself and laid the half-elf on the ground.

The claw marks on her shoulder ached with the movement. She needed to sew up her wounds. It wouldn't do anything for the pain, but it needed to get done regardless, and it would pass the time. She reached for her backpack, and realized she'd abandoned that too. Fantastic. She was stranded in the desert without water, again.

Thwap! Thwap! Each slam of waterdrops against stone was another blow of a hammer against her skull. She couldn't think. *Damn this echoey cave.* She knew the sound's grating nature was more likely due to her hangover than the cave's acoustics, but she'd rather blame the cave. This strangely ominous cave with its pool of magical gods-only-knew-what where she had found Zelnor—not gasping or struggling, but lost in a deep, peaceful sleep.

The bottle full of "water" felt heavy nestled against Erianna, hidden in her corset. She hadn't been able to see the liquid through the layer of mist. Maybe she should open the bottle up and take a peek. She had little else to do while Zelnor slept—aside from remembering every excruciating detail of her breakdown the night before. Why was it that the most shameful memories were always clear as crystal? The world really went out of its way to make her feel terrible about herself. Not that she didn't deserve it.

Erianna's eyes welled up. *Oh no. Absolutely not.* She refused to go back down into that pathetic spiral in front of Zelnor.

Erianna uncorked the green, glass bottle. A pungent, metallic scent wafted out. Blood. The smell rested at the back of her mouth, so strong that she almost thought she'd bitten the inside of her cheek. It was nothing like the caked mass on her claw wounds that had mostly dried. It was fresh. The water shared the same powerful scent that she had smelled in the vial Lia had given them to ward off the vaal'akkar.

Erianna closed one eye and peered into the bottle. The contents glowed. A flash of gold. Bright, blinding gold. Golden threads knitted across teal arms, burrowing beneath teal skin. The threads disappeared into flesh. Hidden magic shredded muscle.

Erianna slammed the cork back into the bottle neck. What in Kalkor's Eternal Punishment! It was her nightmare. The water had shown her snippets of her *nightmare.*

Was the "water" a window into her worst memories? Had it caused her nightmare? Maybe the liquid *was* nightmares, a fragment of Celrelborain distilled into tangible terror.

Erianna barely stopped herself from chucking the bottle across the cavern. She tucked it back into her corset instead. If there was even a chance that this substance was the same stuff that warded off vaal'akkars, she had to keep it.

Zelnor gasped and flung herself upright. The mage clutched at her tunic. If just being near the "water" had given Erianna the worst nightmares she'd experienced in years, then what about Zelnor? The mage had *bathed* in the stuff.

Erianna reached for Zelnor, but the half-elf flinched away from her. Zelnor mumbled something through her stuttered breaths, shaking her head vehemently. Erianna's nails bit into her palms. Every instinct told her to get closer, but she respected Zelnor's wishes, staying back until the mage's breathing steadied.

"Where's Lyle?"

That was the first question Zelnor asked? Really? Was this the gods punishing her for abandoning a child? How was Erianna supposed to tell her? *Oh, Lyle? You mean our friend? He saved me from a vaal'akkar. It probably ate him.*

"He's around," Erianna lied. "Are you all right?"

"I just had a bad dream. A really bad dream," Zelnor said.

"No, I don't mean what *just* happened. I was talking about before," Erianna said.

Zelnor cocked her head, fixing Erianna with a vacant gaze.

"The water," Erianna prompted. "You know, the strange glowing liquid I pulled you out of? Magical? Possibly acidic?"

Zelnor rolled up her pant legs. She wasn't seriously considering stepping into the pool again, was she? For Liscuntia's sake, Erianna had only just rescued her, and the half-elf was already attempting to throw herself right back into that accursed liquid. Erianna would never understand how someone so smart could act so dumb. Zelnor's curiosity was going to get her killed.

Erianna prepared to hold Zelnor back, but the mage never got up. Instead, Zelnor stared at her legs. Jagged white scars snaked between tufts of fur, disappearing beneath her clothes. She placed her hand gingerly on one of the marks, yanking it away seconds later. Erianna's own hand hovered over the scars. An unnatural chill radiated from them. With Zelnor's nod of permission, she touched the bleached skin. The cold burned her fingertips.

"I can't feel anything in those spots. It's just numb," Zelnor said.

"What in Thorns' unspoken name happened to you?" Erianna whispered.

Zelnor described everything she'd seen in the water—bizarre visions of multicolored dots and figures swimming in a white void that had been … consuming her? A memory had protected her from the corrosive, white light. Zelnor refused to discuss its contents, letting her story come to an abrupt end. So, Erianna supplemented it with her own journey through Kialma'keer.

Zelnor stayed suspiciously silent at the mention of Lia but audibly gasped when she learned she'd been gone for a month. Apparently, she had spent the entire time suspended in the nightmarish fluid. Zelnor was lucky the stuff hadn't killed her.

Erianna heavily altered the ending of her story, omitting the vaal'akkar attack, her drunken breakdown, and Lyle's fate. Her skin glowed brightly with guilt, as she wondered what had happened to the little ghost. Zelnor's eyes lingered on Erianna shoulder, and the bard realized her mistake too late. She had inadvertently provided Zelnor enough light to see the swollen claw marks that *hadn't* been a part of her tale.

"Vaal'akkar," Erianna said before Zelnor could ask.

"You survived a *life* beast? How? When? What do they look like?"

"It was a narrow escape. I'd rather not dwell on it."

"But how did you escape?" Zelnor pushed.

"This seems like a conversation we should have as far from this pool as possible. Don't you think?" Erianna said smoothly.

Zelnor dropped the matter without protest. Fortunately—or maybe unfortunately—they had more pressing issues to deal with than the holes in Erianna's explanation. They were out of supplies and facing immanent death from dehydration. And on top of that, Zelnor could barely stand.

"Want me to carry you?" Erianna half-joked.

"No!" the mage said.

The adamant refusal came off more embarrassed than annoyed. Rather than tease the weakened mage, Erianna hooked an arm through Zelnor's and let the bearded woman lean some weight on her.

Erianna was grateful for the kunari paintings on the walls marking their exit. She wasn't sure she could've navigated the tangled labyrinth without them. It was a testament to how exhausted Zelnor was that she didn't comment on the drawings as they ascended through the tunnels. Maybe she simply couldn't see them. Erianna only provided enough light to keep the mage from tripping on the uneven floor. Any more than that would have been visible from a distance. They needed to be cautious until they knew for sure the vaal'akkar was gone.

Scritch. Scritch. Something scratched at the entrance to the cave.

Had the monster found them? Erianna was sure she had broken its line of sight, but maybe the creatures used other senses to hunt. What if the vaal'akkars could smell them? Were these monsters the type to ambush their prey? If only she had asked Lia more. Why had Erianna had been so Thorns-damned confident she could avoid them?

Only the strip of bright sunlight streaming in from the cave mouth prompted Erianna to move forward again. The vaal'akkars slept through the day. Whatever waited for them wasn't a vaal'akkar. It couldn't be.

Erianna held her breath as her eyes adjusted to the daylight. *Eli?* The scraping was webbed paws scrabbling excitedly against stone. Eli's chest rumbled with a deep purr at their approach. Lyle hovered just above the cathmal's back. *Oh, thank the gods above!*

Erianna sprinted ahead, dropping Zelnor. The mage yelped and hastily braced herself against the wall, but Erianna couldn't be bothered with even a half-hearted apology. Lyle was alive! Or, well, as "alive" as he had been before. And somehow, he'd found Eli and brought him to the cave.

Erianna started to hug Lyle but aborted mid-motion. She held her arms awkwardly between them. The ghost smiled, but the normally warm expression was stretched thin. She couldn't tell whether he gazed at her with thinly veiled disappointment, or if it was the natural melancholy of his downturned eyes.

Lyle lifted a canteen into her hands. Water—real water—sloshed enticingly inside. Erianna hadn't realized how thirsty she was until the ghost offered it to her. Her hand paused over the stopper. The ghost had brought her a canteen, and it wasn't just a single canteen either. Erianna's backpack sat at Eli's feet, intact and fully packed, with her um'prakta resting on top.

The ghost hardly had the energy to carry the statue of Thermoren a few feet at a time. How had he carried himself *and* her things all the way here? Eli might have returned after the danger had passed, and maybe Lyle had managed to place the statue and bag on the cathmal's back. But without a way to communicate, Lyle couldn't have led the cathmal to the cave. For that matter, how had *Lyle* found the cave? How had he escaped the vaal'akkar?

Lyle's tight-lipped smile transformed into something genuine when Zelnor stumbled out of the tunnel. Erianna bit back her questions. She didn't deserve those answers after what she'd done.

"Zelnor!" Lyle exclaimed. "How long were you down *there?*"

"A month, apparently," Zelnor said. "Is that—"

"A cathmal! His name is Eli."

Zelnor draped herself over the cathmal. She whispered something in the beast's ear, and Eli nuzzled her cheek. The two seemed far too familiar with each other for a first meeting. Zelnor knew Eli, which meant she knew *Lia.*

Erianna had been right. The elven woman was Zelnor's mother, and Erianna could tell Zelnor missed her desperately. Erianna had never felt homesick herself, but she recognized it well enough in the mage's wistful sigh.

Well, lucky for her, Zelnor would get the chance to return home very soon. Retracing Erianna's steps was the fastest way back to Alaspinor—much faster than sailing up the coast—and without Erinna, the mage had no reason to avoid Nirdeem. The route was practical, and Zelnor was nothing if not practical.

It wasn't without its dangers. The way back to Kezeek Mesa would take Zelnor through Vaal'akkars' Wrath, but with her elemental magic, she could defend herself against the vaal'akkars. Lyle would want to go with the mage, of course. He would watch over Zelnor the way he had watched over Erianna. They could take some of the pool's water too, as a last resort. Together, the two of them wouldn't have any trouble.

Now that their journey together was finally over, Erianna needed to move on. She supposed she would continue on to Bokest al'Bar. She had no other option, really. Perhaps she'd sail somewhere other than Alaspinor, get herself as far from Plindurin and the Broken Claim as possible. Once Erianna left Bokest al'Bar's port, she could put everything that had happened on Eltun behind her.

"I'll make you a copy of the map." Erianna said. "The route back to Kezeek Mesa is fairly simple. And you'll need—"

"I'm not going back," Zelnor interrupted.

Erianna's hand rested on the bottle of strange water. Had she heard that right? She couldn't have.

"I thought I'd go to Bokest al'Bar. With you and Lyle. I've always wanted to go," Zelnor said, "and I don't have any reason to go back the other way."

"But—It'll take longer," Erianna said. "And your mother ..."

Lia acted stoic, but she obviously cared about her daughter. She missed Zelnor. She was worried about her. A mother like her deserved more than to be passed by without a word.

"I can't," Zelnor said.

"Really? You can't?" Erianna repeated.

"Trying to get rid of me already?" Zelnor asked.

"I'm not going to Alaspinor," Erianna said.

"Fine! That's fine," Zelnor said.

Fine. Far be it from Erianna to butt in on anyone's relationship with their mother. If Zelnor wanted to avoid hers, then so be it. The mage would regret it, but she obviously didn't want to hear what Erianna had to say on the matter. It was always like this with her. She wondered why she'd wanted to find Zelnor in the first place.

Chapter Nineteen
Halfway

Since leaving the cave, Erianna and Zelnor hadn't spoken a word to each other. They'd spent the entire day riding Eli in silence, and now they unpacked their supplies in complete silence. The stillness of the desert made every unspoken word so much louder. It was killing Lyle! If ghosts could die, then the tension between them would've done him in hours ago.

That said, part of him also welcomed the quiet. He couldn't describe his relief when the last whispers from that cave finally faded. There was something really, really wrong with that place. A mix of sweet voices had called to him from within its depths. The whispers were so kind, so familiar. Loved ones who he'd already forgotten called him closer. They had promised peace, but they wanted to destroy him. Lyle didn't know how he knew, but he was sure of it.

And yet, at the same time, he had wanted to go. Desperately. With every passing day, he remembered less of his past. Even his parent's features had gotten hazy. He tried to imagine his mother's hair, her eyes, anything. Did his father have facial hair? Had he been kind or imposing? The harder Lyle grasped for his memories, the more they slipped through his fingers, like water through cupped hands. Only a few faint memories remained now. What would happen when even those faded away? Would he start to fade away too?

The voices promised he would become whole again, and Lyle almost believed them. Only his tether to the statue and his desire to reunite with his friends had held him back. But were they really his friends? Would a friend have left Lyle with a vaal'akkar?

It wasn't her fault! Erianna had been terrified, delirious with sleepless hallucinations. And there was also the fact that she had disappeared. She had only taken a few steps before she vanished. Perhaps the monster had teleported her away, or maybe Zelnor had.

Those were good reasons. Perfectly good reasons that Erianna couldn't have saved him. She wouldn't have done what she did otherwise, would she?

Lyle couldn't answer that question in any way that felt satisfying. Did the answer even really matter, if he was forgetting everything anyway?

Lyle needed to focus on more important things. Erianna hadn't been the same without Zelnor. For a month, Lyle had clung to the hope that once they found Zelnor, everything would go back to the way it had been before. But it hadn't.

Zelnor and Erianna argued all the time, but this fight seemed worse than the others. Maybe they'd been apart so long that they'd forgotten how to make up again. That was something Lyle could definitely fix.

Lyle's two friends rolled out their bedrolls so far from each other that they almost couldn't call it one camp. Zelnor leaned against Eli, her head resting against him as she stared at the stars. Erianna had started humming a sad song under her breath.

The two of them were hopeless.

Lyle flew over to Erianna first. She had her head buried in her large backpack. Lyle waited patiently for her to finish. The bard finally fished a sewing kit out, but she dropped it into the sand when she saw him.

She smiled just a few moments too late. It was the same feeble expression she had worn when she emerged from that cave. The one that cracked partway through—not ingenuine, just *broken*. This was exactly why she and Zelnor needed to make up.

"Lyle. I…"

"I had an aunt and uncle who used to fight all the time," Lyle said.

He couldn't remember their names anymore, but he did remember their quick-paced arguments—so similar to Erianna and Zelnor's. Like his friends, his aunt and uncle's fights were never that serious, but their constant bickering had made Lyle wonder why they got married in the first place. His mother had taught him that not everyone expressed love the same way. Lyle repeated her words to Erianna.

"Sometimes when people love each other and can't say it, they fight instead."

"I don't love Zelnor. I barely know her," Erianna said.

"Are you sure? You really wanted to find her. A lot," Lyle pointed out.

Erianna's eyes drifted toward Zelnor, but Lyle wasn't sure she saw the same thing he did. He could only hope he had planted the right idea, because pushing Erianna any further might lead her to stubbornly resist the obvious. Still, he had faith in her. She would realize how badly she wanted to cross that gap between them, but she couldn't do that alone. Zelnor had to meet her halfway.

Zelnor hadn't noticed Erianna's gaze. She held Eli in a tight embrace, her head turned toward the cathmal. She scrubbed her sleeve across her eyes. Zelnor had been crying. Lyle had never seen her cry before.

"I didn't want to travel with her anyway. We weren't supposed to stay together this long," Zelnor muttered.

"Is that why you're so sad?" Lyle asked.

"Thorns' name!" Zelnor cried. "Where did you come from?"

"I've been here for a while…" he said.

Zelnor hadn't noticed him. Of course she hadn't. Even while he was alive, he tended to fade into the background… But that was fine! As long as his friends were happy, he was happy.

"And no, of course I'm not upset about her. I just think it was stupid to ask her to come with me. How could I even *think* about traveling with her after I—?" Zelnor stopped.

"After you…?" Lyle prompted.

"I dreamed about an old friend," she whispered.

Zelnor looked like she was about to start crying again. Her friend must have left. Now that Lyle thought about it, that made a lot of sense. She never let herself get too close because she thought that, eventually, Erianna would leave too. That's why Zelnor was always keeping her at arm's length.

"She's not gonna leave you, you know," Lyle said.

"Did you miss our conversation yesterday?" Zelnor asked.

"I know what she said, but—"

"Why weren't you with Erianna when she found me?" Zelnor asked.

"That's not really what I came over here to talk about," Lyle said.

"She wouldn't answer the question, either. She did something bad, didn't she?"

It took no time at all for Zelnor to immediately mistrust Erianna. The bard had worked so hard to find Zelnor. They were so close to finally admitting they belonged together. Lyle didn't want to foster more animosity between them.

"We got separated," he lied.

A white lie. Just a little one. A necessary one.

"How did you find her again?" Zelnor asked.

"I didn't. Someone dragged me to the cave," Lyle said.

That part was true. When the vaal'akkar had turned its hollow, eyeless stare back to him, the frail hope that the beast couldn't see ghosts had shattered in an instant. Just when he was sure that the monster would kill him, it had suddenly lost interest.

Then, Erianna's stuff had vanished, but it wasn't gone. Just invisible. He knew it was invisible because he could still see the trail the backpack left as someone—or *something*—had dragged it through the sand. The tether had pulled Lyle to the cave, where the backpack, all packed up, reappeared again. Erianna's hat and Eli had appeared at the cave mouth a little while later.

Lyle had thought it was Zelnor somehow. Her magic was strange and powerful. He'd thought that she had summoned him to her, but the dumbfounded expression on her face made it pretty clear that wasn't what had happened. Who else could it have been, though? The High Mage? But if he couldn't even see Lyle, he'd have no way to know the ghost was in danger.

A ripping sound filled the air between them. Erianna laid a piece of pale pink cloth covered in little white flowers across a wide-brimmed hat.

"What in the Eternal Library are you doing?" Zelnor asked.

"Thought I'd better sew up the hat before I tackle my shoulder. Wouldn't want to get blood in the stitching," Erianna said.

"You're making an um'prakta?" Zelnor asked.

"I don't have a spare," Erianna said.

Erianna had ripped up one of her dresses *and* used her only hat to make an um'prakta for Zelnor. It was the sweetest thing Lyle had ever seen Erianna do for anyone. That was a sign if Lyle had ever seen one. Erianna was finally starting to bridge the distance between them!

Zelnor had to realize what this meant, right? But she only nodded, barely acknowledging the gesture before staring at the stars and getting lost in her own head again.

Lyle would have to try again later. They had to realize how much they needed each other before they actually split up. Although they kept inventing reasons to continue traveling together, Lyle knew that wouldn't last forever. He needed to help them while he was still around to do it, because once he was gone, they wouldn't have anyone.

Zelnor might have idealized her childhood more than she'd realized, because the last few weeks in the desert hadn't been nearly as pleasant as she remembered. Sweat stuck her ful'prakta to her in all the worst places. Sand slipped under her clothes and chafed against her skin. And although Zelnor appreciated Eli's hard work, she missed walking. There was something so much more satisfying about traveling on your own two feet, not to mention the jostling. Zelnor did not remember cathmal riding being this jarring. She blamed Erianna for that; the woman was clearly an inexperienced rider.

Between the bumpy ride, the heat, and the damned sand, there were times when it was difficult to do anything other than focus on her own discomfort. Probably because there was so little to distract her from it. She loved her home, but it wasn't exactly scenic.

Mountains. Sand. The canyon. A distant mesa town. More sand. Gods, Zelnor was sick of sand.

Erianna's stories were the only thing that made the journey bearable. She'd started sharing anecdotes from her time as a traveling singer, and each tale was wilder than the last. Zelnor had acted disinterested at first, as a matter of principle more than anything, but something about the way Erianna told her stories made it impossible not to be drawn into them.

"He wouldn't stop bothering her. So, I grabbed a knife from his plate and pinned his undergarments to the wall," Erianna finished.

Zelnor snorted as Erianna described the stuck-up merchant gaping in horror at his silken underpants, with their "unfortunate holes," displayed for the entire tavern.

"I got kicked out after that," Erianna said. "But so did he."

"How did you get his undergarments?" Lyle asked.

"He left them in my room," Erianna said.

Lyle asked how exactly *that* had happened, and Erianna brushed the query off as carelessness on the man's part. The bard had clearly left out some of the raunchier parts of the story for Lyle's benefit, but she turned and winked at Zelnor. Zelnor was searching for the dryest reply possible when she spotted something sparkling.

Zelnor leaped off Eli and scanned the ground for the glimmer. *Thwump.* Erianna tumbled off the cathmal. The sudden shift in weight must have unseated her. Zelnor wanted to laugh, but she couldn't let the accident distract her from following the glittering light. They were difficult to spot again, but after a few moments, she found them. Zelnor gathered a handful of sand speckled with little orange crystals.

"You knocked me off Eli for some rocks?" Erianna asked.

"I did not knock you off Eli," Zelnor said. "And these are more than just 'some rocks.'"

Zelnor flung the sand aside and dug into the ground, packing the edges of the hole as she went. Her um'prakta slipped forward as she worked. Erianna had a big head, literally and figuratively; of course the hat she had loaned Zelnor didn't quite fit right. Zelnor set it aside while she worked.

A few moments of digging and her efforts bore fruit—literally. She exposed a patch of short, flattened grass growing out of dark earth. The greenery stood out starkly against the sea of sand, but Zelnor uprooted it without any guilt. It would grow back, as would the round, rich purple fruit buried underneath it.

Lyle flew closer, fascinated by the plant.

"How does it grow under the sand? And where do those patches of grass come from?" he asked.

"No one knows. There's plenty of them scattered everywhere, but they're rarely near water," Zelnor said.

"So, you stopped us for a big, purple rock," Erianna said.

The bard clearly knew it wasn't a rock. She was just being difficult. As usual. Zelnor tossed the fruit to Erianna, and the bard caught it.

"It's a duur'een fruit. I used to dig them up with my friend," Zelnor said.

"You have friends?" Erianna asked.

Erianna apologized immediately. Zelnor knew she had only been joking—just another quip about her awkwardness—but it still hurt. And why had Zelnor brought Heeden up as though he were just an old friend that she had lost touch with?

Zelnor had continued having nightmares about him for a few days after Erianna had rescued her. Her hands had fizzled when she awoke, burning like they did on that night, and she had to fight against an inexplicable urge to return to that pool. But now that she had gone back to her usual, strange dreams, Heeden's fate had nearly slipped her mind.

Zelnor's magic wriggled inside her at the reminder. The energy had built up so slowly that she hadn't noticed it until now, but her magic had gotten strong. Even stronger than it usually was after a few weeks. Technically, if she counted the time spent in the pool, it had been nearly two months since she'd last cast something. Her elemental magic was going to get out of control soon. Just like it had with Heeden.

Zelnor didn't have to address her magic right now, though. She would be able find a moment to sneak away before they entered the city.

Erianna handed Zelnor the um'prakta she'd set aside. Every time Zelnor looked at it, the hat appealed to her less. The fabric around the brim wasn't nearly as effectively as plain white. And the pink with white flowers? That sort of thing looked pretty on Erianna but had never been Zelnor's style.

"Can we switch um'praktas?" Zelnor asked "The pattern on this one is a little…"

"I ripped that from my favorite dress! Gods, you are terrible at receiving gifts," Erianna grumbled.

"It was a gift? I thought you just made a spare for yourself and gave it to me."

"What? Liscuntia, you are such an idiot," Erianna said.

It did sound pretty stupid when Zelnor thought about it, now. But at the time, the conclusion seemed more reasonable than Erianna tearing up her own clothes *for Zelnor*. Not just her clothes, but apparently her favorite dress.

Zelnor toyed with the edges of the pink fabric.

"What is that? And should we be worried about it?" Lyle pointed to a cloud of dust gathering at the base of the mountains in the far distance.

Zelnor was surprised they hadn't encountered any sandstorms before; the two of them had been lucky, if this was the first one they'd run into. The sandstorm headed toward them was still small. Zelnor doubted that it would cause any problems.

"It'll dissipate before it reaches us," Zelnor assured them.

Zelnor watched Erianna shift in the saddle, holding her shoulder at an awkward angle. She'd tried to make light of it, but Zelnor knew the vaal'akkar wounds weren't healing well. They were puffy and purple, oozing with a strange gunk. And her stitches kept breaking. She had resewed them with the deftness of a professional seamstress, but a few had already snapped again.

Zelnor knew some methods of nonmagical wound care—thanks to a book about apothecary alternatives to light magic—but nothing that would do them any good. There was a specific type of thread and needle used for suturing. Neither of which they had. Zelnor wished she could heal Erianna. She wished her elemental magic could do some good for a change instead of constantly ruining everything.

Thankfully, their group was only a few days away from Bokest al'Bar. They could find help there. *No, Erianna will find help there.* Their journey together would end once they got to the city. For some reason, Zelnor kept forgetting that.

Zelnor's stomach flipped. It had to be her elemental magic. She'd put off expending it. Admittedly, not the best idea, but she had waited this long. She could probably last a few more days. She would rather cast after Erianna and Lyle left, anyway.

"And there's the sandstorm, heading straight for us," Erianna said.

Gods, the bard didn't have to sound so smug about it. The sandstorm could have dissipated. There had been a good chance of it. But of course the winds had shifted direction and picked up strength. The sandstorm had gotten even bigger. By the time they realized the storm would cross their path, it was too late to avoid it. It was like the gods themselves were trying to prove Zelnor wrong.

The cloud had gained an alarming amount of speed by the time it reached them. Erianna steered Eli into a gully they'd had their eye on for the last half-day. Eli slid down into the depression, as sure-footed as only a cathmal could be. The wind roared above them. They had just made it.

Sand had filled the old gully over time—rendering it almost too shallow to fit two people and a cathmal. Errant sand poured down from above them, feeling like a thousand tiny cuts across Zelnor's cheeks, neck, and hands.

Zelnor could feel warmth radiating off the woman next to her. Their shoulders nearly touched. She was acutely aware of the familiar urge to cast, pooling at the base of her stomach, writhing against her grip as it struggled to reach her fingers. Her magic was nearly impossible to suppress when it got this agitated.

The gully was too small. There wasn't anywhere else to go. She needed to keep her magic at bay for the duration of the sandstorm, which meant she would likely have to wait hours before she could slip away. Zelnor wasn't sure she could last that long.

Zelnor's um'prakta flew off her head. Erianna caught it, just before it left the gully. The pink, flowery fabric flapped in the wind. Erianna put it back on Zelnor's head and tilted it to the perfect angle to block the incoming sand.

What if the sandstorm was the solution to Zelnor's problem? She could quell the magic inside her and direct it toward something positive for once.

Zelnor rose. Erianna grabbed her wrist, preventing her from clambering out of the gully and into the storm.

"Where are you going?" Erianna asked.

"Walk," Zelnor said.

"Funny," Erianna replied.

The bard didn't budge. She didn't seem all that amused.

"I'm going to do something about this storm," Zelnor admitted.

"You're going to *cast?*" Erianna asked.

The bard only let go for a moment, but it was enough. Zelnor climbed the sloped wall, and Erianna's protests were lost in the violent bluster. The winds bent Zelnor backward like a broken reed. She wasn't nearly far enough, but at least the others had some cover from her. *They should be safe.*

White light bloomed in her hands. The six bright dots around her were the only thing visible against the maelstrom. Then, the sand cleared in a pocket around her. She jogged forward, getting a few more steps away before more elemental magic surged impatiently out of her.

Every grain of sand stilled. Miles and miles of suspended specs, much farther away than Zelnor had intended. Her legs trembled. Her heart felt too heavy in her chest. She had only meant to stop a small portion of the sand, but in her haste, she had overextended her reach. Her magic flowed freely, sustaining the spell well beyond the limits of her capacity.

Zelnor stumbled forward. A teal arm caught her right as her knees buckled. Erianna, Lyle, and Eli had joined her. The sand fell around them with a sudden *whoosh.*

"Dammit, go back to the ditch," Zelnor muttered.

"I'll be fine," Erianna said. "You're not nearly as dangerous as you think you are."

"Erianna!" Zelnor snapped.

"I am not leaving you here in the dirt, *alone,* just to escape a flurry of flying flowers or bubbles shooting out of your ass."

Zelnor tried to push Erianna away, but her grip only tightened. Zelnor could almost see the bard's mildly annoyed features shift into a familiar, pockmarked face. The dots impacted Zelnor. She couldn't stop it. It was happening again!

The ground quaked beneath her. It jerked violently left. Zelnor's head swam. She prayed to Felsha'kor that it was just dizziness unsettling her footing.

CRACK.

The ground gave way in a perfect circle around Zelnor. Erianna plummeted into an inky, bottomless void.

Zelnor thrust out her hand, seconds too late. But her magic extended beyond her reach. Erianna hovered, fixed in the air. The elemental magic tapped depths Zelnor didn't know she had.

Erianna slipped, falling half a foot. *Shit.* Apparently, the magic was coming from depths that Zelnor really *didn't* have. Her limbs weighed a hundred pounds each. The spell dropped and Zelnor pitched forward, following Erianna into the void.

They both froze mid-air before they were unceremoniously tossed to the outer ledge of the circle. Zelnor thought she'd lost her grip on the spell, but had it only been delayed?

"Are you all right?" Lyle asked.

His voice was strained, and his form rippled like a mirage. Lyle had saved her, saved both of them. Zelnor didn't even have time to thank him before she felt the second set of dots hit her. She scrambled blindly away, but her limbs were heavy with exhaustion.

Squelch. Zelnor plunged into something thick and viscous. She pulled back her hands, covered in red. *Erianna.*

Zelnor's magic always ruined everything. No matter how she tried to help, every effort would always end in tragedy. She shut her eyes. At least with Heeden there hadn't been anything left. She didn't want to see Erianna's body.

"Why didn't you try this in Vespar? You made such a fuss about wanting food."

Her eyes flew open. Erianna stood in front of her. Alive. Unharmed. Well, a couple of her stitches had ripped again, but other than that, she was unharmed. And she was holding a pie?

The dots had created a dozen duur'een pies, identical to the one in Erianna's hands, arranged in two neat rows in front of Zelnor. Their perfectly baked crusts blended in with the golden cast of the sand in the setting sun. The closest two had caved in, revealing a dark red interior. Zelnor smelled the sticky goop on her palms: sweet and tart, a little smokey, and decidedly *not* blood.

Why was elemental magic like this? Why couldn't it be something she could plan for, something she could predict? Why did it propel her from one ridiculous scenario to the next? One spell had sent Erianna plummeting into an endless abyss, and the next had summoned pies. Pies!

Zelnor let out a hysterical laugh. She wasn't cursed. *She* was a curse. A curse to every poor soul who crossed her path. She had been an idiot to think she could control it well enough to travel with someone again. Anyone who stayed with her long enough would end up just like Heeden.

She wobbled to her feet, accidentally smacking Erianna's arm and smearing duur'een filling on the bard's sleeve. The pie Erianna held splattered onto the ground.

"I was going to eat that," Erianna joked.

The bard spoke in a mild, pitying tone, as if something as mundane as dessert could possibly mean anything after what had just happened. Sand was still pouring into the circle that Zelnor's magic had carved into the ground.

Zelnor gripped the front of Erianna's ful'prakta with her red-stained hands.

"What is wrong with you?" Zelnor asked.

"Nothing. I'm fine," Erianna said. "Your magic did its worst, and I'm fine."

"Only because Lyle saved you," Zelnor said.

"Technically, *you* saved me, and then Lyle saved both of us," Erianna said.

"You're missing the point! This isn't the first time this happened. It's going to happen again. You can't—You can't—"

Erianna lowered them both to the ground. Zelnor only realized how shaky her hands were when she let go of Erianna's ful'prakta.

"You'll need more than a sandpit if you want to get rid of me," Erianna said. "I've dealt with worse."

"Worse?" Lyle asked.

Erianna paused. Something flashed quickly across her face. She clearly couldn't think of anything worse than Zelnor.

"Rowdy patrons are no joke." Erianna chuckled half-heartedly. "More importantly, Lyle and I aren't going to leave you."

Lyle crossed his arms. He wouldn't meet Zelnor's eyes. She could tell he didn't agree with the sentiment, and she didn't blame him. He might not have a life to lose anymore, but for all he knew, he might face an even worse fate. And if even a *ghost* didn't want to stay with her, then why in Thorns' bloody, unspoken name was Erianna fighting Zelnor so hard on this?

As much as it pained Zelnor to admit, Erianna wasn't stupid. At least, she wasn't this stupid. Was it arrogance? Pride? Something had clearly clouded Erianna's better judgment.

"Thank you," Zelnor said. "Thank you for everything, but this is over."

"We're still going to the same place," Erianna said.

"But we don't have to travel there together," Zelnor said.

"Thorns' bloody name, can't you just trust that I can take care of myself? Do you have that little faith in me? After everything?"

"You nearly died because you didn't stay back when I told you. Why are you still here?" Zelnor snapped. "We keep saying we'll split up, but it's been over a month!"

"If I'd listened to you, you'd be at the bottom of that pit right now!" Erianna shouted. "You need people. Admit it or not, I don't care. But you can't make me go, and you know it."

Erianna was right. Short of casting a spell on her, Zelnor couldn't make the woman do anything. Zelnor certainly couldn't get rid of her by physical force, and the woman had proven herself immune to any kind of logic or reason.

"I just don't understand why," Zelnor said.

"It's because I—"

Erianna cut herself off. Her face twisted. What if Erianna only stayed because she felt she had to? She had admitted once that she felt responsible for Zelnor's pact with Torrin. But that wasn't enough of a reason to stay together anymore. She had to know that.

"It's because I don't *want* to leave," Erianna admitted. "And I don't think you want me to, either, do you?"

Erianna wanted to stay with her.

Zelnor was an idiot for not realizing sooner. The stubborn bard hadn't turned around when Zelnor had disappeared. She had a chance to leave the whole situation behind, but instead, she'd trekked through Vaal'akkars' Wrath to find her. The woman's actions extended far beyond courtesy or duty. Erianna had risked her life, more than once, to help Zelnor.

It was selfish—so painfully selfish and irresponsible—but Zelnor didn't want Erianna to leave, either. In all honesty, she had never wanted her to leave.

"I don't," Zelnor whispered.

Erianna flashed the smuggest, most obnoxious grin Zelnor had ever seen.

"I knew you liked me. You like my gifts, my stories, my unfailing optimism, my radiant presence."

"I'm liking you less by the second."

Erianna slapped her hands on Zelnor's cheeks, smushing her face.

"I love it when you try to lie. It's adorable," Erianna cooed.

Lyle giggled, and the bard jerked backward. Her face flushed faint purple. Was she blushing? Before Zelnor could mock her, the ishlanian swung, a touch awkwardly, onto the cathmal. Erianna held out her hand, and Zelnor took it.

"Right, let's go then," Erianna said.

The bard drove her heels a little too sharply into the cathmal, and Eli lurched forward, nearly knocking Zelnor off and forcing her to grab onto Erianna's waist. After a moment, Zelnor regained her balance and let go.

"Sorry," Erianna muttered.

Even though the ishlanian was facing forward, Zelnor could tell she was embarrassed from her faint teal glow.

Chapter Twenty
Bokest al'Bar

A tall dune blocked their view of Bokest al'Bar itself, but Zelnor could finally see the odd shape at the top of the mesa on the far side of the city. She recognized it immediately from her dad's description: *"a GIANT sea monster pierced by three harpoons."* Though she knew it was a building, she couldn't help but see the ball of interwoven tubes as a mass of tangled tentacles lined with suckers. Just as he'd said, the sphere was pinned to the top of the hill by what looked like three spears. The landmark was unmistakable.

Erianna peeked past Eli's horns.

"What is that?" she asked.

"It's so… weird looking," Lyle said.

"That is Zoh'kret University," Zelnor said with a fond smile. "The largest hub of research, study, and teaching in all of Tularien."

"I assume you'll want to visit? Considering how obsessed with books you are," Erianna said.

"We need to find a healer for you first. But if we have time after, maybe we could stop by," Zelnor said.

"I wanna go too," Lyle chimed in. "I have to see what's inside!"

"Well. If *Lyle* wants to go, then I guess we have to," Zelnor said.

"All right," Erianna said. "We'll go to your nerd place."

"It's not a 'nerd place,'" Zelnor grumbled.

Erianna's shoulders shook with laughter, and Zelnor nudged her so hard the teal woman nearly fell off their cathmal.

Just as the sun was beginning to dip close to the horizon, the group finally reached the edge of the sprawling port city. It was different from anywhere Zelnor had ever been.

The city rested on a bed of compacted sandstone, sloping gradually up around the far mesa. Hundreds of ships of all sizes were moored at the enormous harbor. The ground around the docked vessels was alive with the constant movement of sailors and seaside merchants. Her grandparents (on her dad's side) had been sailors. Zelnor wished she could remember the stories her dad used to tell her about them.

The harbor was only a third of the grand city. The rest was a labyrinthine patchwork of architecture. A flood of color washed over the otherwise dull sea of sandstone buildings. From a distance, it looked like a field of flowers growing in the sand, but as they drew closer, Zelnor realized it was actually silks. The vibrantly dyed fabrics decorated homes and stores alike, strung between windows and stretched tightly as awnings for reprieve from the merciless sun. There was a soft boom in the distance. A blast of bright red fire flew into the sky and burst, dissolving before it could hit the ground again. The fizzling light drew Zelnor's eyes back up toward Zoh'kret University.

Of all the stories her father told, it was the tales that took place in the university that had captured her imagination. Zelnor had wanted to see Zoh'kret University for as long as she could remember, but she had hoped to reconcile with her mother first. No matter how angry she was with her, it didn't feel right to set foot in Bokest al'Bar when they were still on bad terms, not when she knew how much this city meant to her father.

Now that she was here, though, mere steps away from the city that her father was born and raised in, how could she possibly turn back? She was so close to finally learning more about him. Besides, they needed a healer and a ship willing to take them back to Alaspinor, both of which waited for them somewhere in Bokest al'Bar.

Walking into one of the most populated cities in Eltun was reckless, especially considering how many catastrophic near misses she'd had recently, but she was in as good a position to visit the city as she would ever be. Quelling that sandstorm and holding up Erianna had nearly drained her completely. Her elemental magic was just a gentle ripple between her stomach and chest that faded into the background. And all she'd needed to do for this momentary reprieve was nearly kill her traveling companion. Who wouldn't want elemental magic?

The sooner Zelnor returned to Alaspinor and finally washed her hands of her accursed powers, the better. The longer she waited, the more casualties would build up in her wake. Briefly endangering one city for one day with the currently low risk that she'd cast something was surely worth all the people she could spare later.

Maybe Zelnor was fretting over nothing. Things had gone all right in Nirdeem. Well, sort of. They would only be in Bokest al'Bar for a day. How much trouble could they possibly get into in just a day?

Zelnor dropped to the sand before their mount stopped completely. Finally, she crossed the boundary between the city and the surrounding desert. She reveled in the shift from deep sand to firm stone. She had officially entered Bokest al'Bar.

Erianna brought Eli to a proper halt before she dismounted with a surprising amount of grace for someone so new to riding cathmals.

She let go of the reins and nudged Eli, trying to prompt him to leave. The cathmal tilted his feline head and stared at her. Zelnor pursed her lips to hold back a laugh. She stepped in front of the singer, shooing her away and addressing Eli.

"Go back to Lia," Zelnor said.

Eli stared plaintively at her. He knew the Path. He'd been trained to take the same routes and stops that he had on the way here. Cathmals were well known for their impeccable memories. He was more than capable of going back by himself. He just didn't *want* to.

"I've missed you too," Zelnor whispered. "But you need to go home."

Eli stared at her for a moment, before he huffed. He licked her cheek with his scratchy tongue and waddled back into the desert.

Erianna watched the exchange with tightly crossed arms and a little pout.

"I could've convinced him to leave too, if you'd given me half a chance," she said.

That was horseshit, and they both knew it. Eli clearly liked Zelnor more. Granted, she did have an unfair advantage, given she'd raised the cathmal, not that she'd ever tell Erianna that. It was too funny watching the charismatic bard struggle to connect with Eli.

"Don't give me that look," Erianna said. "I know you have some sort of trick."

"If being likable is a trick," Zelnor said.

"Why don't you take charge, then? Find us a ship," Erianna said.

"No, no. I would never take away a chance for you to practice your people skills."

"Try not to fall behind while you're busy charming people."

Erianna led the party through the sinuous streets and deeper into the city. The colored silks were even more vivid up close. The fading golden light shone through them, splashing the streets with a rainbow of color. Nearly every building boasted some kind of mural—each painted with a variety of subjects and designs ranging from detailed and intricate, to hyper-realistic, to simplistically abstract. Commercial businesses and homes were nearly indistinguishable; only signs above the doors differentiated the two.

Zelnor could see now why some people called Bokest al'Bar the City of Artists and Academics. There was a certain unrestrained chaos to the place. Every corner burst with imagination unbound from the confines of its skull. She only hoped that the academics were as remarkable as the artists were.

Erianna stopped next to a shop called *Eulfson's Rare Imports and Exports.* A large mural of an ishlanian woman was painted around the door, and it struck Zelnor again just how inaccurate the public perception of ishlanians was. The painting didn't look anything like Erianna or Seshvin.

The woman in the painting had the same rounded, soft face as Erianna and the same longer, downturned ears, but instead of blue or green skin, the painter had made the woman pale white with long, wavy blond hair. A single strip of gray fabric stretched improbably across her bust. She was painted to look as though she were lounging atop the door. Her head was tilted down slightly, and she gazed coyly through her lashes. Waves crashed at her white, sparkling fish tail.

"What's this a painting of?" Lyle asked.

Erianna, who had been gazing at the shop with a blank expression, suddenly looked toward the ghost.

"What painting?" the ishlanian asked.

"…the one right in front of you," Zelnor said.

What had the bard stopped to look at, if not the art?

"Oh!" Erianna gasped, then she scowled. "Oh. That's Ireeshnem, goddess of the ocean."

So, *this* was the goddess of luck and the sea. Zelnor had never seen iconography of her before. In fact, she went out of her way to avoid Temples of Ireeshnem. Zelnor had lost her father at a young age, developed these stupid powers, and gotten stuck in a pact with a dragon. Fortune had never been on her side, and the last thing she needed was to piss the goddess off further and worsen her luck.

"Or I should say," Erianna continued, "it's a shitty interpretation of her."

"What's wrong with it?" Lyle asked.

"She's the only ishlanian in the pantheon and they make her into *that.*" Erianna gestured angrily toward the pale woman. "Why does she have a fish tail?"

"Well, what is she supposed to look like?" Zelnor asked.

"I don't know! It's not like I've met her," Erianna said. "But she can't be half-fish."

"Maybe she is," Zelnor said. "How would you know?"

"She's supposed to be ishlanian. Do I look half-fish?" Erianna asked.

"Well … you do have gills," Zelnor pointed out.

"And Seshvin had scales!" Lyle added.

"You're a bad influence on him," Erianna said.

Zelnor and Lyle shared a glance and smiled, both struggling with barely restrained laughter. Erianna huffed and strode forward, pointedly ignoring them. They'd only walked a couple of steps when a golden blur tackled Erianna.

The attacker dragged Erianna into a nearby alleyway, pulling Lyle along with them. Zelnor raced after them. Her magic leaped to her hands as she prepared a spell. Whoever this was, they were not kidnapping Erianna. Not again. Not on Zelnor's watch!

When Zelnor rounded the bend, she saw the attacker…hugging Erianna? *What in Vel'erma's Eternal Library?*

With an Alvetchian effort, Zelnor forced her elemental magic away from her fingertips. Thankfully, she'd released it recently, or she wouldn't have been able to stop herself. The stranger was a tall woman, almost as tall as Erianna, with pale skin and soft features. The human had long, light blond, wavy hair that flowed over her shoulders all the way down to her hips.

Who was she? Where had she come from? What was she doing here? And why was Erianna hugging the pretty woman so tightly?

Erianna let out a happy sigh, and Zelnor's stomach twisted. Lyle waved his hands in front of her. His little smile shook Zelnor out of her stupor.

"We should go say hi," Lyle whispered.

"They're busy. Let's just go," Zelnor said.

Lyle looked at Erianna and back to Zelnor. His plaintive gaze bore a striking resemblance to Eli's, but Zelnor stayed resolute. Finally, the ghost held out his hand, lifting the statue of Thermoren out of Erianna's large backpack and into Zelnor's waiting palms.

Zelnor clutched the statue tightly. What was she getting so worked up about? Erianna clearly knew this woman, so all this—whatever *this* was—really wasn't any of Zelnor's business. Erianna didn't want to visit the university anyway, so they might as well go without her. Erianna could get herself treated while they were gone. It would save time.

Zelnor turned away, walking quickly from the scene and toward Zoh'kret. It was a huge landmark. It couldn't be too hard to reach it, right?

Erianna still couldn't believe she had almost tried to murder her old friend. Entering Bokest al'Bar, Erianna had felt tense. Over these past few weeks, she had become increasingly sure that they were being followed. It wasn't all in her head, and it wasn't paranoia. She hadn't wanted to worry Zelnor and Lyle, but she had caught glimpses of someone or something following in the desert behind them.

Erianna had thought their stalker was finally making their move, lunging from the shadows to strike. When the blond had pulled her into the alley, Erianna had unsheathed her knife from her boot and held it to the stranger's throat. She was about to draw blood when she recognized the tall woman.

It was Christine! Erianna immediately pulled her old friend into a tight embrace, and the blond laughed. Erianna winced as a sharp pain bloomed in her shoulder. Christine pulled away to stare at the dark crimson splotches on Erianna's sleeve and chest, and the rust-brown stains on the bandage around her shoulder.

"What happened to you?" Christine asked.

"Oh, you know. Danger, daring feats, pie, nothing I can't handle."

Christine accepted her nonchalance, but a keen gleam in her eye told Erianna that her friend expected more details later. She rarely let a mystery go unsolved, especially when it concerned the safety of the people she cared about.

"Dodging the question, as usual, fish girl," Christine tutted.

"Would you stop calling me that," Erianna said.

Erianna shot her friend a sour look, but there was no real ire in her tone. Instead, she felt an overwhelming, warm relief settling across her shoulders. She still remembered the day when Torrin had told Christine he needed her in the war-torn country of Gealtalmh. Erianna had been sure their vicious fight would be the last words they ever said to each other. And yet, somehow, despite spending time in the most dangerous nation on Tularien, Erianna's oldest friend had survived.

But why hadn't Christine contacted her? No letters, no messages passed along at taverns where Erianna sang, no sign or even the barest hint that she was all right. Erianna had gone back to Goldhaven every couple of months for a *year* and never heard a word.

"It's been *four years*. Why in Thorns' unspoken name didn't you tell me you were all right?" Erianna said.

Christine flinched. She pulled away from their embrace and gave Erianna an annoyingly nonchalant shrug.

"I'm sorry, Eri! A lot happened after I left," Christine said. "I did *try*. I came back to Goldhaven a couple years ago, but you weren't there."

"You could have left a message," Erianna snapped.

"I didn't think of that," Christine said.

Erianna sighed. "You haven't changed at all."

"Haven't I?" Christine grinned and tilted her head.

She flicked the edges of a long, walnut-colored leather coat, revealing a darker brown vest, fitted snugly over a white tunic. She wore baggy, faded pants tucked into very practical, ankle-high boots. The last time Erianna had seen Christine, she'd been wearing a lacy dress with a full skirt. Erianna still remembered Christine's grousing when she'd gotten it stuck on a doorway.

Christine *had* changed, and it was more than just her clothes. She still had that openness, that teasing, almost mocking joy to her, but there were hints of their years apart. Little details that Erianna hadn't noticed at first: her once pale skin now sun-weathered; the strange wooden contraption in a holster at her waist; and a wild, overgrown quality to her hair, where it once had been pristine.

Erianna had trouble staying mad at Christine. After all these years, she finally looked happy. She finally looked like herself.

"I like the new outfit," Erianna said.

"You should see the hat!" Christine laughed and grabbed her hand. "Come on! I'll buy you a drink, and you can tell me more about this rogue pie."

"Hold on," Erianna said. "Lemme just check with…"

Erianna didn't see Zelnor. She scanned the alley. She jogged around the corner—but Zelnor was just *gone*. So was Lyle.

Where were they? *Oh gods.* The person following their group through the desert certainly hadn't been Christine; she would have announced herself immediately. What if the stalker had caught up to Erianna's friends? What if…

"They left while we were talking," Christine said.

Erianna patted the side of her bag. The statue was gone. Zelnor had taken Lyle and left without saying anything. Erianna couldn't believe it. Neither Zelnor nor Lyle had thought to let her know where they were going or even that they'd left at all.

Didn't she deserve at least that level of courtesy after everything they'd gone through? Zelnor had literally vanished once. It wasn't so outlandish that Erianna would worry about her when she suddenly disappeared again.

And what about that moment they'd had in the desert? They'd agreed to stay together—in a confrontation that was dramatic even by Erianna's standards. Zelnor couldn't possibly have forgotten it already. After all that, the two of them had really just slipped away?

Maybe Lyle was still mad at Erianna. She wouldn't blame him after what she'd done, but she'd thought that things had gotten better between them.

Christine's eyes sparkled with mischief.

"That half-elf is a shy one. He didn't even wave, just glared at me. Think he was jealous?" she asked.

Jealous? Of Christine? Erianna doubted it. Zelnor and Erianna had a passing attraction between them—well, Erianna certainly found Zelnor attractive, anyway, she'd made that clear from the out-set—but that's all it was, a *passing* attraction. Erianna enjoyed their light-hearted flirting, but Zelnor didn't have any interest in her beyond that, and that suited Erianna just fine. They knew each other far too well now to strike up a casual relationship.

"Zelnor's not jealous. Why would he be?" Erianna said.

"Actually, that's a good point. Why *is* he jealous when you're wearing that potato sack?" Christine asked.

She gestured at Erianna's formless, dusty desert clothes with a bemused quirk of her lips.

"They're called ful'prakta," Erianna said, butchering the name that Zelnor had told her. "Clothes specially designed for surviving in the desert."

"They certainly leave a lot to the imagination," Christine said. "Anyway. Let's get that drink. We'll catch up with *Zelnor* later."

Erianna could already tell Christine wasn't going to let this go. Erianna was hard to embarrass, so Christine relished every opportunity to tease her. As Christine bounded back out into the street, Erianna wondered where Zelnor had gone. Probably that Zokret school, gushing over some book. Erianna would have been bored out of her mind. She didn't really want to go anyway. They were probably better off going without her.

The more Zelnor thought about the encounter with the blond woman, the stupider she felt. Had the mage really been considering using her magic in the middle of a crowded city street? How had she summoned it so thoughtlessly? Who knew how many people would have gotten hurt if she hadn't stopped herself in time. And for what? Erianna could take care of herself. Zelnor knew that. She'd seen the teal woman single-handedly fight off a kidnapper, for Vel'erma's sake.

And to make matters worse, Zelnor and Lyle were definitely lost. The two of them had been walking for at least an hour, but somehow they hadn't gotten any closer to the university. They didn't have a map, and Zelnor was willing to bet that even if she did have one, she'd still manage to lose her way. The streets were deviously circuitous, almost like the city itself had malicious intent. Just when she was sure she'd finally found the right direction, they'd hit a dead end or the path would curve, and they'd end up walking away from Zoh'kret again.

They came to another intersection of three paths: two leading to the right, one leading to the left. Somehow all three of them led away from their destination. She had no clue which one to take. Maybe they should just turn around.

"Should we flip a coin?" Lyle asked.

"There are three paths," Zelnor pointed out.

"I could fly a little ahead and see where they lead?" Lyle offered.

"You wouldn't be able to look far enough," Zelnor said.

The longer they wandered aimlessly, the farther away they were going to get. Erianna always knew which direction to pick, but of course, she wasn't here when they needed her. She was busy with that blond woman. They would have to do without her. Zelnor could do this, right? She just needed to work up the courage to ask a local for directions.

"Excuse me," a voice said behind them.

Zelnor startled and stepped out of the way as an elderly kunari man passed them, his red feathers faded and streaked with white. He struggled to carry two large boxes in his wings.

"Would you like help?" Zelnor asked.

"I certainly wouldn't mind," the old kunari chuckled.

The kunari turned, craning his neck to see Zelnor around the boxes but ultimately giving up, as Zelnor took the box off the top. It wasn't as heavy as it looked, just bulky. *And thank the gods for that, I'm not nearly as strong as Erianna.* Zelnor adjusted her new cargo and turned her attention back toward the kunari, waiting for him to lead the way.

The elderly kunari just stared at her.

Most kunari were difficult to read, as their beaks didn't have the same range of movement that lips did, but Zelnor had gotten pretty good at deciphering their expressions, having grown up around so many. And it almost looked like the old kunari was *smiling?*

"So," Zelnor said. "Where are we taking these?"

"Ah, yes! My shop is close by, follow me," the kunari said.

Zelnor didn't get a chance to read the name of the shop as they walked in, but it was immediately clear that the kunari sold weapons. The interior was simple and practical. Adobe walls with wooden tables and shelves displayed traditional weapons like swords and bows, as well as more that she didn't recognize.

On the opposite side of the store, an elderly half-elven woman with gray hair pulled into a severe bun was furiously polishing a claymore. Her arms were surprisingly toned for her age, and she had no trouble moving the heavy weapon to get to the back side of the blade. The kunari man shuffled over and slipped his box onto the counter next to her.

"You should let Ves'rik do that," the old kunari scolded.

"I am perfectly capable of polishing a sword," she said.

"For the moment you are, darling," the kunari said, "but if you keep pushing yourself…"

"The child never does it right. No attention to detail in that one," the old woman groused. "Always polishes the hilt more than—"

The old woman froze when she looked in Zelnor's direction. The woman's mouth hung open. Her eyes scanned Zelnor quickly, and her brow furrowed. Zelnor stayed absolutely still under the woman's scrutiny, until the box started slipping through her arms.

"What are you doing just standing there?" the woman said.

Zelnor scurried up to place the box on the counter.

"Sorry," she mumbled.

The woman pulled the kunari closer to whisper in his ear. He muttered something back, smiling at Zelnor again. The old half-elf eyed Zelnor with another inscrutable stare, before polishing the claymore with a new intensity.

"Pulling strangers off the street. Forcing them to help, uncompensated," the woman scoffed. "You'll invite a murderer into our home one day."

"I'm not a murderer," Zelnor lied. "Although, if I was, I probably wouldn't tell you…but I'm not."

"I was not talking about you," the older half-elf said.

Zelnor couldn't help wondering what the woman would say if she found out that Zelnor had, in fact, killed someone.

The old kunari cleared his throat.

"Thank you so much for your help," he said. "I apologize. I haven't even introduced myself yet. I'm Zinneon Siebold. Call me Zinnie, and this"—he gestured to the woman polishing the greatsword—"is my wife, Lily Siebold. You can call her Lily."

"Colonel," the woman corrected.

Colonel. The elderly half-elf must be a foreigner. There was no formal military in Kialma'keer. She might be from Nirdeem, or maybe Gealtalmh? With the war going on in Gealtalmh and the woman's thick, lilting accent, the latter seemed likelier.

"Unpack the boxes," the colonel said.

"Of course," Zinnie said. "Zelnor, would you mind helping me?"

Zelnor unsealed the two packages, finding arrows in one and daggers and short swords in the other. Per the colonel's instruction, Zelnor tied the arrows into bundles of fifteen and placed them in front of the bows on display. Meanwhile, Zinnie balanced the blades on the iron hooks installed on the walls. As they worked, Lyle floated around the store examining their other wares.

Zelnor stopped midway through stocking the shelves. She clutched an arrow tightly. It had taken her a few minutes before she realized what the kunari man had said. He had called her Zelnor. And she was fairly sure that she hadn't introduced herself…

"How did you know my name?" Zelnor asked.

Zinnie paused and his shoulders sagged. He spoke without turning around.

"We knew your father," he said.

The colonel's hand tightened around her polishing brush, and Zinnie walked over to his wife, resting his wing on her arm.

"I'm going out again for a while, dear. Will you be all right?" he asked gently.

"Zinnie, you—"

The colonel stopped; her head whirled in the other direction.

"Don't touch anything," the colonel said.

Zelnor jumped, startled by the sudden order. She hadn't been anywhere near anything. The only things she had touched were the arrows in the box, and she had arranged them exactly the way the colonel had told her to.

"Uhhh…" Lyle stammered.

Zelnor turned to see Lyle caught in the act, hands about to graze an especially shiny lance. The colonel had addressed the ghost directly. She could see him. Her husband tilted his head and furrowed his brow. It was clear he had no idea who she was talking to.

"Sorry," Lyle said. "I promise I won't."

The colonel turned her attention back to her husband.

"Don't stay out too late," she said.

"I love you too," he replied.

Zinnie held the door open for Zelnor, ushering her out of the shop and back onto the street. Zelnor hesitated for a moment. She did wonder how the elderly half-elf was able to see ghosts, but … no, there would be time for questions later. She couldn't pass up this opportunity. Zinnie knew her father! She could finally find out more about him, and more importantly, the kunari might know what her mother was hiding from her.

Chapter Twenty-One
Artists and Academics

Christine urged Erianna forward, insisting her tavern of choice would be too crowded soon. When they rounded the final bend, they came upon a glistening beacon that stood out even among the color-soaked streets of Bokest al'Bar. Small lanterns of multicolored glass strung on metal cables crisscrossed over the restaurant. Crushed seashell paths led to large misshapen bowls covered with thick sheets of glass that Erianna only recognized as tables due to the chairs around them. The Ocean's Gems was scrawled in beautiful calligraphy across the ground.

The restaurant had no walls or doors, no structure at all. Just a patio with an open-air cooking hearth and an adobe oven at the far end. Three chefs worked in a flurry of motion, preparing ingredients and mixing drinks at stone tables near the ovens. Erianna had seen kitchens like it in Bimblebarrow, but they were never out in the open like this. Never outside.

Christine guided them to the only available table. The inside of the "bowl" they sat at had thousands of glittering green crystals of varying shades and sizes. It looked like a hazy cloud of shimmering stars as it sparkled in the setting sun. The sturdy chairs were white with green vines and leaves wrapping around the legs and up the back. They were surprisingly comfortable.

"This place is…" Erianna trailed off.

"I know!" Christine said. "Now. Your shoulder."

The wounds Erianna had forgotten throbbed. A full month to craft a better story and her mind still went blank. She'd never had any trouble spinning a good tale before, painting herself in an ever so slightly better light, but she needed more than a few slight tweaks for this one. The longer she dwelled on it, the more the words seemed to stick in her throat. Each explanation sounded worse than the last.

"Attacked by a beast in the desert," Erianna finally said.

"Really? And how were pies involved?" Christine asked.

Liscuntia, the pies. Erianna should never have mentioned that. It had sounded so charming as a little snippet of an anecdote, but it was a piece of a story that wasn't Erianna's to tell. She couldn't share Zelnor's secrets with anyone, especially Christine. The mage already didn't seem fond of her—at least, not yet—and Christine knowing too much, too soon, wouldn't help matters.

"That was separate. My friend spilled some pie on me," Erianna said. "Hence, the stains."

The explanation was as vague as she could make it without outright lying. Christine held her gaze for a pregnant pause.

"At least let Quinn do something about the wound," Christine said.

"Quinn's here?" Erianna asked.

Erianna hadn't spoken to Quinn, or any of Christine's old handmaidens, in ages. Christine's father wouldn't let Erianna back into the estate after his daughter had gone missing, and sneaking in would only get her friends in trouble. She wasn't sure why the man kept the handmaidens on, except maybe to lure Christine back to him.

"They all are! It's a great story. One of my best. I bet yours is better, though," Christine prompted.

"Sorry to disappoint," Erianna said.

"It's been a long time since we last saw each other, hasn't it?" Christine said.

Christine's eyes flashed, and Erianna thought she saw hurt there, but before Erianna could respond, a pretty elven woman with dark curls walked up to their table. She held a small book with a quill poised above it. Erianna stared at the beautiful elf for just a moment too long, and the woman tapped her quill against the parchment.

"Drinks?" the server asked.

Erianna started to speak, but Christine answered first.

"I'll have the chef's recommendation, and she'll have"—She smirked—"a tropical date."

The elven woman nodded and left.

"She was cute," Christine said.

"Mmhmm," Erianna hummed.

"Gonna do something about it?" Christine asked. "Turn on the charm? Because that first impression makes me think you've lost your touch. Or maybe…a certain handsome, older half-elf has—"

"This isn't about Zelnor. I'll admit it has been…a while. But I'm still as smooth as ever," Erianna said. "It's just more challenging in these clothes."

"Speaking of," Christine said, "the Erianna I know would never wear anything that didn't accentuate every pretty, little curve."

Erianna looked down at her ful'prakta, fiddling with the hem of her sleeve. She had never truly felt comfortable in the loose garments, but traveling with Zelnor, she'd forgotten all about them. Now, she wasn't quite sure she hated them anymore. Ful'prakta were hardly her outfit of choice, but they had kept her safe. If Lia hadn't gifted her these clothes, Erianna would probably never have made it across the desert. She supposed the clothes reminded her of the kind elf. The elf who also happened to be Zelnor's mother.

Zelnor's reaction to Lia still bothered Erianna. The stern woman had been so worried about Zelnor, and yet her daughter hadn't shown any interest in going back.

"If there are—If someone, a friend, has a problem with a family member, then you should intervene."

"Is that a question or a statement?" Christine asked.

"I don't know. A statement?" Erianna said.

"It depends on how long you've known Zelnor, and how close you two are."

"How did you know I was talking about—?"

"It was obvious," Christine said. "Anyway, I need more context, Eri. What happened with the half-elf?"

It was a long, very involved story, and more importantly, one Erianna couldn't share without Zelnor's permission. But Erianna desperately needed advice. She rarely stuck around anyone long enough to develop attachments, and apparently, befriending Zelnor came with its own special brand of annoyances and complications. She wished it was easier. Everything had been so easy with Christine, even a little too easy at times. Until it wasn't.

After a pause long enough for their drinks to arrive, Erianna decided to tell a modified version of the story.

"Zelnor went missing for a while, and I nearly died in the desert looking for him. I was saved by someone who I later learned was his mother. When I found him, we were still near his mom. She's kind, a good person, clearly worried about him, but he refused to see her!"

"Are you sure it was about her? Maybe Zelnor didn't want to leave you? He really likes you."

Christine was baiting Erianna. She wanted to rile Erianna up.

"It had nothing to do with me," Erianna said. "You can ask him yourself."

"I'd love to have a few conversations with him. If he comes back in time."

Oh. Christine wasn't staying. Of course she wasn't.

Erianna's drink was orangey-amber with streaks of pink running through it, and it smelled like fresh fruit. Erianna worried it was nonalcoholic as she took a long gulp of the almost overly sweet, viscous fruit juice, but then the burn hit her, along with a sweet smokey aftertaste. This "tropical date" tasted familiar.

Duur'een wine. This drink had duur'een wine. The same alcohol that Lia had given her. The same stuff that had turned her into a blubbering mess, and the same wine that she'd drunk alone, at the bottom of that cave. Erianna pushed the drink aside, resolving to only take small sips. This wine had never done her any favors.

"Lemme ask you this: would you have wanted someone to intervene with your mother?" Christine asked.

"My mother? I gave up hope on that a long time ago."

Christine flinched, and Erianna could almost see the way the flippant comment pained her. "I'm sorry I didn't know you back then," Christine said.

"Doesn't matter. I'm away from her now," Erianna said.

Erianna tried to smile, but she could feel it turn into a grimace. Christine squeezed her arm, eyes filled with pity. Erianna yanked her arm away and readjusted her um'prakta.

"Eri. If you ever want to talk about it—"

"Like I said, I'm fine. So, about Zelnor."

Christine sighed and sat back in her chair.

"Talk to him about it first," she advised. "Family relationships can be messy. You and I know that better than anyone. If you aren't careful, you'll cause more issues than you fix."

"How did you know my father?" Zelnor asked Zinnie the question the moment the kunari closed the door.

"Ah." The old kunari chuckled. "Straight to the point. A lot like your mother in that respect."

"You know my mother too?" Zelnor asked.

How could she not recognize Zinnie when he knew her mom *and* dad?

"I only met her twice. Under the best and worst circumstances," Zinnie said. "But this is a particularly involved conversation. Is there anywhere you wanted to go? Perhaps a sight you wanted to see?"

"Zoh'kret," she said.

"Oh, I see. Did you come here to learn more about Kezok?" the kunari asked.

"I hoped that I would meet someone who worked with him there," Zelnor admitted.

Of course, she wanted to go to the university just for the sake of seeing it—it was the largest university in the world—but learning about her father was the main reason she had planned on visiting Bokest al'Bar. Her mother had refused to tell Zelnor how he died, and the mage was convinced it had something to do with her father's work.

Zinnie started walking, gesturing for Zelnor to follow. Lyle and Zelnor fell into step with him, easily matching the kunari's leisurely pace.

"Kezok's parents both made a living in the Circle of Commerce," Zinnie said.

"The Circle of Commerce?" Lyle asked.

Zelnor repeated his question.

"It's the largest trade route on the Ethnarian Ocean, connecting the port here to Gealtalmh and Goldhaven. Razif'rik, your grandfather, was an old friend of mine. Asked Lily and me to take care of Kezok while they were away, which was unfortunately the majority of the year."

"So, you basically raised my dad," Zelnor concluded.

"He was like a son to us," Zinnie said.

"Then why didn't my dad ever…?"

"Lily and Lia …" Zinnie sighed. "We met your mother first at the wedding, and it was so sudden for Lily and me—the marriage, starting his family so far from his work and his home, on the other side of Vaal'akkars' Wrath… Neither of us were happy about it. My wife fought for him to stay here. Lia didn't take it well.

"Both of them are too stubborn, too similar. Neither wanted to acquiesce because neither wanted to give him up. So, he did his best to split his time between both of them and his work and you, and inadvertently, became just like his own parents…"

The kunari's eyes drifted toward the horizon.

"The next time we saw Lia, and the first time we saw you, was the funeral," he said. "So often, you only realize how much time you've wasted when it's already gone."

The old kunari seemed to get lost in the memory for a moment, before shaking his head and smiling.

"But that's not what you wanted to hear was it?" Zinnie asked. "I'm sure you wanted to know what your father was like as a child, all his embarrassing secrets?"

"I don't know about embarrassing," Zelnor said. "I just want to know him."

"He was a wonderful man to know. Kezok…" Zinnie beamed. "He was bright. A scholar from a young age. Quiet, not because he didn't have anything to say, but because he wanted to listen. To learn. He was incredibly determined, though Lily would call him stubborn instead."

"Mom used to call him stubborn too," Zelnor said.

"More than anything, he loved stories. He loved history, loved old myths, tall tales, and ordinary stories about people and life. For a while, we thought he'd become an author, but then he started studying anthropology and archeology and, well…found his calling."

"I remember the stories he told more than I remember him," Zelnor said. "He always brought me new books and told me about adventures, but they were never his adventures."

"He had his secrets. Especially near the end," Zinnie said.

Zelnor nodded. Her father had seemed more guarded in his final year. The stories that he always told had become shorter and stranger. The ground beneath Zelnor started sloping upward as the kunari led Lyle and Zelnor closer to Zoh'kret University.

"Zinnie… How did my dad die?" Zelnor asked.

It was the question on the tip of her tongue throughout the entire conversation. The question that had plagued Zelnor for a decade now. It caused the infamous fight with her mother that marked the start of her curse and prompted her to finally leave home for good.

"I don't know," Zinnie said. "He changed after you fell ill."

"You were sick?" Lyle asked.

"I don't remember being sick," Zelnor said.

"You were an infant," Zinnie said. "Inflicted with some unknown disease. Kezok worked tirelessly for a cure and must have found something. But not long after you recovered, he became obsessed over some new avenue of research."

"What was it?" Zelnor asked.

"He never told us. Only talked to Lia about it. But over the years, he changed drastically. Until he suddenly stopped visiting us, and I just knew something must've gone terribly wrong. Lily blames your mother, of course."

"Do you?" she asked.

"Well… I shouldn't say this as a scholar, but some knowledge is better left untouched. Some things, when uncovered, do more harm than good.

"I knew Kezok. He would've traveled to the ends of Tularien to find answers for you and Lia, no matter the cost. And I believe…the final cost was higher than he expected," the kunari concluded. "And on that cheerful note, we've arrived."

Their group had reached the bottom of the steep slope. Before them was an enormous contraption. The solid metal frame, taller than the three of them combined, had two hefty steel cables connecting to an identical steel frame at the top of the hill. A large carriage, soldered to the metal ropes, gradually approached the bottom frame, where a small crowd had gathered.

"I see you're interested in the HAMOC," Zinnie said. "Want to know a bit about it?"

Zelnor nodded, unable to tear her eyes from the machine.

"The Horseless Arial Mechanist-Operated Carriage was invented just four years ago. The steel cables are like spools of thread. A team of capable workers turns pulleys to move the 'thread,' and therefore the carriage, up and down."

"That's incredible," Zelnor breathed.

"*Brilliant,* if you ask me. In my day, if we wanted to leave the college, we used the stairs. Took hours and certainly wasn't for the faint of heart," the kunari said. "Most chose to live in the dorms."

"What's the cannon for?" Lyle asked.

"Cannon?" Zelnor repeated.

The mage glanced to her right and saw a narrow cannon with a long stick in the end pointed at the sky.

"Oh. What is that for?" she asked.

"It's called a flash explusor—an integral part of the HAMOC. It shoots a harmless, dissipating burst of fire into the sky to signify to the other station that all the passengers have boarded. Still can't believe he wanted to name it the *dazzle blaster,*" Zinnie laughed.

Zelnor didn't respond, far too enthralled by the HAMOC to pay the joke much mind. She knew that Zoh'kret was a haven for academics, but she had underestimated just how brilliant the minds at this place were. Growing up in Kezeek Mesa, and then remaining in Alaspinor, she'd never seen such an impressive feat of mechanics in her entire life.

Lyle floated up next to the cables.

"Is it *safe?* It doesn't seem safe," the ghost said.

"Would you rather take the stairs?" Zelnor asked.

The mage inclined her head toward the steep, endless steps the old kunari had mentioned. Lyle glanced between them and the HAMOC. Was he actually considering taking the stairs? *Of course he is. He can just fly up them.*

"I think I am a trifle old for that," Zinnie said.

The kunari mistakenly believed that Zelnor was talking to him.

"Wait, you're coming with us?" Zelnor asked. "Weren't you just showing us the way?"

"My son works here, so I've decided on a little surprise visit," the kunari said. "It has been a while, and retirement would get rather dull without some spontaneity."

"CLEAR THE WAY!" a human woman bellowed as the carriage approached.

The crowd backed away from the metal frame, and the HAMOC stopped with a soft thunk, swinging back and forth. The spacious carriage had two tall, barred windows on either side and the word HAMOC printed on the closest side. The door had a large padlock on it. Zinnie noticed Zelnor's curious gaze and explained.

"The bars and lock are safety measures. When they were first made, a couple people fell out when the carriage was jostled in a strong southwestern wind."

Lyle floated back to Zelnor and stared at her pointedly.

"I'm sure it's safe now," she said.

"Quite," Zinnie said. "Hasn't been an accident since."

"Zelnor," Lyle whined.

"What do you care, you're already dead," Zelnor muttered.

Lyle flinched. She realized the comment had come off harsher than she'd meant it to.

"I'm sorry," Zelnor whispered. "I didn't mean—"

"STAND BY," the operator shouted.

The attendant unlocked the door, and a small group of people filtered out; some desperate to get off, others too busy reading a book or tinkering with little contraptions to even notice they had arrived. The operator cleared everyone out, and soon the HAMOC was completely empty.

"NOW BOARDING," the woman yelled.

"Hurry now. The operators aren't known for their patience," Zinnie said.

Zelnor and the kunari stepped inside. Lyle drifted in reluctantly behind them. Zinnie led her to the window, promising her that she would want to see the view. A dozen more passengers filed in, but the space was more than large enough to accommodate them all. The operator shut the door and locked it.

There was a *hiss* followed by a large *bang!* The carriage jolted forward, throwing Zelnor off-balance. She grabbed the bars on the window just as the contraption started moving. The HAMOC swayed, and Lyle poked his head out the top of the carriage to inspect the machinery. Zelnor doubted he'd find anything amiss, but his worrying unsettled her. She tried to enjoy the ride nonetheless.

The view really was beautiful. As they rose, the Ethnarian Ocean sparkled with the last rays of the setting sun. The glistening oranges, deep reds, and lingering pinks caused the water to glitter with what looked like a million jewels. Light from the waves danced across the sea of rooftops between them—making the already vibrant city shimmer with a magic beyond even Zelnor's capabilities. The ride was over all too soon, lurching to a sudden stop. Luckily, Zelnor was prepared this time and managed to keep her footing.

"STANDBY," bellowed a muscly half-elven man.

With a *click,* the door opened and the three streamed out with the other passengers. A strong wind swept across the campus, rattling the carriage behind them. The packed sandstone was unnaturally smooth beneath the soles of Zelnor's leather boots.

There it was: Zoh'kret University.

The massive building was absolutely *fascinating* up close. It was made of the same sandstone as the mesa, but nothing about the structure looked natural. The plethora of tubes that twisted around the building were actually just two tubes. They wound several times around the sphere, crossing over each other until they fully covered the building. But somehow the system of tubes stood completely independent of the main structure! There was a visible gap between the tubes and the main sphere. *How is that possible?*

The little spheres lining the outer edge of the long cylinders were even more implausible. It wasn't just the fact that they managed to stay attached and not weigh down the tubes, despite the sheer number of them. They were also perfectly spaced from each other with gaps at just the right spots, so that the tubes still fit together.

Zelnor couldn't even begin to imagine how much planning had gone into this building. Was a feat of engineering this great even possible without magic?

And what about those three towers protruding from the top? How did anyone get inside them? The two shorter ones to the left and right might have hidden entrances on the other side, since they were closer to the back of the structure. But what about the tall tower directly in the center? That one had to be difficult to access.

Nothing about Zoh'kret University made sense, and that fact filled Zelnor with more wonder than she'd felt since she was a child. She could see why her father described the structure the way he had. It was a difficult building to picture without an outlandish metaphor, and the college did almost look like a castle that a sea monster had strangled with its tentacles. But the description didn't quite do the meticulous creation justice.

The university looked like…a carefully woven knot of pastry with even, perfectly spherical piped dollops of frosting so neat that it would take years of training to achieve. No, that wasn't quite right. Maybe more like a spherical metal cage with wide bars trapping the inner sphere…but it also had tiny spheres on the bars, for some reason? What would that make the towers sticking out from the top? Keys…? Gods, that was a terrible description. She had never been any good at metaphors.

"How has this not collapsed?" Lyle asked.

Zelnor was too enamored to relay the question, and Zinnie had already moved on, striding forward and gesturing to the sight before them.

"Welcome to Zoh'kret University," the kunari said. "Those buildings to the left are the bungalows: dorms for students and nontenured faculty."

He gestured to row upon row of ramshackle buildings to the left of the university. The wooden structures looked one light sea breeze away from collapse. Zelnor couldn't imagine they were particularly comfortable to live in.

"They were only supposed to be temporary, but the funds to replace them are constantly allocated toward research instead," Zinnie said.

"That's awful!" Lyle exclaimed.

"Don't the people who live there get a say?" Zelnor asked.

"Unfortunately, they do," Zinnie said. "As often as the faculty and researchers complain, when the time comes to divvy out funds, they always campaign for their own departments instead of their quarters. The price of letting academics set their own budget."

As the three moved farther into the campus, people of all kinds started pouring out of the university. Zelnor recoiled a little at the sudden throng of students surrounding them. Despite its popularity, she somehow hadn't expected the college to have so many students. There were more people here than the entire town of Bimblebarrow.

"As for the college itself, there are six floors. The teaching halls and library are in the interior of the main sphere," Zinnie said. "The tubes are long hallways that allow access to the faculty and researcher offices in the smaller spheres along the outside. The towers are for housing tenured professors, and of course, the headmaster, who traditionally resides in the top of the central tower."

"But how does it all…work?" Zelnor asked. "I mean how does it stay standing?"

"The building has been around as long as anyone can remember, as sturdy and enduring as the mesa itself," Zinnie said.

"I think that means he doesn't know," Lyle said.

"But he does seem to know a lot about Zoh'kret," Zelnor said.

"Well, I have guided a prospective student or two," the kunari said. "Regardless, that one was Kezok's office."

Zinnie pointed to one of the spheres on the far-right side of the college, near its base.

"You'll need the key, but I'm sure you'll get it somehow," he said. "And if you want to chat with this old kunari again, come back to Wisdom's Weapons any time."

"Wisdom's Weapons?" Zelnor asked.

"My wife's weapon shop," Zinnie answered.

"Right. We'll probably be leaving soon, but maybe next time," she said.

"Until then," Zinnie said.

The old kunari wandered off, leaving Zelnor and Lyle to explore the greatest house of knowledge ever established.

Erianna, despite her best efforts to drink slowly, had finished her first "tropical date" and ordered a second. Considering the added juice in the blend, she figured there wasn't any harm in it. Even with the addition of duur'een wine, she highly doubted she'd get drunk off a cocktail like this one.

Erianna had avoided asking Christine about her time in Gealtalmh and Torrin's mission, and in return, Christine didn't press Erianna for details about Zelnor or the "beast" that had attacked her. They were hardly lacking for conversation, though. After so long apart, they had plenty of other stories to share.

Christine's story was as exhilarating as promised. Her daring rescue of her handmaidens from her devious father's employment would have drawn nearly as many people to a tavern as Erianna's songs. Maybe an even larger crowd, if Erianna were entirely honest. Christine would have made an excellent bard, if she weren't so set on a life of adventure and piracy.

Christine leaned forward, bracing her hands on the glass surface of the table. "There I was, in the dead of night," she said. "I used our old signal."

"Three flashes from a hooded lantern," Erianna said.

"You remember!" Christine said.

"Of course." Erianna chuckled.

They'd gotten into so much trouble back then. *I suppose we both still get into trouble. Just separately.*

"Then, Annette opens the window, and—"

"How are things with Annette? Any progress?" Erianna asked.

"I'll get to that part." Christine smiled coyly. "So, Annette opened the window and shooed me away, because apparently my father had an unexpected visitor that night."

Erianna nearly lost it when Christine dramatically announced that Jörnn Eulfson, Christine's fiancé, had rather unfortunately picked that evening to discuss her disappearance with her father. Jörnn and Christine had been engaged since her birth, and she absolutely despised him, as did Erianna and anyone else that had the misfortune of meeting the bastard.

"Are you still engaged to him?" Erianna asked.

"It's complicated," Christine said.

"Is it? You either are or you aren't," Erianna said.

"Ha! Wish someone would tell *him* that," she scoffed. "Anyway. I needed a new plan. And that's when I ran into this strange ishlanian named Otto."

Erianna would have accused Christine of exaggerating, but even she couldn't make up someone so peculiar. According to Christine, Otto was an ishlanian man with ram's horns, and as strange as his appearance was, his mannerisms were apparently even stranger. He had spoken as though he were the protagonist in an adventure novel, proclaiming that he would right the wrongs committed against the merchant's daughter. Amused by his antics and lacking better options, she had hired Otto to occupy her father.

"He claimed to specialize in distractions," Christine said.

Despite his assurances, the odd ishlanian had nearly bumbled the whole thing, but in the end, he'd managed to give Christine's friends the opportunity to slip past her father. Thanks to Otto's help, the handmaidens had managed to escape the house undetected by Master Glymnoire, but unfortunately, someone saw them flee the estate: Jörnn. On his way out, he spotted the group heading toward the wharf.

"The bastard followed us all the way to the quay," Christine said. "He was probably waiting for the perfect moment to drag me back to my father."

"Did you shake him?" Erianna asked.

Back when they were friends, Christine had no trouble losing the many tails hired by her father. She had a knack for getting them out of tight spots—a talent that the two troublemakers had most certainly abused.

"We did, of course, but he was still close-by, and he'd blocked off the streets. The ocean was our only escape," Christine said. "And we had to leave fast."

She took a long swig of her drink.

"We couldn't exactly ride the barge I came in on. We needed something subtler, and we found the perfect little ship," Christine said. "But we didn't have any money. So, I tried sweet-talking the owner, flirting a little, but she clammed up."

"*Really?*" Erianna said.

Christine's persuasiveness was legendary.

"Turns out, she wasn't the owner." Christine paused for dramatic effect. "She was a guard."

Erianna laughed. "No…"

"Yes!" Christine slammed her hand on the table, and the server glared. She waved apologetically before continuing.

"The guard was suspicious, and we had no idea what to do. Eleanor was seconds away from knocking her out, Amelia barely holding her back. Elizabeth snuck away to steal the ship, while Camilla tried to play off the whole thing as a joke. It was chaos!"

"What happened? Did you get caught?" Erianna asked.

"That's the best part." Christine grinned. "Annette stepped forward, put her arm around me, and said, 'Why are you keeping my wife from boarding her own ship?'"

"That worked?" Erianna asked.

"Not at first… The guard demanded paperwork proving I owned the boat. But Annette said," Christine spoke in a gruff tone, "'We already showed you the paperwork. Just yesterday! You have got to be the most incompetent guard I've ever met.' And then the guard scampered off to check her records, and we stole the *Scarlette Wind.*"

"Brilliant!" Erianna exclaimed.

"I know! And the whole time, I was just a stuttering *idiot*. All I could think about was her arm wrapped around me. And later, when we were out at sea, and Goldhaven was just a little flicker of torchlight, Annette and I kissed."

"Congratulations! You two deserve it," Erianna said.

"Thank you! It was amazing. And a few months ago, we got married."

"And you didn't invite me?" Erianna asked.

"It wasn't anything official," Christine assured. "More like a promise to each other. Until I can break off the engagement with Jörnn."

"Right, Jörnn." Erianna's lip curled.

"Damn bastard won't let me go. But I promise when I've finally shaken him, you'll be invited to the real wedding. And"—Christine smirked—"you can bring along that handsome half-elf, who's 'definitely not a crush.'"

Erianna ignored her old friend's not-so-subtle implication.

"You really have to leave tonight," Erianna said.

"Is that a question or a statement?" Christine asked.

"A question," Erianna said.

"You already know the answer, Eri."

The pirate picked up her glass.

"Let's have a toast! To love," Christine said.

Erianna rolled her eyes. So *predictable*.

"Absolutely not," she said.

"Fine," Christine sighed. "Then, how about to old friends?"

"To old friends," Erianna agreed.

She clinked her drink against her old friend's cup and downed the remaining third of her tropical date. Erianna's head started feeling a little floaty. That…probably hadn't been the wisest choice.

"It's Jörnn's fault I can't stay. Hard to stay in one place when your ex is constantly chasing you," Christine said.

"No one likes being chased," Erianna said.

She stared longingly at her empty glass. She wanted to drink until she forgot all about the shitty people pursuing her.

"So, Eri. I've got some unfinished business you might be able to help with."

Christine cackled. Erianna was almost afraid to ask. She recognized that evil spark in her old friend's eyes. *In for a silver, in for a gold.*

"All right. Unfinished business?" Erianna asked.

"Remember Dirk?" Christine asked.

"Jörnn's brother? The creep who flirted with you?"

"And called me the embodiment of Ireeshnem, his 'aquatic goddess.' Yes, *him.*" Christine shivered. "He's in charge of Jörnn's import, export shop here, but he's out of town. I thought I might pay their shop a visit before I set sail again."

"So, it was the same Eulfson. I passed by that shop earlier

when—Wait, did you say *sail?*" Erianna shouted.

Some of the other patrons glared at her, and she slumped self-consciously into her seat, glowing bright teal.

"Yes, sail." Christine laughed. "I've mentioned the *Scarlette Wind* several times now."

"Zelnor and I are looking for a ship," Erianna said. "So, if you're headed in the same direction—"

"We don't have any travel plans," Christine interrupted with a huge grin. "We would be happy to take you anywhere. I'm sure Annette wouldn't mind!"

"This is perfect!" Erianna said. "Oh. But I should probably ask Zelnor first. One of us should show a little courtesy, at least."

Where had that pesky half-elf got to? Oh right, that college place thingy… What was it called again? Zegra, Zeggo. Ziggy. ZOogLiE. Erianna giggled.

"Of course, but first." Christine leaned in, bouncing up and down in her chair. "First we do some crime."

"Just like old times," Erianna said.

"Melinda!" Christine called to their server (whose name was definitely *not* Melinda). "Another round of drinks for OLD TIMES!"

The pretty elven server frowned at them and sighed as she finished taking the order of a human man with dirty blond hair. The man had his steely, brown eyes fixed on them. He looked familiar, but Erianna couldn't put her finger on where she'd seen him.

As the server relayed their order to the bar, getting them their third round of drinks, Erianna decided she didn't care who that man was *or* why he was judging her. Nothing would ruin the long-awaited reunion of the two rowdiest criminals in Tularien.

Chapter Twenty-Two
Dr. Kezok Çahra'keen

Zelnor idled in the quad of Zoh'kret University. She allowed herself a moment to take everything in. Lyle seemed strangely fascinated with the giant constellation etched into the middle of campus. She knew a fair bit about astronomy, thanks to the odd book here and there, but she didn't recognize this particular constellation, and she was certain her father had never mentioned it either.

The carving showed a single star surrounded by five others. Star constellations were usually represented with straight lines, but these lines curved into loose spirals that joined the five outer points to the center. Two large concentric circles surrounded the design. Simple depictions of fire, lightning, rock, water, and wind were carved in between the two circles, each above a star.

In an odd way, the carving reminded her of the university itself—curving, circular, and wholly unexpected in its unique design. It clearly symbolized something…maybe some sort of elemental harmony?

A figure knocked into Zelnor's shoulder, apologizing profusely as she hurried off. The stranger inadvertently directed her attention back toward Zoh'kret University, and she saw something she'd missed before—three curtain-covered archways at the base of the main sphere. They fluttered a bit before settling back into place.

Why would they choose curtains instead of doors for their main entryway? Considering how regularly they must need to replace them, it hardly seemed worth it. At least they maintained them well. Unlike the dingy, dismal bungalows, the yellow, gray, and orange fabrics were still bright and distinct. Did that combination of colors also represent something? Maybe they were just the school's colors.

Zelnor wished Zinnie were still around to answer more questions, but his absence was probably for the best. She could spend days here, and a proper tour would only make it harder to leave. Even with her magic so docile, she'd prefer not to push her luck. For now, she needed to focus on finding a way into her father's office.

Zelnor scanned the crowd. Some of the students and faculty had gathered on the quad in small groups, having debates or checking their bags. A surprisingly large number of people plopped down right there on the mesa floor, laying out books and studying them intently. Didn't they have a library for that?

A kunari woman with an absurd number of books spread in a semi-circle around her caught Zelnor's eye. She tugged at her pale brown feathers, her eyes only pausing on each page a minute before flicking over to the next one. Zelnor wondered if she'd overestimated the appeal of attending a university. It seemed…more stressful than she'd pictured.

The kunari woman scooped her books up into a teetering pile and staggered to her feet. Behind her, a middle-aged human man scribbled in a small journal as he walked. His beige coat must have had a hundred small pockets. He didn't look up once, despite getting dangerously close to crashing into several harried students.

The absentminded man continued striding forward, heading straight toward the kunari woman. Unlike the other students, the woman couldn't see beyond the stack of books in front of her. The student turned and crashed right into the man.

The kunari pitched forward but managed to keep ahold of her books. For a half-second, Zelnor thought it would be all right. Unfortunately, the middle-aged man was not nearly so coordinated.

The man's notebook slipped out of his hands as he toppled over. Ink soared out from an open inkwell, staining the pale mesa floor with dark spots. Items flew out of nearly every pocket. A couple of stones hit nearby students, leaving nasty bruises in their wake, and a rotten fruit splattered across a distinguished-looking elven professor's face. The professor pulled lumps of fruit out of his salt and pepper hair.

"Watch. Where. You're. Going. *Archibald,*" the elven man spat.

"Hah, sorry about that," the middle-aged man said. "Suppose I should stop keeping snacks in my coat..."

When the man with pockets spoke, Zelnor recognized a slight Alaspinoran accent.

"I'm so sorry, Professor Ludlark!" the kunari student squeaked. "It was all my fault!"

The professor growled and stomped off in the other direction, not bothering to acknowledge her apology.

"I'm so sorry," the student repeated. "So, so, so sorry! Let me just—let me help clean it up."

The kunari bent down and started to help, but froze, her beady black eyes staring at the setting sun in horror.

"It's all right," the middle-aged man started, "I know that you—"

"By the Eternal Library, when did it get so LATE?" the student screeched.

The kunari woman sprinted away, and the middle-aged man ran a hand through his auburn hair, streaking it with black ink. The silver at his temples was almost completely black. The man must get annoyed fairly often, or maybe he was just in the habit of bumping into people and flinging ink everywhere.

"I know you didn't mean to," the man finished. "They never do."

He glanced down at his belongings, strewn all over the mesa: innumerable rocks of all shapes and sizes; three iron keys; a series of full and partially full notebooks, accompanied by several quills; and two inkwells and an inkpot—all empty, with their contents flowing over the ground. He sighed and crouched down, putting everything back into its respective place.

Zelnor stooped down next to him, piling his items in a little heap for easier access. Lyle used his power to lift a limestone chunk back into the man's top pocket. A few people wandered closer to help, but seeing the various objects floating on their own, they quickly retreated. Somehow, the academic didn't notice the flying rocks or the scared students. Zelnor couldn't help but marvel at his focus as she stacked scratched pieces of quartz onto the pile.

"This guy has a lotta rocks," Lyle said.

"Yeah, he's got a pretty comprehensive rock collection," Zelnor agreed.

"I should hope so," the man said. "Though I'd call them specimens rather than a 'collection.'"

He put a small scraping tool back into a pocket near the bottom of his coat. He picked up all three iron keys and frowned at them. Holding one and comparing it to the rest, he shook his head with a sigh and dumped them all into the same pocket.

"So, he studies rocks. Cool!" Lyle said.

"What is there about rocks to study?" Zelnor asked.

The man's eyes lit up. "SO MUCH! Stones, minerals, and crystals can tell us...about..."

When he finally looked up, he trailed off. Zelnor glanced over her shoulder, expecting to see the angry professor again, but the redheaded man was staring at her.

"Kezok," the man said. "You're alive?"

The redhead reached out and put a hand on Zelnor's shoulder.

"I'm so glad. Why didn't you say something sooner?" the man said. "We have so much to speak of! I finished my paper. And I kept your office inta—"

"I'm not, um… My dad is dead," Zelnor interrupted. "Sorry."

"Oh," the man said. "Of course, he is. I had hoped… I should've known better."

"Sorry," Zelnor repeated.

"I wasn't aware Kezok had a son," the academic said.

"Yeah. Hi. I'm Zelnor."

She stuck out her hand.

"Zelnor? Huh." He shook her hand. "Archibald Gossimare, well, Archie. Geoarchaeological researcher and an old friend of your father's."

"Nice to meet you," Zelnor said.

"I've actually been holding onto something of his for a while. I think you should have it."

Lyle and Zelnor followed Archie to the start of the tunnels surrounding Zoh'kret University. The ends of each tunnel were as tall as a house! Zelnor inspected the circle on her right. She couldn't see any entrances, just the same smooth packed sandstone. How were they meant to get in?

She heard a faint rustle. The three curtains that led into the main building rippled gently with the wind. Up close, the archways were at least twice her size. Standing at the base of the imposing university was an almost overwhelming experience.

Lyle waved to get her attention. He flew to the top of the arches and pointed out a phrase carved above the entrances. Zelnor couldn't read it from her current angle.

Archie paused when he realized what had caught her attention.

"The school's motto," he said. *Lux mentis illuminat mundum.* No one knows where the language came from, drives the linguistics department crazy. We know what it means, at least: 'the light of the mind—'"

"'— illuminates the world,'" Zelnor finished.

"Yes! You… You can't read it, can you?" he asked.

Zelnor had finished the phrase on instinct. She had forgotten it until now, but those words had haunted her father in his final moments.

"It was one of the last things my dad ever said," Zelnor said.

That night, ten years ago, the tiniest sliver of Parenus had cast the pale sands in a dim white glow. Her father was home for the first time in months, and yet he'd scarcely left his office. The little bungalow her mother had built for him was only a few hours away from Kezeek Mesa, but her mother didn't want Zelnor making the journey alone. And every time she asked to go see him together, her mother would find a new excuse to put the visit off.

In hindsight, Zelnor understood why. Her father hadn't been well. His hair had gone prematurely white, and his hands trembled. He was always muttering something under his breath. Sometimes, she caught him drinking from a flask while he worked. And yet, despite all that, he was still her father, the person she loved more than anything. She had been determined to see him, whether her mother approved or not.

Zelnor had trekked out to his office, nearly getting lost in the process, and crept up to the door. She heard yelling from within. Her fist froze mid-knock. Slowly, she nudged the door open and saw her father shouting at an empty space.

"Lux mentis, lux mentis! The light of the mind illuminates the world. The light of the mind. The light. How is it connected? Tell me! Please."

Suddenly, he had turned toward the door, and Zelnor saw his eyes—vacant, glistening pure white in the dim moonlight. She ducked out of view, pressing her back against the frigid wall.

Her heart beat too loudly. She was terrified he'd discover her. But after a moment, he started his relentless chant again, and Zelnor scurried away, shaken to her core.

The next day, a villager found him a few miles away. Dead. Zelnor remembered the confusion that ensued and the subsequent funeral. But how could she have forgotten that night? No matter how many years had passed, how could she forget something so, so…

"What does it mean?" Lyle asked.

Zelnor thought, at first, that Lyle was talking about her father, but the boy was still staring at the inscription above the archways. She explained the phrase the same way her father once had.

"It means that smart people make the world better," she said.

"That's one interpretation," Archie agreed. "But you know scholars, the only thing they like more than learning new things…"

"…is arguing about them," Lyle and Archie said together.

Zelnor laughed at the pout on the ghost's face.

"Where did you hear that?" she asked.

"It's just a little joke among us academics," Archie responded with a grin.

The group turned back toward the large sandstone tube on their right. Archie pressed his hand onto the giant circle and another smaller circle appeared inside it, as though it had been instantly cut from the stone. The newly formed circle rolled out of sight, leaving a large opening.

Zelnor leaped through it, immediately examining the other side. There was no sign of the door. The stone circle that had rolled away had seemingly vanished. She stuck her head back out again to check the inside of the gap. The wall was pretty thick. She wondered if…

Aha! The door slid *into* the wall. But how? There must be some complex machinery pushing and pulling it.

"I would move, if I were you," Achie said. "They close on their own."

Zelnor quickly withdrew her head, and the researcher led the two through an uncomfortably warm hallway. There was a *CCRRR* and a heavy *THUNK,* as the stone sealed shut behind them.

They walked alongside a row of round, wooden doors. She noted that all the doors were on the right side of the walkway. She had suspected that additional, smaller offices secretly connected the tunnels to the main building, but apparently her theory was wrong.

Some of the doors had increasingly ridiculous "do not disturb" missives tacked onto them. Zelnor paused briefly, as the bold letters of one of these notes caught her attention. *"And if Professor Ludlark asks, I've died. I suffocated in a pile of my students' term papers, and it was most certainly his fault."* Zelnor snorted. She was about to ask Archie whose office it was when she realized he was already several feet ahead of her.

Zelnor jogged to catch up to the surprisingly fit man. It only took a few moments before she was falling behind again, and she was grateful Archie stopped a relatively short distance from the entrance. The walkway was much steeper than it had appeared from the outside.

Archie stuck his hands into one of his pockets and produced the three iron keys from earlier. He squinted at them, scratching his chin.

"Can you tell the difference?" Archie asked Zelnor.

"Aren't they three copies of the same key?" Zelnor asked.

"They do look it, don't they? But no," he said. "One's my office and one's my room."

"What about the third one?" Lyle asked, and Zelnor repeated his question.

"And that is the main problem. The third should be for this door," Archie said.

He gestured to the office in front of them, which was, apparently, not his own.

"And this office is…?" Zelnor trailed off, hoping she was right in her assumption.

"A surprise," Archie said.

The researcher looked back at the door and tried the first key. It slid in to the lock, but wouldn't turn. He jiggled it a couple times, claiming it had a tendency to stick, before switching to the second key.

KRRRRRRRR.

A scraping sound echoed through the hallway.

KRRRRRRRRRRRRR.

The sound grew louder.

"Blast it! He's at it again," Archie said. "Hug the wall!"

Zelnor pressed her back against the wall. The sound crescendoed into a rushing, thundering *WHOOSH KRRRRRRRRRRR*. A red blur sped past her and crashed into the door at the end of the hallway with a *thud*.

A few moments later, they heard the grinding sound of the door opening. Zelnor stifled a laugh. Even Lyle giggled.

A young half-kunari with red feathers on his cheeks, arms, and exposed shoulders lay in a crumpled heap. He had just the barest hint of a point to his ears. As he turned, she saw his cheek was swollen with the beginnings of a large bruise.

Zelnor immediately felt bad for laughing.

"Oh no!" Lyle gasped.

"Agerat!" Archie shouted.

Archie jogged back down the slope to help the half-kunari up. Agerat pushed his dark hair away from his face and beamed, taking the middle-aged man's hand.

"Uncle Arch! Did you see? The roller-slate! It *worked*."

The half-kunari held up a wooden contraption with a couple of levers and four wheels. The bottom was covered in complicated looking machinery.

"You crashed into the wall," Archie argued.

"True, the brakes did malfunction," Agerat said. "But with just a few modifications—"

"Have you ever considered *not* practicing indoors?" Archie asked. "You nearly killed me, and yourself. Again. And you've probably broken something."

"I feel fine. And you know that I *tried* practicing outside, but my roller-slate mark one almost carried me off the mesa," Agerat said. "I'd rather crash into a wall."

"I suppose you have a point. Just…go get patched up." Archie nudged the half-kunari toward the door. "And please, test your inventions with a dummy next time."

"Can't. Professor Ludlark said that using first-years to test my machines is unethical." Agerat snickered.

"That isn't funny, *Headmaster* Siebold," Archie said pointedly, shooing the half-kunari out of the tunnel.

Headmaster? Did he just say "headmaster"? The half-kunari was only a few years older than Zelnor. Lyle and Zelnor shared a baffled look as Archie returned, shaking his head.

"That boy. So reckless," he said.

"So, he's the…?" Zelnor trailed off.

"Headmaster?" Archie smiled fondly. "Agerat doesn't act like it, but he's a genius. Smarter than people three times his age."

Zelnor had so many questions, but Archie had already gone back to the door and opened it with the last of the iron keys. As soon as the wooden door swung inward, everything she had been thinking about ceased to matter.

The small spherical office probably looked identical to every other office in Zoh'kret University: a notice board suspended from two cables, hanging above an adobe desk built into the far wall with a wooden chair in front of it. But there were so many little touches that instantly reminded Zelnor of her father. Stacks of history books and fables littered the room. A second, rickety wooden table had been brought in and subsequently covered in broken vases and crumbing scrolls. It was exactly the sort of controlled chaos her that her father loved to keep.

A crudely done picture of a family stood out in the center of the mess. Zelnor didn't remember drawing it, but it was clearly a child's drawing. Her father had put the doodle in a hefty, ornate frame. The frame was impractically large—far too bulky for a single piece of paper. That wasn't like him.

Her dad used to say everything always had a place and a purpose. Zelnor still remembered how angry he'd gotten at her mother when she'd commissioned such a large painting for their house. Somehow, their fight had ended with her mother pushing him into quicksand. He'd nearly died! After that argument, her father had started researching in earnest, leaving home for months at a time.

Her mother had torn their family apart that day, and Zelnor would never forgive her for that. Although, truthfully, her mom had only started the tear: she had driven him away, but Zelnor was the one who'd ripped their small, struggling family to shreds. Not that it mattered. Without him holding them together, they were hardly a family anymore.

Every available surface on her father's desk was absolutely covered in parchment containing his distinctive scrawl. She rifled through the loose pages, attempting to organize them in chronological order. There was just so much: daily logs, research notes, paper outlines, more about her father than she could even *dream* of squeezing out of her mother.

A pattern emerged as Zelnor sorted through her father's work. Everything her dad had written in the last eight years or so of his life was about a single cave. The cave had paintings depicting a race of ancient kunari that had lived in the desert over a millennia ago. He'd tried and failed to replicate their ancient art in his notes. Apparently, he wasn't a particularly good artist.

Based on the dates on his expedition notes, Zelnor's father had visited this cave many times before. He was determined to uncover the ancient kunari civilization's secrets and find the truth behind their "holy celestial waters." As the entries progressed, his writing grew more frustrated and harried.

According to the latest writings, her father had returned from his most recent trip with two pot sherds in "pristine condition," which he'd labeled artifact seven. Zelnor leaped up from her chair and ran over to the nearby table. There it was! Two pieces of a broken, clay drinking vessel, labeled A7H1 and A7H2.

The artifact showed the same ancient kunari performing several different actions: dipping a vessel into water, bringing it to his beak, drinking from it, and gasping as bright light erupted from his eyes. Zelnor's father had scribbled some cryptic notes on a paper underneath the sherds that read: "metaphr or instrct? sight = side eff or intent?"

Why was her father so single-mindedly obsessed with this old race of kunari and their "celestial water"? Why was it so important that he discover their secrets? Something must have happened to give him a sense of urgency, but what? Despite sifting through a mountain of notes and observations, she couldn't find anything that ever directly stated the reason behind it all. Occasionally, his notes made allusions to another journal that she hadn't managed to find. Every question led to more questions. The only thing she could reasonably deduce so far was that the design on that vessel was very important to her father.

Zelnor grabbed a half-empty inkwell and quill from the desk. After some digging, she managed to find a page with a blank back. She stared at the drinking vessel. How should she even begin going about drawing this? A bead of sweat dripped from her brow onto the page.

"Why is it so hot in here?" she grumbled.

"Not sure," Archie answered.

Zelnor jumped. She had completely forgotten he was there. He stood in the corner, examining a rock and noting something in his journal. He continued speaking as he removed a scraping tool from one of his many pockets.

"The whole place is unbearably hot in every season. No clue why. We're near the ocean, so it should be cool in theory. I think they keep it hot on purpose. Keeps us from working too long and dying of starvation," Archie joked.

Zelnor went back to the blank page. She wouldn't be able to do the drawing justice. She glanced at Archie out of the corner of her eye. He was still focused on his work, slowly shaving away layers of rock. Zelnor beckoned Lyle over.

"Can you draw?" Zelnor whispered.

"Yeah, pretty well," Lyle whispered back. "Want me to draw the broken pot?"

"Just the kunari, please," Zelnor said.

Lyle nodded and fixed his gaze on the quill. It rose into an upright position and began moving in fluid arcs across the parchment. Zelnor watched him draw for a moment, before she returned to her father's worktable. She dug deeper in the pile and found some of his older work, before his obsession over this cave. His older studies had information that the cave studies lacked: formal sections indicating his initial hypotheses and goals, and his interpretations of his findings.

There was no doubt about it. Some of her father's work was

missing, and his office, cluttered as it was, had no real hiding places. He must have brought that part of his work out of his office. Her father was obviously keeping the bulk of his last project a secret. This wasn't exactly news, since Zinnie had said as much, but considering this was her father's personal office, Zelnor wondered who her dad had been hiding from.

Unfortunately, there wasn't much more she could learn here. Zelnor would need to visit this cave herself. A glance at the map above the desk told her that the cave was in the middle of the Kialma'keeran desert. Somewhere south of Moons' Dance Oasis but north of Bokest al'Bar.

"Dammit," Zelnor said. "We might've gone right past it."

"Right past wha—?" Archie started, then gasped. "*What* in the bloody name of Thorns is—is—!"

He pointed at the quill, his hand trembling slightly. Oh shit. Archie couldn't see Lyle, so he just saw a quill moving on its own. Zelnor would need a really convincing lie to explain this one.

"It's a self-writing quill that I invented. It's, uh, mechanical," Zelnor said.

"That's incredible!" the researcher marveled. "Would you mind if I just…?"

Archie wandered closer, holding out his hand to touch the quill. Zelnor's eyes widened. If he examined it, he'd immediately discover it was just a normal feather.

"I wouldn't do that!" Zelnor shouted, getting between him and Lyle. "The, uh, power source is unstable. It could explode."

"Oh." Archie stopped in his tracks. "I think I'll wait for you… in the hall. But, maybe, um, talk to Agerat or another inventor about that problem while you're at Zoh'kret."

Archie fled the room, and Zelnor exhaled with deep relief once the door closed.

"You know," Lyle said. "You could've just told him about me."

"Could I? No one in Kialma'keer believes in ghosts. Not even children," Zelnor said. "He would probably think I'd gotten sun fever."

"He saw the quill moving on its own. That's proof," he argued.

"You would be surprised how far people will go to explain the unexplainable," she said. "At least we can talk to each other now."

"Well, that's true." Lyle frowned and stuck his tongue out as he worked. "I was wondering, why am I drawing this?"

"It's part of one of the last projects my dad worked on," Zelnor said.

"Oh, all right." Lyle was quiet for a few moments, then spoke again. "You don't talk about him very much."

Honestly, Zelnor avoided the topic on purpose. For a decade, she had wondered what really happened to him, but she had to set the matter aside in favor of doing everything possible to rid herself of her powers. Ignoring the mysterious circumstances of her father's death had always felt like a betrayal of his memory.

"I guess I don't," Zelnor said.

While Lyle continued copying the design on the sherds, Zelnor returned to the notice board with the map in its center. The mage brushed her fingertips against the site on the map. She desperately wanted to mark the location down on their travel map, but of course, Erianna had all their maps. If only the bard had come with them…

She probably would've hated it. Maps and research notes—none of it really seemed like Erianna's thing. She was probably having a better time with that pretty blond. Zelnor wondered what they were talking about. Probably laughing over something and drinking. Maybe the two had even gotten a room and—

"Oh! I know that place! Is that where the pot came from?" Lyle asked.

Zelnor cleared her throat, grateful for the distraction. Gods, where was her head these days? It had been too long since she'd traveled with someone, and it was making her oddly possessive. She would scare Erianna off at this rate.

Wait... Zelnor startled as her mind finally caught up to what Lyle had just said.

"Lyle...have you been to this cave before?" she asked.

"Well, yeah," Lyle said. "You have too. It's where Erianna found you."

Vel'erma's wisdom! Zelnor had been so out of it when Erianna rescued her that she'd had no sense of where she was. She had been right there, and she hadn't even glanced at the walls or searched for broken pottery! She couldn't have known, but how could she not have known? Shouldn't she have felt it somehow? She had stood in the very same place as her father.

"That pool was the ancient kunari's 'celestial holy water'! I need to go back," Zelnor said.

"Zelnor I—" Lyle bit his lip. "I don't think that's a good idea. That water is *really* bad."

"I won't touch it," Zelnor said.

"You almost died in there! And I..."

Lyle wrapped his arms around himself. He wouldn't meet Zelnor's gaze. She almost put a hand on his shoulder, before remembering it would just pass right through.

"Lyle." Zelnor crouched to get his attention. "I'll be careful. I promise."

"All right..." Lyle nodded but still wouldn't meet her eyes.

Two sharp raps, and the door opened a crack. Archie peeked his head in.

"Are you done using your, erm, contraption?" he asked.

Lyle pointed to the completed sketch. It looked perfect—an exact replica of the original.

"It's done," Zelnor confirmed.

Archie let out a long exhale and slipped back into the room.

"Well, it's getting late, and I still have something to give you."

"Is it late?" Zelnor asked.

"Hard to know for sure," Archie said.

He fumbled through his pockets, discarding rock after rock as he looked for something. Lyle stuck his head through the wall, pulling it in again a second later.

"It's nighttime," he announced.

"Already?" she asked.

Where had the time gone? Erianna would probably be looking for them. That is, provided she wasn't spending the night with that blond, which was completely fine, of course, but the bard would still want to let them know where she'd be. Well, probably. Checking in with each other was what friends did… wasn't it? Though, now that she thought about it, Zelnor had left Erianna without a word. Shit.

"We—I mean, I really have to go," Zelnor said.

Zelnor gathered up Lyle's sketches, blowing on them to dry the ink.

"As do I. But please, just a moment—Aha! Found it." Archie pulled something out, keeping it concealed in his palm. "Don't know how I lost it. I just used it. Should really label my pockets. Anyway, here."

Archie handed Zelnor the iron key that he'd used to open the door. The key to Kezok Fahra'keen's office. She clutched it tightly.

"I've been keeping them from cleaning out Kezok's office and giving it away," Archie said. "This space is in high demand, being so close to the entrance."

"Thank you," Zelnor whispered.

"Well, it wasn't wholly selfless," Archie said. "I was hoping you'd take over his office someday. Hoped you were as brilliant as your father, and it seems I wasn't disappointed."

"I'm nowhere near as smart as he was," Zelnor said.

"I wouldn't be so sure. I think, with time and study, you could easily surpass him."

"Are you sure you want to give the key to me? I don't know when, or if, I'll be back," Zelnor said.

"Of course. It belongs with you. I had hoped you would stay," Archie said. "But I suspected you wouldn't. You have the look of an adventurer. I hope you'll consider enrolling in Zoh'kret once you settle down."

She just smiled, looping the key through a leftover cord from some pendant she'd sold. She slipped it over her head and hid the key under her tunic. It rattled softly against Torrin's amulet.

Zelnor picked up the framed drawing of her family: an elf, a human, and their child. It felt strangely heavy in her hands.

Archie's offer was everything she'd dreamed of since she was little—becoming a student at Bokest al'Bar and uncovering Tularien's secrets, one book at a time. She'd long since given up on that dream, but with Devlin's help, maybe it really was possible. Maybe after she closed those pools, she could finally have the life she'd always wanted.

Zelnor stuffed her father's research journal and the heavy, framed drawing into her satchel—leaving a few light magic books behind to make room. As desperately as she wanted that life, she would be foolish to get ahead of herself. One day she hoped she could use her father's key, but today, she needed to track down Erianna and hope that the ishlanian had found a boat and a captain willing to take them.

Chapter Twenty-Three
Secrets and Lockpicks

"Crime time!" Christine cheered. "Oh, that rhymed."

Erianna and Christine had arrived at *Eulfson's Rare Imports and Exports*. The double crescents of Cytho and Parenus illuminated the horribly inaccurate ishlanian mural on the building's front, tinting the painting's skin an ethereal blueish white. In the faint moonslight, the illustration almost looked like a proper ishlanian with blue-gray skin, but the fish tail ruined it. Dirk *would* commission a mural of that damnably wrong-looking goddess. What idiot had decided Ireeshnem looked like that anyway?

"Stupid fish girl," Erianna muttered.

"Aww, Eri," Christine spoke in a baby voice. "Don't beat yourself up."

"I'm not a fish girl!" Erianna shouted. *"She's* the stupid fish girl."

"Ah, ssszzhhhh," Christine slurred the sound. "Shush! Don't want people thinking we're doing anythin' illegal."

"Breaking into a store *is* illegal," Erianna said.

"Don't tell them, 'kay?" Christine winked.

"I swear." Erianna giggled.

"'Kay. You got the door?"

"Mmhmm," Erianna hummed.

She pulled her lockpicks from the bottom of her backpack. It had been a while since she last used them. She pressed them in and tried to maneuver them, but they stuck in the lock. She just barely managed to get them out again.

"You're rusty, Eri." Christine laughed. "Lemme."

"Nooooo! I got it, I got—"

Christine tried to shove Erianna out of the way.

"Stop it," Erianna snapped. "Let me work!"

Erianna pushed Christine back and tried again. The lock clicked, but the door still wouldn't open. Erianna pulled her tools back out with a huff. She narrowed her eyes and glared at the lock. She was great at picking locks. Why wasn't it working?

"This's taking too long!" Christine said.

A small sapphire light glowed faintly from behind Christine's curtain of wavy, blond hair. Her eyes glowed the same bright sapphire. Then, in a flash of dark blue mist, she disappeared.

"Christine!" Erianna shouted.

Erianna's hands trembled. It was happening again. Another friend had disappeared. Why did this always happen? Why was Torrin doing this? SHE WAS GOING TO DESTROY THAT EVIL LIZARD IF HE DIDN'T RETURN CHRISTINE RIGHT—

Christine threw the door open.

"Got it!" she said.

"How did—? Oh," Erianna said.

Erianna emitted an embarrassed teal glow. How could she have forgotten? Torrin's pact gave Christine the power to teleport. She had *teleported*. Ugh. Erianna was so dumb. That was nothing to get upset over.

"Huh," Erianna muttered as something occurred to her.

Back in Nirdeem, mist had surrounded Zelnor and then she had suddenly disappeared. Erianna had assumed Torrin was responsible, but now that she thought about it, could Zelnor have teleported herself away on purpose? *But why would she teleport into some random, evil cave lake?* And then, there had been that strange white light that had overtaken the sapphire mist around Zelnor. That definitely wasn't normal.

"Eriannnaaaaa," Christine whined. "We're gonna get caught if you just stand ou'side!"

"All right, all right. Sorry," Erianna said. "What are we here for anyway?"

"Oh…you'll see." Christine grinned menacingly.

"Ominous." Erianna chuckled.

Erianna only had seconds to see the initial state of Dirk's shop before Christine ransacked it. She toppled the artfully placed pedestals, shattering rare, expensive-looking antiques on the varnished wooden floor. She snatched jewelry from the counter and chucked it at the ground. A pearl necklace broke apart, scattering little white spheres in front of the entrance.

Erianna picked her way around the carnage, torn between concern and amusement. She had forgotten just how wild her old friend could be. Usually, the level-headed Annette and the admittedly less sensible Erianna fought to rein Christine in, but Dirk and Jörnn absolutely deserved this act of revenge. And far be it from Erianna to deny her friend closure.

Christine gleefully bounded to the far corner of the store—the only untouched area. The last two intact shelves held figurines for every nation's interpretation of the deities, excluding The Lord of Thorns, of course. Christine took a statue of Ireeshnem and tossed it to Erianna.

"We'll throw 'er back in the sea where she belongs," Christine said.

"Oh, *Afterworlds* yes!" Erianna cheered.

"Now… There's one more thing that we needa get…"

Christine skimmed her hand along the shelves for a moment before pulling a figurine of Liscuntia down. The obscene goddess was nestled between Fleurepa (the version of Her worshipped in Nirdeem) and a figurine of two cuddling bunnies that Erianna didn't recognize off-hand.

"Ha! Found it. Pervert like him doesn't deserve this. 'Sides"— Christine smirked—"I think Annette and I could use Her blessing *more.*"

"Doubt you need a goddess for *that* with the way you lusted after her." Erianna snorted.

"Maybe I just wanna see the look on her face."

"I doubt it'll even get a rise out of her," the bard said.

"Oh, it will," Christine said.

Erianna heard footsteps outside. It should be fine. No one knew they were here. They'd been careful not to be followed and had broken in when no one was around. The footsteps were likely just a passerby. That said…it wouldn't hurt to head out while the way was still clear.

"Chrissy, I think we should go," Erianna said.

"Fiiine. Just need to find Dirk's expense ledger first."

Christine ducked behind the counter and waved a black leather book over her head triumphantly. She started scribbling something inside it, but before she could finish, the door burst open.

A man stood in the doorway, his weaselly features twisted into an ugly scowl. Why had the angry man from *The Ocean's Gems* followed them here? Unless…*Dirk.* He must have gotten back early. Oh gods, they were idiots.

A couple of low-ranking guards from the Sundry flanked the

owner on both sides. Of course he'd brought guards, that honorless coward knew he would never win against them in a battle otherwise. The three of them blocked the only exit.

"Come and get us," Christine said.

The sundries took one step forward and immediately fell on their asses. Erianna's sluggish mind struggled to catch up. *Why did they…?* The pearls. They had tripped over the pearls.

Christine leaped over the two sundries and shoved Dirk aside. Erianna followed closely behind, and the two women thundered through the twisting streets. Christine hooked a sharp left, then a right and another left.

"Do you know where you're going?" Erianna shouted.

Christine glanced over her shoulder and grinned. "Of course! But I thought we'd run them around a little first."

Christine pulled Erianna into a narrow alley. The blond held a finger to her lips, and they waited until they heard Dirk and the sundries run by. They looked at each other and broke into giggles.

"This is even more fun than I remembered," Erianna said.

"It's been too long since I was chased out of a city," Christine agreed.

The two darted back into the street. Christine was surprisingly coordinated for a drunk. Erianna needed to pick up the pace, if she didn't want to lose her.

Erianna's foot caught on an uneven patch of road, and she pitched forward. Arms encircled her waist. She looked up, expecting to see one of the guards, but it wasn't a sundry in front of her. Instead, she saw a familiar bearded face.

"Zelnor!" Erianna beamed. "You're here! I missed yooou."

Erianna looped her arms around Zelnor's neck. The bard straightened up, getting her feet back under her, but immediately had to crouch over again. Zelnor was significantly shorter than her. That was fine, though! The shorter woman just needed to be the one putting her arms around *Erianna's* neck. And then Erianna could put her hands under the half-elf's thighs and hoist her up. That would be fun. She should ask Zelnor if they could do that later.

The half-elf slipped out of Erianna's loose hug.

"What are you doing?" Zelnor asked.

"Just saying hello," Erianna said.

Zelnor flailed a little, before tucking her arms back at her sides. Erianna grinned. How could Erianna *not* smile at the mage's flustered face? Gods, she was so cute.

Lyle peeked out from behind the half-elf's shoulder.

"Is she…?" he asked.

"Yep. She's drunk," Zelnor said.

"Mm-mm, am not." Erianna shook her head so quickly that she got a little dizzy. "Whoooa! Haha. Whoops."

Zelnor's hands shot out to steady her.

"Fine, I am just a little bit *tipsy,*" Erianna admitted.

"More than a little," Zelnor said. "I guess we'll stay the night."

"Oh no. We can't do that."

"Should I even ask?"

"Wellll…" Erianna hiccupped. "So, we got in a just a little bit of trouble."

A figure in a dark gray cloak appeared at the other end of the street. She pulled down her hood to hide her face, but Erianna still caught a flash of red hair and a crooked nose. The woman ducked back out of view almost as soon as Erianna saw her, disappearing down the road.

But the figure wasn't fast enough.

Erianna had gotten a good look, and she was *sure* of it. That was the same redhead she'd seen at Moons' Dance. The woman had been following her since she'd left Nirdeem!

The stranger had to be from the Broken Claim. She was missing their traditional blank mask, but only someone from the Claim would have followed Erianna across the desert. The bard had been a fool to think the vaal'akkar would stop them. Plindurin had a wealth of resources. She could easily hire someone who knew the Path through the beasts' dens.

I need to take care of this. Erianna broke out of Zelnor's grasp and moved to chase her pursuer. But before she went even two steps, Christine jogged back into view.

"Eri, they found us. And they brought friends." She turned toward Zelnor and Lyle. "Speaking of! It's nice to see you two again. Let's talk more on the ship."

"Two?" Zelnor asked. "Can you—? Wait. *Who* found you?"

"Tell you later," Erianna said.

The little group tore through the streets, heading straight for the harbor. Erianna could see some of the taller ships peeking out over the buildings. The bustling wharf had finally gone quiet, only a few stragglers packing up their wares or loading the last of their crates onto vessels. She really hoped the Sundry wouldn't guess where they were headed.

A clamoring shattered the still air. As they turned the final corner, Erianna's worst fears were realized. Another battalion of sundries advanced from the other end of the harbor. They would be surrounded in mere moments.

In a burst of dark blue mist, Christine teleported to the top of a nearby ship that was a few yards away from the dock. The ship had deep red lettering across the side: *Scarlette Wind*. Was Christine really going to leave without them? After everything?

"Liscuntia's tits, Christine! What in the unspoken name?" Erianna screamed.

"Hold on!" Christine turned and shouted to her crew, "ALL HANDS ON DECK!"

"We're already on deck!" someone shouted.

"THEN MOVE YOUR ASSES!" Christine yelled.

Erianna recognized Annette's commanding voice: "You heard the captain. To your stations!"

There was a flurry of activity, and Erianna counted at least six different women scurrying across the deck. The Sundry closed in on either side, as Erianna, Zelnor, and Lyle waited at the dock's edge.

"Teleport us up!" Erianna yelled.

"Can't!" Christine shouted. "I've used them all up already!"

"Zelnor! Erianna!" Lyle pointed to the guards, now just a few yards away.

One sundry pulled ahead of the rest, speeding toward them. He would be on them in seconds.

The *Scarlette Wind* sailed slowly forward, carving sluggishly through the water. Even so, Erianna and Zelnor had to jog to keep pace with the vessel. A rope thudded against the ship's hull.

Erianna leaped for the rope and easily caught it. She hoisted herself up, boarding the boat with ease. Not the most graceful ascent but not bad, considering she was slightly drunk and still clutching the Ireeshnem figurine in her other fist.

Zelnor was not nearly so proficient. She dangled from the bottom of the rope, her hands tensed as she struggled to pull herself up. Lyle hovered next to her. He tried to use his power to help her but started fading around the edges. He must've used up his energy at that university.

Zelnor had only managed to climb a few feet when the closest sundry launched himself from the dock and onto the rope's end. The rope swayed dangerously, nearly throwing the mage and ghost into the waves.

This was a disaster! The ship had left the dock, but Zelnor was still flailing helplessly and the guard was gaining on her.

Annette started hauling the rope back in. A muscly handmaiden joined her. *Eleanor!* Erianna only spared a moment's excitement at seeing the two of them again before Zelnor's frantic cries sent a new jolt of fear through her.

"Help me pull him up," Annette said.

"What about that sundry?" Erianna fretted.

"We can take one guard," Eleanor said with a wolfish grin.

"But if he gets to them first, he could pull them into the water!" Erianna said.

She stared over the side, her skin glowing. The sundry climbed effortlessly, scaling the rope faster than the half-elf could. This was *really* bad. Zelnor could barely swim. She couldn't afford to fall into the water. Even if she got away from the guard, who knew where the current would take her and Lyle?

If it came down to it, Erianna would rather fight the sundry on the ship than see the three of them get lost beneath the waves. They just needed to get Zelnor up before the guard reached her. Erianna grabbed the rope and heaved. Her shoulder burned, skin stretching painfully around her wound.

"Eri, pass me Ireeshnem," Christine said.

Erianna immediately tossed Christine the figurine. Christine leaned over the side, closed one eye, and chucked the statue. It hit the sundry square in the forehead and sent him tumbling into the ocean with a splash.

"That's our captain!" someone cheered behind them.

"Focus, Camilla," Annette snapped.

Christine joined them at the rope, and between the four of them, they hauled the mage up and into Erianna's waiting arms. Zelnor heaved with exertion, and Erianna was breathing just as heavily. Erianna pulled her close. She felt as though a weight had finally been lifted from her chest. Her shoulder throbbed, but Erianna tightened her arms anyway.

"Thank Liscuntia," Erianna whispered.

"I'm fine," Zelnor said. "I'm fine."

The mage squeezed Erianna back briefly, before carefully removing herself from the embrace. Erianna stood there for a moment, glancing between Lyle and Zelnor and just basking in the relief that they were all right.

"Throwing the goddess of fortune at a sundry? Your luck is going to get even worse now," Annette said.

The stocky human woman crossed her arms, trying to look disapproving and failing miserably.

"Impossible as long as you're by my side," Christine crooned, pulling her closer.

"Your lines don't work on me anymore," Annette said.

"Then I'll just have to come up with some new ones…"

Christine kissed Annette. The two stayed like that long enough that Erianna wondered if she should give them some privacy, but suddenly Christine broke away—breathless and beaming.

"I still need to introduce our new arrivals," the captain said.

"Well, I recognize one," Annette said wryly. "Nice to see you again, Erianna."

Finally, Erianna had a moment to take in Annette's new appearance. The stocky woman had cut her fine, brown hair. It was shoulder length now, and it suited her much better than the long braid she'd had previously.

"Annette. A pleasure," Erianna said.

"And this *handsome*, half-elven gentleman is Zelnor, I'm told." Christine gave an exaggerated bow and took Zelnor's hand in both of hers. "Erianna has told me a *lot* about you."

Zelnor turned an accusing glare toward Erianna. Oh, for Liscuntia's sake. The mage had absolutely no faith in her.

"I've told her nothing," Erianna said.

"Nothing?" Zelnor asked.

"Nothing! Well, almost nothing."

Annette nudged Christine away from the half-elf and stuck out her hand. "Don't mind her. I'm Annette, the first mate."

"She's also my soulmate," Christine chimed in.

"Nice to meet you," the mage replied. "And thank you, all of you, for helping me with the rope."

Zelnor glanced away, clearly embarrassed at her abysmal lack of physical strength. Erianna sniggered.

"Happy to help!" Eleanor said.

Eleanor strapped her club onto her back and scooped Zelnor up into a bear hug, as the first mate introduced the burly woman with short, curly black hair. Erianna had already recognized her, of course. She looked almost exactly the same, although her attire had changed drastically. Gone was the ill-fitting handmaiden dress; instead, she wore a simple baggy white tunic—with long sleeves that stretched a little too tightly across the woman's thick arms—and matching pants.

The rest of the crew wore similar outfits, with a few variations here and there. The strangest part about their clothes, though, was the messy splatters in a rainbow of colors strewn haphazardly across them. The pattern reminded Erianna of her father after a long day sequestered in his painting room.

"And now, I believe there's one more member of your group I've yet to meet." Christine stared directly at Lyle.

Christine could see ghosts! That was new. Did it have something to do with her time in Gealtalmh?

"The stern!" someone shouted from the crow's nest.

Annette spun around. A large ship had followed them from the port, still far enough away that it wasn't a problem yet, but it had started gaining. The Sundry weren't usually so persistent, certainly not over petty theft. Erianna wouldn't be surprised if the Eulfsons were lining the Sundry's pockets.

"Introductions have to wait until we've shaken the Sundry," Annette said.

The *Scarlette Wind* lurched as it crested a large wave, nearly knocking Erianna off her feet. Eleanor caught her shoulder—the wounded one—and Erianna yelped.

"That can't wait, though," Annette said. "Quinn!"

A lithe figure slid down the rigging and landed with a *thump*. Quinn flicked a tricorn hat away from her eyes. A few frizzy tufts of black hair flew wildly with the motion. The woman grinned, uncharacteristically excited.

"Eri! It's good to see you again," Quinn said.

"Does *everyone* call you that?" Zelnor grumbled.

Quinn snorted at the comment, but her eyes lingered on Erianna's wounded shoulder.

"Getting into trouble without us?" Quinn asked.

"What can I say? Everyone's attracted to me, even trouble," Erianna joked.

Quinn gestured to a trapdoor that led below deck. Erianna wobbled over and slipped through it. She nearly tumbled down the stairs, but Quinn hooked her arm through Erianna's just in time, downgrading the stumble from a minor injury to a major embarrassment. Damn that duur'een wine.

The lower deck was a simple space, just fully stocked shelves and stacks of wooden crates shoved into a corner. Erianna threw her large backpack off her shoulders, rifling through it until she found her bedroll. She spread it across some boxes and flopped onto it.

"All right. Let's get this over with," Erianna said.

As Quinn prepared the wound for healing, she complained

about the little bits of sewing thread that had melded into the cuts and called Erianna's stitchwork *messy*. The comment hurt Erianna more than the hand digging around in her shoulder. In fact, the cleaning itself hardly hurt at all. Erianna had always struggled to picture the lackadaisical woman training to become a professional healer, but despite her complaints, Quinn worked efficiently.

Soon, golden threads drifted from Quinn's fingertips. Erianna braced herself, but she still flinched when the woman's hand neared her. The light faded. The handmaiden let her arm fall back to her side.

Quinn didn't know about Plindurin, or Erianna's distaste for light magic. Very few people did, and she intended to keep it that way. Erianna could stay the flirty, cheerful bard everyone expected. It wasn't hard. It only took a few bright assurances and a well-placed smile to show people who they wanted to see.

Erianna laughed, twisting her expression into something more apologetic.

"I've never been healed before," she lied.

"Don't worry. It doesn't hurt," Quinn said.

Quinn brought her golden threads back to Erianna's damaged shoulder. Light looped around the edges of the cuts, knitting them together. The skin around the wound settled from raised purple to smooth teal. The throbbing eased as lines of scabs blossomed in the light's wake.

Weeks of healing condensed into a few minutes, and Erianna had hated every second of it. But she was confident she hadn't let it show.

Annette summoned Quinn abovedeck. The handmaiden instructed Erianna not to pick at the scabs and to rest—if she could—before leaving her alone.

Erianna lay back on the bedroll. Pale moonslight filtered through the planks of the deck above her. Her mind buzzed with everything that had happened. For the first time in years, Erianna was surrounded by friends. She'd reunited with the handmaidens. Christine was alive. *Zelnor* was alive—in no small part thanks to Erianna's efforts.

Lyle had been right. Erianna did care for the mage. She wouldn't call it love, but she had gone back to Nirdeem to help Zelnor and nearly paid the price for it when the Broken Claim had cornered her. Erianna wouldn't take that sort of risk for just anyone.

Gods, that had been a close call, even closer than she'd initially realized. Why hadn't Erianna noticed the crooked-nosed woman following her through the empty desert? At least she could confidently say she had lost her stalker now. There was no way that woman could follow her out to sea.

Something shifted. Erianna thought she saw movement out of the corner of her eye, but no one was there. It was probably just the cargo moving with the ship. There was nowhere for her stalker to hide. The lower deck was too open. Still, she would swear she felt someone watching her… She was jumping at shadows again, and who could blame her after everything she'd gone through? It had been a shitty two months.

But I'd do it all again to meet Zelnor and Lyle.

The sappy thought made her feel warm inside. Or maybe that was the alcohol. Those tropical dates were pretty strong… Still, it felt nice to have a purpose beyond just surviving, to have people who relied on her.

Although, could Erianna really call herself reliable? Leaving Lyle with that vaal'akkar was almost unforgivable. She *would* find a way to make up for it, somehow. She had to. Because eventually, Zelnor would seal up the pools, and when the mage inevitably moved on and the ghost had to pick between the two of them, Erianna wanted Lyle to choose her. She couldn't go back to traveling alone again.

Thankfully, that choice was still a long way off. Between the

Broken Claim, the High Mage, and Torrin, they still had plenty of excitement and danger ahead of them, and Erianna would be damned if she wouldn't enjoy every moment they had left.

Definitions and Pronunciations Glossary

Archibald Gossimare
Zoh'kret University
27th of Theolrin
Passing Season, 3rd Quarter

Herein I have compiled a comprehensive list of terms found throughout this tale at the behest of its author.

I sourced my definitions from various tomes across Eltun, including but not limited to: religious manifestos, astronomy textbooks, anthropological research, the testimony of local inhabitants, and my dear friend Kezok's notes. My pronunciations are based on conversations with locals, both observed and initiated myself. My references list will be provided upon request only.

Linguistics was never my subject of study so I pray, please be patient with me. Without further ado, I present this Definitions and Pronunciations Glossary for *The Dragon's Emissary*.

Alaspinor [Ah–lass–pih–nor]: The rainy country on the northern end of the continent of Eltun, ruled by The Five and composed mainly of small farming villages.

Agerat Siebold [Ah–jehr-at Sigh–bold]: The youngest headmaster in the history of Zoh'kret University and son of Zinneon and Lily Siebold. (Also a brilliant yet annoying pain in the you-know-what.)

Apalandis [Ap–uh–lan–diss]: One of the prevators of the Court of Kings and Queens in Alaspinor.

Alvetchian [Al–veh–key–in]: A term derived from the god Alvetch [Al–vehk], whose domains are weakness, humility, lost strength, and arrogance. The only member of the pantheon to have once been mortal. He presides over the Afterworld of Downfall, sometimes called the Divine or Eternal Embarrassment. His name is part of the idiom "Alvetchian effort" meaning a nearly impossible feat, and "Alvetch's heel" meaning a weakness or vulnerability.

Archibald Gossimare [Archibald Gah–sih–mare]: Well, me! A geoarchaeological researcher at Zoh'kret University and an old friend of Kezok's.

I am responsible for not only this list of terms but also, for sourcing the maps in the front matter of this story (for which I have gone uncredited, it would seem). You can call me Archie.

Bokest al'Bar [Bow–kehst al Bar]: The largest, southernmost city in Kialma'keer, home to Zoh'kret University. A hub for artists and academics alike with one of the most prosperous ports in all of Tularien.

Bimblebarrow [Bim–bull–bear–oh]: One of the largest towns in Alaspinor and a culinary haven for aspiring chefs.

Cathmal [Cath–mall]: A Kialma'keeran mount and beast of burden characterized by its feline features, stout and sturdy body, webbed feet, and distinctive hump. The creature's ability to go two weeks without food or water makes the cathmal an ideal mount for long desert journeys.

Celrelborain [Cell–rell–bore–ain]: One of the two First Deities of Tularien: creators of mortal life, Death's Many-Faced Attendant, and the seven gods that rule the Afterworlds. They represent eternity; darkness and eternal cycles; dreams; mysteries and the unknowable. The people of Eltun depict Their physical form as pitch black, covered in stars with Parenus and Cytho as Their eyes. They hold the sun in their cupped hands. Unlike the other members of the mortal pantheon, Their depictions do not vary across the continent and They are always worshipped under the same name.

Cytho [Sigh–thoh]: The smaller blue moon that orbits Parenus. Its visibility depends on its position in orbit around the larger celestial body of Parenus and its phase. (Why you would need a definition for this term, I cannot say. But it was on the list the author provided.)

Daeyarus's Flower [Day–are–us's Flower]: A toxin derived from a plant of the same name. Discovered first by the famous Alaspinoran apothecary Aithlin [Ay–thlin] Daeyarus, the poison causes exhaustion, dizziness, and mild to moderate dehydration. While nonlethal, it does render its victims unconscious if left untreated. Its effect on ishlanians is particularly severe due to their predisposition to dehydration.

Delaith [Duh–layth]: One of the mortal gods, the mistress of storms and soft rainfall. The goddess represents change and the dual capacity for anger and forgiveness. She rules over the Afterworld of Absolution. She is one of two goddesses most commonly invoked and worshipped by sailors.

Devlin Devereaux [Dev–lin Deh–ver–oh]: The only other known practitioner of elemental magic. He is also Nirdeem's High Mage.

Duur'een Fruit [Door–een Fruit]: A sweet fruit with a naturally smokey aftertaste native to the Kialma'keeran desert. Its thick, syrupy juice is often fermented into a strong wine or baked into jams and pies.

Eltun [El–tune]: The continent that houses Alaspinor, Nirdeem, and Kialma'keer.

Ethnarian Ocean [Eth–nar–ee–in Ocean]: The ocean along the eastern coast of Eltun, that stretches between Eltun and Gealtalmh.

Felsha'kor [Fell–shah–core]: Death's Many-Faced Attendant, created by the two First Deities to collect and shepherd souls to The Lord of Thorns for Final Judgment. This god represents funeral rights, nourishing flame, and rebirth after tragedy. This name refers to the Kialma'keeran variation of the goddess—depicted as a giant bird with golden feathers wreathed in flame.

Fleurepa [Flooreh–pah]: The goddess of pleasure. She is also worshipped under the names Liscuntia and Zelerbix. Generally speaking, she represents the domains of promiscuity, indulgence, and physicality. She rules over the Afterworld of Pleasure, sometimes called the Divine or Eternal Brothel. The deity's variations each have different pronouns, names, and appearances. These variations of the goddess were born from differences in how mortals interpreted the domain of "pleasure" within each country on Eltun.

Fleurepa is the variation worshipped predominantly in Nirdeem. Like her Alaspinoran variation, this goddess is associated with brothels and prostitution; however, Fleurepa also represents the sheer physical pleasure that money can bring and wealth itself. She is more closely associated with revelry and partying than sex.

The goddess is depicted as a human woman with her face obscured by shadow and hair. She uses one hand to expose her breast and has so many gold coins piled in her other palm that they spill over onto the floor beneath her.

Ful'prakta [Full–prahk–tuh]: A set of heat resistant, baggy white clothes developed and traditionally used in Kialma'keer.

Gealtalmh [Guhee–el–tallmuh]: A snowy, war-torn country northeast of Eltun, across the vast Ethnarian Ocean.

Also see, Gealtalmhn [Guhee–el–tall–muhin]: From the country of Gealtalmh.

Glymnoire [Glim–newour]: The surname of the wealthiest and most powerful merchant family in Goldhaven. They deal primarily in fine silks and dresses. Christine Lenore Glymnoire—sole heir to the family's legacy—has been reportedly seeing the world and "studying the business practices of other cultures to prepare for her duties."

Heeden [He–den]: Zelnor's childhood best friend. Deceased. Zelnor refused to give me any more information about him.

Hrik'nar [Here–ick–nar] and Sreet'nar [Sir–eetuh–nar]: The names of Bimblebarrow's most reputable blacksmith and his daughter respectively.

Ireeshnem [Ear–ee–shnehm]: The goddess of fate and navigation, the ocean, and the tides of luck. She rules over the Afterworld of Capriciousness. One of the two goddesses most frequently invoked by sailors, her form is depicted as a blond woman with a fish tail instead of legs and considered the only "ishlanian" deity in the pantheon.

Ishahnan [Ish–ah–nan]: One of several ishlanian nations underneath the Ethnarian Ocean.

Ishlanian [Ish–lawn–ee–an]: A reclusive, semiaquatic race rarely seen on Eltun. They hail from several distinct nations deep beneath the Ethnarian Ocean. Due to a lack of information, they are widely believed to be humanoids with fishtails instead of legs. In actuality, this race looks more like a semiaquatic variation of elves.

In addition to their angular features and long ears, ishlanians are taller than other mortal races, and they possess bioluminescence and gills. Their skin and hair are always shades of green, blue, or purple. Their eyes are pitch black with no sclera, and as they mature, scales grow over parts of their body (most often the shoulders and chest). Ishlanians do poorly in direct sunlight, as they are considerably more sensitive to heat and light than the other mortal races.

Kalkor [Kal–core]: The mortal god of war, guilt and grievances, cruelty, vengeance, and torture. Also, known as the King of Grudges. He rules over the Afterworld of Punishment, sometimes called the Divine or Eternal Punishment.

Kezeek Mesa [Keh–zeek Mesa]: A small town in northern Kialma'keer near Nirdeem's South Gate.

Kezok Fahra'keen [Keh–zahk Fah–rah–keen]: An Anthropologist at Zoh'kret University who lived in northern Kialma'keer on Kezeek Mesa. A dear friend of **Archibald Gossimare,** and also the son of **Razif'rik** [Rah–zif–rihk] and **Flueriet** [Floor–ee–et] Fahra'keen. He was adopted by Zinneon and Lily Siebold after his parents' passing. Kezok died suddenly ten years ago, leaving behind his wife, Lia, and their child, **Zelnor.**

Kialma'keer [Keyal–mah–kear]: The desert country on the southern end of Eltun.

Kunari [Coo–naree]: An avian race characterized by their beaks, small black eyes, wings, and feathers of various colors. Though they originated in the Kialma'keer, and many still live in the desert's mesa villages, they are now found throughout Eltun.

Liscuntia [Lie–sun–teeuh]: The Alaspinoran variation of the goddess of pleasure. Of the three variations of the pleasure goddess, Liscuntia is most focused on the enjoyment and fulfillment found in sex. As such, she is also the most closely associated with brothels and prostitutes.

Her worshippers pray to her for a satisfying sexual encounter. She is depicted as a naked woman leaning back with her legs spread wide. She is very occasionally rendered in profile, but more often from the front, fully exposing herself. Her name is considered the most profane word in Eltun and is the strongest swear word used on the continent.

The Lord of Thorns: One of the two First Deities of Tularien: creators of mortal life, Death's Many-Faced Attendant, and the seven gods that rule the Afterworlds. They are the divine leader of all the Afterworlds and determine every soul's place in the Final Judgment. They represent mortality, finality and order, and light and reality.

Mortals do not have a physical representation of The Lord of Thorns, even though all major cities on Eltun have temples devoted to Them. To speak Their true name portends a swift demise; therefore, They have been referred to only by Their title for all of known mortal history. As a result, Their true name was lost.

Nirdeem [Near–deem]: A small city-state situated in the only valley in the Reindune Mountains. The nation's standing army and vital location make it a strong political player on the continent despite its size.

Opeli Leaves [Oh–pell–ee Leaves]: A rare, medicinal herb with white leaves and blue veins found in Alaspinor.

Orvash'na [Or–vah–shnah]: Erianna's last name.

Parenus [Par–en–us]: The large white moon in Tularien's sky. (Again, I ask you Robin, which of your readers doesn't know the names of Tularien's moons? Is this a children's book?) *Get back to work Archie, and please stop using this list to air your personal grievances against me.*

Prevator [Preh–vah–ter]: An Alaspinoran legal status and title conferred to one member of every noble household within the Court of Kings and Queens. The title is granted upon a noble's marriage and the birth of their first child. Prevatorship is required for suffrage within the Court and property ownership. Only a marriage between a man and a woman is recognized for the purposes of this status.

Primitha [Prim–ee–thah]: The goddess of nature, balance, and new life. She is deeply revered by Alaspinoran farmers, who regularly pray to her for bountiful harvests. She rules over the Afterworld of Abundance.

Reindune Mountains [Rain–dune Mountains]: The expansive mountain range that splits Eltun in half and extends down through the western and eastern coasts of Kialma'keer.

Torrin [Tore–in]: An emerald and sapphire dragon whose lair is a few days away from Bimblebarrow—just off the eastern coast of central Alaspinor. He has a keen interest in the intentions of the High Mage of Nirdeem and appears to be the only one on Eltun (besides, perhaps, the High Mage) with knowledge about the origins of elemental magic.

Thermoren [There–more–in]: Death's Many-faced Attendant, created by the two First Deities to collect and shepherd souls to The Lord of Thorns for Final Judgment. This god represents funeral rights, nourishing flame, and rebirth after tragedy. The Alaspinoran variation is depicted as a broad-shouldered warrior without a helmet, holding a sword, hilt clutched in one hand and blade resting on the other palm.

Tularien [Two–lair–eean]: The name of the entire world.

Um'prakta [Oom–prahk—ta]: A traditional hat invented by Kialma'keerans to protect against the desert's heat—part of a set of ful'prakta.

Vaal'akkar [Val–uh–car]: The word has changed very little from its origins in ancient Kialma'keeran. The name's literal meaning is "beasts of life," as they are unkillable. These four-armed, skeletal creatures with strange magic roam Kialma'keer and slaughter every mortal on sight. They are nocturnal and very territorial, always staying within a certain distance of their dens.

Vel'erma [Vel–air–muh]: The goddess of resourcefulness, survival, practicality, preparation, and utility. She is also the goddess of knowledge and exploring new horizons. She rules over the Afterworld of Acuity, also called the Divine or Eternal Library.

The goddess's name is sometimes spelled Velerma by countries who do not have the glottal stop in their native language to reflect the slight alteration in the name's pronunciation.

Vocarii [Voh–car–ee]: Soulless, reanimated corpses under the control of the Broken Claim. Few interact directly with them, and even fewer know the tragic circumstances behind their creation. (Myself included. Erianna was not forthcoming with details on this creature.)

Vespar [Ves–par]: An Alaspinoran town with a vast produce market. It is the largest settlement south of Bimblebarrow, and the closest town to Nirdeem's borders.

Weareely Marshes [Wear–ee–lee Marshes]: A flooded grassland marsh in northern Alaspinor that spans many miles. It is very near to the Court of Kings and Queens.

Zinneon Siebold [Zin–ee–on Sigh–bold]: A kunari man who lives in Bokest al'Bar with his wife, Colonel Lily. He was the headmaster of Zoh'kret University for over fifty years.

A few years ago, the elderly kunari retired, replaced by his son, Agerat. Zinneon—affectionately known as Zinnie, by those close to him—currently works in his wife's weapon shop, Wisdom's Weapons. A close friend and father figure to Archibald Gossimare.

Zelerbix [Zell–air–bicks]: The Kialma'keeran variation of the deity of pleasure. They represent overindulgence in sex. More specifically, they represent a focus on sex so intense that it diverts attention away from all other aspects of life. They are depicted as two rabbits huddling so close together they are almost indistinguishable from each other.

Historically, Zelerbix is evoked in both a positive and negative light. For instance, honeymooners are thought to be blessed by Zelerbix, but the deity is also referenced when speaking of sex-addicts. There is no explicit gender assigned to the rabbits; however, their genders are sometimes assigned to match the couple being compared to them.

Zoh'kret University [Zoh–kreht University]: The largest and most prestigious university in the world. Located in southern Kialma'keer, mortals travel from all over to attend this school. It has—rightfully—gained a reputation for hosting and producing the brightest minds in Tularien, including **Kezok Fahra'keen, Archibald Gossimare,** and **Zinneon** and **Agerat Siebold.**

Acknowledgements

All the way back in 2018, I came up with Zelnor—a character I played in my first "serious" Table Top Role-Playing Game. Life happened and that campaign fizzled out, its story left unfinished before it even really began.

Three years later, bright-eyed and looking for a novel concept, my old character from that unfinished story grew into my first fully fleshed-out idea. Soon Zelnor lived and breathed again in an entirely new world of my own design, sprinkled with loving references to those action-packed sessions with my friends.

Without that campaign Zelnor wouldn't even exist, let alone be one of the stars of my first novel. But a book is much more than an idea, and The Dragon's Emissary wouldn't exist without the support of these amazing individuals. As such, I absolutely have to give these incredible people the credit they deserve.

First, and most importantly, I'd like to thank my mom. Thank you for listening me talk for hours about my ideas, for providing your superb edits, for your formatting guidance, and most of all, for encouraging me not to quit all together. It's impossible to describe how important your advice and editorial insights were. My book truly would not exist without you.

You had faith in me long before I had faith in myself, and no matter how many slips and stumbles I have, your confidence in me never waivers. That's not just something difficult to find in a mom but in a person. I hope you understand that you're not only special to me; you are special to everyone who has the pleasure of knowing you. I love you deeply. Not because of everything you've done for me, but because of how deeply you love me.

Thank you so, so much to my sister, Amye, who crossed state lines more than once to exchange my manuscript in a several spy-style hand-offs. She read the first very, very rough draft of this book and was the first to witness its rebirth in my full rewrite. She delighted me by asking when I thought I might finish a sequel. I'll try to finish it (relatively) soon for you, Amye.

I cannot thank Katie Bucklein enough. She has been absolutely invaluable to the final stages of my process and has only strengthened my belief that every book not only needs a great editor but deserves one. She elevated my story from very good to professional, and we became friends along the way. We're both committed to putting more queer media out into the universe, and she was essential in helping me do just that.

Thank you, Rebecca Sutherland, for helping me make a truly polished book, for combing through my work and finding everything I missed. Your proofreading was essential, your advice about my book blurb was life-saving, and your instruction about the finer details of interior design made a world of difference. Your patience and kindness saw me through my final edits.

How do I begin to thank Sean and Victoria Hilferty? Uncle Sean helped with every single aspect of graphic design in the print version of this book—from labeling my maps to helping me turn my mock-up into a stunning cover. He even offered his expertise on my website. He took the time to not only help with the many tasks I had to complete that were beyond my scope, but also taught me along the way, so that I could stand on my own two feet.

And Victoria Hilftery, my Aunt Viki, has been so kind and supportive, ready to help me wherever she can. She taught me how to manage my frizzy hair and took hundreds of fantastic shoots for my "About the Author" photo. Those are only a couple of examples among the many ways she is supporting me. She has always been there for me, every step of the way—as a cheerleader, as a role model, and as a kickass aunt.

I'd like to thank my dad for believing I could do this, even when I didn't believe it myself. And for supporting me when I decided to do the most insane thing I could think of—writing a book full-time.

My friend May Bee Trist deserves a lot of love for being the Game Master that inspired this story in its earliest stages and for letting me borrow her characters: Torrin, Christine, Annette, and the handmaidens.

Our first campaign still has a special place in my heart, and this series is partly my way of honoring it. I hope some of the adventure and excitement we experienced together bleeds through these pages. Thank you, May, for a wonderful campaign back then and here's to many more in the future!

Similarly, thank you Rody Villagas for giving me permission to use Otto. Even just the small reference to the chaotic man was a joy to write, and I look forward to him terrorizing Erianna, Zelnor, and Lyle in future books. I hope I have done your character justice.

Kay Calder also deserves my deepest thanks. Thank you for working with me on the aspects of a novel that no writer wants to deal with. Your fantastic eye for design and great writing suggestions helped me shape my work into something beautiful. And on top of all of that, you're an amazing friend. Thank you for being my writing bestie!

Acknowledgements

Thank you to my brother, Michael, for still listening to me even after I asked him a million variations of the same question with the same worried intonation. How he hasn't throttled me yet, I'll never know. I hope, in the end, you think that this book was worth all the aggravation.

I'd also like thank my friend Korrin Schriver for always supporting me in everything I do. She's one of my loudest, most adamant cheerleaders. Whether it's offering to promote me to anyone who will listen or having in-depth conversations about gender identities.

Of course, I want to give a huge thank you to Alina Lalik for the wonderful art in this book and her immense patience as I neurotically insisted that every single detail in each illustration be just so. Her art brought my characters and world to life with a magic that still takes my breath away.

I'd like to thank Julie Belote for encouraging me to commit to splitting my (increasingly long) single book into a trilogy. You helped convince me to put my work out into the world and for that I'm grateful.

Thank you, Danielle Van Alst, for so kindly and genuinely answering my questions about self-publishing and copyright. Your advice about putting pictures into my manuscript was invaluable.

And finally, a very special thank you to Kim Scott for helping me through the darkest periods in my life when I wasn't sure my book was worth writing at all. Thank you for reminding me that, no matter how scary it seems, it's always worth taking those last few steps to cross the finish line. Thanks to your encouragement and compassion, I've made something I'm proud of and that means so much more to me than the lofty overreaching expectations I once cradled close to my heart.

You didn't just help my book get better; you helped me get better. And for that I am deeply grateful.

About the Author

Robin Arnette enjoys reading fanfiction, playing video games and TTRPGs, and overanalyzing TV shows with her little brother. If her writing ever inspired new creations in any of her passions, she would implode from joy.

Robin graduated from CSUN in 2021 and was the first recipient of The Deborah Averill Award in Creative Writing.

The Dragon's Emissary is her debut novel and the first book in her series, *Legend of the Fragmentum.*

Learn more about Robin and the world of Tularien at www.robinarnette.com